Praise for
Saint of the Shadows

"The external plot weaves with the romance seamlessly! The love triangle is steamy, Marisol is unforgettable." *E.K. DARNELL,* author of *A Bond of Blood*

"There's a new hero in town—and only one person can bring him to his knees! The Patron Saint is a realistic, vulnerable, sympathetic hero. This literary take on the superhero genre balances action, empathy, and heat perfectly. Marisol and the Patron Saint's dynamic is both tender and powerful; their partnership redefines what it means to save and to serve. A bold, genre-bending debut—this author is one to watch." *AMAZON UK REVIEW BY DAMON LORD*

"A heart-racing tale of courage, love, and forgiveness... an amazing ride." *REEDSY DISCOVERY* REVIEW BY DIAMOND HARRELL

"Wish I could give more stars! I felt like I was there or watching it unfold. The universe needs to make this story into a movie—it's a must-read!" *GOODREADS REVIEW BY PRETTYLADYMAINE WRITES*

"So good I stayed up way past my bedtime! Think *Daredevil* meets *The Princess Bride*—a swashbuckling vigilante MMC, an unstoppable badass FMC, and a nefarious city underbelly. Loss and hope, vengeance and steam—if this were a movie, I'd totally watch it." *GOODREADS REVIEWER*

"Smart plotting, intense action, and sexy intrigue. Equal parts fantasy and romance with a heavy dose of mystery. Throw away your expectations and be pleasantly blown away." *GOODREADS REVIEWER*

Content Notes

My content notes for book one, *Saint of the Shadows*, were not as direct as this one for book two. *Deus Ex Umbra* goes into darker places and feelings, which although set in a world of superheroes, cuts closely to our reality. Your mental health is of the utmost importance. Be mindful and take care of yourself.

- Abuse between MCs
- Blasphemy and sacrilege
- Colonialism
- Cursing
- Death of a minor character due to pregnancy complications
- Decapitation
- Discussing of pregnancy (doesn't happen)
- Drug dealing
- Dub-con
- Estranged parent
- Explicit sex (for type of acts, see **ADDITIONAL CONTENT NOTES** at www.jonesyelise.com/books)

•Foot and shoe worship

•Gang violence

•Graphic violence

•Homelessness

•Human trafficking (mentioned)

•Infertility (mystical variety)

•Misogyny

•Murder (on and off-page, descriptions of crime scenes and autopsies)

•Pet mouse

•Police brutality

•Police shooting

•Pregnancy loss (minor character)

•Rape (mentioned, off-page, occurs in the past and not to MCs)

•Sex workers

•Slut shaming

•Substance abuse (alcohol, marijuana, and fictional drug)

•Suicide/ideation (mystical variety)

•Brief moment of vomiting

•Zombie-like creatures.

For the teachers, caregivers, advocates, and survivors who risk their safety and livelihoods so children may live in safety, knowledge, and acceptance.

Against war.

Against hunger.

Against censorship.

Against silence.

You are the true superheroes.

Prologue

One Hundred and Fifty Years After the Curse

I pour the last of the oil along the dock. The slick stream shimmers in the moonlight, a beautiful path of destruction to rob slavers of their means of transport. Everything is going to plan.

"Alto!" a man shouts. It has come from the direction of the shipyard that Adhara claimed for herself when she'd axed open a few kegs of gunpowder and chopped apart mastheads.

The voice means trouble. That Adhara is in trouble.

I run. I'll twist the guard's neck until his forehead flops against his shoulder blades or gouge his eyes until the *squelch!* becomes a *pop!*

I clamber over the wooden skeleton of a ship. *Mierda!* No death tonight. No death to the loggers who chopped down trees, to the shipwrights who built the vessels to carry human cargo, to the guards who protected their stolen property, or even to the men who counted their coins after selling a shackled human in the market.

The plan had merely been to ensure the guardsmen drank an entire jug of rum earlier that night. I had even joined them. Although my cursed situation makes any sort of drunkenness a brief dizzy spell, those mortals should've slept through theirs as planned. The plan should've worked. Those guards had loved my conversation, and my rum even more. Adhara said I play a good deceiver because I have the face of the god my people promised would save her. "People trust your eyes, " she had whispered before kissing my eyelids.

It must've been the boy who woke from his drunken slumber. Fresh into manhood, he'd sipped while the others drank long pulls, burning our throats and chests with each swallow.

Boom! Smoke from a musket flies into the air. I break into a sprint. A musket ball had never stopped us before. Our bodies have a way of rejecting them. A direct shot might take a little longer to heal from, but we always heal. Except when a cannon had crushed Nando's chest and left him a rasping revenant.

My temples pulse, a faint echo of all that rum, as if a sliver of mortality lingered. The thick, tropical air suddenly chokes me. Sweat soaks the bandana over my face; my heartbeat thunders in tandem with the throbbing of my head. Do I worry for Adhara? No. Under most circumstances, she handles herself all too well. I panic for the young guardsman who dared to fire at her.

When I near them, Adhara and the guard's shadows move among the stacks of lumber. Between my quick breaths, I hear a glottal, soft grunt followed by a splatter—the sound of a slit throat. Why hadn't I run and climbed faster? It must've been the headache. Or the reoccurring problem I had after spending a day with mortals—I sometimes forgot my super-strength.

I dart, using all of my power, but I arrive too late. Adhara stands above the boy, her prized sica sword dripping blood as he gurgles through the last seconds of his life.

"I cleaned up your mess again, my Rubio," she says flatly as she wipes the blade clean and returns it to its sheath.

"You didn't have to kill him," I say. Even in death, the boy's eyes are wide and pleading. A sour taste rises in my mouth. If only I had pushed the boy to drink more. Mistakes pile onto others, forming the mountains of mistakes I had committed since arriving in the New World—a long list of *if onlys* spreading out in a vicious cause and effect. If only my people had treated the West Indies like any other port city with its *quaranta giorni*[1]. If only my people worshiped our god the way they did power.

If only I hadn't drunk from the Fountain.

After the lifetimes since the curse, I've ached to look into the glazed eyes of those meeting their end and feel nothing. To my dismay, I always feel something, and even more acutely after the transformation. No matter

---

1. Forty days, origin of quarantine

how hard I try to change the outcome, Death follows me.

Adhara and I jump into our rowboat and head toward the open sea to meet the Padre's ship. When we reach a safe distance between the boat and the shipyard, Adhara strikes a flint and lights a torch. With supernatural strength, she hurls the flame over the black water to the dock. Fire sprawls, carried by the tributaries of oil.

Flame meets gunpowder and explosions reach the sky, bathing us in heat, even from the safe distance of the rowboat. The gunpowder does its trick.

Adhara lowers her bandana to her chin. The fire dimly casts a celestial copper shine over her umber-brown skin. Her lips move upward slightly, the widest her smile ever has been since the curse. Churning flames reflect off her pupils.

"That should send a message and slow them down," I say, rowing.

I dwell on the dead boy. What was his name? Did I forget it? Did I bother to ask? Even when I had worried about the other nameless faces that met their ends from our interference, Adhara would respond with a lecture about balancing the scales of Justice and the unfortunate collateral in pursuit of the greater good, a lesson I could recite, but never learned.

She stares at the ever-growing destruction. "I will not slow down. I will know no peace. They will know no peace. Not while they abduct people from their homes and treat them like beasts of burden."

With each slicing row into the water, my muscles burn. I am tired from the rowing, the running, the hauling of oil, and the drinking, but my earlier labors aren't what drags at my insides. To be tired the way mortals become, some stronger force binds me. No, my body resists my new mission: to stay ahead of Adhara so that those who stood in her way were brought to Justice.

And not to Death by her blade.

I

I've Been Here Before

Vincent Varian scanned over the sweating, dancing bodies shining in the dim lights of the nightclub. Unlike the cool shadows of his home city, the heat hung in the air in the country of La Isla Reina. No breeze came to offer respite. The ceiling fans spun in vain. The heat multiplied among the dancers and stuck to his skin. When was the last time he'd been here? A distant memory of explosions, blood, and flames snaked through his mind. *When I was a different man and went by a different name.*

Spotting his target, Vincent slipped into the partitioned area of the club, elevated off the dance floor. Wealth afforded him unfettered access to *VIP*, to *private*, to *yes, sir* with nary a phone call or a double check.

The target was Grant Durant, a trust fund multi-millionaire whose depleting fortune had compelled him to invest in running for Congress. As fitting as it might be for a sentient slime ball to represent the city he called home, Durant's corruption was the last thing Shadowhaven needed.

And that wasn't the reason Vincent hunted him.

"Varian!" Durant called out. Each of his arms was hanging around the neck of a semi-conscious woman, barely out of girlhood, judging by their narrow body frames and soft faces.

Vincent realized he was wearing his mask—loose linen pants, guayabera shirt, and huarache sandals. Targets called out to him because he was the face they could trust.

"Durant." Vincent forced a smile and reached out to shake Durant's hand.

Freeing an arm, Durant let one of his human accessories flop to the couch. "You escape Shadowhaven to come here alone?" Durant flashed a toothy grin. He'd had his teeth capped since Vincent last saw him at a fundraiser, and with his vacation tan, his smile was a ridiculous neon white.

"I'm not alone," Vincent replied, his gaze traveling over the dancers.

"The nurse still?"

Vincent nodded. Naturally, Durant was the type to keep tabs on Vincent's personal life. Vincent hadn't helped the matter. He practically shouted about his new relationship from every rooftop in Shadowhaven with interviews and staged photos, much to the chagrin of his girlfriend.

"If you ever need to sneak away and really party, let me know. My stable can show you a good time." Durant slid a hand down the thigh of his drowsy companion and patted her knee. "Young and willing to do whatever you want."

Vincent released a sigh and smirked. Smirked because he couldn't immediately rip Durant's larynx through his neck. Justice had to be methodical, especially when carried out by a masked vigilante like himself. But the temptation to slaughter enemies always threatened to surface since his transformation long ago. He'd kept that aspect of himself hidden from his friends and now, from his spirit, the woman he loved. He acknowledged the impulse, imagining a bloody melee that would wake Durant's "dates."

Not yet. He breathed in and held his breath, a trick to calm the vagus nerve. Love kept the urge at bay.

His love for her. He found her, back to him as she stood at the bar. The humidity kinked her long, black hair into waves. Her white floor-length sundress skimmed over her curves, made practically obscene as she swayed her hips to the music. He rubbed his lips together and tasted the salt of his sweat, delighting in how he'd gripped and guided those full hips.

She turned to face the crowd, sipping what looked like rum on the rocks. Her bright brown eyes winced and teared a tiny amount. Her drink was too strong, but she continued to sip. He adored watching her tough act give way to moments of humanity. Her, the brilliant mortal woman who had captured his heart. Her, the nurse—Marisol Novotny.

Her gaze flicked up as she sipped again. She found him, and he locked eyes with her. She narrowed her eyes and licked a drop of rum off her sensuous lips. It sucked the breath from his lungs. Any small gesture from her was a knife held to his ribs that became a serrated stab every time she crawled between his legs, straddled his lap, tied him up, choked, slapped, and spanked him. The delicious pain when she forced him to beg for what he wanted and violated him until his mind blanked, reaching what had to be Aaru, Nirvana, Heaven, or Omeyocan.

A light flashed, and he found its source behind the dancing bodies. Paparazzi. The clueless fop of his alter ego had its setbacks. He signaled to Marisol using their agreed-upon code, *Target located. Careful. Photographers.*

She tilted her head and pulled on her ear. *Sneak out the back way?*

He shook his head and signed, *Let's give them a show.*

She winked and finished her drink, but didn't wince this time. She plucked an ice cube from her glass and ran it down her neck, over her collarbone, and across the tops of her breasts. She popped the melting cube into her mouth, sucking on her index finger and thumb. The show was for him, not the photographers, and he answered her seduction with a single, arching eyebrow. An arched eyebrow because he couldn't immediately teleport across the club, lick where she dragged that ice cube, hike up her skirt, and help her come on his fingers and then his mouth. Society had rules. If the rules didn't harness him, being on hunt definitely did.

But a hunt never stopped him from savoring his lover. The huntress became the hunted.

"Good luck with the campaign!" Vincent called back to his target. He jumped down the stairs, hopped over the velvet rope, and prowled through the crowd.

The drumbeats picked up in rhythm and the guitars drove harder and louder. Marisol knotted one side of her skirt to free one of her sculpted, golden-brown legs. She closed her eyes and danced, circling her hips and skimming her hands over her torso. Her body rolled and contorted to the beat, and she opened her eyes. *Do you like that?* those eyes asked. With 500 years of experience, he was more than ready to show how much he did.

The crowd parted around him, forming a line straight to her. He took her hand and pulled her in a spin. She turned into him with a breathless smile. Another veneer of cool slipped away from her. Their dancing, like their fucking, was a duel. Someone would submit while the other struck. Side by side, he had the upper hand as he traced his nose along the velvet-soft underside of her upper arm. The scent of musk, sweet floral, and the hint of her sweat stoked his desire. His fingers glided down her arms, and he guided those arms to hug his neck. She stepped in close with bent legs. Her knee wedged his knees apart. Or was it the other way around? The duel reached a standstill as the graze of her thigh against him weakened his defenses.

He held her gently near the bottom of her rib cage. Her elbows rested lightly on his as he directed her swaying body. Answering his lead, she arched her back and kicked up a leg. Not so easily bested, he ghosted his hand along her calf and knee. The teasing worked. She bit her lip and twisted the hair at the nape of his neck. However, his advantage crumbled for her mouth begged to be kissed. But that wasn't the dance. The dance rode along the edge of indulgence. Denying pleasure built their desire into a sharp ache that when finally satisfied would bring them both beyond the little death and into rebirth.

And that's what he loved about dancing with her or making love to her. Both thrust him into a world of life and connection, something he was never given by his inability to age or die, both quite inevitable for her. Yet she carried herself with such fearlessness, it was she who felt eternal.

He never felt life's hope with other dancing partners. Death's specter hung over the wild bursts of energy. It was there when he'd danced *la volta* before the defeat of the Armada[1] and when he performed a minuet during the Reign of Terror. He danced a quadrille in Jamaica and Bhangra in the Punjab province on the eves of rebellions, waltzed as war tore through Virginia, and foxtrotted while assassinations threw the world in tumult in Sarajevo[2] and Yekaterinaburg[3]. He'd madly kicked and flipped to big brass bands during the blitzkrieg of London and grooved to music before the fall of Saigon. In Tehran, he hustled to a disco beat with women in miniskirts and sequins, before another revolution, before another transformation.

1. The English navy defeated the Spanish Armada in 1588.
2. Where Archduke Franz Ferdinand was assassinated
3. Where the Romanovs were assassinated

She completed a half-turn and grinded her ass into him. Her gaze focused on Durant and his entourage leaving. "Target's on the move."

Vincent switched their positions and disguised observing the target with a kick and ball-change. "We have ten minutes. Time for the grand finale."

The music crescendoed and drums rattled to an end. He guided her hand down his chest and twirled her into a dip that hovered her over the floor. From here, he pulled her up into a crushingly deep kiss. At first her body went rigid, caught in the surprise. She moaned into his mouth, and her limbs grew heavy. The kiss and the friction of his thigh between her legs released the tension just enough to resume the hunt. Lights strobed as paparazzi snapped photos like fireworks.

"Shall we take this elsewhere?" he murmured against her lips.

Mouth parted in a daze, she nodded.

He led her by the hand toward a door marked *Private* and slipped a handsome sum of money to the security guard blocking the pathway. The guard opened the door for them. Cameras still aimed at them, so Vincent drew her into another devastating kiss that persisted until the door closed after them.

The room was small and dark, hardly bigger than a broom closet. He pushed her against the door. She gasped. He jammed the lock of the door.

He stepped back, unzipping his fly and unbuttoning his shirt, and watched her with her heaving chest and swollen lips. "Go time."

Her eyes flickered—once, twice—until she followed his lead once more and slipped out of her dress. "I forgot what a tease you can be when you're showing off. I think you gave me blue ovaries."

"You started it." He bolted to a window in the back, opened it, and whistled. A buzzing drone holding a suitcase flew inside. "Thank you, Staci," he said, to one of the many manifestations of his faithful computer system.

The drone chirped and headed out the window. He opened the suitcase, revealing their uniforms. Marisol braided her hair back; Vincent tied on his mask that covered his whole head except for his lips and chin. She yanked on her Kevlar pants; he, his Kevlar suit.

The unzipped gap of his uniform exposed the fleur de lys-shaped scar on his upper back, the place where she had sewn him together and cauterized the wound with silver nitrate almost a year ago. She placed a kiss there and zipped his uniform. Perhaps she wasn't super-powered like him, but her protective love surrounded him. The least he could do was return the same.

From the suitcase, he lifted out her heavy, silver-hooded chainmail shirt. He eased it over her torso, shielding her in his affection. His uniform came together as he clicked on his utility belt. She stepped into her utility harness, which secured over her hips. The metal O-ring over her pubic bone served another exciting purpose, so he gave it a playful tug.

"Safety check?" she asked. When he'd added it to her costume design, she assumed it was to support her in scaling and rappelling. He hadn't corrected her.

He laughed, "In a way." Someday he'd tell her what it was for and expand their bedroom horizons. Unfortunately, today was not the day.

They squeezed on their gloves and jammed their feet into combat boots. Finally, he clasped his cape to his shoulders, and she put on her domino mask and flipped up her hood.

They had become the Patron Saint and the Silver Spirit.

One after the other, they crawled out the window and leaped through the sunroof of his matte black sports car. Staci couldn't open the doors in the narrow alleyway. Adjusted and buckled in, they headed off on the mission.

Vincent said, "One of us will take out Durant's armed guards and the other will follow him to find his laptop. Obviously, I'll take—"

"Durant duty?" she interjected and cracked her knuckles.

Her eyes gleamed with a familiar hunger for Justice. Deja vu all over again. Where had he seen a look like hers before? Distant memories echoed throughout his unnaturally long life like barely lucid dreams.

"There's enough guards with semiautomatic guns to make a deadly basketball team," he warned. Her mortality raised the stakes, but she couldn't support him from the safety of home nor would he wish the transformation on her, even if it were possible. Those choices would make her another woman altogether, either a caged bird or a cold mercenary.

"You think I'm being foolish, but believe me, my saint, I'm afraid of what I might do if I were alone with Durant." She nuzzled her masked nose against his masked ear.

"Very well."

The car stopped, and she slipped out of the passenger seat. She sidled along the shadows and bushes until she reached the outer wall of Durant's vacation fortress. After shinnying up a palm tree, she vaulted over the barrier.

"Staci? Where is Durant?" The screen in the car switched to footage of his limo creeping past the gates to his home. Staci's drone had surveilled him since he left the club.

Vincent stepped out of his car and sprinted toward the gate, squeezing through as it closed. The darkness swallowed him. No one could see him.

Durant exited the car, bolstering one of his dates as she staggered along the driveway. The other followed him with an unsteady gait. "Does something smell funny to you?" she asked sleepily.

The strange smell must be the chemical agent Marisol had released. Some guards were getting a heavy dose, and if the air was thick with it, were already passed out. Vincent had nothing to worry about when it came to his spirit.

He crept across the yard and peered through a window. Inside, Durant disabled the security system. Time to make another move.

Using a laser from his utility belt, Vincent cut through the glass and jumped through the hole in the window.

Durant's voice traveled from the hallway. "Get yourselves changed and meet me in the pool." He swatted each woman on the ass. The force knocked them forward into a doorway, where they disappeared. Durant drew out his phone and pressed buttons; lights came on.

Joder! Vincent darted to a shadowy nook. Blending into the murky shapes, he followed his target slowly. He kept a close trail after Durant through hallways and doorways, swiftly moving as Durant disabled security measure after security measure. Durant finally entered a windowless study and switched on a lamp. Almost automatically, Vincent pulled his cape around himself as a shield from the light.

Durant turned around suddenly and appeared to scan the empty room. How precious. He thought he had a tail. A reasonable person—an innocent person— would conclude that passing through armed guards and high-tech intrusion detectors would be enough to talk themselves out of paranoia. Nine times out of ten, the shadows were only shadows. Guilty people, however, could never be fully assured.

Durant sighed and headed towards a large painting of an anglicized Jesus radiating gold and handing the

U.S. Constitution to a blond boy standing in front of a crowd of modern Americans. Vincent stifled a laugh. If Durant only knew the Framers had squabbled over word choices and ideas in stuffy rooms sweltering from the summer heat or in dark, musty pubs. Vincent knew. He had witnessed the discussion of a draft, and one of those famous men had spilled beer on it.

Durant moved the work of art to reveal a safe locked with a keypad. He entered numbers, and the safe clicked open.

All Vincent had to do was follow the plan: get the laptop. But the abyss rose within him, and he craved vengeance. "Empty the safe on the desk behind you," Vincent growled.

Durant's face turned as white as his teeth. "Who's there?"

Vincent's suit powered up, glowing with blue lightning. "Your reckoning."

Durant reached into the safe. *Click.* He grabbed a handgun. *Zzt!* Vincent struck him in the hand with two Taser darts. Predictably, Durant yelped and dropped the gun.

Vincent launched a cable that wound around Durant's hands and ankles. The captive struggled against the bind and toppled over, cracking his chin on the desk.

Durant spit blood as he wriggled like a worm. "So you're the Patron Saint of Shadowhaven. Aren't you a little outside your jurisdiction?"

"I don't have a jurisdiction." Vincent hurried to the safe, which held a laptop—*the* laptop. He placed the computer on the desk and opened it to search through files. A quick scroll confirmed dates and names. Lots of important names.

Durant moved his jaw from side to side, presumably checking if it had been dislocated. "That isn't going to prove shit."

"Maybe not, but some of these names will start singing something to the tune of Grant Durant, skeeve turned human trafficker—anything to get heat off their well-lawyered backs."

"Trafficking? I provided a haven to those whores and runaways."

Vincent punched him in the ribs and didn't hold back as he usually did when combating mortals. At least one rib broke. "Fourteen is still a child in your jurisdiction." All the meditative exercises and years of wisdom failed him in tolerating insult directed at victims.

Durant took in a wavering breath and wheezed. "Are you going to kill me?"

Vincent patted him on his cheek. "No. I'm taking you home." He hoisted Durant over his shoulder and walked out of the study. In the hallway, Staci's drone joined him, flying close like a trusted falcon. It carried a copper box. With his free arm, Vincent stored the laptop in the box. "Okay, Staci. Give the place a scrub."

The drone chirped and a large, blue electrical pulse emitted from its tiny body. The pulse combed over the walls and ceiling, sending a magnetic wave strong enough to reboot the security system and erase camera footage.

He stalked through the yard and the gate. His car arrived in front of him with an abrupt squeal of the brakes. The passenger window lowered.

Marisol sat in the driver's seat. "Hey hot stuff, need a ride?"

"Pop the trunk."

She tipped her head towards the tied-up man on his shoulder. "He wasn't the plan."

A sniffle and whimper came from the backseat—Durant's companions huddled together, hugging. In shorts and T-shirts, they appeared even younger, not women but girls.

"They weren't the plan either," Vincent said.

"I sobered them up with a shot of adrenaline, and they cried for home. He kept their passports from them so they couldn't escape," Marisol said.

"Hm." The sound from his chest came out like an annoyed grumble, but it was all he could muster. In truth, he was proud of her and a little ashamed of himself. She never lost sight of the people caught between the schemes of villains and the heroics of the mighty. That's why she was his hero. With her, he had an overwhelming sense the never-ending battle of good versus evil might end—that he'd break the everlasting curse. The feeling was enough to weaken him to his knees and offer a prayer, but he loaded the trunk with a screaming asshole instead.

He lowered himself into the passenger seat and turned to the cowering girls. "Your names?"

"J-J-Juniper," one answered.

"Danielle," the other replied, wiping her nose with the back of her hand.

"Juniper? Danielle? We'll get you home." He turned to Marisol. "Hold your breath, my spirit."

Marisol inhaled and stiffened. He reached inside a compartment of his utility belt, procured an aerosol can of his sleeping agent, and pressed the valve. *Whoosh!* The girls fell fast asleep. "Staci, roll the windows down a crack?"

Marisol exhaled, "Thanks for thinking about me."

He nodded. "We'll rendezvous with Staci at the airfield. Next stop, the club." With a tap, the screen traced a path back to where they started. Staci drove them to the alleyway, and they climbed back through the sunroof and window. They changed into their normal clothes, and he fixed the lock. The other masks back on, they were ready to return to the dance floor.

Marisol turned the doorknob, looking far too put-together. The show had to continue.

"Nuh-uh," Vincent said, "the story is in the details." He loosened her braid into messy waves and pulled the strap of her dress down until it fell loose at her bicep.

They returned to the dance floor, walking past the security guard. Onlookers giggled at Marisol pulling up her strap and running her fingers through her hair. Another photographer aimed his camera. Vincent zipped his fly. Cameras wildly snapped photos. To the gawkers of the world, reformed playboy Vincent Varian and his girlfriend couldn't keep it in their pants during a night out on vacation.

A perfect cover for assault, breaking and entering, kidnapping, and robbery.

Vincent settled back into the pilot chair. Another safe landing in the quiet Shadowhaven airfield. Marisol kept her seat buckle fastened until he taxied into his private hangar. There, they reemerged as their alter egos.

As the Patron Saint and the Silver Spirit, they continued the next leg of their mission: Operation Girl Return. He cross-checked Juniper and Danielle's names in the missing person database and located their home addresses. Staci drove them to their destinations. Vincent carried a sleeping Danielle to a suburban porch swing and climbed up a building to prop Juniper against the sliding door of her family's apartment balcony.

Staci drove them to their final destination, Police Precinct Four. His stomach tightened as he faced the part of their plan that hung around his neck like an albatross—he had to confirm the contents of the laptop. "We're in Quinlan's neck of the woods," he said in an attempt to distract Marisol. A visit to Detective Tobias Quinlan was always in order after a night of hunting.

She leaned her head against the passenger window of the car. "I guess we are."

"You should visit him. Tell him what to expect at work today, so he doesn't get any surprises." He tensed and relaxed his jaw over and over again, hoping she didn't hear or see his deception.

"Sure you wouldn't like to come with me? Make this a couple's outing?"

"People are more suspicious of screams coming from car trunks around here."

"Got it. I'll keep it brief, monosyllabic, and I'll disappear the moment he turns around." She nuzzled her mask against his and headed into the night.

A case against Durant wasn't going to stick without knowing what was on those files. With Marisol gone, he opened the laptop and braced to see the worst of humanity.

2

Mea Culpa

In the dark, Cesca moaned, "Harder, deeper."

Barely awake, **Tobias** did as he was told, slipping inside her wet heat. Her legs hugged him closer.

Her hot breath met the shell of his ear as he cradled her head and drove in. Hips met hips in a frenzied rhythm.

"You're so good to me, baby," she wailed.

He thrusted with more power.

"So good."

Her moans reached a higher pitch; her core pulsed, squeezing every sensitive inch of him. He liked her in this mindless state, greedy for what he could give her. And he could give it.

She screamed and slapped him on the back. Sure, he and Cesca had achieved encyclopedic carnal knowledge of each other that made this stage of dating more fun, but she'd never screamed like that before. Somebody give him a medal.

A couple smacks on his back gave him the encouragement to thrust deeper, but a few more said it wasn't working. Something was wrong. He stopped. "What is it?"

Streetlights reflected off the outline of her lips, trembling. "I heard something. Outside."

He studied the streaks of light on the floor of his room. Something outside moved, a familiar trick of the shadow.

He sighed, slipped off the condom, and threw it in the trash. Fucking Vincent. He'd stand in the window to his fire escape, gesture to his dick at half mast, and wave the few wafts of pussy in the air toward the vigilante to communicate that whatever he'd come for could wait a half hour.

Kicking around the floor, he searched for his boxers. They weren't where he thought he had whipped them off. Aggressive nudity might send a stronger message. He stumbled into his living room, the blood finally traveling back to his legs. He gave the latch at his window a flick and opened it.

Marisol as the Silver Spirit stood waiting for him. Her dark hair whipped in the wind. The city lights glittered over her armor. He stepped back, inadvertently exposing more of himself in her view.

Heat prickled over his skin. He followed the burning trail of it with the tips of his fingers across his chest and abdomen as it formed into an itch. She stared, unmoving. Would her true love want this? Her sweet little brown eyes tracing the path of his hands over his body? Emboldened, he adjusted his balls, his thumb ghosting underneath the root of his shaft. His breath quickened. He had made whole stories from those stolen glances. Those were enough for him. Enough to draw him drum-tight and seek release. He dug his teeth into his bottom lip and unlocked his gaze from hers. Shining with arousal or Cesca or whatever, his cock was ready. He gave it a pull and glanced up.

She was gone, vanishing like magic as if she were the Patron Saint. Tobias shook his head. The heat from within subsided. His addiction almost controlled him, but he wasn't a mindless brute grabbing the nearest bottle or falling into the most convenient bed. This time, he was going to be different.

He slammed the window shut and returned to the bedroom. Cesca sat up, her knees tucked into her chest. "What was it?"

"A cat."

"I guess my imagination gets the best of me." She held the edge of the sheets against her collarbone and with her other hand, tucked a phantom strand of hair. Her pixie cut was never out of place.

He ripped open a new condom foil and rolled it on. "Now get on your stomach and raise that ass in the air. When I'm done with you, you'll not only be seeing things, you'll be hearing them, too."

The sheets fell away as she presented herself to him. He plunged into her fiercely, and he disappeared into the sensations of hot and slick. She greeted him with a breathy laugh.

He came thinking of Marisol's hair flickering in the wind.

Vincent studied the contents of the laptop. First, he found boring items like budgets and spreadsheets. It'd be helpful to freeze Durant's accounts and even make a case of campaign fraud. Next, there were videos of bacchanal-like parties, perhaps some signs of drug use and underage drinking. All charges Durant could weasel out in the court of public opinion.

But then he found them—the hidden camera footage of drugged girls and the things he and his clients did to them.

"Staci, stop!" He burst out of the car and bent over, propping himself over his knees. He inhaled and exhaled as if he'd run a marathon without super-strength.

"I couldn't bring myself to bother the old man. He had a lady friend over." Marisol returned, and earlier than he had expected. The twinkle in her eyes disappeared. "Are you okay?"

He straightened himself and nodded. How much had she seen? How much of the truth would he have to tell?

She whispered, "What were you doing?" and petted the back of his mask.

He counted in his mind as he breathed in and held his breath. With a sigh, his body relaxed. After 500 years, it still wasn't easy witnessing the evil humans did to each other. His pain was the necessary part of the work, the collateral damage when it came to balancing the scales of Justice. "What I had to do."

She searched his eyes until he could no longer avoid the prying. "What'd you see?"

He didn't answer. A white lie was difficult to put together when her brilliant eyes attempted to read him.

"Is it that bad?" She took a glove off and rubbed her thumb over the cleft in his chin.

"Oh, you know, it's never actually as bad as you imagine," he answered, but he couldn't hide the quiver in his lips.

She narrowed her eyes. He'd been caught.

The broken images that cut into him in La Isla Reina suddenly pieced together. He had seen the look in her eyes before—not in a dream, but in a memory. Adhara. Her bloody sica sword. The dying boy. The memory froze him in place. What would it mean if she followed the same path as Adhara? Not even losing her head had stopped Adhara. Could he bring himself to stop Marisol?

Marisol opened the car door. "Staci, the trunk."

The trunk opened.

"About time! I pissed myself!" Durant whined.

She dragged him out and threw his bound body to the ground. Another rib snapped. Durant howled again. But this time, in an alley in Eastside Shadowhaven, someone might wake up and call the emergency line.

She pulled him up by the collar and socked him in the face. Durant whimpered. Fresh blood from his nose mingled with the dried blood on his chin. She seethed,

"You've got two seconds to tell me why I shouldn't stuff you in a cement box and push it in the river!" *Crack!* His jaw broke under her might. Durant spit out some of his capped teeth.

Her violence wasn't Justice but vengeance, the swell of a bloodthirsty tide, which had consumed Adhara but would not sweep his Marisol away—not if he stopped it. Vincent lunged and shoved her in the middle of the alley, standing between her and Durant. "Because it's bigger than him. We could get people even higher up the food chain. It could change things. Really change things. We could build a better world, but it's not going to happen if we kill him."

She paced to the car, leaned against the passenger door, and buried her head in her arms. Her hurt shook him. Had he done the right thing?

"Thanks for putting your bitch on a leash," Durant mumbled through his slack jaw, wiggling from his place in the gutter.

The insult unleashed the shadow within, a rapidly thumping urge to cave his face in. But the break of dawn encouraged him to save two souls this morning. He released another aerosol of sleeping agent. The now toothless bastard slumped into a heap.

Vincent stuffed him back in the trunk. He said, "I wonder if they offer cosmetic dentistry in prison." Despite his levity, Marisol did not move from her defeated position. He slammed the lid shut.

The sky grew lighter, and the city began to awaken. They didn't have much time for their last stop.

Outside Tobias's precinct, **Vincent** duct-taped the laptop across Durant's stomach. The copy would be in Vincent's safekeeping until he studied all the names on it. Until Justice was served.

The Patron Saint and the Silver Spirit tucked a confession in his front shirt pocket and dosed Durant with an amnesia drug. He'd shuffle in the precinct, confused. The cops should find that a bleeding sex trafficker paired well with morning coffee.

What story would make this seem like a clean investigation? Maybe Grant Durant turned in his computer for repairs, and the IT person reported it? And a guilt-ridden Durant turned himself in? That story might receive a district attorney's approval. Maybe throw a story to the fringe media about the deep state putting Durant up to it? That would keep the public frothing from the mouth.

Vincent and Marisol arrived in their hideaway under and between the Varian Family Research Hospital and Clinics and the new penthouse apartment across the street. Both were far from the antique finery of his estate, smack in the heart of the city, just as she had asked. However, she remained slumped in the passenger seat.

He reached out and touched her shoulder, hoping that it would bring her back to the funny, sexy, and powerful woman she was mere hours ago. "We're home."

She threw her mask to the floor of the car. "I should be over it by now—this anger."

"It's a cycle that's never truly over. And I mean that as a positive. You haven't failed if you feel it as strongly as when it first arrived."

"But I lost myself." She rubbed her temples and held her breath.

The truth that made him fear his own reflection emerged. "I feel the rage, too." He untied his mask and removed it. "You ask me how I can be good when the others, the ones in my freezer, are deathless rage monsters? The truth is, I'm not different. I still feel the hatred, but I choose not to become it."

She chortled. "Sounds like a good bumper sticker."

"Truths have a way of being catchy." He gently lowered the chainmail hood from her head, gathering it at the back of her neck. How could he show her he had the super-power to always save her, to shield her from corruption? He kissed the top of her head. "If you're lost, I'll find you."

She rested her head on his shoulder. "And if you're lost, I'll find you, too."

The dance returned, back and forth. He was saving her, but she was saving him as well. "You'll never have to," he said, a promise he most assuredly could keep. What else was he going to do during her lifetime and his eternity? He'd dedicate every ticking second to her, as long as she'd allow it. As long as time had length.

3

Inquisition

Adhara enters my thoughts more now than in a century. I haven't seen her since the tail-end of the eighteenth century. Time and space provides the tools for erasure and rebirth, and Adhara is someone I want to erase. Yet she's lingering in the twists and turns of my mind.

In comparison, I barely remember my actual family. I have ideas of them—my mother is wavy hair the color of saffron and hands dusty with flour; my father, a shadow in a doorway. My baby brother is an old man in robes, blinded from cataracts. My condition challenges the notion of linear time, flipping effect and cause.

Because of my issues with time and memory, I'm a bad storyteller. For instance, mother's floured hands most likely belonged to a servant. Her hair color probably more a guess explaining my own gold curls than to an actual memory. The people of my first life have ever-changing traits as I attempt to understand myself. To explain my yearning for adventure, my mother is a young and free spirit who chased me around the orange orchard. To explain why I never felt at home in Spain, my mother is a bedridden ghost. All can be true. Or none of it. Or some.

These memories flood my mind strangely today while I comb my golden mustache with my fingers reading, once again, *The Brothers Karamazov*. I reach my favorite part, the part taking place in Sevilla during the Spanish Inquisition. The chapter scratches at the surface of my old arguments with Adhara. Maybe this is why she's here even when she isn't.

Leonard shuffles into the study and rubs his bald head, groaning. Leonard, the only one who knows what makes me different from other men. Leonard, who was once my adopted son, grown into a friend, and now posing as my father. Effect and cause. He turns on the green-shaded brass lamp and moves to the window, where he ties back the curtains with sashes, mumbling in Lithuanian about the dark ruining my eyes.

The old man is already in a mood, so I'm not going to needle him further. Okay, maybe a little bit. I lay the book in my lap and relax against the tufted back of the sofa. Clearing my throat, I say, "Reading that chapter again. I'm still not sure whose side I should take."

Predictably, Leonard shakes his head. "There's no 'side.' It is the inquisitor who believes there is some dichotomy, either offering earthly bread to the hungry or the bread of Heaven to the damned. Are those choices truly in opposition? *Ne!*[1] The chapter is about the hypocrisy of the Church, demanding obedience

1. No!

rather than nurturing free will. Do you expect fealty from the people you save?"

I shake my head, cocky grin growing as I entertain the absurd idea of holding out a collection plate whenever I wear the mask.

"*Žinoma*[2], I may be a devil." Leonard taps an arthritic finger against his nose.

He continues lecturing, "If you can turn stones to bread, I believe you should feed as many people as possible." The old man sighs. "*Prakeikimas*[3], I didn't come here for philosophy." He throws a wrinkled, yellow envelope in my lap. "This came in the mail for you, I think."

"You think?" I study the envelope. Someone has addressed it to Rubio, care of V. Varian. *Rubio*. I haven't heard that name in almost 300 years.

My heart drops. Can't be. I've tracked uprisings and violent protests all over the world, and it has been a solid century since anything bore her mark. I've even had fleeting moments of hope, because silence meant she'd done it—she'd broken her curse.

Adhara.

My hands tremble as I scan the envelope for a return address, but it's covered in postage. Adhara has sent it from halfway around the world, back again, and finally to Shadowhaven. She never made anything easy for me. "You're not trying to rile me up now, are you?"

Leonard shrugs. I open the envelope, and a *Journal of Particle Physics* slides out. Nothing else is inside. Sections of the journal are highlighted and marked

2. Of course
3. Damn

with sticker flags. What is Adhara trying to tell me after all these centuries?

Then one of the highlighted words registers in my mind: *Antimatter*. I feel like my body is sinking, suddenly aware of gravity's force.

"You look like you've seen a ghost," Leonard says.

I nod. Since the curse, I and the others I'd entombed in cryofreeze are the textbook examples of the Law of the Conservation of Matter, never to be destroyed, only changed. Yet the universe is asymmetric. What throws it into imperfect asymmetry? Antimatter.

According to the journal, physicists are able to isolate antimatter for microseconds. Soon, it'll be longer. And from there? Possibilities opening into other possibilities. "Aut inveniam viam aut faciam[4]," I whisper as I stand. *Brothers Karamazov* tumbles from my lap to the rug. Leonard snatches the journal before it, too, falls from my shaking hands.

"She found a way," I say, gripping the arm of the sofa as the room moves around me. The spin dizzies and dizzies.

"She? Who's she? And what did she find?" Leonard opens the journal and perches a pair of reading glasses on the tip of his nose.

No amount of violence has accomplished it. Fire, explosions, nuclear fusion? No. But this? A laugh emerges from my belly.

"Freedom!" And I run out of the study to begin the end.

4

Herein Lies the Problem

Marisol stifled a yawn as she entered the treatment room. She'd managed four hours of sleep and a half-assed shower before heading into her new job at the Park Medical Clinic. Of course, her workload wasn't as exciting as the emergency room, but she more than made up with her moonlighting job.

Her patient, Yesenia Lopez, slouched in the chair across from the exam table. The teenage girl dressed in baggy gray sweatpants and a plaid button-up shirt. Her love of creating graffiti murals covered her clothes in paint splatters. When Marisol was a teenager, her mother would have preferred her to leave the house in something so shapeless and covered. Now the kids just did. How times had changed.

"You're not pregnant, but your blood tests confirmed you have low hemoglobin levels, which is probably why you missed your period. I can get you a week's supply of iron supplements from here, but you will need to get some at the store. If the problem persists after that, you can let me or any of us here know."

The girl fidgeted in her seat as if she had an itch on her ass she couldn't scratch. "Got it." She loudly sniffed before blurting, "Last time I was here, we talked about birth control?"

Hell yes, another teenager getting her life in order. "Right. Do you think there's a method that works for you?"

"What do you use?"

Her method was a cursed immortal with a wonder dick. All the fun without the hassle, not exactly something she'd preach to the city's teenagers. "Everyone has different needs and goals. What features are you looking for? Long-term? Nothing to remember? Low hormones?"

Yesenia pinched her face together. "I was thinking of the arm implant one."

"I could convince the doctor to squeeze you in today's schedule, so we can get that started today."

Yesenia nodded, cueing Marisol's pivot out of the room. "There's one more thing. We also talked about the problem I was having with that guy."

Marisol cracked the knuckle of her right index finger. "Are you having any more trouble?"

"That's the thing. We hadn't heard from Juniper in almost a month. She posted a video about how she woke up at home, far away from that creep."

Ah, her and Vincent's handiwork with Grant Durant.

Yesenia continued, "I've met a lot of people who tell me they're listening or they'll see what they can do. You're the first person to say those things, and things actually change."

A swell of pride overtook her, the feeling of a job well done. "I'm just a nurse worried about your hemoglobin levels."

Yesenia shook her head, and she squinted as if she were looking straight into the sun. "You know him, don't you? The Patron Saint. The real one."

She checked if anyone else in the clinic had heard Yesenia. Vincent really needed to train Marisol on her poker face if every other adolescent with an inkling held suspicions. In a hushed tone, she replied, "I've seen my fair share of masked people. None who I've treated fought any terrorist group." Echoes of last year's Bloodsucker drama still rattled her.

The corners of Yesenia's mouth lifted. "Maybe I have an overactive imagination."

Marisol bandaged the girl's upper arm and loaded her with a goodie bag of iron supplements and condoms. She escorted the teen into the waiting room.

Yesenia called out, "I told you not to wait for me."

A teenage boy in an equally baggy hoodie and jeans stood up from the vinyl seat. "I wanted to make sure we were okay." The sigh and concerned creases on his forehead on his otherwise boyish face begged for the good news.

"Not pregnant. And now I'm on birth control." Yesenia playfully smacked his upper arm with her small plastic bag. "Marisol took care of me."

Marisol finally got a good look at him, and the moment they made eye contact, she immediately broke it off. Shit, he was the kid from last year. The one flanking Tiny's side when the Shadows, her brother's gang, put the Bloodsucker's minions on the ropes when she'd saved Vincent from the abandoned slaughterhouse. Now, Tiny led the Shadows as they managed their growing control over Shadowhaven's local drug trade. It wasn't a flash of recognition she expected at her day job.

"Marisol." She extended her hand out.

He took her hand and gave it a single shake. "Guillermo. We met before."

Fucking kids. Her brother would've gone ham on him for blabbing about the Shadows so publicly. "Oh yeah?" Marisol tested how long she could play dumb before she dragged the boy into an alley and told him what was what. No, they hadn't plucked the bleeding Patron Saint off a meat hook and Molotov cocktailed a rival's hideout into oblivion. That had been someone else.

"I'm a welterweight at your dad's gym."

"Right on." How a year had changed things. Her dad's after-school program at his once-fledgling gym made him a paragon of the Westside neighborhood.

"Marisol is the one I've been telling you about. You can tell her shit."

Marisol nodded. Not much she could do with the hyperbolic admiration of a teenage girl.

"See you around." Guillermo's lopsided smile activated a dimple.

"Call if you need anything." Marisol directed her concern toward Yesenia.

The girl waved goodbye, and the couple left the clinic.

One fire put out.

"I can tell her you're here," the receptionist said, "but you are not her boyfriend. She's dating Vincent Varian."

Another erupted at the check-in desk.

"I didn't say I was her boyfriend." Tobias's increased pitch gave away his annoyance. "I said—" Marisol snuck up beside him. "I'm her friend." His expression melted from pissed to pleased.

She had to admit the sudden shift in him was adorable. "Try not to give Detective Quinlan such a hard time. He had a late night last night."

Mischief flashed in his eyes. "Didn't we all?" He raised a white paper bag to his cheek. "I brought you a sandwich."

"Working lunch?"

"Yep."

"I'll go clock out."

A bounce entered **Marisol's** step as she and Tobias strolled in the direction of their pickup point. The waning winter cold bit a touch of pink into his nose. "We need to set some boundaries about you two and your night visits. You scared the shit out of Cesca."

The name drew a blank. Tobias rarely brought a companion around. Probably because he had a revolving door of them. "Who's Cesca?"

"My girlfriend!"

Despite his emphasis, not as clarifying of a descriptor as he intended. "Which one is she again?"

"The yoga instructor who someone in AA set me up with."

Now that he mentioned it, she had seen him with a quiet workout enthusiast possessing the sour face of someone who'd had her coffee made with cow's milk rather than the usual almond. "Is she the one who's always scowling at me when we hang out?"

He shrugged, unhelpfully oblivious.

She snorted. This *Cesca's* screams last night were of the orgasmic variety. "She didn't seem that scared."

"Figured a woman in a committed relationship such as yourself would understand the importance of the adult sleepover."

She flinched as if a fist was moments from her face, a strange, irrational, and automatic human response. Yes, she had everything and the kitchen sink with Vincent, but a small part of her mourned the end of Tobias's crush on her. "And not much sleeping going on, either."

He placed his hands on his hips, flicking back his trench coat. "She slept all over me nine times."

The rise of his fuccboi ego abated her jealousy, which she had no problem greeting with an eye roll.

Vincent's shining limo pulled up to the curb. She opened the door and dropped into her seat next to Vincent. Tobias followed her, sitting across from them.

"We're calling our meeting into session?" Vincent asked.

"Yep. First order of business: you guys are goddamn assholes," Tobias grumbled.

Marisol scoffed. "Uh-oh, Dad's mad."

"When a bleeding Congressional candidate has to get his jaw wired shut, even the baby they got working as the assistant DA knows we got a confession under duress. You were supposed to get me the hard drive. You know, a clean case? Not this." He leaned forward. "The whole thing's got stink lines."

Her leg bounced until it became a full-blown stomp. "This case is clean." She pointed an accusing finger at Tobias. "He hurt those girls! On video, no less! If more men like him had to drink out of a straw for their crimes, the world would be a better place."

He didn't even blink. "Lawyers are flies to shit, kid. If they get a whiff of us getting something dirty, they'll bury it. Even if it's on video."

Dressing up and fighting crime was a way to circumvent the bullshit of the city's justice system. Now, here she was with the same bullshit but a different flavor, no thanks to her best friend. "The thin blue line never fails to disappoint."

Tobias shook his head and jutted his chin toward Vincent. "What do you think?"

Vincent dropped his head. "We may have gotten carried away."

Tobias threw his arms out. "Exactly!"

Why were her men turning on her? Yes, she'd lost her temper, but Durant deserved to be roughed up. More than that, even. Marisol pushed herself against the car door, creating as much space away from them as she could with no real means of escape.

"But not for nothing. What he did was" —Vincent sighed— "reprehensible, to put mildly. Sometimes following the rules doesn't send the message we're trying to communicate. Those who do evil will have their reckoning." His rich baritone dropped into a growly bass.

A hint of his Patron Saint mode with his heightened Justice speak calmed some of those worries, fan-service for a fangirl.

"If he entertained people like the ones on the list you shared with me, there will be people after him. Even in the relative safety of jail." Tobias softened. "How do we polish this turd?"

The corners of Vincent's mouth curled, becoming the cat who trapped the mouse. "How Vincent Varian handles everything. We'll have a big party."

5

Step Nine

Tobias fidgeted in the booth of the bustling coffee shop. He'd already drained half his coffee—drip, none of the fancy stuff. According to his watch, Diedre was ten minutes late and counting. His daughter had the other half of his coffee before he gave up.

Diedre entered the coffee shop. Someone should buy her new clothes. Her baggy jeans were frayed at the bottom hem, and her thumbs poked through holes in her gray sweater's sleeves. One thumb wedged under the thin backpack strap at her shoulder. Flecks of auburn highlighted brown hair she had clipped back in a sloppy French twist. She scanned the place with a concerned, lost look.

She finally made eye contact. He had expected the relief of finding him to iron out her concern, but instead, her expression soured further. Today's meeting wasn't going to be a sweet father-daughter moment.

To-go cup in hand, she sat down at the booth and plopped her backpack next to herself. "I'm on a deadline. You have until I finish my tea today."

Arrive late and leave early? She must've learned the trick from him. "Deadline?"

She sat back, almost as if she were finally relaxing a bit. "I'm working freelance cybersecurity. Businesses hire me to hack them, so they can predict attacks."

Watching the defensiveness slide away made evident how much she looked like him, the fragment of brown in her otherwise blue eyes, the twitch of her nose moving her tiny freckles, and the bushy curl to her hair.

His daughter, brilliant and independent. Those qualities had nothing to do with him, though. Thank god Laura and her husband had their heads on straight. "I know who to call if I click a link in a suspicious email then."

"Please don't click links," she murmured into her cup of tea.

He reached into the inner pocket of his trench coat and drew out a stuffed envelope. "This is for you to read later."

An exercise in sobriety was apologizing to those he hurt when he was lost to his addiction. He had written Diedre a multi-page letter, which documented his more egregious wrongs. Missing sport games and performances, skipping custodial weekends, and the countless nights he avoided family dinner or story time —the actions separating a father from a sperm donor. Except it wasn't all whiskey and following his drunken dick around. A lot of those times were for the job. It's not like he could turn away from Shadowhaven's record-breaking murder rate.

She took the envelope and immediately tossed it in her bag without flinching. In silence, they sipped their drinks. If anything proved that time was relative, it was this interaction. Awkwardness slowed it down; her looming early exit sped it up.

He scratched the back of his neck. What did he have for small talk? He couldn't quite tell her about working with a super-powered, 500-year-old vigilante and his girlfriend, but he could give her certain details. "I'm going to a ball hosted by my friend. Someone you may have heard of, Vincent Varian. I get to wear a tux and everything. I was wondering if you'd like to be my plus one? We get to rub elbows with the elite. Maybe you could hack into their bank accounts?"

Her eyes narrowed.

"Joking, obviously. About the hacking, not the ball."

Crossed arms joined her scowl. "Aren't you dating someone? Wouldn't you want to take her instead?"

"I thought it could be a father-daughter thing, something cool you get to do with your old man."

"Let's be clear, I don't need to do things with you. Yeah, you missed out on a lot with me, but Mom showed up double to make sure I never felt what was missing. I'm glad your new friend has been around for you to turn this new leaf, but you can't throw a tuxedo and some sequins on the past and expect to make amends."

He hadn't thought of extending the invitation to her as making amends. Nothing he could do would change the past. Taking Diedre to the ball was a chance to build a future, to have something more than a mountain of fuck-ups with her. The truth, as bitter as his now-cold coffee, was that he'd have to build a careful future on the shaky foundations of his past.

She hoisted the strap of her backpack onto her shoulder and scooted to the edge of the booth. Shit, she was making her exit already.

"Deeds, I get it, and I thank you for making time for me when I've given you plenty of reasons not to, but—" Jesus Christ, he was trying his best. What was he supposed to do? Build a whole baseball field in hopes they'd play a game of catch? He took a moment to breathe. "—your tea smells good, and it would be a waste of perfectly good money to leave it here."

She slid a few inches back into the booth. Her backpack strap dropped from her shoulder. She raised the cup, and Tobias toasted his mug against it. "Cheers," he said.

She buttoned her lips to one side, a Quinlan way of holding back a smile.

Vincent's measuring-tape-wielding hand brushed against Tobias's crotch. **Tobias** jumped back, squinting in the mirror. "Does it have to be so tight?"

Vincent called out the measurements to Staci, which the computer recorded. Deep into the underground hideout of the Patron Saint, the superhero and his computer conducted the important business of dressing Tobias for the upcoming ball.

Drawers sprung from the recesses in the wall, presenting fabric bolts. Black, black, and more black, all variations of some kind of blend.

"It's not tight." Vincent clicked his tongue. "It's custom fit." He ran his fingers along the bolts of fabric and picked one out of the lineup.

"The last time I wore a tux was on my wedding day, and I'm pretty sure I rented it from someplace with the word *emporium* in the title."

Vincent wound a strip of black silk around his fingers, staring at Tobias's reflection. "The shirt is all wrong. Try flat front, no pleats."

Tobias unbuttoned the white dress shirt, peeling it away from his body. The life of a modern-day prince was an oddity to him, how easily image became a carefully curated story.

Another drawer opened, presenting a collection of white dress shirts. Vincent picked one out and held it out as if he was going to dress Tobias. Tobias hooked the dress shirt by the collar with one finger and took it off the persnickety billionaire's hands. "I got this." The fabric glided over his arms as he slipped them inside. Vincent reached out to button the shirt for him, but Tobias stepped back, quickly fastening the shirt himself.

"Much better," Vincent said. He approached the platform and hugged Tobias around the neck.

The thrill of the other night returned—Cesca's joyous wails blending in with Marisol's shadow, which now merged with the pressure around his neck. "What are you doing?"

"Bow tie." His bright blue eyes focused on Tobias's throat.

He gulped at the searing sensation. "I can't tie one of those."

"Nonsense. It's like tying your shoes. A loop, a knot, a little tug." The bow tightened around his neck. Vincent straightened it and glanced up at Tobias, flashing a smirk.

The blue of his irises called to him. *Confess. Your girlfriend watched me naked.* The admission developed into little stings across his tongue. He swallowed his guilt back. What would an admission do? Create tiny fissures into a relationship built on trust, friendship, and loyalty. The confession would expose him as some jealous extra waiting in the wings. He was better than his worse impulses. Better than making mountains out of molehills of misread cues and poorly channeled desires.

Vincent stepped down from the platform and watched him in the mirror. "Marisol and I...we need you."

Had Vincent seen right to his hopes? His heart raced. Maybe he hadn't heard him correctly. "What?"

"When you live on the edge as I do, it's easy to lose sight of the laws we've put into place. Doing too much of what we do, and we can disappear into the vengeance. She's not angry with you. She cares."

Tobias sank a bit. They needed him for the job and nothing more. "Not the first woman to give me shit. She certainly won't be the last."

A beat passed as Vincent seemed to study his twitches. "Woman," he said, followed by a hum. "Take your shirt off. Staci will have your tux ready for you in no time."

Vincent waved around the shirt and fabrics like a flag as he disappeared around the corner of the hideout. Tobias leaned against the wall of drawers as he steadied to put his pants back on.

"Tobias Quinlan recognized," Staci announced over her system. A drawer popped out from behind him, and cool clouds wafted from it. The drawer contained the wonder drug that had caused him to puke his guts out, but had sucked the gray out of his beard back when he and Marisol emptied the hideout almost a year ago. He picked up a vial and studied it.

"What are you doing?" Vincent asked, having returned to the main part of the hideaway.

Tobias nudged the drawer, and it disappeared into the wall with a click. "Nothing." He pulled his pants on. "Staci opened up one of these things. I'm still in your system, remember?" He punctuated his question with the zip of his fly.

Vincent's steely gaze cut through him, as if he were decoding every one of Tobias's nervous tics. "Yes, you're still in my system."

The memory of Marisol on his fire escape mixed with Vincent. All those nights of Vincent appearing in the dark and needing him—needing his help, that was. The prickling heat returned. What if it were Vincent who had been on Tobias's fire escape instead of Marisol that night?

Tobias walked away from the downtown high-rise, tie loose and his dress shirt buttoned unevenly. He left in a hurry, carrying with him the burden of the answer.

It wouldn't have mattered who had been waiting on the landing for him. Vincent or Marisol, he'd still feel the wave of desire, followed by the guilt.

A month of practice and **Tobias** still couldn't tie the damn bow tie. Hopefully, Cesca would help him. He knocked on the door of Cesca's apartment. She greeted him at the door dressed in a slouchy sweatshirt, sports bra, and leggings. Hardly the gown he had expected.

"Not feeling well?" Tobias entered her apartment, his head dipping slightly under the doorway to avoid bonking his forehead on the frame.

"No." She paced her beige living room, mouth pursed together. After enough stomping and wiggling, she announced, "I spoke to my friend today, the one from AA."

The hairs on his neck stood up. "Oh yeah?" He leaned against the arm of a chair. What corners of his darkness was she going to delve into?

"She said members are discouraged from entering new romantic relationships until six months. Something about vulnerability and recidivism." Cesca crossed her arms and kept her gaze downcast.

He held back a smile. "I didn't start dating you until seven months in." Standing up from the chair arm, he reached for her chin, rubbing the point at the end of it. "See? I'm a good boy."

Cesca blinked rapidly and lifted her chin away from his touch. "I'm not talking about me."

Vague words and angry body language. He'd been swept up in the passive-aggressive dance of a relationship hanging by a thread.

"When she told me that, I knew what's been holding us back." Tears pooled into her eyes.

What reassurances did she need? If anyone had received an unbroken promise since he turned things around, it was her. "I haven't wanted a single drop since we've dated."

"It's not the drinking. Answer this question—what are we going to do at the ball?"

"Stand around and look pretty with—"

"Them, right?" Acid poured into her words, landing like an attack.

A constant on his path to becoming a good man was the support and encouragement from Vincent and Marisol, as complicated as his feelings were for them. "They're my best friends." The claim faltered as he said it. He hadn't acted like a friend. Not when Marisol visited his apartment. Not when Vincent tightened silk around his throat.

She nodded and headed to her door, opening it. "I'm not going."

"Not going as in I tell them you're sick or—"

"Not going because I can't stand being the odd one out on these supposed double dates."

"Do I need to point you to the direction of the news? The shit we've been through together? We're practically comrades-in-arms."

"But it isn't just that, is it? There's no room for me in your codependent relationship."

Had to hand it to Cesca. She was perceptive.

Tobias left her apartment and settled back into the driverless limousine. He could whip off his tie, run back into Cesca's apartment building, and declare he'd be a good man and let them go.

Yet, his reflection warped in the darkened glass of the window. He was doomed to follow them like the twisted dog he was.

6

All That Remains is You

Vincent double-checked the speech notes safe in his tuxedo jacket's breast pocket. They were there next to the small box for Marisol. Surprises like these were difficult to keep—the notes even more so when they contained his yearslong announcement of a technology promising freedom. Freedom from the fuels destroying the planet. Freedom from the poverty and squalor dragging the city down. Freedom from the rules of matter.

He could spout a speech off the top of his head no problem, and if he stumbled over his words or drew a blank mid-sentence, people would chalk it up to another adorable faux pas from the city's golden idiot, but he wanted to say the words perfectly for her, the woman who was currently posing in the mirror of the vanity across the room from him.

She studied her appearance with a serious expression, as if she was trying to find a flaw. He felt like a guest in his own estate home now while they lived in the city, but he kept the estate in adequate working order with Staci's help. He couldn't let a good ballroom go to waste. How else was Shadowhaven's supposed elite going to choke down his hierarchy-shattering news? By greasing their gullets with a party.

She fidgeted with some tendrils, which had escaped from her elaborate updo. Her dusty blue silk chiffon gown swirled around her. It had a fitted bodice with off-shoulder sleeves and a layered skirt, which flowed away from her waist. His favorite part of it was the hidden splits in the skirt, flashing the occasional sight of her golden-brown legs.

He turned on the Tiffany lamp next to the untouched canopy bed.

"With the way they braided and pinned my hair," she said to her reflection, "they made me look like a pastry."

"Nonsense." He had stroked her hair enough to know what she worried about only she could see. "I am all of sudden hungry looking at you."

She snickered.

"You look beautiful but—"

"But?" She put a hand on her hip, the thin bangles at her wrist jingling.

"Something's missing." He feigned scanning and thinking, though he had the very thing resting against his heart next to his speech notes. "Ah, I know!" He reached inside his jacket and revealed the jewelry box.

She shot him an admonishing glance. She'd routinely lecture him when he lavished her with impractical gifts.

He stepped closer to her. "I know, but I promise this is necessary."

She raised a skeptical eyebrow. He could already see her listing the causes and programs in need of funding. After his the reveal tonight, she needn't worry.

"Indulge me," he said.

Her expression shifted subtly—her pupils wider, a visible pulse from her neck. Usually, she indulged him with a spanking or stuffing her underwear into his willing mouth, so opening a box posed fewer problems and taboos. She lifted the lid, revealing a gold, spiked ear cuff. He plucked it from the cushion and clipped the cuff gently over the shell of her right ear. The spikes shot out like rays of sunshine. She smiled at her reflection.

"You look divine."

"Thank you." She took his hand and raised it to her face. "I'm a bundle of nerves. I get so edgy around these blue bloods. Ridiculous because you're the one with the big speech, and I'm the arm candy."

He rubbed his thumb along her jawline. "I just picture the audience naked."

"Gross."

He drew her in closer and hugged his arms around her waist, pressing his chest against her back. "Now I'm picturing you naked." He kissed behind her bare shoulder and breathed in the light, sweet musk of the perfume she had dabbed on her neck.

They should ditch the party and spend the evening naked. He'd trace his nose over every inch he could smell her sweet scent. The big announcement of his could be easily blurted over social media between a cat video and a photo of a setting sun with a quote from *The Art of War* imposed over it, as the other billionaires did with life-altering news. Too bad he had hosted the event and guests were already gathered downstairs.

She laughed but wriggled away from him. "Don't start. We have to go soon."

He tucked lurid ideas about convenient leg slits away. They were better used later at the party, so he could experience the thrill of watching her bite her lip as she attempted to come quietly, while people around the corner made small talk over flutes of champagne.

She breezed past him to the chaise lounge, her skirt flitted behind her. She slid her right foot into her gold stiletto sandal and struggled to tie the straps into a bow around her ankle. He took his jacket off, threw it on the bed, knelt down before her, and retied the straps into a secure, symmetrical bow. "These aren't the shoes I bought you."

She shrugged. "I returned that pair and got these on sale."

"You're saving my money?" He beamed with admiration for how easily she had his riches at her disposal but snuck sensibility into the fun of them. His frugal little hedonist.

"There are better uses for it." She extended her left leg from the layers of silk. Her legs and feet shimmered with her body oil, and her toes were tipped with pearlescent polish.

"What could be better than supporting this foot?" His touch ghosted alongside her foot. A touch he punctuated with a kiss of her arch.

"You're misbehaving."

"I am?" He slipped the heeled sandal on her other foot and tied it delicately at the ankle. His rising inner heat forced him to loosen his bow tie and unbutton his collar. He returned her foot to the floor, pushed back the silk of her dress, and kissed the side of her knee. "I thought I was being very, very good."

Her breasts heaved as she sighed. "Want to please me?"

He performed an internal backflip, because he did want to please her. Oh so very much. He nodded.

"*Sálvame*?"[1] She checked for their safe word. He repeated it to confirm his understanding. "Now show me how much you love these shoes."

He placed her left foot on his shoulder and kissed the strap at her ankle and the criss-cross at her forefoot, never breaking eye contact with her. She dug the stiletto into his pectoral. The pain stirred into the first ripple of pleasure, yet he was already edging as the heel drove harder into his muscle. If he couldn't control himself as a man, at least his super-powers gave him another sort of super resistance. Though, *joder*, if she didn't have a way of wrecking his strength, too.

She lifted his chin by her big toe. "Pathetic little smooches. Is that how you show love?"

1. Save me.

He shook his head. His love could be a devastating deluge. He ran the flat of his tongue over the strap across her toes.

"I said love, not drool. You better not ruin these with your sloppy spit." The stiletto stabbed into his shoulder again.

Mierda. His body pushed out a moan. She'd punish him if he didn't do a good job. And she was getting so good at punishments, his balls tightened at the potential. The tip of his tongue traced along the side of her shoe until he reached the stiletto. He lifted her foot higher and kissed the tip of the pointed heel. The ball of her foot rested on his forehead. He was no better than the ground she walked on.

Demeaning him stripped him of his illusions and power, made him something elemental and free. He was no longer Vincent or the Patron Saint or even a man. He was the formless, primordial ooze in meiosis, sharing and dividing himself until he was something new. He opened his lips and sucked the entirety of his lover's bargain stiletto into his mouth.

"That's it," she soothed. She pinched one nipple over the fabric of her bodice and stroked her silk-clad inner thigh with the other hand. Her body arced and rolled as nerve endings connected to places they hadn't before—nipple to stiletto, stiletto to clit. "You're doing such a good job."

He answered with another moan.

"Take off my panties."

His hands glided up her calves, along her thighs to find a stretch of lace across her hips. But nothing. He teasingly explored the curls along her pubis, gave her ass a squeeze, but found not one scrap of fabric. Those panties were either unbelievably tiny or— "You're not wearing any."

"I know," she answered with a playful grin. "It was a surprise for the party." She looked down and wet her lip with her tongue. Lifting her gaze, she offered him wide-eyed vulnerability. "I wanted to show how much I love you by fucking you senseless right under their noses, but I can't wait."

He embraced her, burying his nose against her apex, still covered in a waterfall of silk. He pulled her closer to breathe in the ripe and ready smell of her. He draped the silk of the skirt carefully around them, like she was the center of a blue flower. She opened her legs for him.

"Lap me up, " she ordered.

He parted the curtain of silk to nibble and lick the inside of her thighs. She clawed at the back of his neck, so he kissed her at her sweet center, ran his tongue back and forth over it, sucking, changing pressure. All to show her he was good. She trained him so well with her shoes.

She opened more to him and he probed her entrance with his middle finger. She was dripping wet. He added another finger and formed the two into a hook, pushing in and up against her. He plunged gently until she writhed and hummed. With his free hand on top of her belly, he suckled on the berry of her clit and fingered her harder.

"Oh fuck. Vincent, you'll stain the dress."

"Hm." He didn't care. He'd go to the party with her all over him. His guests would ask him where they could find his cologne. *Custom made,* he'd answer but leave off, *from the divine nectar between my lover's thighs.* They'd see the mess he made of her on his pants, his shirt. Tipsy, they'd think, spilled his champagne, but he was only drunk off her.

Her muscles pulsed around his fingers, and he savored the sweet taste coming from her center. He didn't stop drinking until she pulled the hair at the back of his neck.

"You're too good," she murmured as she panted. "Too fucking good. Would you like your reward?"

Earning her possessed him. He got up off his knees and yanked her to her feet.

"The bed," she breathed, heading in its direction.

He couldn't wait to move the few feet and he spun her around, bending her over the back of the lounge chair. She braced her arms on the velvet seat. He freed his cock from his fly and sheathed himself in her. Deep inside, he stilled, listening to the soft gasps escaping her lips. She moved her hips, but he pulled out.

"Dammit, Vincent," she whined.

"I'm enjoying my reward." He drove back in slowly and then picked up pace. Pounding, rapid thrusts shoved the chaise lounge into wall and scraped divots into the damask wallpaper. She turned her head, glancing at him. Her eyes glowed ever wilder with every pump he gave her. He couldn't hold back much longer. The beautiful mess they made was going to end.

She lifted her leg and kicked her heel into his hip bone. He jumped back, the cool air on his shaft tearing apart the force building around his pelvis. She dropped to her knees, her silk skirt spread around her.

"Give it all to me." She took the crown of him into her warm, wet mouth and jacked the base with a firm grip.

Her cheeks hollowed as she sealed her lips around him, sucking and stroking him with her tongue. Her hands moved to his ass, and she took him farther and farther in her mouth. He threaded his fingers in her hair, unraveling her updo into untamed curls.

He was seeing stars—burning red giants expanding into oblivion and crushing him into the center of a black hole. He pushed the back of her head, felt the squeeze of her throat and... and... he came over and over, until he was reduced to his atomic level, until he was the absence of matter. She swallowed his orgasm and licked him clean. Her tongue prodded his raw nerves, and he whimpered. She laughed and licked him again; he shuddered.

He had been completely rebooted, back to his default settings. "*No queda nada,*" he whispered, "*más que tú.*"

"*Nosotros.*" She kissed him, her tongue pushing against his, combining the different flavors of their sex in his mouth. "Nothing remains but us."

Us. What was the feeling when someone euphoric felt more happiness? He stumbled to sit on the chaise lounge and catch his breath. Even with super healing, he had to wait until he stopped floating to return into solid form. She collapsed next to him. "Eventually, I'll get up to fix my makeup and hair."

"Sorry about that." Eyes closed, he feebly gestured with a wet noodle arm toward what he believed was her hair.

She giggled. "No worries. I'm no longer nervous."

"That was part of the plan all along." He sighed, still lost in the dream state.

"Oh shit! We're late!" Her weight left the seat, and she rummaged around the vanity.

He interlaced his hands behind his head and leaned back. "Nothing important will happen without us."

"Yeah, but it's the principle." A pause. "Is this why you're always late to your parties? The ball, last winter?"

He fluttered his eyes open. Usually, he arrived late to parties because he had a special delivery for the police, and criminals never followed a set schedule. No legendary bedroom escapades disrupted his lives. Before Marisol, sex was a means to an end, a tool like a pick for locks. "A gentleman never kisses and tells."

"You're not that gentle, either, man."

"I am whatever my lady desires." He studied her in front of the vanity as she reapplied her lipstick and touched up her eyeliner. She brushed her hair, which now fell into silken waves. Instead of twisting and braiding her hair back in the bun, she pinned the right side up with a simple hair comb.

He finally had a word for euphoria plus even more happiness. *Home.* He was home, and not in the literal sense of the word. For now, he no longer needed to run or find answers. The world spun, and he could be still. Home.

7

Past and Future Collide

Marisol clung to Vincent's arm as they made their way into the ballroom. From the shadows of his estate's east wing, she entered the grand ballroom full of Shadowhaven's purported best people. Vincent had pulled out all the stops. Caterers in black and white weaved among the masses, serving plates of delicious decadence and flutes of bubbly escape.

A large, blank screen contrasted against the old-school gold and lush red decor and gilded marble. The incongruent setup promised Vincent's secret project—even secret to her.

Predictably, cameras flashed. Marisol adjusted her shoulders and the angle she stood. She hadn't been like this before, self-conscious around the paparazzi, but after finding enough websites and newspaper pages featuring her, she suddenly became aware. Aware of the sweeping silk chiffon of her gray-blue dress about her legs, the boldness of the spiked golden ear cuff emphasized by the half-pulled-back hairstyle.

A camera flashed. Vincent kissed her shoulder. "All that remains is us," he whispered in her ear. A flurry of photographers snapped photos.

As much as he tried to reassure her that she belonged at these high society events, she scanned the crowd for a familiar face standing out from it. Someone else who suffered these silly gatherings along with her. But there was no sign of Tobias. She smoothed the fabric along her hips, burying her disappointment.

"Ready to share about your project yet, Mr. Varian?" a reporter shouted over the crowd.

Vincent responded in a catlike smile and jerked his chin in the direction of the blank screen. An audio-visual expert manning a board of knobs, slides, and connections nodded. A few flicks at the table, and an image projected onto the screen.

Scientists, dressed in white coats, gathered onscreen.

"Good evening, Mr. Varian and the people of Shadowhaven. We come to you via satellite from the Varian lab built beneath the Micah Forest." The scientist adjusted his glasses and sighed. Crowds didn't seem to be his forte either.

Whispers among the party goers echoed, "Underground lab?" or "Secret?" or "I told you. Varian is so mysterious."

Another white-coat emerged to the forefront of the group, centering herself in view. Her dark, angled bob reminded Marisol of the ball almost a year earlier, her best friend Annie cooing over Dr. Sandra Faraday.

"Our physicists are excited to show Shadowhaven our years of hard work, and I'm sure the press will be delighted to hear the rumors of a secret project were true," the doctor said to the camera. The group behind her dispersed to stations at a giant computer.

Vincent gestured toward the screen. "My grandfather, Leonard, was a dedicated physicist. He witnessed experimental mushroom clouds and committed his life to understanding the atom. He refused to accept his path of study in nuclear energy had only to do with destruction. In that way, he was much more like my medical doctor father than I'd care to admit." His knowing smile grew, the joke being Vincent Varian was all of these incarnations—all of them but his adopted son turned father and eventual grandfather figure, Leonard. "Under the research and development wing of my company's name, we attracted brilliant minds from CERN and gifted physicists, all in trying to understand the power of the atom."

He continued, "We built upon the technology of the world's premiere Hadron collider. Where they pursued physics to understand the beginning of life, recreating the Big Bang, we sought to harness that life's explosive force."

With another snap of his fingers, the electricity went out in the ballroom, leaving only the screen and camera. A small generator hummed to power them. Terrified gasps and wails burst from the crowd. Marisol herself clutched onto Vincent's arm, but a faint blue sparkle from his eyes told her this was all in the plan. Count on Vincent to create all sorts of mischief to watch the elite crowd react.

His sonorous voice boomed over the chatter. "We have cut the estate's power from the grid."

The partygoers cowering in huddles stood straighter, perhaps a sign of their fear subsiding.

"Dr. Faraday," Vincent said.

She walked to a computer panel set up before a giant glass window, thick in its gargantuan structure. Faraday pulled a lever.

Nothing.

Marisol checked Vincent for a tic indicating disappointment. He hadn't even blinked. Instead, he seemed to study the crowd like some god who knew the waves and troughs of a journey while the mere mortals were tempest-tossed.

The camera lens appeared to have developed a smudge, but the smudge moved. A faint aura shimmered behind the thick glass. White light flashed. The scientists, including Faraday, ducked for cover. The light grew in intensity. The crowd in the safety of Vincent's ballroom reeled back as if they were in the lab.

Dancing magenta sparks emerged from the white light. The rosy hue was less of a retina-scorcher. The dark pink fuzzies seemed to quit vibrating and froze in place.

"The atoms are moving at such a rate, to the naked human eye, they seem still," Dr. Faraday announced.

The light fixtures in the ballroom flickered to an ember glow. People witnessed the change and pointed. The dim glow grew brighter and brighter until bulbs shattered from the sudden surge. Glass pinged against the floor like tiny, ominous chimes.

"My estate is now powered by the life created in my particle collider. In a few more minutes, the energy produced by the collider will be self-sufficient and will no longer have to rely on old-fashioned dinosaur grids."

The crowd hummed, moderately impressed.

"Dr. Faraday, please tell my guests what else they can expect."

"With the collider operating, in a twenty-four hour period, Shadowhaven will have enough green energy to be powered for one hundred years."

Marisol gripped Vincent's hand, her fingers linking between his. Green energy for a hundred years? Her home, her Shadowhaven, could possibly be a city of the future? He turned to her, his pupils moving rapidly and finally fixing on hers.

"And with an updated grid system, Shadowhaven could power the rest of the country, the continent. When people think of Shadowhaven, they will see it as a beacon of clean, sustainable energy." His statement came out quietly, as if it was only for her. He had breathed life into what she had always dreamed: the way to save her city was not by fighting crime, but by empowering it.

"Power the country?"

"The rest of the continent?" News reporters echoed him, catching on to the promise.

"Our work powering a large swath of the Western Hemisphere will sustain Shadowhaven and its citizens.

As municipalities pay us for our reliable energy, we will have funding for housing, schools, infrastructure. Soon, our city will have income to provide every one of our citizens. We can show that life has dignity not for what it can produce, but for merely being alive."

Shadowhaven becoming a place where anyone could prosper? Marisol had never believed she'd see the day. The crowd devolved into murmurs. How would the powerful assert their dominance if all life lived equally and had equal dignity? What innovations and knowledge would burst alive from the rotten depths of the Westside if people actually had full bellies? Fed souls? Vincent wasn't just providing Shadowhaven with power, he provided the mallet to destroy the whole power structure.

People swarmed Vincent. Questions attacked him in a flurry.

"What inspired your soft heart?"

"My spirit, my Marisol inspires me to love this city as much as she does."

She bit her lip to hide her smile from the crowd's prying eyes.

"Income for everyone? Even criminals and drug addicts? Immigrants?" one of the faceless journalists called out.

He whispered, "You have my permission to hide now."

In a darkened entryway toward the back, she saw Tobias, halfway between the dark room and the crowd. He wore his bow tie loose around his neck. Ever since

Vincent started doing his shopping, his suits looked damn fine on him.

Marisol darted through the crowd to greet him. "I thought you hadn't come."

"Observing from afar, more like."

"So you saw the big reveal?"

"Didn't miss a thing. Who would've thunk, Shadowhaven, a bastion of energy."

Her hope broke containment, and she hugged him. He smelled clean with a hint of sweet clove, no longer rocking drugstore artificial pine. He was missing the woman who scowled at her every time she went in for hugs like this. He was alone. Where was his date?

"I thought you were bringing what's-her-name?"

Tobias stepped deeper into the unlit room and sat on a tufted divan. "Ah. She isn't coming."

"When I last saw you two, I thought you were enjoying each other's company," she teased. Remembering his naked greeting on the fire escape spread heat to her cheeks.

He scratched the back of his neck. "You know me. Good at some things, not others."

"You two broke up?" She laced the question with too much joy.

"Pretty much. She said. . . nah, I won't say anything."

Marisol kicked the divan's cushion, nudging her foot against his knee. "C'mon. What'd she say?"

"She said" —he rubbed his thick, cropped beard— "there's no room for her when I'm already in a codependent relationship."

She scoffed. That felt brutally clinical.

"I told her that the three of us have been through the equivalent of a war together. Not divulging any magical details, but a war."

"Maybe we are a little bit." She nudged him more with her foot. He scooted over, and she sat next to him on the divan. The skirt of her dress split to reveal her shining thigh. "Codependent, that is." She toyed with the bangles at her wrist to avoid the gaping hole of honesty from opening. Something more than friendship existed between them, but it was the mask thing—the whole way they started that caused the confusion.

She stopped playing with the bangles and focused her attention to his jawline, the strong and sharp feature slightly resembling Vincent. Now that he'd grown a beard, she no longer could excuse the confusion. Just admire the fleck of auburn in the dark brown.

A jolt of eye contact caught her studying him. What'd be her excuse this time? "Sporting the loose tie look, now you're a single man?"

"Vincent showed me how to tie it. Been hiding back here because my fat fingers can't seem to do it myself. I wind up looking like a hack comedian with one side of the bow poking my chin."

"I got you." She buttoned his top button. His Adam's apple bobbed. For a guy who wore suits and ties on the daily, he sure seemed insecure having anything tight against his throat. She pulled on the ends of the tie. His torso turned to her as she wound the fabric just right around his neck. The knot secured at the center of his collar. "There. Dapper as ever."

"Thank you, kid."

She blinked, her gaze looking up to his. In the meager lighting, she couldn't make out his strange eye color, blue with hints of brown. He smiled, but the crinkles around his eyes seemed sad. It was a longing she recognized if she glimpsed at him while leaning on Vincent's shoulder.

"Are we getting along now?" he asked.

"We get along most of the time."

"You know what I mean. The case with—"

"Our methods may differ, but I know we have the same goal, my friend." She squeezed his upper arm. Vincent had made it possible—a Shadowhaven which was no longer a burden, lifting people and fulfilling promises. The change would echo through generations. "It's strange living in a world where true Justice can happen. Maybe I'm still seeing things the old way."

Her skirt had split too much while sitting, her bare hip exposed, and the way he looked at her left her naked. She pulled at the fabric to cover her leg. He bent his head down, studying the movement of her hands and perhaps the playful peeks at her legs.

A server entered the room. "The host requests guests gather in the ballroom." They turned on the lights. "Ms. Novotny, I apologize. Do you and your guest want a drink?"

"Seltzer with a twist of lime," Tobias ordered.

Shit, she hadn't considered Tobias had been invited to never-ending temptation. People in the ballroom were guzzling flute after flute of champagne. "Same," she stated in a concerted effort of solidarity. "I'm proud of you, you know."

"What? For the sobriety?"

"You've seemed to handle it with relative ease."

"It hasn't been easy." He turned his head away from her and squinted at the gallery surrounding them. "What is this room anyway?"

Golden frames glittered in the hazy light. "A gallery?" Vincent's estate always felt like a creepy inconvenience, a part of him she hadn't reconciled with the vigilante do-gooder cosplaying as a billionaire himbo. "We don't hang out here often since the move to the city."

His eyes narrowed in the direction of a larger piece. Not one of Vincent's fake family portraits, but some religious reenactment. "What's that one?" Tobias asked.

They walked to it carefully, as if the sounds of their footsteps would upset the people in the paintings. Closer, she could make out the details, a fair and naked muscular man with white cloth draped strategically over his thighs. Long, golden blond hair curled around his face with his lips parted in agony. A woman tended to his wounds, which appeared like gaping mouths. The attendant was dressed in eighteenth century work clothes, her breasts heaving, because women of the past always seemed to have heaving breasts. "Looks like Saint Sebastian."

"No arrows, though."

The waiter returned with their drink order. She sipped the crisp bubbles out of the highball glass and licked her lips in consideration of the painting. "Still him. The woman is his nurse who performed the miracle of healing."

"Religious paintings always seemed like everyone was secretly pervy in the name of the Lord. Look at him, open mouth, holes. Seems like the only miracle here is... penetration." His eyes had an ember of mischief, needing the oxygen of her high heel on his chest to become a full flame.

"Be a good boy," she whispered.

His breath stuttered. What would make him her good boy? She considered. Cleaning the sticky sensation courtesy of Vincent from her thighs with his tongue? Forcing him to smell her gloriously used pussy and name the scent notes? Semen, slick, sweat, saliva— some of it hers, some of it his.

The lure of sin broke when Vincent entered the room. "I've schmoozed. Now I need to decompress with my favorite people."

Tobias cleared his throat. "We're admiring your art collection."

Marisol squeezed Vincent's shoulders and nuzzled her chin into his upper arm. "Especially that one." She pointed to Saint Sebastian.

"It's me. Posed for it. Paris" —He looked up, calculating— "250 years ago?"

She entertained the desire to watch the men in her life squirm, to deflect her sin and underscore theirs. "Tobias said it reminded him of penetration."

Vincent locked on Tobias with his predator's glower. "How interesting."

Tobias scratched the back of his neck, a blush rising above his beard line. "I didn't know I knew the model." Something else captured his attention, and he bolted to it. "Like this one. When did you have the time to pose for a portrait, kid?"

She cocked her head to one side. "I didn't?"

In the back of the gallery was a smaller painting, bigger than printer paper but not by much. It was of a woman with long, dark hair sweeping in the wind, golden-brown skin, a blue shawl swimming about the curves of her body. Slivers of her skin appeared in the folds of the fabric. The woman reached out from a beam of light, surrounded by barren trees. Religious for sure, but the subject in no way appeared like any of the saints she'd grown up with.

She could see how Tobias made the mistake. The resemblance was strong.

"I commissioned this, " Vincent said. He rubbed a thumb over the cleft in his chin. "I don't remember when. No model, but—"

His body seized. He zoned out this way more often than she liked, as if the deeper he dug into the past, the more it hurt. A trauma response, perhaps, and one she barely understood. She exchanged a look of concern with Tobias.

"Yes, no model, as I recall. A vision I had? Before building the estate. Yes. Before. Not sure how long ago exactly."

Tobias teased, "You're glitching, Vinnie."

Reconciling Vincent's long past overtook Marisol in a suffocating, uncomfortable itch. "I need to step outside for a bit."

Marisol stormed past the French doors and leaned against the balustrade outside. She took in the familiar sight of Shadowhaven over the trees.

She loved Vincent. Loved him after peering into the darkest parts of him, but there were times their conversations seemed overly alien to her. She loved him completely, but with only knowing him partially. She'd never know what he was like as a child. Hell, she barely knew what he was like in most versions of his adulthood.

The hair on her arms twitched. Was Vincent behind her? She turned to lock eyes with a woman at the corner of the balustrade. A puff of sweet smoke hovered over her, the source a cigarillo hanging loosely from her lips. Her hair, in blond braids, was coiled on top of her head in an elaborate bun. A thick gold choker adorned her long, thin neck. She wore a black jumpsuit that highlighted her muscular shoulders, and her bare arms glistened with gold streaks against her deep brown skin. The streaks looked like tree branches. As she turned to ash her cigarillo, Marisol confirmed she wore a backless jumpsuit, emphasizing spine-like body jewelry creeping up the middle of her back.

The woman waved.

"You're staring," the woman called out.

Bold. And playful. "I like your jewelry."

She spewed a breath of smoke. "Not jewelry."

What could the gold be if it wasn't jewelry? Marisol waited to be told more. Instead, the woman pushed what looked like white fabric over the edge of the balustrade. Whatever it was, the estate's bushes swallowed it.

One of the servers burst out of the French doors. "Hey, cigarette breaks are not allowed while on client property."

"Excuse me?"

"And your break was over ten minutes ago."

"I don't work for you. I'm one of Mr. Varian's guests." And the most interesting guest of the lot. She didn't seem like the Shadowhaven elites.

"Funny joke. Now get back to the bar."

"You must be confusing me with someone else."

"I've had enough of your games."

Marisol had heard similar condescension and hostility from doctors and even patients who thought less of her. She stomped over to her strange new friend. "You've obviously confused her with someone else. Mr. Varian would not be understanding of you chastising his guests."

"I'm sorry, Ms. Novotny. But she—"

"I know it can be confusing for you, but not all of us are the help."

The server bowed his head. "Forgive me." He walked slowly inside, shaking his head.

The woman chucked the stub of her cigarillo over the ledge. She held out her hand, the movement of her lithe arms seemed accompanied by an electric hum. "Thank you for the assist. I'm Adhara."

Marisol shook her hand. "Marisol."

"I know who you are."

"I forget I'm becoming well-known."

"Not from the gossip. Varian and I go way back." She had an accent Marisol didn't recognize. Perhaps she was an acquaintance from Vincent's jet-setting days, because apart from her and Tobias, Vincent's friends' list was zero.

"I apologize. He hasn't mentioned you before."

"To his credit, he probably thought I was dead. Or as dead as people like us can get."

A lump formed in Marisol's throat. She'd experienced these sensations before—her hair standing on end, the odd conversation implying a bigger picture.

"I've been following your partnership for a while. Two masked vigilantes fighting crime, questing after the true Justice which will free him from his curse."

Marisol crossed her arms, anything to help her poker face. She and Vincent were so careful, and any confirmation of their late night activities could threaten their whole livelihood.

"I knew him before the transformation. Apart from the zombified friends he stores away, I may be the person on this planet who has known him the longest." Adhara smiled wryly. "You're shocked. I get it. You're probably scanning me for a sign of knowing him, making sure I'm not some wolf in sheep's clothing."

Marisol no longer froze to be indiscernible to this intruding stranger. She was now genuinely confused by Adhara's openness.

Adhara continued, "To know Vicente is to lose something of yourself. What did you lose to know him?"

Annie. Her messy updo, cat-eye glasses, her silly jokes, her unwavering friendship suddenly had been ripped from her by three blasts from a gun. What had Marisol lost? Her best friend. Her eyes welled with tears, and she hid the sting by feigning interest in the stars. "I don't understand your question."

Adhara's playfulness faded. "I think you do. The way I know hundreds of years haven't dulled my pain."

From her sorrow sprouted anger, coming at her in rapid-fire questions. Hadn't Vincent said there were none like him left? That all that remained of his past were men frozen like icicles in his basement? She hadn't thought to find inconsistencies in the brief, monosyllabic statements Vincent made about his former lives. The lies were supposed to be over once she saw behind his mask.

What did the similarity to Adhara mean about his love for Marisol, especially when Adhara was so beautiful?

"Ease the crease in your forehead. We've fucked, sure, centuries ago, but I'm not looking to steal your man."

As forthright as Adhara was, the truth didn't provide much comfort either.

8

History Lessons

Vincent searched for Marisol in the crowd. "It appears we chased her off."

"She's outside." Tobias gestured to the French doors leading to the large balcony. The silvery shine of the full moon illuminated Marisol, along with another who had captured her in conversation.

At first, he swore he was seeing things. Many women had rich umber skin and long, muscular arms. But it was the unique details which jostled his memory —hair blond like his and the gold choker around her throat, a way to attach her detached head to the rest of her body.

Blood, smoke, screams. "Adhara," he murmured.

"I didn't think you were capable of looking any whiter. What's wrong?" Tobias asked.

"That woman, she looks like someone from my past. My distant past. I last saw her over 240 years ago."

"An ex that won't quit."

"*Ex* seems so diminutive after spending centuries together." He ran his fingers through his wavy hair, upsetting its collected, cool style. "Never completed the paperwork, so *wife* isn't technically accurate either."

Tobias patted him on the chest. "Come, I'll buy you a drink."

"It's open bar."

"Three fingers of your finest Scotch."

Oh, no, had Tobias fallen off the wagon? "I thought you were a teetotaler?"

"It's not for me. It's for you. Your girlfriend is talking to your ex, which means in the matter of minutes, you'll have two women thinking about what a piece of shit you are."

"Make it four fingers, then." He drank the smoky alcohol in three gulps, the burn disappearing as soon as it arrived. Vincent slammed the empty glass on the counter. "Another." He slung the drink back and rubbed the back of his lips with his hand.

He walked outside, turning on his mask. "Marisol, my love, please introduce me to your friend." He hugged Marisol from behind, nuzzling her nearly black hair. Up close, there was no mistaking the woman was Adhara.

"You know me, Rubio." Hundreds of years, and yet, she sounded just as annoyed with him.

"Been a while. Eighteenth-century France?"

"Head's back on." She rubbed her thick golden choker. "In fairness, that wasn't the *last* you heard of me."

His hold on Marisol loosened as he searched Adhara for highlights of her last century. The best clue placed the recent development in her accent with Soviet Russia. "The ice axe in Trotsky's eye[1] seemed familiar."

"Wasn't me. I liked the man."

Now that she mentioned it, ice axe felt too merciful for Adhara's thirst for violence, especially against the ruling class. "Basement with the Romanovs seemed more your style."

"I'm neither confirming nor denying."

Marisol fully slipped out of his arms, her expression frozen in surprise or concern. "I'll give you two time to catch up. Sounds like it's been awhile."

Marisol joined Tobias, observing them from the French doors in the ballroom. She placed her hands against the window frame as if she were observing them from the other side of a cage—and he and his ancient counterpart were the exhibits.

"I must admit, I am at a loss. The last century didn't seem to show many signs of your handiwork. I thought you had figured out the curse and your revenge was not telling me." His heartbeat grew louder in his ears. The deafening silence from her over the last century worried him. Surely, she had found a loophole out of the curse. However, standing before him answered the question. There was no way out...yet.

"I hypothesized, Rubio, but I hadn't the means. No thank you for me? After all, your green energy project was my idea." She air-quoted *green energy,* always one step ahead. Adhara understood his atomic collider

1. Exiled Bolshevik leader assassinated in Mexico by a Stalinist agent in 1940

existed to not only study the Big Bang of life, but also to grasp how everything degraded over time, including him.

The ridiculous, crinkled envelope lurched from his memory, traversing the world with its stamps and addresses. "Mailing the pamphlet to me thirty years ago? Not sure if it counts as giving me the idea." It was not as if antimatter appeared at his word. The collider took years and years of development, failure, and his money and research.

"Calm down. I'm not taking you to court over it." In show of how effortlessly she dug under his skin, she draped herself along the balustrade, looking in at the ball through the window. "I like her. She reminds me of our lab assistant in Calais."

"Now, now, I love Marisol. Our French girl was a fling, who I warmed up and you got off."

"You remember her well. Our Venetian blond with the skin like milk."

"Yes." A night of candlelight and elaborate costumes, the eager, high-pitched sighs of their shared lover. But her thighs were golden brown, her hair near black. She was Marisol, but couldn't be. His past had been corrupted by the present.

Adhara opened a golden case in the palm of her hand. "Smoke?"

A handful of cigarillos laid evenly along the velvet interior. A gap indicated she had already used some of the tightly rolled tobacco. "You know what smoking does to us," he admonished.

"I give myself time to heal between hits. Not going to end up with lungs turned into ash like Nando."

She lit the cigarillo and puffed a cloud of sweet smoke into his face. The scent brought him back to a simpler time of tobacco and sugarcane. Of cigars and rum. At least those memories were clear and vivid.

"One couldn't hurt." He held the cigarillo unlit between his lips. Instead of striking a match or offering a lighter, she leaned forward with hers dangling. He puffed as the glowing end sparked his alight.

"I'm disappointed in you, Rubio," she said from behind the muffle of the cigarillo clenched between her lips. "500 years of human relationships, and you pair off with a woman. How predictably cishet of you."

He yawned out a short cloud of smoke. As it dissipated, he studied the two silhouettes watching them from the French doors, his knight and queen. "I haven't felt alone in almost a year."

Adhara snorted. "Look at you, free from that martyr complex. One might mistake you as happy, even while the rot of injustice spreads." She shook her head. "I tried it once, the love of a mortal. They help you forget you're different. Well, until they tell a joke or sing a song that you don't quite understand. Until your frozen and crushed body is the only thing to make it out of an expedition alive." She chucked the stub into the garden and sucked on her teeth. "What's the plan when you leave them?"

"Plan?" He had at least three decades left in his current identity, and the hope Marisol gave him promised an end to the cycle. His mortals helped him forget, indeed.

"It's quite obvious, Rubio. You don't use your cuckold chair only for fucking. You get off letting another man live the life you can't." Adhara lifted her chin, as if a newer angle would offer a better inspection of him.

A fear licked at the edges of him and stuck to the grooves of his tongue more than the taste of ash. He was forever on the outside of humanity looking in. A god with no power to create or destroy, but some feeble puppet master unaware he pulled strings drawing Marisol and Tobias closer together, preparing for the inevitable day he could no longer live among them. As much joy it gave him to feel and foster human love, he built futures where no one needed him. Unable to age, unable to father, the only thing he had to chase the pain of immortality was the fight, which burned like the cigarillo's last puff.

"Try observing us at a different angle. You'll see the hope. You? Me? We're living our last lifetime."

Yet when confronted with Adhara's smugness, he no longer believed it.

The caterers packed the last of their supplies into their van and took off down the gravel driveway of the estate. **Vincent** pivoted off the top of his main entrance's stairs and walked to the study, where Marisol, Tobias, and now Adhara waited for him. She perched on the couch beside Marisol, relaxed, one arm draped across the back—far too comfortable in *his* study.

Marisol looked up at her, face lit with awe. "And then we stuffed him into the trunk."

Adhara laughed, full-throated and unrestrained. Marisol regaled her with the capture of Grant Durant... and in doing so, invited Adhara into the inner circle.

Tobias squirmed, leaning against the bookshelf, his discomfort echoing Vincent's. With a tilt of his chin, only the detective offered Vincent any deference when he entered.

In the safety of privacy, Vincent could take his mask off and talk business. Or rather, put the mask on.

Vincent handed a smartphone to Tobias. "During the party, I clandestinely downloaded the cellular information of the guests into Staci's cloud. Cross-check Durant's list with the phone's data. We could end up with piles of circumstantial evidence or some incriminating files. Use them to leverage a stronger case against Durant or get him to turn on someone bigger." Marisol and Tobias beamed, erasing any sense of inadequacy about his usefulness and lack of mortality.

Adhara, however, burst through the moment with derisive laughter. "That's all you can do. Collect data? Cross-check? Build cases to maybe get people to turn?" She made sure she held Marisol's attention, her gray eyes boring right into Marisol's soulful brown. "History's arc isn't toward Justice. It's toward boredom."

Tobias mouth quirked as if he were considering jumping to Vincent's defense, the ever-loyal knight, but Marisol's brows furrowed, giving Adhara's naysaying generous consideration. A bitter rage seethed through Vincent. He fixed their problem, and Adhara dared to tear it up with her cynicism. "Think you can do any better?"

Adhara leaned forward casually, elbows meeting her knees. "Think? I know I can." She held her tongue between her teeth, teasing the impotence of Vincent's attempts at Justice. But her jabs were never playful. Adhara's ways of doing things invited chaos and bloodlust, despite its efficiency.

He'd save himself and countless others a headache if he kept her close—the better to stay one step ahead of her. That and he couldn't let Marisol slip into the glow of admiration, as entertaining as Adhara's promises could be. "It's the twenty-first century, Adhara. We don't solve our problems with terror and executions."

Adhara shifted back in her seat, an unspoken admission that he'd scored a hit. Vincent won this round.

"We should reward our hard work with a little bit of fun," Marisol said.

Tobias held his hands up. "No more trouble tonight."

"No hunting. Good trouble." The single arch of her eyebrow invited divine temptation. What could be in store for them tonight? Perhaps they could scale the city's tallest building and play out a scene—the Patron

Saint imprisoned by the nefarious Silver Spirit, seducing his way to an escape.

"Dancing," Adhara suggested. "Our Rubio always likes dancing." The golden outer veins of her arms glinted as she flicked her hand in the air.

"Dancing it is then, but our Rubio must forgive me. I'm changing out of this dress."

As she left, Marisol mouthed *Rubio*? He had a lot about his past to explain.

The tension between the former paramours was thick enough to cut with a chainsaw. **Tobias** had to have a history textbook open to catch the shifts in conversation.

Marisol called out, "I'm ready."

She emerged from her dressing room in a strappy, white minidress. The hem ended halfway down her thick thighs, and the fit not only hugged her luscious curves but also emphasized the shape of her muscles— the ridges of her abs, the powerful lines of her hamstrings. And the places he wanted to know with his fingers, such as the divot of her belly button and the enticing pebbles of her nipples. With her every breath and rise of her chest, a burgundy areola threatened to peek over the dress's edge.

"Holy shit," Tobias said.

"You look like an angel." Vincent placed his tuxedo jacket over her shoulders as they left the estate grounds.

Adhara followed behind the couple closely. "Which kind? Messenger from God or fallen?"

Marisol turned her head back. "I don't know about you, but I want to raise some Hell tonight."

"Yeah, that's what I was worried about," Tobias groaned, as he forced his eyeline away from the hem of Marisol's dress.

9

Frailty Thy Name is Man

Marisol finished in the stall and pulled the skirt of her white minidress down. She joined Adhara in the mirror. Marisol fingered her wavy hair whereas Adhara checked the smell of her armpits with dramatic sniffs. The super-powered woman raised her muscular biceps and posed in the mirror. Tufts of hair grew from her underarms. Marisol shaved, waxed, plucked to perform the role of a shiny, soft-skinned woman. Lucky Adhara to be so free from the bullshit.

Marisol busied herself, washing her hands, but taking more glimpses of the mysterious woman who'd known Vincent the longest. Adhara helped herself to the perfumes made available in the private bathroom, spraying and squirting to test the scents.

"What do you think of Vincent handing all his evidence to the police?" Adhara asked, distracted by a cloud of perfume.

"Tobias isn't your typical police." Tobias may get on Marisol's nerves when he went by the book, but he was she and Vincent's greatest ally. The way he'd protected them during last year's Bloodsucker debacle made it easy to forgive her best friend for being a part of the force. "Working together, I think we're changing things."

Something sweet with vanilla and tobacco earned Adhara's nod. She dotted the perfume along her neck and wrists and casually asked, "So it doesn't bother you?"

"Why would working with Tobias bother me?" The recent memory of their bickering about the mess she'd made of Grant Durant's dental work suggested, at least, something bothersome happened between them.

Adhara moved on to a gloss and flexed her mouth in the mirror, smearing the colorless shine on her full lips. "Where I come from, a cop's a cop. Mark my words, they'll fail. Trusting the police means entering a broken system, and doing the right thing is buried in negotiations."

So far this evening, she'd watched Adhara make sport of getting reactions from Vincent. Maybe even her. Marisol nodded, suddenly aware of any break in her expression. Hadn't she and Tobias buried the hatchet with formalwear and awkward glances?

She wasn't a fool. Tobias was one man in an entire justice system that had no problem framing her brother for murders he didn't commit. Of course, the whole city was indifferent to it. Who cared if a murderer was in prison for the wrong murder? The beauty of negotiations was the details mattered little. But if one technicality caused any of those rich, slimy assholes to slip away from Justice? Marisol might need to flip more than some tables.

Adhara spun around to face the real Marisol, not the one in the mirror. "Why not destroy these so-called untouchable rapists and traffickers in the court of public opinion? Share those files with the people. The people will rip those assholes to shreds. Believe me, I saw what happened in September of 1792."

Marisol bit the inside of her cheek—anything to maintain her poker face, preventing her smile at the idea of watching Grant Durant bleed. After all the suffering he caused, it had felt good to hear bone crack. Sometimes running a criminal's red insides into the gutter set the world in balance. If she told Vincent how she fought a smile right now, he'd spout an adage about revenge consuming the soul. Between Tobias wanting to keep the cases clean, and Vincent practically becoming the pacifist with a punching fist, Marisol was outnumbered by her angels on the shoulder.

"I have faith in them."

Adhara's laughter resonated throughout the bathroom.

Oppressive electronic music pounded through the darkened club. From his place in the cushy VIP section, **Tobias** could barely make out Marisol and Adhara dancing. Lights strobed over them. Their bodies undulated wildly to the techno beat. They raised their arms above their heads and held hands. Marisol's hair shook around her as each woman rolled her hips. It was like witnessing the sides of the yin and yang hump each other like they were in some erotic thriller he'd watch on cable as a kid.

Tobias finished the last of his water from his sweating glass. The cubes shook at the bottom. He leaned back in the plush couch to enjoy his view, however strobed and murky. Hot ladies writhing together? He'd be an idiot to not impress the images to memory. But Vincent watched them as if ready to pounce. The angry way. Not sexy.

Tobias had never seen someone attempt murder with a look before. The super-powered man's jaw ticked and nostrils flexed, homing in on Adhara grinding against his woman.

"They look like they're having a good time," Tobias said to break the tension.

Vincent pinched his lips together.

If Tobias wasn't mistaken, the green snake of jealousy had possessed Vincent.

Vincent leaped to his feet and prowled through the crowd. He breached the wall of dancing bodies and pulled Marisol against him. She met him with a smile and kiss. And all was right with the world.

Lost in the happy ending, Tobias shuddered when Adhara seemed to teleport next to him on the couch. She helped herself to Vincent's tuxedo jacket and dabbed her sweat with his sleeve.

Tobias sidled down the couch to give her as much room as possible. Her gray-hued gaze followed him and seemed to judge him, filling the space between them.

"I'm trying to understand how you fit in with them," she said, eerily casual.

"Comrades-in-arms," he croaked. Cesca, hours earlier, had nailed him as the pathetic fanboy he was. And the way Adhara stared at him, she was going to get an accurate read of him, too.

"No. That's not it." She pointed a gold, claw-tipped finger in his direction. The gleaming sharpness of them was not lost in the dim lighting of the club, and their looming threat froze him to the spot. "I know. You're the failsafe."

Tobias snorted and made a feeble attempt at sipping the melting ice from the bottom of his glass. "Gotta hand it to you immortals. I need a Rosetta Stone to understand half the things you say."

She performed a laugh. "Do you always have a wiseass answer when you're uncomfortable?"

Tobias finally had the bravery to face her. "I also have dumbass ones."

She bit on her lower lip. It slowly emerged from her teeth. "I'm not sure what he's told you about our abilities and inabilities. Strong, can't die, but we also can't have children."

He hadn't heard about that caveat. Why was Adhara telling him this?

Her metallic-capped fingers moved in the air as if they wove the meddling question within him. "He wants you around to be the failsafe. When he can't grow old with her and give her the life you mortals seem to crave, he'll pass her off. Or maybe he wants to try fatherhood out this lifetime, which makes you the stud."

Stud cracked open the friendship like lightning. The earlier glares Vincent had directed at her all made sense as a complicated anger overwhelmed him.

Diedre, his daughter, didn't call him Dad. The honorific belonged to her dopey stepdad. Ninety percent of the problem had been on him. Homicide detectives didn't get to have happily ever afters while working double shifts in Shadowhaven. Losing himself to drinking and women had cost him the family he had. He wanted to be a new man now.

Yet, a pesky notion throbbed. Why did Vincent and Marisol, who seemed to be the happiest couple he ever knew, keep him around as a third wheel?

He studied them dancing. Beautiful, smiling—the both of them. He wasn't one of them. He was...the stud.

"Have they not discussed this with you?" she asked.

Tobias shook his head. A sour feeling rose within him, the kind he'd typically temper down with shots of whiskey. He needed to separate himself. Fight the urge. Find peace.

He headed to the dance floor to say his goodbyes. Stumbling and bumping through the sweaty crowd, he lacked the swift elegance of Vincent.

Vincent noticed him first. He had been nuzzling Marisol's neck, but stopped to blink at Tobias like a cat as he approached. Marisol's eyes were closed, back to her man as she danced with one arm raised, her other arm draped behind Vincent's neck. She finally opened her eyes, and her face lit up. Her excitement heartened and wounded him.

"Tobias!" she shouted over the music.

He stooped, lips near the shell of her ear and Vincent's mouth. "I'm beat. Taking off."

Her fingers bristled along his arm. "You can't. You haven't danced yet."

Her pleading brown eyes shot down his defenses. His face softened. "Kid, I got two left feet."

"But I can make you look good." She was in a blissed-out state, eyes narrowing.

Her husky voice enraptured him, drew him taut—just like the night when she stood on his fire escape.

She took his hands into hers and shifted her shoulders to the beat. A spell had been cast over him. His feet felt lighter. The music took over, and he bobbed his head, matching her rhythm.

His gaze met Vincent's, and he froze. Shit, he was third-wheeling. Sinning. Whatever he called it. He anticipated Vincent's fierce jealousy, but the billionaire instead watched Tobias with an amused crook to his eyebrow.

So he followed their lead, discovering his hips, too, could sway. Marisol placed a possessive palm on his chest, right over his heart. Vincent directed her other arm to go back around his neck. His long fingers trailed down her underarm to the curve of her breast. Tobias's gaze followed the path of Vincent's hands, lured by them groping and pinching where he had dreamt himself doing the very same. He inched closer, his thigh wedging between Marisol's legs. She was warm against him. Blood pounded in his ears, edging out the music.

Her eyes fluttered shut, and her mouth parted. A sigh escaped her lips. "Be a good boy."

His cock jolted. His breath became shallow. Before desire seized him, he thought of Cesca and Adhara—seeing him for what he truly was. He had to escape it.

Just as he took a step back to leave, she spun into him and rolled her hips, the cleft of her ass finding the right spot to give his erection a pump.

Her eyes opened wide. She stopped dancing, and the furrow in her brow brought on a string of *fuck*'s. Fuck, she knew he hadn't changed. Fuck, he was always the hound dog, hungry for her. Fuck, he was never a good man, despite what she insisted on seeing in him.

She rubbed her lips together as if she was working out the sensation. Her head lolled against his chest. Vibrations shook her upper body. She was laughing. Her body undulated to the beat, rubbing him in the most intimate of ways.

Whatever kind of dancing this was, it was better than any sip of whiskey. Maybe she was always on his wavelength, a sinner just like him. They'd draw each other further down.

A hand pushed against his chest. Tobias looked down. It was Vincent's hand. His electric blue eyes shocked Tobias back into reality, so he took a step back. Now would be the time to say sorry, beg for forgiveness.

"I'm sor—"

Vincent's fingers curled, gathering the fabric of Tobias's shirt in his hand. The powerful grip pulled him closer back to the fire-hot grind of their dancing. A phantom tie knotted around his throat. A dark truth surrounded him. Tobias stuck around, not only for those stolen moments from her but to feel them from him, too. A memory—or a dream?—of a whiskey-fueled kiss with the masked man swept over him.

Something seared into from afar. It was Adhara's gaze. *Pass her off. The stud.* He broke away from the two of them and charged through the crowd. They haunted him. They suffocated him. He wanted to burn it away with alcohol, but he needed air.

"I gotta go."

He burst out of the club doors and bent over to catch his breath. His ears rang—a shrill throttling of his ear drums. Where was he? The sidewalk. He slowly inhaled, filling his lungs with chilled air. He released his breath. The sound of tires rolling slowly down the street centered him. The night air cooled him, inside and out.

He needed to cleanse himself longer. A walk home would make do.

"Sorry for the sudden exit. Had an urge"

Hitting send, he noticed he left his sentence unfinished.

"To drink."

Three dots pulsed as he waited for her reply.

"I understand. Take care of yourself. See you soon."

As he continued into the night, the hair at his neck stood on end. Someone was watching him. He had a sneaking suspicion the someone had gray eyes.

Vincent took one step inside the dark entrance of his penthouse and pinned Marisol to the wall. He breathed in the scent of her skin, recognizing the scent of sweet musk. Entwined in her dance floor-induced sweating was another scent—clove like Tobias. Sharing her was like sharing the Good News, a joy to know Tobias adored her and wanted her the way he did. Where else could he track Tobias's scent and award every inch of it with a kiss and a flick of his tongue?

"I can smell him on you." He lowered his face into her breasts and inhaled. Fuck, not only the clove but his sweat, too. He bit her nipples through her white, clingy fabric.

"You like that, don't you?" She threaded her fingers through his hair.

He nodded, dropped to his knees, and smelled the divot between her thighs. Arousal. Dancing with him turned her on too, feeding into his hunger for her. He had to be nearer to her, taste her. The skirt of her dress rode higher with his hasty kisses to her center. A thin layer of synthetic fabric separated his mouth from her experiencing the ultimate pleasure.

"I need him to warm me up. A good boy to show you how it's done."

He moaned as he pushed the skirt from her perfect ass. Her soft skin still carried his faint scent of clove.

"You're so worthless, unable to please me." She pulled down the top of her dress, pinching at her nipples.

The past echoed, carrying with it Adhara's tears and anger. *Useless*, she had said.

He leaned back on his haunches, "*Sálvame.*"

Marisol straightened and adjusted her dress back into place. "Staci! Lights!"

Don't belong, shouldn't be here, if only it could end. Each shard of self-hatred cut into him. He winced and held his eyes shut. "Um, I'm sorry. I think what you said triggered something in me."

She guided him to the sofa. "Wait here. I'll get you some water."

His thoughts kept cutting. Cutting and cutting and cutting. He rubbed at his collarbone to bring him to the present. *Sofa, Marisol, water.*

She handed him a full glass and sat next to him, tucking her legs to one side. A reassuring rub of his back quieted the negative spiral. "Want to talk about it?"

"I think calling me worthless brought me to a place I didn't want to be."

"I'm sorry. I should've checked if the roleplay was okay. I'd never want— I mean, I don't really think—"

He took her hand into his. "I know." A sip of water calmed his nerves. "Adhara showing up out of the blue reminds me of the regret I have over what happened between us."

"You can tell me anything."

Approaching his memories of regret struck a livewire nerve, a pain more profound the longer he held it. Tell her? No. Instead, he lay in her lap, and she stroked his hair. "I'd rather you hold me right now."

"Of course."

He nearly pushed the intrusive thoughts away, until he smelled sweet tobacco on Marisol's skin.

The smell of Adhara.

Tobias flipped on the lights of his apartment and entered his bedroom. Automatically, he opened the lid of his laptop and signed in. Without sitting down at his desk, he entered *You up?* in a chat box.

He didn't wait for an answer. Instead, he furiously unbuttoned his tuxedo shirt and unbuckled his belt, whipping it off and tossing it on his bed. He stormed into the kitchen and opened his fridge. The old him would grab a beer at this moment. In place of the beers were a handful of tiny vials. He pocketed one and made his way to his bathroom where he kept the syringes, pocketing one of those, too.

Back at his desk, the person on the other end of the chat had replied.

Been a while. I'll always be here when you need me.

The ceremony could begin. He opened a desk drawer containing a lighter and incense sticks. In the matter of a spark, swirls of sweet and woodsy smoke licked around him.

He typed, *Sorry. Been busy. Do you remember my request?*

I can take care of it right now. A few minutes until I'm ready.

He filled the syringe with the liquid in the vial and gave the cylinder a flick, setting it down next to his keyboard. In a flurry of typing, he sent his payment information—$500 for custom content.

Get the money?

A link appeared in the chat box, and he clicked it. A video screen opened up on his laptop. On the other side was the performer LilyG1RL in a sparkling silver mesh shirt doing little to hide her dark nipples, and wearing a domino mask. She had dyed her hair a deeper shade of brown—practically black—since he'd last ordered content from her.

I like the hair.

She ran her fingers through it and gave her head a shake. "You have such good taste, baby."

Call me good boy.

She broke into a smile. "Does this good boy need to come?"

His fingers hovered over the keyboard. Was it release or resistance he needed?

He entered *N O* in the message, but deleted it.

"I see you're thinking about it. No need to feel shy about wanting to pop." She caressed her tits, squeezing them together.

You're missing a part of the request.

"Be patient, my good boy. He's getting ready for you."

Another joined her, a naked, wiry man wearing a black half-hood mask. Not a touch of body hair on him.

They performed an exaggerated kiss with wide open mouths and lapping tongues. The small things called his dick to attention. The way her incisor stuck out as she smiled between kisses. The way he'd hold her chin between his index finger and thumb. They could be Vincent and Marisol.

LilyG1RL turned to the camera, her lips swollen. "Are you touching your cock now?"

Yes.

He unzipped his pants and pulled them down to his thighs. But he put his hands flat on the desk and leaned back in his chair. His dick jutted out and throbbed, but he ignored it.

"Good boy. I'm sure it's so big, you have to take long strokes." She obliged her masked man with the sensual pulls Tobias denied himself.

Her throaty laughs turned into moans. She lowered herself to her knees to lick and suck. The masked man pulled her hair back in his fist, showing off her hollowing cheeks and batting eyelashes. Her mouth worked up and down. He moaned. Too tenor, too excited to be cool in the face of heat like Vincent. His grip on her hair loosened. She practically swallowed him.

She released her companion from her mouth. A strand of hair stuck to the saliva on her lips. The toss of her hair—it reminded Tobias of Marisol on the fire escape.

Tobias's balls tightened. Arousal leaked out from his tip, but he did nothing. Nothing but breathe in the sweet smoke, hoping the sacred scent would cleanse him. Nothing but watch, begging to feel nothing. Watch the pretend Marisol and pretend Vincent go through the show of hands, mouth, pussy, so he could burn his desire away.

"Don't you dare come yet," LilyG1RL grunted out. Her friend rhythmically pounded into her. "Tell me where a good boy wants to blow his hot load."

Your face.

She dropped to her knees in front of the camera. The masked man was nothing but a desperately working hand on a red-hot dick. Her mouth opened and her tongue lunged out like a yawning cat.

Tobias popped the cap of the syringe off and stabbed the needle into his hip. The serum burned through every vein of his body. Pain wound tight in his belly. A tear escaped his eye.

"That's a good boy. All over my—"

Tobias slammed the laptop shut and wrapped his hand around his cock. He fucked into his fist as the agony peaked, and the serum twisted the ache into ecstasy. He came, a filthy mess into his hand.

He used his tuxedo shirt to clean himself and tossed the soiled thing into a corner. The ceremony ended as carefully as it began. The used syringe was disposed. The incense was snuffed out. He scrubbed his hands over his beard—even softer now as the serum worked its magic.

Kneeling, he clasped his hands together and rested his head against them. The substance—the healing medicine he stole from Vincent's stash—tempered down his craving and pushed out the sins of lust and gluttony. He prayed tonight would be the last time. He'd go clean the hard way, the way everyone else did.

The last of the incense's sweet smoke dissipated, but a sin lingered.

Tobias Quinlan was a fucking liar.

10

Town and Country

The exit door slammed shut behind **Marisol**, and she gave the handle a wiggle. Everything locked.

The security light over the alley shone along the surface of the robot-chauffeured car waiting for her. A few more steps across the alleyway, and she'd be in the luxury of safety.

A shadow moved. She jumped back. Stupid, nothing was there. After all her nights of vigilantism, the shadows should fear *her,* but without the mask, she was plain ole scaredy-cat Marisol.

This time, not without reason.

The shadow moved again. Squeezing her hand into a fist, she lowered her weight to her back leg to throw a heavy punch, if needed.

Many years ago, it was her brother Caz who was the shadow in wait for her. He had a bullet in his leg, and he'd demanded treatment to keep him out of the hospital and away from police and the ever-circling rivals. At first, she'd told him to fuck off, and that keeping her nursing license was better than helping his sorry, limping ass. But he'd raised his gun and lined it up to her forehead. It didn't matter they were family. Caz had protected her from the rest of the Shadows only to threaten her himself.

When all was said and done, she wasn't sure what hurt more, tending her brother's leg at gunpoint or Mom telling her she'd exaggerated the whole thing. Dad, on the other hand, gave her a crowbar and said, "Next time, swing good."

She had sardonically laughed at him. What good did a crowbar do against a gun?

In fatherly fashion, he told her about an encampment roughly ninety years ago of protesting coal miners who lived not far from Shadowhaven. They'd been dropping like flies from lung disease. When they objected to their conditions, the coal company rode the train to their camp site, and from the open boxcar, fired indiscriminately into their tents. Thankfully, no one had died, but when the company tried it again, they found the train tracks destroyed by the wives of the miners—using nothing but crowbars. Crowbar beat gun.

She never had to "swing good," but tonight, she wished she had more than her hands and a vigilante boyfriend on speed dial. The shadow lurched forward, and she raised her fists. The thing entered a beam of light.

It was Guillermo—this time holding his ribs, lip split open, and one of his eyes swollen shut.

"Help me," he groaned.

Safe inside the closed clinic treatment room, **Marisol** applied anesthetic to the gash above his eyebrow. Guillermo cringed. Welts dotted along his upper body, turning even more purple while he sat.

"Who did this to you?" She threaded the needle to sew his wound shut.

"Ever since Izzy left town, some New York gangsters, the 86ers, been creeping into our territory."

She thought the Shadows had stopped relying on the young ones to fill their rosters. Following on the heels of the memory of Caz, sisterly disappointment fueled the way she speared Guillermo's skin with the needle. "I thought you were done with the Shadows. Going to school. Boxing."

"You tell me what I should do if someone comes after my best friend with a two-by-four."

She didn't have an answer. Even when she walked the straight and narrow as a nurse, Caz and the Shadows had a way of sucking her in. On the Westside, Justice was rare.

"If the 86ers take over, the whole city will have a mess on its hands. I figured that friend of yours could help us out. We helped him out last year. It's the least he could do."

"The deal I struck with the Patron Saint was he'd leave the Shadows alone if they kept to themselves and made sure more of you guys finished school."

Guillermo sneered. "School? Really?"

"It wouldn't hurt finishing, especially when you have such a smart girlfriend." She pulled through the final stitch and knotted the end carefully.

"Yesenia said you could help me."

Having a young admirer made her feel a sense of obligation. She only hoped her hero self met the girl's high expectations of her. The Shadow young'uns deserved a better and safer Shadowhaven, even if a two-by-four knocked them back into the gang. "I'll see what I can do." Her thumb smoothed over the Steri-strip protecting his stitches. "What do you know about the New York gang?"

"Rumor has it their second-in-command and some street lieutenants been hanging out in one of the old warehouses by the docks."

"I might need to give the Patron Saint more information."

"That's all I got." He cradled his bruised ribs, and his breath stuttered.

Guillermo was no good here. "Know anyone who lives outside the city?"

"My grandma lives out past the county line. Where all those bugs make that weird-ass sound?"

She forgot how noisy the world outside the city was. It was one thing to block out the traffic and rumble of crowds. At the estate, the cicadas and frogs were like jackhammers in her ears. "I'll take you there."

Marisol overrode Staci's orders and rerouted the driverless car to Guillermo's grandmother. They reached the county line, pastures and farm homes and country living.

The car turned into a long, gravel driveway. A white home with a screened-in porch stood at the end of the drive. A stout woman with thick arms waited, propping the screen door with her hip. Guillermo was safe here. Marisol could sense it.

"You stay out here and finish school, got it?" she said.

The teen boy struggled with his injuries, opening the car door. "Yeah, yeah, yeah."

"If you need some lovey-dovey time with Yesenia, I'll pay for her bus ticket. You don't need to be going into the city getting yourself into stupid trouble."

"Anything else, Mom?" he asked.

After spending her night treating wounds and giving him a ride out to the country, smart-mouth teen garbage was the last thing she needed. "Hey."

"Thank you, Marisol. Yesenia's right about you."

Marisol smiled crookedly. She was only doing her job. Whatever Yesenia said, Marisol doubted she came close to the hero the teen had imagined. With high expectations though, Marisol vowed to herself to never disappoint Yesenia—or worse, put them in further danger. In the face of the hard knocks Shadowhaven schooled most people in, the fighting chance they needed was more people just doing their jobs.

Staci drove the car up the driveway until they encountered another moving shadow roving the countryside. This time, a sexy, not-so scary shadow—a concerned Vincent in his Patron Saint gear. She rolled down the window to hear him growl, "When I saw the car route change, I grew worried."

Marisol ordered the car to stop and stepped out onto the abandoned road. "A kid got in between the Shadows and the 86ers territory dispute. I'm getting him to safety before the city puts him through the grinder. Sorry to worry you unnecessarily. Duty called." She wrapped her arms around his neck and gave him a kiss. "The poor kid said they attacked him and his best friend with a two-by-four."

Vincent broke away, narrowing his eyes. "You're thinking something."

"I'm thinking we should chase this New York crowd off. Shadowhaven supports local business, not a money-grubbing franchise."

"We are discussing drug dealers, right?"

"I don't know." She propped herself against the car door, practically collapsing in the exhaustion brought on by the unexpected evening. "They helped us out last year when you were between a meat hook and a hard place."

"And I've turned a blind eye if they kept their activities isolated, and Vincent Varian's funding addiction treatment and clean needle exchanges. The Patron Saint isn't going to choose a side in a gang war except for the side that keeps all of them off the streets."

"It's not the bigwigs who suffer in a territory war. It's the kids. They're just kids trying their best with the shit deal they got."

"We're not honorary members of the Shadows, in case you forgot why your brother is paying his due."

She cracked her knuckles, anticipating squaring up for a punch. Really, her brother? She lived with the burden of his crimes every day. If not from her own guilty conscience, then from the way Shadowhaven's finest gave her an up and down look when they learned she grew up on the Westside. It was a costume she'd be unable to shed.

Of course, she'd never forget. How easy it was for him to be holier-than-thou when they could go through his extensive past and count the cardinal sins. "I'm heading back to the city. Don't follow me!" A solid hour of pouting in the backseat of an auto-driving car ought to do the trick.

The Patron Saint sped away on his motorcycle into the dark cover of the country night. Marisol got out her phone and pressed Tobias.

"What's up?"

"I had a boy come to my clinic after hours. He was part of the Shadows gang when they helped us take out the Bloodsucker. Some New York gang, the 86ers, is in town and roughed him up over a territory dispute. What can we do for him?"

His exaggerated sigh rustled the phone's speaker. "Best scenario, SPD works with the FBI to build a case against some of the 86ers' leaders. Maybe in a few weeks, we have some targeted arrests that hobble the gang so they don't keep rearing their head around the city. If the boy knows anything, we could negotiate his testimony in exchange for some protection—maybe a get out of jail free card for some misdemeanor. Worst case? Police send some dum-dums to rip and raid. Great way for some grown men with badges to give an eighth grader a black eye."

"Forget it." She hung up the phone. Vincent wouldn't get his hands dirty, and all Tobias could promise were maybes. Guillermo deserved more for laying down his safety for them. She adjusted Staci's route and headed to the address of the storage facility, Space 4 Rent.

Marisol double-checked the number written on the torn piece of paper before she banged on the corrugated metal garage door. The door rolled up, and Adhara's makeshift crash pad was on the other side. The ancient woman's claws clicked impatiently on the garage frame.

"Can you help me with something?"

Adhara's face lit up as if she were opening a birthday present. "Of course."

Marisol recounted how her alley visitor needed patching up after a bully rival gang attacked him. Adhara blinked slowly and said nothing. Had Marisol overestimated the ex's willingness to help?

The super-powered woman's golden veins shone with a pulsing light. The lightwaves called pieces of an armored suit to her. Each fragment flew and attached to her exoskeleton until they covered her limbs with rocket-propelled shields on her arms and legs. Over the year, Marisol's own dark, urban fairytale had come to life, yet as Adhara's chest plate clicked into place, awe prickled throughout the mortal's body. Sure, magic was real, but Marisol had forgotten the beauty of it when it became commonplace. With Adhara, wonder was still possible.

"Let's party," Adhara said.

11

Climax

Marisol ditched the auto-driving car in the penthouse's basement hideout. Here, she slipped on her Kevlar, chainmail, and mask, becoming the Silver Spirit.

Outside and free of all the trackers Vincent placed on her, Adhara and Marisol readied to confront the 86ers. "I'll show you a trick," Adhara said, as fire breathed out of the bottom of her ankles. "Wanna ride?"

Marisol jumped on Adhara's back, and they shot out above the buildings. Adrenaline pumped in her veins, the same speed the air whipped over her. Lights below glittered like magic, and cars and buildings looked like toys. Up here, they were invincible. "Let's kick some ass." Marisol's awe of Adhara twisted into malicious glee. She couldn't wait to fight beside Adhara. The super-powered woman pointed her right arm to the direction of the warehouse district.

Hell hath no fury.

Tobias's name appeared in giant letters across the motorcycle's screen. **Vincent** answered over the pounding of the force as he zoomed along the highway. "Yes?"

"I got the strangest call from Marisol."

"I'm passing by your apartment. Care to tell me in person? Bring your cattle prod and ski mask."

"Be still my heart, Vinnie. I thought you'd never ask."

Vincent pulled the motorcycle into the alleyway. Tobias slid down the ladder of his fire escape, landing on his feet with a grunt. He had his cattle prod slung behind him on a strap, and his ski mask pulled down. "My knees are too old for this superhero shit."

Instead of the detective's trademark trench coat, he wore a black leather bomber jacket—straight out of a biker bar Vincent had cruised in a past life. He greeted his friend with a smirk. "Haven't seen you in leather before."

"I'm trying out the alter ego thing." Tobias patted his chest.

A little too daddy for Vincent's taste. He rolled his eyes and nodded toward the computer. "I'm watching a dot of her move over half the city in minutes."

"Lover's quarrel ending in her swiping that helicopter of yours?"

"Worse. She's teamed up with someone who has rocket propulsion."

"The ex?"

"That's my educated guess, and judging by her location, they're aiming for the old warehouse district."

"This wouldn't have to do with the 86ers showing their faces in Shadow territory, would it?"

"We have to stop her." Vincent moved forward on the cycle, making more space for Tobias.

Tobias swung his leg over the seat. "When I begrudgingly took on the role of sidekick, I didn't think I would be sitting bitch."

Vincent throttled the engine and jolted the motorcycle forward, tripping Tobias into an awkward stumble. "Your hurt ego could always walk."

Marisol and Adhara landed gently on the tin roof of the warehouse. Through the skylight, they looked down at the gangsters below, wearing green and black —the colors of the 86ers. It was sweet how some made the giant warehouse home, gathering around an old box television on some worn-out furniture or playing a round of pool on a scuffed table. They may have tried to take over corners in Shadowhaven, but they hadn't hired an interior decorator. Interestingly, Marisol noted, some half-naked rubes in the corner packed and weighed a hefty amount of heroin. After her Patron

Saint dealt a blow to the B'Lee trade last year, the gangsters returned to the old reliable narcotics.

"What's the plan?" Marisol asked. Vincent and Tobias never entered an unfair fight without one.

"Jump down. Start swinging." Adhara blasted out the skylight. Glass shards sprayed the gangsters below. The 86ers froze in place, gaping cluelessly. Marisol couldn't back out of this now, as much as her shaking limbs wanted to.

Adhara flew down to the ground and strutted. *Clank, clank, clank.* Her rockets clicked the ground like cowboy spurs. Marisol scrambled among the rafters, scooting her way toward a metal pillar she could use to get down.

A gangster sprang up from his beat-up easy chair. "What the hell is this?"

"Doping the masses and sending children home with bruises so you men feel grown. You make me sick." Adhara drew a curved sword from her back and pointed it in the direction of the speaker. "Where would you like to bleed from?"

He guffawed as her metallic gait moved closer and closer.

"Ear? Nose? Hand?" Adhara sliced the air with her blade.

Marisol leaped to the pillar. Guns fired with abandon. Bullets ricocheted around the warehouse, the tin walls reverberating the tiny explosions. She clamped the metal column with her arms and legs, resisting gravity's pull. Sweat beaded on her forehead.

At least Vincent couldn't say *I told you so* if she died. The gunfire ceased, and bullet casings landed in successive pings.

Adhara stood unharmed, but her blade gleamed with freshly shed blood. She had kept her word. Three of the 86ers nursed slashes to their ear, nose, and hand, respectively. Drawing blood was wrong—should be wrong—but watching them cradle their wounds felt so right.

Chaos cut the ooey gooey feeling short. One of the pool players sprung from his crouched position, gun in hand. Marisol slid down the pillar and landed on him, her feet crunching into his spine. His gun skidded across the empty floor.

Marisol raised her fists, keeping her back to Adhara, who seemed to have a handle on these shitheads. She slowly stepped back until her back kissed Adhara's.

"Who sent you?" A sickly looking gang member shrieked. Slicing his hand really drained him of a healthy pallor. If the 86ers tossed their guns to the side, Marisol would suggest gauze and pressure. She was a good nurse, after all.

"The never-ending abyss, opening wider to accept your soul." Adhara's eyes widened furiously. She raised her sword, readying to strike.

A side door flung open with a *bang!* Ski mask Tobias, wielding his cattle prod, entered the vast room. "Evening, friends! I get it. You think I'm tonight's headliner, but alas, I am not. You have three seconds to drop your weapons. Three...two..."

Tough crowd—these bozos weren't following reasonable orders. Marisol smoothed her thumb over her callused knuckles.

"Close your eyes, kid! Fucking one!" Tobias yelled.

Marisol squeezed her eyes shut. A flash-bang burst into the room, showing up as a blood-red glow under her eyelids. Another body had jumped down from the open skylight—Vincent. She opened her eyes, and his cape swept about him.

"Hi, my saint," Marisol greeted sheepishly, the maimed 86ers the sign of her and Adhara's shenanigans.

"Duck," he said.

She hit the floor. An 86er toppled over her and into the grip of the Patron Saint. Vincent flung him in the air, crashing him into a table of heroin.

The chaos scattered the half-naked packagers. Ain't no way those dusty things looking like Jules Verne's Morlocks were getting away. **Tobias** pulled the exit shut, looking around the room to find something to jam the door. Adhara went in on the assist and punched a dent in it. Opening it would be a challenge for anyone. "Thank you, ma'am," he touted.

She snapped right around, facing the feeble throng. "Cower or meet my blade!"

A little Shakespeare in the Park for this crowd, but effective. The packagers shuffled into a corner, away from the mayhem.

The air vibrated as Vinnie used a magnetic pulse from his utility belt to disarm some of the gangsters. Guns and knives clanged to the floor.

Now the fight was going to be *mano y mano,* and the thrill of a little fist in face gladdened Tobias's heart. Sure, greater good meant these jabronis should be going out in bracelets and led into a police van, but there was something beautiful about a mug shot with a black eye. These jokers had no idea who they were messing with—especially some prize fighter who thought he could take on the Patron Saint.

It was like watching boxing training in reverse. The fighter punched and punched with dynamic footing and attacks. Every jab, hook, uppercut, the Patron Saint met with a stone-faced dodge or block. The super-powered man looked as if he hadn't broken a sweat. Honestly, someone had to put the delusional 86er in his place. It was like watching a mosquito take on a rhinoceros.

So Tobias sucker punched him.

"I didn't need your help," Vinnie said in his vigilante growl.

"I was getting bored. Thought I needed a piece of the action."

"I warm them up, and you finish them off?" His eyes glinted with mischief, which stunned more than an unexpected jab to the nose.

Luckily some 86-dingbat was scrambling for one of the handguns scattered on the floor. Cuffs would pair well with his stupidity.

An elbow to the throat floored the next goon who probably expected the woman to be the group's weak one. **Marisol** eyed Vincent, her dependable backup. Usually, any threat to her set him off, but he was currently distracted preventing Adhara from slicing another appendage off a gangster. He grabbed her sword by the blade and punched it, cracking it into pieces.

"Keep it clean," he said through clenched teeth.

Adhara laughed, throaty and sinister. She clacked the golden tips of her clawed hands together. Each curled from the ends of her knuckles like talons, emerging from the golden branches growing from her wrists. A punch from her slashed the face of her next victim.

An 86er raised his gun to meet Vincent at point-blank range. Vincent grabbed the gun in his fist and the metal crunched in his hand. He tossed the useless hunk of metal to the side. The gang member gawked at the sheer horror of the powerless force of his gun against a practical god. In a matter of microseconds, Vincent had dislocated his elbow with a meaty *snap!*

Marisol kept her back to the support pillar to take in the looming threats. An idiot parried with her, seeming to take glee in attacking a poor, defenseless woman. She quickly elbowed into his neck and kicked him at his knee with enough force to hear a *pop!* Safe to say, he wasn't going to be coming after her anytime soon.

Tobias, however, wasn't as swift. A ricocheted bullet knocked his cattle prod from his hands. Unarmed, he tackled an 86er with a gun. They rolled onto the surface of the pool table, wrestling for the gun. Marisol cracked a pool cue over the assailant's back. He reeled away, and she slid the cue between his chin and throat, holding it against his trachea. Tobias scrambled from the pool table, grabbed his cattle prod, and shocked the gangster Marisol held in a chokehold. He dropped unconscious to the ground.

"Thanks for the backup, kid," Tobias said between wheezes.

"My pleasure."

The 86ers scattered to the exits, but the claws of Adhara and the fists of the Patron Saint ensured none would escape Justice that night.

From behind the waffle knit of his ski mask, an earpiece lit up on Tobias. "Police are coming. We got seconds to move it."

Marisol bolted to rejoin Adhara across the floor. Vincent hooked her by the elbow, and her hair fell loose from its braid. Her masked gaze locked on to his piercing blue one. He inhaled and kissed her, a frame of stillness among the melee until he peppered his kisses down her neck. The high of the fight conjured a desire only he could quench. "You're coming with me." His voice rumbled against the soft spot behind her ear.

Adhara jumped onto a table of packed and loose heroin. "See you around!" She flew toward the broken skylight. A stream of flames shot from her feet, lighting the drugs in a flash of fire that died as soon as it appeared.

Vincent shot a grappling hook from its launcher, attaching it securely to his belt. The line to their broken skylight-exit pulled tight, and he swept Marisol close to him. "Hang on."

She squeezed her arms around him, bracing for liftoff.

Vincent whistled, sharp and loud. On cue, Tobias raced over to them. "Would it be inconvenient to ask for a ride out of here?"

The trio awkwardly embraced each other before they zipped toward the roof. They tumbled into a pile. Marisol grunted, "I always thought I was a lucky lady, surrounded by a couple of good-looking men, but this is verging on *careful what you wish for* territory."

Tobias picked himself up and regained his footing on the slippery tin roof. "Don't count your blessings yet, kid."

Vincent led them to the edge of the roof. The motorcycle was parked below. How were the three of them going to fit on the thing? "As much as I think we can make a variety of positions work, I'm not sure how we'll go about it on a two-seater," Vincent said.

Bratty vindication curled Marisol's mouth into a playful smirk. "I told you we needed a sidecar."

The smog in the sky turned red and blue. The authorities were encroaching, which put a damper on the superhero retorts. Tobias said, "I'll slip in among the officers to make sure none of these boneheads try anything funny."

Vincent leaped to the ground, hitting a three-point brace. He sprung back up and held out his arms. Turning to face Tobias with her back to the edge, Marisol teetered into a trust fall into the Patron Saint's heroic embrace. Tobias wobbled over to nearby drainpipe and skidded down. He threw off his stocking cap and tucked it inside his leather jacket. He ran his fingers through his hair and beard, as if to smooth away any signs of vigilantism.

Marisol hopped onto the motorcycle with Vincent at the controls. She gave Tobias one last look over. The fight unleashed her hunger, a craving left untamed on the dance floor between Vincent and Tobias. She ran her teeth over her lower lip, a staving of her desire. Tobias tipped his head. And with the whir of the electric engine, the trio broke apart.

The motorcycle zoomed at top speed. Marisol hugged herself tight to Vincent. He turned over the accelerator, popping the cycle on to one wheel. They rode along the edge of her destruction. Marisol laughed, intoxicated by the danger. *More, more, more.*

She kissed his neck. "Want to play?"

He nodded.

"Keep driving," she ordered, smoothing her hands over his chest. His rapid pulse thundered under her fingertips. She kissed the side of his mouth, and he returned weak kisses, maintaining his focus on the road.

She stood on her knees and, sliding her leg over his, maneuvered carefully from the back to the front. Her intensifying exhilaration shook her more than the force of speed. She faced Vincent, straddling his lap. His mouth parted. The thrill of night consumed her. The kiss she gave him—lips, then tongue, then hungry teeth—was enough to catapult them onto the road, but he took one hand off the handlebar and drew her closer to him.

Her hips undulated, grinding herself against his armor. She could take his pleasure giving him only a facsimile of the power of her hips.

The city passed in a blur. She closed her eyes, disappearing into the sensations of her mouth. He bit her lower lip and sucked on her tongue. A moan escaped her, traveling from her chest. Their loving was always a high-wire act, teetering between death and delight. The greater his speed, the more she gyrated against him to twist the stunt into greater bliss.

But the cycle came to a halt. She opened her eyes. Brick wall. Wet pavement. They were in the alleyway next to their hideout.

He pointed a finger at her. "Don't run off like that again."

She bit the tip of his finger and flickered her tongue against its tip. "What? And miss all the fun I'm having?"

"What you did was dangerous."

She gripped him by the clasps of his cape and pulled him toward her mouth. "And you aren't? Dangerous?"

He tore off his gloves and lifted her chainmail to her throat. The weight of the metal links pinned her to the handlebars. His greedy teeth pulled down the edge of her bra, his mouth finding her hard nipples. She gripped the tie at the back of his mask, pushing him into her breasts. Taking her direction well, he thrust against her. The grinding brought her to the brink of release. And teased the kind of fucking he'd give her.

She breathed in the scent of the alley. Dirty, wet, and complicated, just like her. "I want you exactly like this," she said with a sigh.

He ripped open the crotch of her pants. She heard a similar tear.

She joked, "I'll make you buy me a new—" He plunged into her, seizing the breath from her lungs as his hips met hers.

The handlebars dug into her back. The impact most definitely left a bruise. She loved it. Loved the twist of pain in her pleasure. Loved the mark to prove how much she stretched to take him. Her heels dug hard into his ass. *A bruise for you, too.* "Give me danger, my saint. Give it all to me."

Violence entwined with sensuality. Flashes of flames and blood, of speed and broken bones, of bites and bruises, of bodies grinding together on the dance floor. Her chainmail confined her pulse inside her head, blood feeding the high. Her climax shattered her, leaving her limp. "Is that all it takes?" she panted.

He answered with a laugh.

"I love the way you make me feel. I'm alive with you," she crooned against his ear.

And from their place in the alley, she watched the stars and moon shining above her like gods.

12

Falling Idol

Vincent caved. With Marisol's lip biting and eyelash batting, Adhara earned a tour of his hideout. He was never one to deny oxygen from his beloved's fire. Logic wasn't completely sacrificed to his passions, though. Last night's teamwork against the 86ers proved Adhara did good under his watchful eye. A team was forming again, a force powerful enough to set cargo ships aflame, to echo their reckoning beyond the city.

And perhaps this vigilante team would free him.

He showed Adhara the drawers of weaponry, gadgets, and medicine that helped him fight crime. Adhara's expression barely moved, as if she already knew the layout and rigamarole of crime-fighting in the contemporary age. Vigilantism hadn't changed much in 200 years. Humankind obviously functioned on a predictable algorithm.

The only device which seemed to crack into any of Adhara's emotions was the cryostasis chamber. She peered inside from its glowing blue window and tapped a golden claw against the glass.

"Nando, Alvaro, and Raul. The fourth? Is it?" She lowered her brows and brought the talon-like tip to her lips.

No, the fourth was not who she was thinking about. "Stone Ruthven, the Bloodsucker," Vincent said. "A science experiment attempting to unlock my traits, who accidentally unleashed them."

She dismissed the disaster of last year's villain with a blink. The Bloodsucker had promised someone or something more powerful coming for Shadowhaven. So far, nothing until her arrival. Did she know something Vincent didn't? "Last year, the Bloodsucker said he wasn't working alone. That a *Charlie* said hi. Does the name sound familiar to you?"

"I don't know any Charlies. Do you?"

Vincent shrugged. Names from his past eluded him and sifted away as time disintegrated them.

Adhara's eyes narrowed as if she were deep in thought. He had been guilty of the same unfocused daze when considering his past. The glitch, as Tobias had so affectionately called it.

"We're studying the curse with a little furry friend, A.J.," Marisol announced from across the hideout, pulling Adhara from her all-consuming rumination. Marisol indicated the reinforced cage of the super-powered mouse. The wild thing unearthed its deathly shriek.

Adhara held her hand against the mouse's fortified dwelling. "How cute." She made kissing noises at the ferocious creature. "Can I borrow it? To help us understand our curse?"

The cursed mouse in negligent care forecasted consequences spiraling into catastrophe. Yet more of Marisol's lip biting and eyelash batting told him to lighten up. If he continued to treat his vigilante half as if he were the authoritarian who knew better, he'd lose her. He'd be better to allow a safe amount of danger. "It mustn't leave its cage. Otherwise, you'll have scores of dead rodents and reports of mysterious animal attacks in the city."

"Anything else I should know, mouse daddy?" Adhara asked. She drummed her claws on his counter playfully.

He met her mocking with an exaggerated scowl. The pursuit of Justice wasn't all smart-ass quips and antics.

"You're not taking A.J. back to the storage shed," Marisol protested. "I've been keeping my old apartment. Stay there. Wi-fi, climate control, secured entrance—sure beats a garage."

Adhara clicked her claws rhythmically against the top of the mouse's cage. "All right, you've convinced me." She clutched the cage between her underarm and hip.

The women left, taking with them their excitement. He was alone again in his vast hideout, but it was a feeling of no consequence. His plan to draw Adhara further into his orbit was working, and the lab mouse had been subjected to another experiment—one about trust.

He moved to prepare for tonight's watch, but paused. A sudden pain drove into him like a spike. He bent over and caught himself against the counter. He searched his body for the source. It wasn't physical. It was his past. The voices returned, evil whispers humming like a gnat near his ear. *Useless. Don't belong. Shouldn't be here.*

"No!" he answered them. His defiance echoed throughout the basement.

A calm voice broke through the malevolent chatter. *If only it could end.* His mind's clamor quieted, and the sharp pain left just as quickly.

He checked in with himself. Toes curled inside his shoes, recognizing the insole cushion. His fingertips pressed, one by one, against the counter's cool surface. He took in a breath and released it. He was once more in the here and now.

Adhara's return had brought a strange side effect— the worst of him he had tried to forget.

Marisol helped Adhara move into her apartment. It wasn't hard. The super-powered woman only had a couple of boxes, but Adhara insisted Marisol stick around until she emptied them. She spread her computer system over the dinner table and arranged A.J.'s cage on a coffee table in the middle of Marisol's former living room. The setup required Marisol to move a photo of her and Annie to another shelf.

Adhara reached into one of her boxes and pulled out a baggie of what appeared to be fish food. "A snack for our friend."

"A.J. prefers live things, like what people usually give to snakes."

"I know." Adhara scooped the feed into one of her claws. She lowered her hand into the cage. A.J. nibbled at the golden tip.

"What are you feeding it?"

Adhara bolted to the computer on the dinner table. From the tangle of wires, she freed a mechanical-looking spider. Living 500 years made Adhara just as much of a wordless weirdo as Vincent. She sprinkled the fish food into the center of the robot spider.

"The powder is fungi. They can mimic neural pathways of the brain, sending signals." The mechanical spider crawled to the edge of the table and toppled onto the floor. It flipped back onto its feet.

"You're telling me fungus is moving that thing?"

"Yes, but I coded the commands and tuned them into the fungi's communication wavelength." Adhara adjusted the knob of a speaker. The noise sounded like a turkey gobble crossed with an angelic choir. "But if I reverse the command..." She typed a code into the computer. The pitch of the warbling changed.

In the cage, a calm seemed to wash over A.J. It darted to the other end of its fortress to the reinforced wheel and scurried in place.

"I told A.J. to go exercise," Adhara announced. "The creature no longer has to be a slave to its curse. We can control its power so that the next time we take on a bunch of crooks, we can have a mouse with super-strength chew the faces of n'er-do-wells. All at our command."

Marisol crouched down and watched the mouse scurry about the cage normally, as if last year's chemicals had never unleashed its viciousness. "Cool." She had missed times like this, where Annie clicked and coded her way into doing something brilliant. Pursing her lips together, she fought the onset of tears. Adhara's gray gaze bored into her, the same way Vincent's blue eyes would. He never missed the nuances of her emotions, and as it turned out, Adhara didn't seem to either.

"I can enjoy Annie's hard work rather than cringe away from it."

Adhara stared at her blankly. She didn't know about Annie, only allusions of havoc caused by the Bloodsucker. Marisol picked up the frame she had moved. "Annie. She made the substance, which turned our mouse friend into a raging zombie. The Bloodsucker killed her for it." The tremors of the fateful night of Annie's murder returned. Marisol chased them away with a little box breathing and picturing a leaf holding dew drops signifying her problems, floating downstream. See? She was letting go, just like her self-help guides told her.

"We all lose something when we're close to him." Adhara drew invisible arcs over Annie's picture and placed the frame back where Marisol had moved it.

Marisol nodded. Grief expanded from a muscle knot she could ignore to the prickly onset of crying. More breathing, leaves, and waterfalls, anything to make it go away. She blinked rapidly, hoping her eyelashes caught escaped tears.

"You know, you deserve a housewarming party." The more she changed the subject and shut out the trauma, the better she felt, self-help be damned. The remedy to the pain was there, because she had another chance at friendship with someone who understood the strange going-ons in the city. "Maybe another girl's night out? This time less gunfire and maiming." The sadness subsided.

"I was thinking something decadent." Adhara scooted a postcard across the table, avoiding the wires of the computer. "I want to feel like royalty."

The hot pink postcard advertised the Pink Curtain, the Westside strip club promising naked ladies, champagne on ice, and a combination of block and script lettering promising to *FEEL LIKE A KING*.

Marisol and Adhara entered the Pink Curtain. The rowdy audience whistled and tossed ones in the air. Magenta lights cast purple shadows over the crowd. More cash flitted through the air as a dancer slid down a pole into a straddle. Her ass cheeks bounced as she hit the stage. Thanks to the bank account of Vincent Varian, Marisol got her and Adhara a couple of stacks to go wild with. Champagne, dancing, and pretty ladies, what more could they ask for?

At the bar, they popped a bottle, which the bartender put on a bucket of ice. They clinked their flutes together.

"To living among 500-year-old scientists and their creations," Marisol toasted.

Adhara finished her flute in one gulp. "Does it bother you? The reason he made the collider?"

Marisol realized Adhara did this—found weaknesses and needled them open. Marisol tensed, the same way she did when she anticipated a punch from an opponent. "Providing the city with green energy? Not at all."

"Oh. You don't know, then." There it was, the first strike. Adhara helped herself to another pour of champagne. "The energy is a side effect. Do you ever wonder why he became a doctor? The identity before this one?"

Marisol inhaled, preparing her answer. For Justice. For helping people. For being the good man.

"He was studying cancer, how the cell destroys itself. Before then? So-called nuclear energy, but we can crack open a history book and know it was always about nuclear destruction. Splitting an atom with enough force to face oblivion."

Marisol had prepared to counter, but found Adhara in an altogether different fight. "You lost me."

"The collider creates the same energy that began the universe, yes, but it also creates antimatter. How does something like us, who can never be destroyed, defy such a Newtonian principle? The answer is antimatter."

Marisol's chest tightened, her body connecting dots her brain hadn't quite registered.

"He says it's a green energy, but it exists to fulfill the one thing he's wanted since the day we took our first drink from the Fountain—a chance to die. A suicide machine."

Marisol sank into a tunnel, lights and music drowning out. "Restore the balance of Justice," she murmured.

"You believe that rubbish? There is no balance to be restored. As long as the world has spun, it has been conquerors and conquered. Peace and freedom are momentary lapses before they seek to find something or someone to exploit. The only way to end the cycle is to remove yourself from it."

The version of Vincent that Adhara painted didn't make sense. Why was he trying to make the world better? Not only in fighting for Justice in her city, but through his philanthropy? He was a man with hope, not hopelessness. "You can't believe that. What's the point in fighting, then?"

Adhara finished her glass of champagne and licked a droplet off her lips, which she formed into a wide grin. "It's too much fun being a pain in their asses."

Marisol finished her glass and poured herself another to the rim of the flute, finishing the bottle of champagne. "You're wrong about him." She slid off the barstool. "C'mon, let's look at titties."

They moved deeper into the club, toward the main stage. The dancer finished her set and walked off the stage with a garbage bag of cash. The lights in the club shifted to blue. The DJ announced, "Next dancer to the main stage—Wheels!"

The men in the front row seats left and headed to the bar, opening up prime real estate for Marisol and Adhara to sit. Marisol watched the audience. Those near the stage seemed deep in conversation with the others around them. It was as if Wheels had repelled them.

A quiet song began playing. It was of a woman singing opera, not typical for riling up the strip club crowd. A rail-thin woman emerged from the backstage. In the lowlights, she was only a shadow, long, bony limbs and hair molded into two giant space buns. Her shadow skated to one of the three poles on stage and spun in a slow arc around it.

She repeated the motion on the other pole.

"Skates and pole dancing. Not something you see everyday," Marisol called to Adhara over the music.

Adhara was enraptured. Wheels gracefully slid, weaving between poles with twirls. The beat of the song picked up. Wheels leaped onto a pole, squeezing it between her supple thighs, her skates crossed at her ankle. She spun, extending her lithe limbs, landing in a pose which seemed to be the fantasy of any skate princess.

The song charged on. Wheels climbed the pole, the skid of skin shrieking over the music. From the top, she rotated upside down. Holding herself only by her arm strength, she moved her legs as if she were walking on the ceiling.

Marisol should be reaching for her stack of cash and releasing it into the air like confetti. Yet she waited with bated breath as the woman toyed high above them, unable to tear her attention away. The beat of the song halted. Marisol gripped Adhara's arm, feeling the cool metal of her gold veins.

Wheels tumbled down the pole.

Marisol stomach muscles tightened. She gasped. Was the poor dancer's head going to crack like an egg before them? Wheels skidded to a stop inches off the floor. She posed like a crane.

Marisol laughed. The dancer defied odds. The lights turned up, revealing more of the dancer's face. She rolled to the edge of the stage and extended her legs into a straddle, giving Adhara a 5D view of her crotch. Nestling on her elbows, she fluttered her eyelashes, neon yellow like her string bikini. Her skin from her face to her golden-brown shoulders, Marisol noticed, was covered in blue glitter.

Adhara offered her a giant wad of bills. Wheels threw the wad in the air. The bills fluttered about her. A handful, she smoothed over her small breasts and down her ribs.

Her glitter covered scars—a web that spread over half of her face and stretched from the top of her right shoulder to the middle of her collarbone like a supercontinent. The dancer tugged at the tiny, bright yellow fabric over her breasts and offered a peek of her dark nipples. The show was only for Adhara.

Wheels cut the enticing glimpses of her body short. She rolled to the back of the stage and picked up speed, using the torque to spin upside down on the pole, a feat of daring that ended with untying of her top and flinging it in their direction. Adhara snagged it on her claw.

Wheels landed in a backbend and kicked a long leg overhead, rolling into a split at the edge of the stage. She lowered her eyes, indicating the strap of her G-string. Adhara wedged a twenty in the string. The dancer's delicate hand glanced along Adhara's jawline.

The song reached its end. The dancer waved toodle-loo, gathering the cash in her arms before skating off stage.

"She was amazing!" Marisol said. The Pink Curtain, what a strange place to host someone so gifted.

"She's a goddess," Adhara said, staring at the back of the stage.

Marisol chuckled to herself. The half-naked roller skater had captured more of Adhara's attention than Marisol ever could. "I could buy her for you."

The silence stretched between them until a realization stiffened Adhara's expression into concern, seeming to scrutinize Marisol. For stealing attention from Wheels? For suggesting she could buy another human being?

"Not *her*. I mean, I can buy a private dance for you," Marisol corrected.

Adhara's gaze still hadn't moved from the back of the stage, even as another dancer arrived, and the men returned to flock to the more conventional big titties and platinum blond wigs.

The promise of a private dance hadn't moved Adhara. Marisol tried the last outlet to impress her. "I know the owner. I could see if I could introduce you to her."

Without hesitation, Adhara said, "Give me his money."

Marisol handed her a stack of ones.

Her gold tips shimmered as she wiggled her fingers. "More. Your boyfriend is a billionaire."

She forked over a few hundreds. If Adhara needed more, it was a visit to the ATM to barely put a dent in Vincent Varian's savings.

"Wait here. See you in fifteen minutes." Loaded with Vincent's cash, Adhara disappeared behind the beaded curtain, which led to the private dancing rooms.

Marisol retreated to the bar. Instead of champagne, she went for tequila on the rocks. The bartender offered her a wedge of lime, but she liked working through the burn of it. A little discomfort made the buzz worth it.

Scanning the interior of the club, nothing struck her as entertaining enough to note, just clacking heels and shaking asses. If she was lucky, maybe she'd catch the flash of the main stage dancer's strobing butt plug. The occasion required a smart-ass quip about lights decorating sphincters, but there was no audience around who operated on her wavelength. Not Vincent or Tobias.

And not Annie.

She was alone. Marisol stabbed at the ice in her drink with the tiny plastic straw. Jealousy gnawed at her. The stripper had Adhara's attention. Everyone else in the world still had their best friend. She ordered another tequila on the rocks.

Adhara emerged from the dark red, labyrinthine insides of the club. She bit her lip as if she were holding back excitement. Wheels had written her a note. *Meet me outside.*

In the alleyway outside the Pink Curtain, **Marisol** and Adhara huddled around the beat-up metal door of the hidden exit. Adhara busied herself with a cigarillo, filling the sour air with sweet smoke. Marisol had been pulled into two parts. The winning half stayed with Adhara, playing the role of wingwoman to strengthen the newly minted bond of friendship. The other part ached to return home and talk to Vincent—to search for the truth of what Adhara had said. But the answer felt like a box she didn't want to open. Schrödinger's Suicide. If she never looked, she would never know, and life could go on as usual. Hence, alleys and strippers.

The door swung open. Out poked an arm holding a can of bug spray. "Shoo, pests!" a familiar bass voice called.

A tall, broad figure strutted out of the exit, the bug spray aimed straight at Marisol. The defender tossed her hair and clicked her tongue, none other than Mijo

Ray. "Marisol Novotny, never thought I'd see you out here creeping." Mijo Ray called back, "It's safe!"

"Not intending to creep. We were..." All of a sudden, trying to pick up a stripper for a friend felt as embarrassing as it sounded.

"I'm meeting—" Adhara paused as Wheels rolled to the exit. She still wore her blue glitter and hair in space buns, but had changed into cutoff denim shorts and a purple faux fur coat. A pair of thigh-high athletic-style socks protected her slender legs from the cold.

Adhara's gaze never lifted off the scrawny woman, a head taller than Marisol thanks to the roller skates. "I'm Adhara. This is Marisol."

The woman blew a giant bubble of pink bubblegum until it popped. "I'm Wheels, and you can buy me dessert."

Someone gruffly shouted, "You're not fucking leaving." Tiny, the club owner, filled the entire doorway. "Club gets a kickback, and you're supposed to share your tips with the DJ."

Wheels reached into the small pockets of her shorts and handed him a roll of bills.

Tiny counted it right there and then in the alley. "I had it on good word you made double this tonight. You finally found an audience for your art school shit."

Wheels stared at Adhara as she dug into her pocket again, conjuring up more bills, which Tiny more than happily snatched.

"All right, you can leave now." The door slammed behind him.

Adhara said, "Join us. I'll get you something sweet."

Marisol picked at her plate of fries. Wheels and Adhara shared a milkshake and slurped it to its disappointing end. As annoying as being the third wheel could be, Marisol couldn't look away from the night's entertainment.

Wheels' neon nails traced along the gold branches of Adhara's forearm. "These aren't jewelry, are they?"

"How observant. They serve many purposes—a skeletal system, nervous system, and circulatory system. The structure holds my body together and sends signals to my brain to help them move. Tiny needles throughout inject bio-fluid into my body so that I appear...fresh."

The bizarre explanation lit up Wheels' face in the same way a child would express awe if they were told the Easter Bunny was real. "What happened to you?"

"I lost my head in France over two hundred years ago and became broken and mummified in a Himalayan avalanche almost a hundred years ago."

Wheels grimaced, as if she was unsure of how to react, a feeling Marisol was growing accustomed to around Adhara. "Do you always make such strange jokes?"

"I never joke about those things."

Wheels interlaced her fingers with Adhara's over the top of the table. A fry dropped from Marisol's mouth as she could do nothing but watch the two come together like magnet poles.

Wheels raised an eyebrow, coy in its curiosity. "Do these claws ever go away?"

Adhara snapped the fingers of her other hand. The claws retreated into a bracelet-like structure on her wrist. "Does that answer your question?"

Wheels drew Adhara's hand to her face and nuzzled against her palm. "You may have answered the question I asked, but not the question I was thinking."

The awkward day when Marisol walked in on her parents mid-coitus arrived brutally at the forefront of her memory. At least then, she could back out of the room quickly. Now, she regretted taking the inside seat of the booth.

But the budding lovers didn't mind her. Adhara's fingertips traced along the webbing of Wheels' glittering scars. "What about you? What happened to you?"

Wheels sat back, releasing herself from Adhara's affection. Her neon-yellow-tipped eyelashes flitted low. "Someone thought I belonged to them. When he realized I didn't, he tried to destroy me."

Adhara's eyes shone with tears. "People tried to destroy me, too. I sent their souls to oblivion."

Wheels' posture straightened, and her eyes became watery. "Cool."

The pair were on a wavelength far from Marisol and the rest of the world. Their bond reminded her of the beginning of her and Vincent, coming together over centuries and distances to belong to each other.

They parted ways on the cold sidewalk outside the diner. Adhara and Wheels left together, hand in hand, barely acknowledging **Marisol**.

Back to one again.

Marisol bummed a ride from Staci. Annie would never ditch her for a woman. Or a man. Or anyone. Every night had ended in two stops in whatever order—Annie's then Marisol's. As she wallowed in her self-pity, even the driverless car seemed to mock her. No friend. No small talk. At least the long, silent drive gave her time to think.

All thought-roads led to Vincent—how she'd kiss him when she arrived home and how she'd tell him about third-wheeling with Adhara and Wheels.

And how she'd ask him about the suicide machine.

Like a good little Novotny, she shoved it down and asked Staci to play some music instead.

13

Star-Crossed

Marisol padded out of the bathroom, towel-drying her wet strands. Dawn was in another hour, so it was time to get some much-needed rest. "It was nice to have some girl time," she called out, "but I realized how much I miss—"

Vincent, however, wasn't in bed.

She spotted him through the glass doors, sitting with his arms and legs stretched out on the floor of his penthouse balcony. He was staring up at the few stars glittering through the city's smog.

The rumble of her moving the sliding glass door jostled Vincent from his gazing. He turned to her and flickered a smile that didn't quite reach his eyes.

Adhara's explanation for the collider haunted Marisol's thoughts. Asking him about it—suicide—tangled itself in her vocal cords. Instead, she asked, "You coming to bed soon?"

"Soon."

Brief and monosyllabic, like he always was, but loaded with unstated emotion. "If it's any comfort, I think my days hanging out with Adhara are limited. I spent the night witnessing her fall in love with a roller-skating stripper."

He answered her with one chuckle and returned his focus to the stars above.

She joined him on the floor, but didn't know where to look when it came to stars. "It blows my mind you lived in an era without detailed maps or GPS. How'd you ever find your way by looking at stars?"

He sighed. "It's sort of soothing. These were the same stars that guided me here."

"Sort of how I know Willie's Corner Store by the crack in the sidewalk and the grease spot in front of it."

In his right hand, she noticed something sparkling between his fingers—her abuelita's cross necklace she had given to him. Love passed from her abuela and from her to Vincent, creating a force field around them and protecting them. "You have my necklace."

"It's always with me. Sometimes I hold it when I miss you."

She nuzzled against his shoulder and breathed in the sweet scent of him. Of electricity and sandalwood. His warmth surrounded her and shielded her from the sunless chill of night. He was forever. This love was never going to go away.

He pointed toward the sky, to a speck which shone brighter than the others. "Polaris, the North Star. No matter where I was or when, it stayed firm and true through the night." His expression went blank, and he swallowed. "It called to me."

Called to him? A memory came to her of when she was a child. "I couldn't have been older than ten. I don't think Nicole was born yet. Mom and Dad kept Caz and I awake, yelling about money. They carried on as if we couldn't hear them through those thin walls. I got out a flashlight, pointed it out the window, and turned it on. I knew lighthouses and codes spoke to people when nothing else could. I didn't know any signals, but I flickered it, off and on, thinking I'd call on someone or something to fix the fear I heard in my parents' voices." She turned her head, facing him. Her lips anticipated the gentle comfort of his reassuring kiss. "And then you finally came into my life."

He blinked, his stained-glass eyes sparkling a hint of his inner light. "Do you know what else they call the North Star?"

She shook her head.

"*Stella Maris* or *Our Lady of the Sea.* But I like to think of it as the Stella Marisol."

The familiar glittering light feeling came over her, a common occurrence with Vincent. "I'm your star."

His gaze searched among the tiny dots poking through the electric night. "Wherever, whenever you are, I know where I'm supposed to be."

"I'll call for you by flashlight. One, two, three." Three pulses of light, *I love you.*

"My point on the Ursa Minor. One, two, three, four." Flashing beams, his way of saying, *I love you, too.*

She spoke through a yawn. "Your sidewalk crack and grease spot."

He chuckled as his free arm drew her the few centimeters they sat apart. "My Stella Marisol."

Vincent wouldn't leave her. Not in the way Adhara had theorized. The whole idea was preposterous.

14

Good Cop, Bad Cop

Predictably, days passed before **Marisol** heard from Adhara again, and then a text. *Come over It's an emergency.*

She arranged for someone to cover her shift at the clinic and rushed to her apartment. Though she buzzed herself into the building and had a key to enter, she knocked on her apartment door. It was only polite.

Wheels answered with A.J. perched on her shoulder. The mouse peacefully chowed a leaf of lettuce. Adhara's fungi had worked its magic on the thing.

The dancer wore a plain T-shirt and running shorts, her curly hair brushed out from the last time Marisol had seen her. Without makeup on, her facial scars were slightly pale and raised compared to the rest of her clear complexion. She didn't say a word as she turned away from the door, leaving it open. Marisol interpreted it as a sign to come right in.

Nothing was on fire and neither looked ill. The emergency wasn't obvious to her. "What's going on?"

Adhara sat next to the loose wires and computer on Marisol's kitchen table. "Thank you for coming over. Wheels, tell her what you heard."

Wheels handed the mouse to Adhara, who stroked the creature's fur. She sat on the middle seat of the sofa, her small frame dwarfed by the plush cushions. "I was working last night, giving a lap dance to some customers. They were saying while the 86ers' command rot in jail, a large supply of heroin sits in a container on the docks, unclaimed. They know which container has it, and they want to unload it to move the drugs themselves."

"Enough drugs to keep Shadowhaven out of its mind for the next six months," Adhara added.

"That's a lot of money. We could tip the police."

Adhara scoffed. "About that—"

"Their haircuts and bad tipping meant one thing. They're cops," Wheels said.

"They know the 86ers ate it last week, thanks to us. Gangsters are like a hydra. You cut off one head and more sprout up, except this time, it's the city's bluest," Adhara explained.

Marisol had learned how the Shadows functioned practically by osmosis. Wheels' customers blabbed like amateurs, not the nefarious criminals worthy of the Patron Saint. Throw a banana peel their way and call it fighting for Justice. "Not the smartest, planning everything in front of a captive audience."

"The scars. People treat me like I'm not there or I'm too stupid to understand. You'd be surprised what I've heard."

Marisol had to give her credit, she raised a good point. "Did they give a time?"

"Nothing specific. After dark, they said."

She stifled incredulous laughter. "Moving a hefty supply at night after the dockworkers clock out? It sounds like something out of a movie." During her dad's days at the docks, more insidious stuff passed during the day, loaded straight from ships to semi trucks—business as usual—rather than organized criminals sneaking into a container yard at night. The planned crime stunk worse than garbage juice.

"Catching real criminals isn't a battle of wits," Adhara said. "It's blunt force."

In the basement hideaway under the penthouse, **Marisol** explained the corrupt cops' plot to Vincent and Tobias.

"Let me get this straight," Tobias said, his feet propped on the table, "you went to the Pink Curtain without me?"

"After hearing the idiot conspiracy, that's what concerned you?" Marisol feigned a sigh. "I'll invite you next time."

Tobias raised his eyebrows, amused by the promise of champagne and lap dances. He shifted his posture, grunting in old man. With his feet flat on the floor, he'd become serious. "There's been rumors about a group of cops taking a little contraband off the top, siphoning stuff into the suburbs and operating right out of their garages."

Some Shadowhaven cops descended her neighborhood into chaos with their rip-and-raids, which had been successful in injuring a kid but not getting drugs off the street. Now, some were dealing themselves? And Tobias knew about these guys? Her rage powered her mouth. "So you hear about drug-dealing cops and carry on like it's another day at work?"

"More like I add it to a long list of shit I have to deal with, but I have to shift priorities when dead bodies pile up." Tobias stood. "I know this may come as a surprise to you, but the police I know don't like corrupt little shit bricks either."

Adhara's warning echoed through her mind. Tobias was a cop and could only be trusted as far as his limited system allowed. "Hear that, Vincent? He suggests we punish them by transferring them to another town they can fuck up."

Tobias's jaw ticked. "How selective would your empathy be if we were plotting against some Westside teenagers?"

Marisol shifted her weight, considering where a punch might devastate Tobias the most.

Vincent cleared his throat, breaking the rising tension. Marisol's muscles relaxed, and she stood down. Vincent sighed, looking strangely defeated. "We patrol the docks at different points. If anything raises suspicion, one of us will see them."

Marisol opened her mouth to speak, but Vincent stopped her with a raised hand.

"The Patron Saint brings all criminals before Justice," Vincent added.

Tobias smiled weakly. "We're on the same side, kid."

Was ignoring corruption on her side? Her answer was torn. Torn between Vincent's desire for peace and her need to be heard. Torn between her distrust of an institution and Tobias's neutral good balancing along the law and vigilantism. Torn because she so wanted a friend—him—to understand her. Dramatic, but it ate a hole in her heart.

The tearing drained her energy, so she somberly said, "Don't make me regret involving you."

15

BLACK HOLE

Each member of the trio manned a different vehicle to survey the docks. Covering the south side of the docks, Tobias took off in his beat-up sedan. He had assured them that such a car helped him blend in. Assigned to the north side, Marisol started the electric engine of Staci's SUV. Even behind the vehicle's darkened windows, her silver armor sparkled. **Vincent**, as the Patron Saint, pulled up beside her on his motorcycle.

She rolled down the window and took a long look at him. "You don't seem like yourself."

"How am I not myself?" Vincent chortled, the irony of wearing the mask not lost on him.

"I don't know. Low energy. Is it because this plan is Adhara's baby?"

His head sank low. Jealousy twisted in and out of him as Adhara and Marisol bonded. Petty feelings impacted how he saw the past. Adhara had different ways of approaching similar problems as he did, but her help so far was good for the team.

200 years had to have changed Adhara, because he had to believe he had changed too, to someone better

and worthy of Marisol's love. Serving Justice finally filled the hole vengeance carved in Adhara, because it filled the vengeful abyss within him. Didn't it?

If he intervened upon a budding friendship a year after Marisol's best friend had been murdered, he would be the bad guy. He considered himself better than the boyfriends from Hell who told their girlfriends not to hang out with their friends. Marisol deserved better than control. "I'll be fine."

"We both know what *fine* is code for."

"I've been a little jealous," he said, his voice thin.

"Of who?"

He swallowed. It wasn't only Adhara, who had strength and friendship, but it was Tobias, too. He had caught the stolen glances and tense words disguising their feelings, which at first, he attributed to the aftereffects of her once believing Tobias was the Patron Saint. Normally, he found their dance of temptation thrilling. Why did it hurt now?

Because Tobias had something else, too. He was someone from her time, who was as devoted and mortal as she was. Marisol and Tobias were meant for each other in a way he and Marisol never could be. He was a man who didn't belong. Yet, he chastised himself further for daring to think it. He had moved on from the insignificant feelings of mortal humans centuries ago. His weakness brought their return.

His silence spoke for him.

She said, "You don't need to be. I love you."

He gave a closed-mouth smile. Duty called, and he had to let go of these complicated feelings. He gazed at her, glittering in her armor, a star guiding him, and he straightened. "I love you too."

She rolled the window back up and drove away. The engine lit his motorcycle in blue, and he followed close behind her. Yet as she turned in the direction of the docks, a force seemed to take over him. His muscles locked in resistance, but a trembling took over. He turned his motorcycle in the opposite direction.

Why was he doing this? To leave the way he had left Vincent/Victor behind. And Leonard, Verne, Virgil, and the rest of them, the men he used to be. Vincent was going to be another one he ran from. Sure, Marisol promised this lifetime would be different. He claimed they would beat the curse. A part of him knew, though, it was a hope he let her have, so they could pretend not to be fools in love.

Confronted with the pain of the truth, he gripped the handlebars to fight it, yet he zoomed past the city limits, deep into the Micah Forest. *Turn around*, he begged himself. *Be a fool a little longer.* But something possessed him to accelerate toward the Varian Energy and Particle Physics Center. At night, no one operated the unused powerful machine. No one except Staci, who dutifully opened the entrances and turned on the lights.

The voice telling him to turn on the collider was the same one he had heard in the numerous nights of his despair. Not only the sharp mantra activated by *useless*, but also a chronically painful message he carried his entire unnatural life. It first appeared when he wanted to outrun the blood and smoke. Whose blood? What fire? He lost the answers in the labyrinth of his memory. It was the voice wishing to be free of the curse, begging for God to take away the Faustian bargain. It was the voice he ignored as he wished the masked man would fix what he had broken. The voice prevailed as he pursued the oblivion of the mushroom cloud, the destruction of cells, and now finally his newest innovation.

The man he thought he could be had already been replaced—Marisol, hero, Adhara, friend, Tobias, lover. As the machine awakened under his trembling hand, euphoria lifted the weight of the centuries of suffering. At last, the voices would be silent.

Marisol sat on stacks of storage containers, Shadowhaven's version of mountains. From her view on the mountaintop, she spotted the valley of smaller stacks and the quiet boats still in the harbor. The jaundiced streetlights cast a sickly pallor over the yard and warped with each ripple as they reflected off the water. She blew out a breath and tapped her earpiece. "I'm so bored."

Tobias yawned loudly. "I may have to stop by the corner store for some energy drinks."

"Cue the Patron Saint to tell us we're using the system to needlessly converse, which could give our locations away." Marisol waited a beat and heard nothing.

"He's been quiet—quieter than usual. Maybe he knows something we don't." Tobias laughed, but then the sound cut off. Lights of a semi tractor shone from the middle of the container depot. He boomed over her earpiece, "Do you see that?"

"Yeah. They're making it too easy." Shifting her weight forward to her toes, she prepared to leap from her perch on top of the container.

Two shadowed individuals jumped out of the giant truck's cab and cut the entrance with wire cutters, opening the chain-link gate far enough for the semi to pass.

"Hold on," Tobias said.

The semi made it a hundred feet out of the yard before a swarm of port authority vehicles descended upon it. Marisol watched as the criminals were easily rounded up. She scoffed. Why were they here on such a weak tip?

Something moved from across the container depot, and she saw people descending from the seemingly abandoned boat. They began to move multiple crates from a nearby container and load them onto the boat. Opposite side of the yard? Away from port authority? The semi and drama of all the sirens had to be a distraction.

"They're unloading a ship across the yard."

"Time for the Shadowhaven surprise?" Tobias asked.

"You bet." Marisol took a running leap onto a container below her. A few more jumps from platform to platform, and she landed with a roll on some containers stacked two high. From there, she dug her boots into the metal and slid to the ground. Her three-point landing prepared her for springing into a sprint.

She neared the dock, where the slew of criminals loaded the crates. Unwilling to confront them alone, she took cover behind the foot of a crane. "Tell me you're near."

A jet pack's roar rumbled above her. Adhara landed in the middle of the throng. "Those who prey on people's weaknesses are no better than scum!" Flames shot from her protective suit, lighting a stack of crates on fire.

Multiple guns clicked in chorus. Adhara flung a boomerang in the air. The arc knocked the guns from hands. Marisol took their disarming as her cue to emerge from hiding.

Tobias met her at the dock. An electric pulse from his cattle prod knocked one of the drug traffickers into the water.

"Promise I get the next one?" Marisol asked. Wish granted, a criminal charged at her. She greeted him with a boot to the gut, sending him to join his friend in the water.

Another foe raised his gun. Adhara threw something white and shrieking in his direction. A.J. gnawed the assailant's wrist, and he dropped the gun screaming. The super-powered furball flitted around the dock, avoiding stomping boots and kicks. Its mousey teeth sunk into some man's ankle, sending another shadowy figure into the water. It scurried up Adhara's leg and sat on her shoulder, safe from harm.

Victory followed victory, but the thrill left the fight. Something was off; something was wrong. Where was Vincent? Suddenly, the watch on Tobias's wrist glowed and pulsed three times. One, two, three. *I love you.*

Automatically, Marisol tapped her earpiece four times. *I love you too.* "Vincent, where are you?"

No answer, but three more pulses. The safety lights lining the dock dimmed. She'd seen something like it before. It was like the electricity had at the ball—the ball where Vincent showed off the collider.

Suicide machine.

Her breath shallowed. He'd activated the machine.

She sprinted down the dock.

"Kid, where are you going?" Tobias called after her.

"It's Vincent!"

The pounding of Tobias's boots followed her, but the blare of ship's horn stopped her in a skidding halt. What the fuck?

Adhara flew from the ship's deck. She had used to horn to call the attention of the port authority's flashing lights. Some flashing lights moved closer to them. Port authority was going to cut short the wannabe drug dealers' night swim in the harbor.

But it didn't matter. She had to get to Vincent.

"Staci, find me," Marisol ordered. She ran through the mazes of storage containers. Her lungs burned, as if she couldn't quite inhale a deep enough breath.

"Wait for me!" Tobias shouted.

She turned a corner around a stack of containers, and the SUV stared her down like a charging bull. "Thank God," she muttered to herself.

The vehicle opened its doors, and she jumped into the driver's seat. "Staci, where is he?"

The dashboard drew a map far outside the city limits—in the Micah Forest, where the collider lab resided. A knock pounded on the other side of the glass. Tobias joined her and slipped into the passenger seat. "What's going on?"

"We've got to get to the collider, now!"

Tires squealed as Staci drove wildly through the yard. Each turn tossed them from side to side. The system led them to a chain-link fence meant to lock them inside. But Staci charged the fence. The electric engine reached a high pitch as it sped. Marisol closed her eyes and braced for impact.

The smooth ride betrayed her preparation. Opening her eyes, she saw the SUV accelerating down the road and into the night. No scrapes or damage? How? She looked back. Staci had cut a precise rectangle in the fence, the perfect size for the vehicle.

Tobias shook his head in disbelief. "Why the collider?"

"Adhara told me the machine makes antimatter. He created it to—to disappear." Panic seized her muscles, constricting her voice to a scratchy whisper.

"I thought he was right behind us when we left."

"I...didn't...say...anything."

"Breathe. We'll get there." He made the Sign of the Cross. "We have to."

The city lights streaked by them, wavering in and out of brightness. The collider was on, she was sure of it.

Every dip or bump in the pavement shook the interior of the car. The city limits sign offered brief respite. A few more miles, and they'd reach the forest.

She clicked her earpiece four times, begging him with each pulse to keep communicating. Three, he was always returning three. He was still there. She could stop him.

The car wound through the trees. They were fast approaching. Up the path, the sign for the Varian Energy and Particle Physics Center stood. The gates opened for the SUV, and it stopped inches from the doorway entrance. Marisol and Tobias tore themselves from the front seat.

"Staci, open those locks for us," Marisol ordered as she ran.

The empty building roared with the echo of unlatching locks. She burst through the door and sprinted, instinct driving her and feet propelling her. Her thighs ached as she ran. Tobias trailed farther and farther behind.

A beam of magenta light shone, casting the sterile hallway in the blinding deep pink. She had to follow the source. He was there. The safety lights flickered to barely a glow. A thunderous sound shook the building. On cue, the lights blazed brightly. Lightbulbs exploded from their fixtures. She shoved her way to the command center. Holding her arm above her eyes to block the magenta rays, she spotted a dark figure standing inside the glass wall collider.

She ran to him and banged on the glass. "Open the door, Vincent!"

He greeted her with a small yet peaceful smile. He mouthed, "Not safe."

She trembled, searching the room for a way to stop him. Approaching the mainframe, she announced, "Staci, stop this at once."

"Process cannot be stopped once initiated," the artificial intelligence coldly responded.

She grabbed an office chair and flung it against the glass wall. It bounced off the barrier, not even leaving a mark. Vincent shook his head from the other side.

No, he wasn't going to give up like this. Though her limbs shook, she grabbed the chair and swung it like a bat against the glass. Nothing. She struck it harder and harder, until the chair broke into pieces.

She moved to strike again. Tobias hugged her in place. "Antimatter? Kid, if you break it, who knows what will happen on our end?"

She sent an elbow into Tobias's gut and dove to the barrier. Vincent held his palm against the glass, her cross necklace wound over his fingers. His lips moved, "It's okay."

No, no, no. It was not going to be okay! She punched the glass, hearing the crunch of the bones in her hand. The pink light rose in intensity until it seared her retinas and blotted out the collider's humming noise with an oppressive ringing in her ears. She closed her eyes. The collider bathed her in a sheet of white light. Then, darkness.

She opened her eyes.

Vincent dissolved, like sand blown by the wind.

She punched the glass again. The blood from her hand smeared over it. *Not again. No, not again.* "No! Fucking no!" Her vocal cords burned from screaming. She stopped to only take a breath. The cold air soothed her raw throat, but her stomach knotted and knotted. She coughed up bile. The ringing in her ears halted, and she heard sobbing. Her sobbing. She was on the outside looking in.

Tobias embraced her. She tried to shove him off, but she registered the pain shooting from her mangled hand. The unbearable hurt sucked the fight from her, and she became dead weight in his arms.

Vincent was gone.

Marisol kept her swelling hand away from **Tobias**. Instead, she sat, knees tucked into her chest. In the last hour, she had stopped crying, but her eyes glazed over, as if she were dead or possessed by a specter. Tobias hadn't left her side.

Boots clicked from behind him. Adhara stood at the room's entrance.

"He's—" Tobias hit his fist against his chest. A bruise over his heart stopped him from becoming like Marisol, like a devastated shell.

"Gone," Adhara said flatly.

"Do you know what happened to him?" he asked.

She leaned into the control panel and typed rapidly. "With every action, there's an equal and opposite reaction. The power of creation also results in destruction." Then she stopped. Her hands jerked back as though the console had shocked her. "The collider created a mini-universe. The resulting antimatter destroyed him." Her voice remained low and steady.

"What about the curse?"

"There is a possibility of a mini-universe the collider created absorbing him—that he's dust at the dawn of time, becoming a star." Her expression darkened, her focus turning inward. "Alive forever."

"So he's something," Tobias added.

"In theory."

Marisol hoarsely replied, "You mean we can bring him back."

"Again, in theory. The kind of calculations to find a speck spiraling into space...well, it's worse than finding a needle in a haystack."

"But it is possible to find a needle in a haystack. So you get on that computer and calculate," Marisol rasped.

Adhara exchanged a look of doubt with Tobias. She took a spot on the computer mainframe and tapped the keys. "Of course. I'll get started."

"Good. How long is it going to take?"

"I don't know. It could be a day, week, a month or...?" Adhara answered.

Marisol's brown eyes grew wild. As if in a trance, she said, "We come up with a believable excuse about his whereabouts to feed the public, and we get him back."

How could Vinnie come back from atomization? Tobias rested his forehead against his clasped hands. God rarely answered his prayers, but he clung to a miracle to do the impossible. The job saved him, giving him something to do when he felt as powerless as he did now.

First job, fix Marisol's bleeding hand. "Come on, kid, I'll take you to the hospital." But after that? The next job? He hadn't a clue. How did one go about patching the Vincent-shaped hole in their hearts?

16

At My Worst

Tobias had become the babysitter of a near-catatonic Marisol. She sat in a chair before the dried spot of blood on the collider. She stared ahead, hands folded in her lap. Her right hand was in a cast.

For the last week, the Physics and Energy Department of Varian Research remained closed. The scientists overseeing the project were placed on temporary leave by the command of a well-worded dupe of an email from Adhara. Now the super-powered woman returned from a week-long vacation, playing the game of "Where in the World Could They Hide Vincent Varian?"

Adhara stood on the grated staircase overlooking the collider lab. She announced she'd planted evidence to explain the billionaire's disappearance—a plane crash. Tobias thanked her for helping, but Marisol remained unmoved. If she didn't need the cast, Tobias doubted she'd ever have gotten up from the lab floor.

Adhara drew out a crinkled sheet of paper from the pocket of her jeans. Margin to margin, the entire paper appeared to contain endless math equations. Adhara waved it in the air, a flag of victory. Tobias gave her a nod, and she turned on the computer mainframe. She typed a few commands, and the collider hummed with life.

Soon, pink particles buzzed inside the tube like a swarm of angry bees. Adhara typed more commands. The buzzing particles vibrated with greater distances within the collider, and at a higher rate of speed as the machine increased in pitch. Ceiling lights inside the center flickered off and on. The light glowed brighter and brighter until a familiar sheet of white washed over them—but instead of particles sifting like sand, it was as if the whole thing had flamed out. The entire computer room fell into in pitch black.

Tobias turned on his phone flashlight. Adhara's brows pinched together. "I don't understand. The whole thing broke down." She clicked the buttons, but nothing responded.

A red light beamed into the room, safety lights coming on. His eyes adjusted in the eerie ruby glow. An alarm blared. Staci warned in its unnatural cadence, "The Staci system will shut down in five minutes."

The alarms shrieked louder. Tobias staggered, but got his bearings when he held his hands over his ears. He shouted for Marisol to follow him, but she hadn't even flinched. Metal shields slid from under the computer mainframe and spread across the keyboard, encasing the panel in thick metal. A rumbling noise traveled across the building, and Adhara pounded on the metal casing.

"The system, it's locking up. If we don't move it, we could be trapped!" Adhara shouted.

With no time to hesitate anymore, Tobias threw Marisol over his shoulder, and the trio ran out of the lab. They scrambled into the black matte SUV, but the thing didn't activate or respond to his commands. The overhead light turned on. That was something good, right? Staci announced, "The Staci system will shut down in two minutes."

"What the hell is going on?" Tobias shouted.

Adhara replied, "I don't know!"

The tow truck dropped them in front of the Varian downtown penthouse. They set the SUV in neutral, and **Tobias** and Adhara pushed it into the underground garage. Marisol trailed behind them, cradling her cast against her chest.

He punched in his code to enter the hideout, but to fit the theme of the evening, nothing happened. No beep. No glow. Everything to access the world of the Patron Saint had died. Tobias smacked the concrete wall, the one he was sure would open. But it didn't.

"We're locked out," Marisol said tonelessly.

Sure enough, from the penthouse to the Varian estate, any location with Patron Saint fingerprints on it was completely shut down.

The time of Shadowhaven's masked vigilantes was over.

Tobias nestled against the back of the plush couch, keeping vigil over Marisol in the elaborate main bedroom. The cushions underneath him had begun to form into his shape over the week, but at least facing the back of the couch mimicked sharing a bed with someone—a room-temperature someone.

She rustled from behind him. She was awake.

"You up?" she asked.

He sighed and rolled onto his back. "Yep."

She stood hugging the bedpost, lightly scratching the small patch of skin between her elbow and the cast. Ambient city light painted a contrast of shadow and light over her, highlighting the parts of her he was ashamed to think about. Her muscular thighs and the generous curve of her hips practically swallowed her tiny sleep shorts, and her cropped tank top barely contained her ample breasts. No, he wasn't thinking about his grieving best friend's voluptuous body and the size of her sleepwear.

"Could you lie next to me?"

"Okay." He stood up and grabbed his pants hanging over the couch's arm. The belt buckle still looped around the waist jingled.

"Stay comfortable. You don't have to put on your pants."

He swallowed. "Okay." Next to Marisol in his underwear? This was God warning him to be careful of what he wished for.

She turned down the sheets opposite from her, and he slid next to her. The sheets were cold on his side and warm on hers.

Marisol curled into him. The weight of her cast pressed over his midsection. He moved his arm around her, and she cuddled closer, her cheek resting against his chest and her smooth leg hooked over his. He'd always wanted to love her this way. So much so, he couldn't help but finger the soft ends of her hair in the middle of her back.

"Why did he...go?"

"500 years is a long time. It's a weariness we can't fathom."

"Wasn't I...weren't we enough?"

For him, addiction had blocked out the people who mattered. His daughter was everything to him, yet the bottle kept calling to him. "We were. You were more than enough. Self-destruction can run so deep, it practically forms in the marrow. It's a war a lot of us never win."

"How do you do it?"

Like a coward, really, supplementing his recovery with doses of Vincent Varian go-go juice, but she didn't need to know about his weakness. He didn't believe in himself enough to recover the hard way. "Minute by minute, day by day. Some battles you win; others you don't."

She hummed as if she was considering what he said. The soft vibration painted him over in calm. She shifted her weight, her body heat inching closer to him. "What are we going to do now if we can't be masked?"

His fingertips glanced hers where they poked out of the cast. "We get back to work, helping people in the way we know how—mending the broken things. Me with the police, you at the clinic. And we keep on keeping on."

"It's as if he didn't exist." She tilted her head up, her breath warm on his neck. With a similar movement, angling down, his lips could so easily meet hers.

"But we know it isn't true."

"Your heartbeat races when you talk about him."

"I'm holding you."

"I raise your pulse?"

"We know that's true."

She rubbed her leg against his, her knee teasing his thigh. "I was thinking."

A shift in his grip, and he caressed the skin between her shirt and shorts. Sharper memories awakened from within—her writhing into him on the dance floor, Vincent's fingers pulling his shirt, the inviting warmth of her soft lips, and forbidden taste of his. The blood coursing through him aimed in one direction, and fuck, he wanted to give in to it.

"We could hire some coders and physicists with his money and make them sign a non-disclosure agreement. Maybe they could get Staci back and then..."

Oh, she wasn't going his direction. Like always. "There's something you're not thinking about, kid."

She sat up. The cold air grew between them. "What's that?"

"What if he doesn't want to come back?"

She cringed, as if a punch had landed in her gut. "Why would you say that?"

Shit, he'd fucked up. He wasn't sure how badly yet.

"I've treated patients who survived...you know. They always say it's a permanent solution to a temporary sadness. Of course he wants to come back."

"I didn't mean—"

"Why the fuck would you say that?" She pulled the covers off him. "Get out."

He'd heard this line from his ex, and he practically had automated the response. "Tobias Quinlan, walking cliche. To the couch I go." He rolled out of bed with a grunt.

"No, leave my fucking house!" She threw a pillow in his direction.

Vincent's house, the temptation to correct her arose. He pulled on his pants and fidgeted with his belt. Unfortunately, his erection hadn't died down, and even in the low light, its presence was quite obvious, impeding his ability to zip his fly. And dammit, he needed to get out of there.

"He's supposed to be your friend, but I'm the only one crying." Fuck, here came a lecture.

"I've been standing vigil by your side. I've barely had time to step away and brush my teeth, let alone shed a few tears for my friend."

She snorted. "Hard to shed tears when you're thinking about your dick."

His zipper and throbbing dick finally reached a truce. He zipped up and looped his belt through the buckle. "Get over yourself, kid." He stormed out of the room. When the door shut behind him, her crying became a wail. It stopped him. *Go back in and say sorry and forgive her. When people feel shitty, they say and do shitty things.*

But the grief he'd snuffed out earlier returned in a consuming flame. Stepping back from the door, he headed home.

Tobias held onto his anger until he reached his apartment. Slamming the door shut helped release some of the rage, but one glance at his empty fire escape and the sadness he ignored all week surged. It came out in messy, stifled sobs and in pounding punches to the chest. Moments like this begged to be chased with a drink.

Instead, he opened his fridge, grabbed a vial, stuck a syringe in his leg, and disappeared in the synthetic euphoria. Of long, dark hair and capes riding the wind. Of the belief the war within could ever be won.

The Birth of Vincent Varian:

Part One

*The abyss, **Vincent** discovered, was like floating in a hallway of memories. He didn't have form, but he had understanding. Each turn in the hallway brought him to another place in his life. Time had distorted these memories, but now he experienced them as they happened.*

The birth of Vincent Varian did not begin the day Vicente Vasquez was born.

Vincent Varian first formed when the oldest Señor Vasquez planned an amalgamation of power and land.

TWO YEARS BEFORE THE CURSE

I am but a pawn.

Felipe, my older brother, has received all the Vasquez property and wealth, promising to fulfill his role as older brother, marrying a good wife and producing many children.

How does a man like my father with two more sons ensure the prosperity of his bloodline? The solution is easy for the patriarch—the youngest, Ignacio, will join the priesthood, further catapulting the Vasquez name higher among the hierarchy of the heavens. As for my father's middle child, me, the one as beautiful as an angel and charming as the Fallen One himself, he's arranged my marriage to a wealthy family without options—all daughters and no prospects.

I marry Susanna, the only living daughter of a wealthy merchant. I do not meet her until I lift her veil. She is a plain woman with pale skin, dark brown hair, and prominent mole above her thin, colorless lips. Although she is older than me, her sheltered life grants her the mannerisms of a nervous girl. The priest blesses our marriage. I give her a kiss and only then, a little color rises to her cheeks.

The consummation of our marriage is awkward and uncomfortable, but we give the interested parties, namely our parents, the satisfaction of properly stained sheets.

The marriage feels more like being a tenant in an elaborate home, not me becoming some new head of a grand estate. We share silent dinners together and not much else. At night, we lie side by side as if there were an invisible barrier between us. Staring at the canopy above our bed, I calculate we have a few months of freedom before the arrangers of our union will demand children, so the invisible barrier remains.

The nights I should be tender to my new wife, I lock myself in my study to read Seneca's plays or Aristotle's philosophy. Languages and ideas spur my passions, not what everyone expects me to love—my new money. Consumed in my books, I no longer have a need for our invisible barrier. My study shuts her out.

Susanna breaks the quiet at dinner and asks to join me in the study. She'd embroider, and I'd read, she suggests. I accept the offer.

Except in my study, she surprises me more. She asks me to read to her so that she understands what brings her husband such joy. I oblige. Not only do I read to her, but she joins me in lively discussions about what Socrates meant when challenging the portrayal of the gods or the hidden critique of Caesar in the writings of Ovid.

Her passion for knowledge brings more color to her cheeks, and in the wonder of my study, I kiss her again. Has it only been the second time? Surely, there has to have been more kisses shared between us before then, but this time is all the more remarkable. I feel less like a pawn and more like a man. I have a choice now, and I choose Susanna to be my wife.

The invisible barrier in our bed disappears, and consummation becomes something akin to sport, excited heartbeats and smiles. After more nights and days experiencing our new favorite activity, to the delight of our arrangers, Susanna becomes pregnant.

"Vicente, I'm finally a good wife," she says.

For the first time, it dawns on me how much society fails the fairer sex, whose worth has been reduced to the men they marry and the children they bear. "You are always a good wife."

The pregnancy takes a toll on Susanna's health. There are no more lively discussions in my study. The doctor prescribes bed rest until the arrival of our child. I rarely see her. Dinner becomes silent again.

But her labor brings the noise back to the house tenfold, filling our home with excitement. My anticipation metastasizes to worry when Susanna's screams fade into quiet moans. The doctor leaves the bedroom with a solemn expression, and a priest arrives to perform the Last Rites. The baby is stillborn, and he can't stop Susanna's bleeding.

I run to her side at the bed we once shared. I kneel beside her, stroking the sweat from her forehead. She apologizes to me—sorry she couldn't bear me a healthy child.

She dies apologizing.

Grief tears a hole into me, and I feel nothing. I feel nothing for the cursed bundle in my servant's arms. I feel nothing toward our families whose demands paved the way of her destruction. I feel nothing when the chatter already speculates who I will marry next.

The sorrow surges like high tide. I already mourn Susanna's smile from discussing philosophy in my study. Holding her warm, lifeless body, drained of its blood, I already miss the way color rose to her cheeks when I kissed her.

The priest who married us oversees the burial of my family I barely know. My servants task themselves with the unseemly disposal of the bloody mattress and sheets, but I tell them to take the day off, plying their pockets with more of my wife's gold.

Alone, I carry the gruesome bedding up a knoll to form a pyre overlooking my wife's estate—my property, but it has never seemed to belong to me. The task of lugging the mattress up the hill takes me hours, as if I am Sisyphus himself. After the day becomes night, I light the pile on fire.

The stars shine so clear this night, even looking at them through the blur of tears and the plume of rising smoke. The brightest star in the black and blue sky speaks to me in an accent I cannot place. Have I become a madman? What do I care! *"Ven a mi, Vicente*[1]. *Encuéntrame, mi amor*[2]," it says. *"Corre, se lo pido.*[3]"

"Yes, I will," I shout, my voice echoing along the hills.

Until the fire fades to crackling embers, I wonder how I'll travel to the stars. Anything, I promise myself, to escape the smell of the blood and smoke.

God has taken my family and sacrificed them. I am no longer a middle son, a husband, or a father. It is here between the stars and the ashes, I am born again.

1. Come to me, Vicente.
2. Find me, my love.
3. Run, I beg you.

One Year Before the Curse

Most of the servants leave when I pay them handsomely. The tavern loves my indirect blessing. The fools who return, the ones who feel sorry for the pathetic rich man, share with me how the townspeople gossiped, claiming the beautiful man in the empty estate threw mountains of his money at people.

The rumors must've reached an explorer who shows up on my doorsteps. The explorer, Alvaro, promises a quest to the New World, a place of unfathomable riches. The investment in the journey will exponentially grow my money beyond the imagination. Such a vow plays empty in my ears. He speaks of being ordered by the Crown to find an ancient artifact so powerful it brings God's gifts to earth, a fountain of some sort. The magic sounds blasphemous, and I prepare to show him the door.

Then Alvaro paints pictures of unseen wilderness, limitless adventures, and stars. He promises to follow the stars.

My heart feels the powerful ache of speaking to the Stella Maris. "Can you bring me to them? The stars?"

"You want to join us, señor?"

I despise the money I gained from Susanna. I'll shed it like a serpent slithers out of dead skin. The artifact? Maybe instead of giving godlike powers to humans, it proves the existence of God, saving souls. Perhaps I will make my father proud. "Whatever you want, I'll pay for it. As long as you bring me to the stars."

For a healthy sum of money, the explorers allow me to join them.

And a rich man becomes a richer man.

Months Before the Curse

I spend most my time in the cabin, going over the observational notes of those who have returned from the New World. Rarely do I take meals with the rest of the crew, dining instead surrounded by the documents. Conversations with Alvaro and the others end in them snickering as they walk away. They call me *Rubio* in obvious mockery of my golden hair. I am afraid they view me as the rich idiot whose only usefulness is bankrolling their venture.

For this reason too, I keep to myself, my wealth affording me a sea captain's quarters. The isolation protects me, but it compounds the loneliness. Surrounded by water for weeks, I miss seeing civilization, the activity of human life. In this state, I find my company is the stars.

The stars must be angels, looking down on us from rose and gold lofts. Night colors have never been painted so vividly back home. Oceans provide a glorious, encompassing view, the way I imagine God sees us. I wait until the others fall asleep, and have trained myself to awaken the same time each night. I go on the deck and lie on my back. Here, I disappear. Disappear in the sound of waves lapping against the ship, in the brilliance above me. Quietly, I whisper to them—the stars—as to not wake the others on the ship, but I am so enraptured, I am afraid to upset the grandeur. The greatest of the stars is the brightest of all, the Stella Maris. *"Ven a mi, Vicente. Encuéntrame, mi amor,"* she calls again.

I promise to meet her.

WEEKS BEFORE THE CURSE

The crew lowers the rowboats. Alvaro insists I ride with their landing party, those who treat me as the beautiful idiot. I hesitate. The water is choppy and dark, and the sun is lowering on the horizon. I am no sailor, but the conditions threaten a safe landing.

Alvaro points ahead. The rowboat of supplies and horses has already kissed the shore. "Don't worry, Rubio. You will understand the sea sometime."

As the sky deepens in its hues, my fear abates. I jump inside in the boat with Alvaro, Raul, and Nando. They bring with them three others who row us, but I have not asked their names.

I should've listened to my instincts. The wind picks up, bringing with it darkening clouds. Waves toss our boat. The rowers strain, unable to fight the raging caps. We are thrown into the dark embrace of the ocean.

Under the weight of the water, my sinuses burn from the salt. The pressure pounds in my ears, obscuring all sound. Kicking to the surface, the water cools around me. How can this be if I'm nearing the surface? I tumble further, feeling the squeeze of the depths. My lungs tighten, begging for air. Bubbles trail above me. I am swimming toward the ocean floor!

I kick with more fervor. The pressure around me weakens, and I surface, gasping for air. Despite the taste of life once more, rain beats down on me, and lightning breaks the darkness. I glimpse at the shadow of our rowboat overturned until another wave churns over me.

When did the storm appear? How did the sun go down so quickly? My strength fades, and I resign myself to a watery grave.

The ocean seethes with anger and swallows me.

I welcome it.

The sea spits me out, and I crawl in the blue-black dark across the sand. Pained groans of the other landing party members sound over the ocean's fevered lapping. I catch my breath and flip on my back to find the comfort of the Heavens again. Nothing but the silver light of the moon. No clouds. Where has the storm gone? *Tell me I'll be okay, my Stella Maris.*

Standing, I search for her, but find nothing. My legs shake so severely, I stagger to my knees. My waning physical strength is not the only thing to hobble me. As I kneel on the wet sand, I discover the moon shines alone. No stars mar the inky firmament. The stars, I fear, are missing.

I point to the sky. "What devil's work is this?"

Raul takes out a compass from his pocket. In the ghostly, meager light, the needle floats, never landing on true north.

We are in a place without location, robbed of Heaven's guidance.

We have washed upon the shores of Hell.

The sun rises, but the moment we feel relief, we sense a discomfiting shift in our shadows. When we look up again, it rises in the west, and again, the north, and once again the south.

At first, the island feels tropical, but as we explore the lush greenery off the beach, we find trees and plants we've found in the Pyrenees. We are in a place that makes no sense to any form of our logic.

Afraid, we resolve to stay on the beach. Yet, people emerge from the forest. Every person is different from the other—some appear like sketches of Ottomans I've seen. Others fit the descriptions I've read from the writings of Marco Polo. Still others appear like faces I've only heard about from the travels of Magellan. Some speak, and I do not understand them. However, the Greek spoken by the Ottoman provides some comfort in our similarity. In his excitement of our understanding, however, he runs away into the forest, returning with a tall, gaunt man with shaggy dark hair and olive skin, wearing the ragged robes of a priest.

"I am Padre Juan Carlos," he says. "I arrived here five years ago when a hurricane separated me from my ship. We are all gifts from the sea here."

"This is not Hell?" I ask.

"No, *mi rebaño*[4]. You have come to Paradise."

The inhabitants welcome us into their village, downhill from a small temple looking like something belonging in the Hanging Gardens of Babylon. Padre Juan Carlos explains the Elders live there, but only Adhara has seen them. "I have been here longer than most, but Adhara has been here longest of all. The Elders found her just as we found you."

Her? The ragtag island inhabitants are mostly men. Does she live in the temple with these strange elders?

The Padre explains they have everything they need here, as if God himself is watching over them. Alvaro asks where the pretty ladies to fuck are. Nando asks if God has sent any of them a ship to return home.

The Padre ignores Alvaro, but smiles when answering Nando. "Indeed we are a navigational anomaly, but every month or so, the celestial bodies return to their assigned places. Some choose to brave the ocean then. Sometimes we never see them again. Other times, we bury their bodies after they wash up on shore."

"I thought this place was Paradise."

4. My flock

The Padre winces much like my youngest brother when he is asked a question challenging his idea of God.

Without satisfying answers, Alvaro leads us to the forest to gather enough logs to make a rowboat. Our first mission is to find a way to escape this Paradise.

As we wait to make a raft, I live with the Padre in his simple home. He offers me a spare bed he made. At night, he asks me about myself. I share what I am willing—my youngest brother is a priest, and I've helped fund the expedition to find the Fountain of Youth.

The next night, he barges into the hut out of breath. "Rubio!" I do not correct his use of my derided nickname. "I know someone who might be of interest to you," he announces with a wild glow in his eyes. "I taught her as much as I could of our language. She has taught me so much about this place. You must meet her."

"Let's go to her—"

"Come in!" the Padre shouts.

The Padre has kept her waiting outside? A lean, statuesque woman enters the tent, making no sound as she moves inside. She wears a barkcloth blouse and skirt, but her hem is too short, ending below her knees as if the clothes belonged to someone a foot shorter. Her honey-colored, undefined curls surround her head like a cloud. Her light hair stands in sharp contrast to her deep brown skin. After she steps inside, she acknowledges the Padre with a nod but casts her gaze downward from me.

The Padre gestures for her to step closer. "Tell him what you told me."

"The ancient language used on this island resembles my own. Etchings on landmarks around here speak of the waters you describe."

"I am not in charge of this expedition. Speak to Alvaro—"

"I don't trust him," the Padre interjects.

I attempt to reply, but am paralyzed by my realization that when greedy, power-hungry men have come to me, needing ships and supplies, I've provided them. From their snickers and my mounting loneliness while we've traversed the ocean, I've already understood this truth. The expedition is about gaining more power. I have lied to myself, forcing myself to believe that the Fountain is for saving people and proving the existence of God. I don't trust Alvaro, Nando, and Raul either, but the Padre is reckless in trusting a coward like me.

"I am here," the woman says, patting her chest. "You are speaking as if I am not here, and I don't like it."

"We are sorry, señorita," the Padre says.

Everything in me quiets. Rarely have I interacted with people who said what they mean. This woman's forthright nature utterly disarms me. I whisper, "I'm sorry."

She bolts straight to the Padre's rickety desk and pushes the drawings aside. She grabs clean paper, dips her long fingers in ink, and draws on the paper with her hands. Once she is finished, she holds the drawing up, the fresh ink dripping in small streaks. "I have a map."

I reach out to take it.

She tucks the paper away. "No!" She points at me with her ink-stained fingers. "I need your word first. I help you find your power, and you take me far away from here. To your world."

I chuckle. This woman blows through niceties like a storm. "Passage to Spain? I'll have to give more money to Alvaro, but I can make it happen."

"No. Say it like a promise. Swear on your god."

I put my hand over my heart. "I, Vicente Vasquez, promise to bring you to my country or my Almighty God will strike me down."

She offers her freshly-inked hand for to me to shake. I sneer at her stained hand but extend mine out.

The woman's grip crushes mine and rubs ink all over it. "My name is Adhara, like the star, and I will help you."

A magical wave sweeps over me. The Padre had brought me to a star.

The Birth of Vincent Varian: Part Two

A Day Before the Curse

Word of our expedition's magical quest takes hold of the village. The Ottoman, who we've affectionately referred to as Pytheas himself, shows the landing party a deep pool in the ground, which glows like turquoise jewels in the sunlight. In his language, he explains the cenote is the healing water we seek.

The landing party ignores building our boat to home. Instead, they bathe and drink from it. With every sip, they insist they feel powerful. Logic eludes them. They express a desire to bottle the water up and take the throne of the king and queen themselves.

But I know they're wrong.

Adhara and I lie and say we are gathering fruit, but we explore the forest, attempting to match landmarks to the squiggles from her memory. In these rocks, we discover hieroglyphics, which appear nothing like I have seen either from the sketches from Egypt I carry with me or the reports from the Americas. I take rubbings of these unique images.

I stop as I notice Adhara is watching me, her head cocked to the side. "Who were you back at your home?"

"A pawn," I reply derisively.

She stares, not understanding my language.

"I am the son of a wealthy man whose marriage to the daughter of another wealthy man was arranged like a trade agreement. We shared a brief time of happiness, but she died along with our child. So back home, I am nothing, a shadow of this golden man."

She embraces me, nestling her cloudlike hair into my chest. I haven't been held this intimately since Susanna passed. Most have treated my loss as easily replaceable. I'd find a new wife, making my deceased family nothing but commodities. In Adhara's tender arms, I finally understand my grief is love. This close, I feel her heart beat with mine.

"And you? Who are you back home?" I ask, my cheek resting on her head.

"It's been so long. I know I am a daughter. I know somewhere, a parent loves me, but I don't remember much since being here. Except I loved to pretend to be the prow of a ship. To be the first to feel the ocean spray on my skin and to see something new on the horizon. That, I remember." She lifts her head, looking up at me. "I am ready to feel that again, and you are my hope—to bring me back to the ocean."

Her love of the ocean, my love of the stars—we are elemental soulmates coming together. I bow and kiss her. She breaks our embrace and holds her fingers to her lips, eyes wide. Her gaze jerks away from me, presumably in embarrassment over my trespassing where I didn't belong.

We return to the village in relative silence. She warns me of minor hazards in our path with such casualness, it's as if she erases my transgression between us. We are back to business partners.

In the safety of the Padre's home, we compare each other's alphabets. Each of our knowledge complements the other. What she doesn't understand, I can decode from my language experience and vice versa. Our collaboration reminds me of Susanna and my discussions in my study back home, and I find myself rapt by her free-spirited confidence. And transfixed by the lovely sinews of her shoulders. And enchanted by her full lips. Yet, her rejection of our kiss shows she does not return my feelings, which is for the best. Like any star, it is better to appreciate her from afar, so as not to burn from the brightness.

One particular carving perplexes me. She taps the shaded image on my parchment and rubs my stomach along my waistband. My breath hitches, body reacting wickedly to her innocent touch. I shrink away from her in my shame.

Her eyebrows pinch together, but raise with almost a delighted knowing of the effect she has on me. She grabs my hand and places it low on her belly. With her other hand, she points to the hieroglyphic. "Womb. The Fountain is in the cave's womb. A stream starts at the mouth of a cave, opening in two to serve the island's water. Like a woman's thighs."

I gulp, the magnet draw of my lust breaking through my careful reticence and the shame born from my earlier transgression.

She lunges over the space between us and crushes her mouth to mine. At first, our kiss is firm, with her mouth tight. I draw her closer in a swift jerk. Her gasping lips part, and I suck on her lush lower one. She hums and melts in my arms, legs parting as she sits on my lap. I edge my tongue into her mouth and glide it over hers. As I deepen our kiss, she grinds against me, sweet pleasure's promise of our bodies joining.

I shift, pinning her between me and the desk. She lifts her head, separating our mouths. Eyes closed, she rubs her lips together, assessing the taste and feel of her well-kissed mouth. But the furrow of her brow indicates worry and hesitation. Has my greed for her intruded once again?

Her eyes languidly flutter open, and she smiles. She wraps her arms around my neck and resumes our kiss, this time exploring my mouth as I have hers. I lift the hem of her skirt and smooth my hand up her thigh. The warmth of her center entrances me. I graze my touch along her intimate curls. She tilts her hips forward, and I glide my fingers through her seam and am welcomed with her wet neediness. I stroke, working the pearl at her dripping apex. She tenses and sighs, high and stuttering. Her delicate sounds possess me, and I need more. My touch becomes rough and insatiable. She shakes but steadies her trembling body by hugging me close. I bury my face into her neck. Her moans catch in her throat. She's holding back. "Don't be scared," I soothe.

My fingers breach her entrance, and she squirms but can't escape from me. I ply her tremulous desire with more fierce strokes inside and out. "I can make you feel so good."

She shakes her head. "They'll...hear...me."

But I increase my speed, and her body seizes. She only gives me a whimper. I stand, lifting her to take her on my cot.

"Rubio, I hear footsteps." I let her go. She adjusts her skirt and leaves abruptly, flashing a tiny smile at the doorway of the hut. I collapse to sitting on my cot and hold my head in my hands, begging my fervor to leave me. But I smell her, and my mouth waters.

The Padre enters, returning from his evening rounds. He says he is proud to find me praying. "But," he adds as he removes his ragged collar and robe, "if He speaks to you, ask Him for help." At his water basin, he slips out of his shirt and splashes water over his hair, neck, and naked torso. He dries himself with his shirt and lies back on his cot. "I worry the others are losing sight of God."

"After all their bathing, turns out cleanliness is not next to godliness," I add bitterly, crossing myself. I glimpse at the Padre's lean form laying on his cot, the V of his hips and the strength in his pectorals. Lust still courses through my blood, a seed planted not only by

Adhara but when studying statues and art celebrating the human body. And like the art, the perfect muscular ridges lure me to touch them.

I stand up, turning away from the Padre.

I too ready for bed, stripping off my shirt and washing my face and hands. The Padre's judgmental gaze roves over me. He knows I am a heathen. He knows I let my baser instincts command me. He knows my glances linger too long on his nakedness. The holy man's notice frightens me, for it warns of punishment following me. I deserve it, the loss, the loneliness, and the terror. I am the nothing, the shadow.

I blow out the candles to hide.

Yet, I can't stop sinning. Under night's pall, I lie back in my cot and fist my cock, mumbling to myself how I am a blasphemer. My god is her cunt. My Heaven is her thighs. I am so close.

"Rubio, are you awake?"

I stop. I fake a weariness. "Yes?"

"When you go with Adhara tomorrow, will you take me with you?"

I audibly sigh. Tomorrow brings a promise of more time alone with Adhara. In the forest, she will cry out my name and become mine. But the torrent of my sinful thoughts, of Adhara's legs around me and the Padre's furrowed abdomen, demands my penance. His godly presence will assure my goodness. "Of course, Padre."

The Day of the Curse

One of the rowers dies of infection.

Alvaro's fury knows no bounds. The inhabitants try to comfort him, but he shakes them off. In his rage, he charges at Adhara. "This bitch has been here the longest. She knows something!"

I try to outrun him to intervene, but he strikes her across the face. She cups her cheek; her mouth gapes in shock. Her expression sinks into a cry, the pain of an innocent experiencing their first cruelty.

He jolts as if to hit her again. But this time I am ready for him. I shove him away.

Alvaro laughs. "The hollow rich man has bite!" He lunges at me with a knife, but I draw mine from my belt, aiming to stab.

"*Mi rebaño!*" the Padre shouts, "We are grieving. Please, no more violence!"

Alvaro's grin widens. Guile glistens in his eyes. His pupils shift from me to Adhara and to the Padre. "I know where your heart lies, you so-called holy man, and it is not with God. You don't have a church here. I am not your flock."

I return my knife to my belt and take Adhara by the hand. We flee to the Padre's hut, and he follows close behind. Alvaro and the rest of his men, Nando and Raul, watch us with dead eyes.

I give Adhara water to wash the blood from her mouth and hold her face in my hand as she winces. My need to protect her sublimates the secret of our growing intimacy in front of the Padre.

"We cannot go to the cave today. They will follow us. I'm sure of it," the Padre says. He eyes outside the hut, monitoring the landing party.

Adhara's eyes narrow as if I betrayed my promise to her by including the Padre. "We'll go at night," Adhara interjects. "Who knows what would happen if we wait?"

We leave the village under the cover of night. At a safe enough distance, we light torches to illuminate our path. We journey until exhaustion looms in my limbs. Our notes guide us to the cave, where the two streams meet.

We enter it. The cave hosts another cenote, and its bioluminescence glows in an eerie blue. The deep pool meets a solid cave wall. Our translations have betrayed us. There is nothing here but mineral water.

Adhara dives in and disappears behind the cave wall.

The Padre and I await in silence. Water drops into the pool in a strange rhythm, counting the passage of time. Our concern and concentration drop into panic. The Padre patrols the edge of the water. I stare into the blue light. I hear my own voice within it. It tells me a path of death brings me here. The Padre jumps in.

Paranoia winds me tight. The voice overwhelms me. *Death,* it warns me. The death of Susanna and the baby. The death of the rower. And more. Hundreds, thousands, millions stretching over centuries. I stand solitary among it all, a never-ending death. "Don't leave me!" I scream.

Splashing water breaks me away from my fear. Adhara has emerged, along with the Padre. "Rubio, there's a tunnel. Follow me."

I dive in and swim, farther and longer than I ever have. The urge to breathe burns behind my ribs. Yet I continue until I reach a rock wall. I flail in every direction, slowed by the embrace of water. A hand grabs the collar of my tunic and lifts me.

I rise from the water coughing. My throat feels raw.

Adhara sits at the rock ledge above me. "We are here, Rubio."

And we are. Lit by an unknown light source, the cave at the end of the tunnel is smooth, pink and white rock with an iridescent shine. A glittering stalactite drops bright, aquamarine blue water into a shallow pool, offset by a similar brilliant wall of pink and white from the tunnel we have emerged from.

Adhara cups her hands in the water and raises them to her lips. The veins in her body glow red as a power radiates throughout her being. Her once gray eyes glow blue like the water. "I see the stars!"

Warmth nestles in where over a year of aching has lived. My destiny, my star has found me, and I am finally free from the fathoms of my loneliness, for she is guiding and protecting me. I bend to the ledge and kiss the surface of the water, which tastes sweet like the finest wine and cools the soreness in my throat. The ceiling of the cave opens up, and I fly among the stars.

Their shine soothes like a summer breeze, but the sensation doesn't stop there. Tingling builds at the base of my spine, mimicking the rare moments in Mass where the ritual awakens the Divine. And yet, the euphoria continues to ascend. My vision blurs into tears. I worry I have grown mad. My body becomes rigid, and I orgasm.

I blink, shame and disbelief bring me back to the Earth, to the rocks, to the cave.

Adhara's lips meet my ear. "You felt it too, didn't you, Rubio?" Her hand caresses the inside of my thigh.

I force her hand to the outline of my cock, straining against my wet breeches. She strokes the outline from the base to my sensitive head. "Yes," I say.

She unbuttons them and reaches inside, running her fingers through my mess. Another stroke, and she raises her hand to her mouth. My sperm glistens on her fingertips. She sucks them, cleaning them with her tongue and lips. Watching her mouth suckle and drag elicits the same spark within as the first sip of enchanted water. I am so hard, it hurts.

As if she knows what I need, her rough and trembling hands work me, drawing me tight. The grooves of her fingertips slide along each sensitive ridge. She laughs, removing her white blouse and soaking it in the blessed water. Sorceress she must be, with hands wringing the water from her shirt as she pumps my cock.

Liberated and wild, she laughs again. Her gray eyes are glorious storm clouds forked with lightning. I am almost swept up in the tempest of them, but she cannot be touching me. The hand is the Padre's. His veins, too, glow red. Amber lightning shatters the brown in his eyes. "Lead me to sin," he breathes into my neck.

I nod. My forehead presses against his. Adhara wrings more water over herself. It drips down her lush lips and small breasts. *I must* are the only words echoing through my thoughts. To drink from her tightly furled brown nipples, I must, I must, I must. The Padre joins me, sucking at her left nipple as I lick the water from her right. One swallow imbues us with the Fountain's power. Another sip snuffs out the light in our eyes, reminding us of our humanity. The intoxication, however, lingers, as if there were also something powerful to be mined from my tongue exploring my lovers' bodies.

Their essences mix with mine every time I drink. Each level of joy surpasses the next. In the endless universe above us, our bodies no longer belong to ourselves. We become stardust, and in this state, I cannot tell her mouth from his or hands or body. His orgasm or hers, I cannot separate them. Our desires are untethered and boundless.

I awake still naked. Adhara sleeps in my arms. The stars are gone. The cave is a cave. The Padre is missing.

THE DAY AFTER THE CURSE

Late morning arrives. Adhara gathers her clothes and bathes in the water separate from the sacred pool. She washes a mark away from the inside of her thigh. The water dripping between her fingers is tinged in red. Blood. My mind races to Susanna dying in our marital bed and then to our first night together. To the stains on our bedclothes that passed our parents' inspection.

Possessed by the Fountain's induced passions, neither I nor the Padre has been gentle with her. A good man would've been slow and tender. I can't believe I didn't recognize her fear the other night, the same hesitation I've seen in Susanna. Neither of us was deserving.

I must've stared too long. She hugs her arms about herself and turns away to put on her clothes. I quickly put on my clothes as well to hide my shame.

Adhara and I do not return to the village. Instead, we walk along the beach, hand in hand. My thumb caressing her knuckles offers the gentleness I should've given her. We stand where the surf kisses our toes. Here, our plan is to enjoy life's beauty before returning the power.

The strange sunlight reflects off her eyes. I tell her I want to be lost in the storm of them. She says my eyes have lightning too, and standing on tiptoes, she kisses each of my eyelids.

For a moment I almost believe the Padre's lie—this place is Paradise. Adhara and I smile at each other in knowing ways, like lovers, or better even, a husband

and a wife. I kiss the velvet softness of her umber-brown shoulder. I'll ask her to marry me. I'll make something good out of the Fountain-induced lust we've shared. The Padre will bless our union, offering a new meaning to the consummation of man and woman with God. I'll take her to Spain as my wife, and my memories of blood and smoke will be a distant nightmare I awoke from.

But when she asks me, "What?" and her gaze meets mine, I only tell her she is my star.

"The Fountain influences your words," she says.

"When we go back and drink again, I'll say it then too."

Silent music plays, and in the enchantment, we dance along the beach. When I am dancing, I am as free as she is. I want to feel the connection dancing brings until the end of my life.

The sky melds rosy oranges with its purple. We return to the cave, but a foreboding hangs in the air. To our horror, the pool at the entrance has a body floating in it, another one of the rowers. Drowned, by the looks of it.

Adhara's face drops. "I hear someone." We run into the thick cover of vegetation.

The Padre leads the others—Alvaro, Raul, Nando and the final surviving crew member—out of the cave. Blood stains his tunic. Have they tortured him? I move to save him or to shout. Adhara raises her finger to her lips and shakes her head. I hold my breath. They pass by. The hair on my arms dances. The bitter knowledge strikes me.

We can sense each other.

They halt, not far from where Adhara and I hide. The magic vibrations of their presence hum over me. Loud and oppressive, a violent nausea overtakes me. I spring out of the brush.

My first thought is to check the Padre. His eyes are sunken with weariness and shame. They do not possess the amber fractals of magic light. He has relinquished the Fountain's powers.

"We were wondering where you were, rich man," Alvaro says.

His sly grin tenses my back muscles, but I force myself to smile. "Señores, we all know we found what we were looking for. I come to you prepared to discuss our return trip home."

"We will return home, Rubio. Where I'll reduce your beautiful estate to rubble, but not before I fuck that whore of yours in your bed and piss on your dead wife's grave."

The nothing within me awakens, a gaping and hungry maw craving vengeance. And as vast and limitless as space and time itself. I emerge from the abyss, holding Alvaro by his trachea, moments from tearing it from his throat. All of us stare at the vicious strength radiating from my muscles.

Alvaro's eyes flash like molten rock, and he snaps my forearm in two. The pain is sickening. I stagger back, and our lightning gazes meet. Another realization strikes me.

We can rip each other apart.

I snap the neck of their minion. Poor man, sealing his fate with the one more drink which had reversed his power. The Padre runs away to the safety of the cave to save himself suffering the same fate, leaving three against one. Never good odds.

Blood spurts and splashes. Bones break and crunch. I hear *Rubio* screamed from the treetops.

The sound fades as I'm lifted and staked to a tree by a branch. My sight wavers into nothing. The nothing absorbs me.

Perhaps we can die after all.

I gasp for air, deep and desperate, rendering me anew. Once again, Adhara is next to me at life's edge. She and the Padre have pulled me from the branch.

"Rubio, you died." The tempest in her irises charges and churns.

My breath and heart stabilize, but my fury returns. "Where are they?"

"They headed to the village," the Padre answers, his brown irises fractured by glowing amber streaks. He must've left to drink his powers back.

Stoking my anger's fire, I have questions for the holy man. Why did he leave us this morning? Why did he give away our Fountain? But the fate of the villagers balances on a knife's edge. We run through the forest, our super-strength propelling us through our surroundings in a blur.

We arrive, and the place is eerily quiet. The smoke of snuffed flames curl to the heavens.

Adhara searches the homes, running in and out of them. I stop by the well to drink water, succumbing to exhaustion for the first time since my transformation. Pull after pull, I raise the bucket to the stone ledge. The water in my hands is strangely warm. I bring my hand to my lips. A metallic scent rises from it, so much so, I check my cupping palm. Something stained it an angry red.

Blood, the water is nothing but blood. I haven't outrun the blood and smoke.

I jump, tripping to ground. The bucket tumbles back, down landing in a thud, not a splash. Horror paralyzes my words. I point a trembling finger in the well's direction.

The Padre peers over the ledge. His gaze downcast, he says flatly, "The rest of the villagers are here."

Adhara flies into a rage. She slaps and beats the Padre. "It's all your fault, you weakling! You betrayed us! Didn't your god give you enough strength?!" She stops to wipe the spittle flying from her lips. Her wrath turns on me, and she kicks at me. "And you! Trying to defy death, but your family is never coming back!"

I beg her to stop, to take the painful accusation back, to forgive me.

The Padre shouts, bringing an end to the onslaught. "Where are the Others?"

The temple door opens. In a crack of lightning, six people appear. Each one is old and young; each is stoic and grieving. The sound of buzzing insect wings infests the air. Their existence drifts among the past, present, and future. Fear seizes my body, and I cannot move. Yet, I tremble on the ground before them.

"We are the Continental Elders, and we have banished the blight. We ail as the human world spins further toward greed and destruction. Your penance, proud miscreants, will be to restore the balance of Justice. You will be frozen in your corporeal vessel until our demands have been met."

"What do you mean?" the Padre calls out. "Please help us!"

But with another crack of lightning, we are on another shore, away from the mysterious island. A caravel sails not far in the distance. The sun is warm against our backs as it lowers in the west.

"What do we do?" I ask.

"Set that fucking ship on fire," Adhara says.

And So The Story Continues...

Nine Weeks Later

Breaking News

President of Shadowhaven State Bank, Skipper Ecklund, allegedly shot and killed his family before shooting himself. The bodies were found by a housekeeper in the morning. Before the shootings, Ecklund had been undergoing an investigation regarding the embezzlement of over a million dollars from the bank.

In other news, the hearing for Grant Durant, the promising Congressional candidate turned alleged human trafficker, is underway after his defense team insisted on a speedy trial. Federal Judge Brown served a blow to the prosecution when he sided with Durant's defense today, stating that key evidence was not legally obtained by the Shadowhaven Police Department.

United States Attorney Penelope Stanwycki argued that when Durant turned himself in earlier in the year, he had voluntarily handed over the concerning evidence, which should make it admissible in the case. Since his arrest, Durant has claimed that the Shadowhaven police used unscrupulous tactics to bully a false confession out of him, including using masked vigilantes and mind-altering substances. Commissioner Peltier denied the accusations, calling them the "desperate fabrications of a guilty conscience."

In additional news, parts of Vincent Varian's private airplane washed up along the shores of La Isla Reina. The billionaire disappeared nine weeks ago after a plane crash during a brief trip to the island. Varian has been declared missing, but the wreckage may confirm what many in Shadowhaven fear—that the city's beloved billionaire is dead.

godspatriot: Vincent Varian was going to turn over evidence about the rich and powerful using the basements of all the city's gluten-free bakeries to harvest the organs of teenagers. That's why they snuffed him.

cloudseeder28: The accusations against Grant Durant are a cheap mudslinging tactic. It's a way to cut a godly man's political career down before he has a chance to defend himself.

fakedmoonlander: Our society has angered the elder gods. More powerful people will die until humankind chooses a righteous path.

17

Denial

Marisol pounded on her apartment door. A pungent, smoky smell drifted from the crack under the door. Neighbors must love her new sublessee. The longer she knocked, the more she toyed with the keys in her pocket.

Adhara flung the door open and immediately spun around, her strange show of a welcome. Since she'd last visited the apartment, more electrical cords and computer terminals filled the place, butting up against an expanded cage for A.J. "You've been busy," Marisol said.

"You'd be surprised the computational power it takes to find an atom moving through all space and time."

"You're talking about him?" Hope formed a knot over Marisol's heart.

"Yes, I'm talking about him."

Him. The scar on her healed hand throbbed, returning with it the final image of Vincent disappearing like sand in the wind. "Thank you."

Wallowing in Tobias's statement—Vincent didn't want to come back—ate at her. He hadn't left a note. If Vincent truly wanted to go, he would've left a note. He wouldn't simply leave her like this. He loved her, didn't he? Another worry to float down the stream. Another sadness to let sift through her fingers. Like sand.

And Adhara was the only one who cared and understood. Marisol sat on her sofa, scooting a few cords out of the way with her hips. "You're probably wondering why I'm here."

"It's your place."

"About that. You see, the penthouse and especially the estate feel haunted without" —the thumping sound of her punching glass echoed in her ears— "and I could stay here, at least until he comes back. You wouldn't have to leave or anything. I'll stay in the spare bedroom."

A not-quite smile reached Adhara's face. "There's no bed in there."

"I'll order a mattress, and until then, I'll crash here on the sofa." She searched the room for space to move the cage and cords.

"I'll move the mouse." Adhara lifted the cage and carried it into her room.

Marisol had planned to rot on the sofa until Adhara yanked the fuzzy throw off her. "You need cheering up. Come with me."

She followed Adhara outside. It was the start of rush hour, and Shadowhaven was alive with activity. People left work and briskly walked, breezing by anything or anyone who impeded their route. Buses and cars chugged away in the streets.

Adhara gripped Marisol by her good wrist and led her to a bench in the middle of the Financial District. There, stuffy-looking people in variations of business casual emerged from their offices.

"What are we doing here?" Marisol asked.

Adhara pointed to the clock. "Give it a minute."

Unsettled by the cryptic answer, Marisol fidgeted in her seat. She and Annie used to go people-watching in their brief breaks from work. Annie would dare her to ask out the man with the quirky patches on his messenger bag or the damn fine jogger with good form, but Marisol would point out messenger bag man had bad taste in shoes or jogger had too flat of an ass for her.

"You're doomed," Annie would say between bouts of hysterical laughter.

"Good thing I got you."

How wrong she'd been. With Vincent gone, what did her newfound loneliness make her? Mega-doomed?

Her next question was going to be what they were people-watching for, especially at 5:14 p.m. The minute hand moved. With the click of the clock, ATMs shot out money like confetti. No, now the next question was going to be, what in the actual fuck?

"Let's go for a walk," Adhara said.

They sifted their way through the chaotic crowds of the city. Some people ran, carrying armloads of cash *toward* the Financial District, which meant other ATMs must be vomiting cash. Increasing crowds grabbed the scads of twenty-dollar bills flying through the air. Adhara kept their walking pace steady, even as more people sprinted by them to find additional free money.

Even at corner stores, people swarmed the ATMs, leaving with generous fistfuls. Adhara seemed to ignore the mounting chaos. Instead, a small smirk crept across her face.

"Did you do this?" Marisol asked.

"What if I did?"

Messing with money and hacking computer systems caught the attention of powerful law enforcement agencies. The worry was enough to knock the amusement out of her. "Isn't it...illegal?"

"And vigilantism isn't?"

Adhara had a point. Marisol had made exceptions when she and Vincent had put on masks and gone for a hunt. Somehow work toward the greater good justified the unseemly aspects of becoming a vigilante for Justice. The fear of law enforcement cracking down on the ATM bandits knotted tension into her shoulders. Whatever Adhara had done, it was bringing the city together, to dance in the whirlwind of money.

Another ATM spat bills onto the street. Marisol stooped to pick up the pile. The giant wad equaled her monthly wages, but compared to Vincent's account balances she had grown used to, the amount was nothing. Only paper.

Marisol threw the money, scattering it in an arc. People surrounded her, and for the first time since Vincent had gone away, she laughed. She laughed until her grief lifted and until she flung another bunch into the air. "How'd you do it?"

Adhara raised a finger to her lips, the tip of her claw grazing under her nose. "You'll never know my secrets."

Marisol was half-asleep on the sofa when a soft buzzing from her doorway awakened her. Adhara answered it, and Wheels glided inside. As soon as she shut the door, Adhara pinned Wheels to the wall.

A wicked interest kept Marisol looking on with one eye open. It was as if she were watching an accident and unable to glance away.

Adhara's sharp, gold-tipped fingers traced along Wheels' neck. "Did you miss me?"

"I did." Wheels answered with confidence, chin up and eye contact unbroken. Adhara ran a claw along the woman's jawline and angled her head down for a kiss, a long, deep kiss that elicited a moan out of the woman.

Marisol jerked her gaze low, feeling a bout of the *oh-fuck-sorrys*. She was making the whole thing awkward, witnessing a private moment. Drawing Abuelita's crocheted blanket above her head, she covered the glow of her phone. She begged the apps she scrolled through to help her disappear into a good book? A movie? Anything!

"Feel how bad I missed you?" Wheels panted.

Marisol slowed her app clicking to focus on their sounds. Witnessing sex mere feet from her would've been something she and Annie would laugh about. *Wanna hear about that time I crashed on a couch and watched a 500-year-old woman fuck a stripper?*

There was no Annie to tell it to, though. No one to label her or to tell her she was guilty of biphobia when a woman turned her on, but she retreated into the arms of a man. Did she go to men like Vincent and Tobias because straight was the expectation? Her desires were only valid if met by a strong jaw, a callused hairy knuckle, broad shoulders, and narrow hips?

A loud, erotic coo claimed Marisol's attention. She peeked out of a hole in the blanket, one Abuelita had knit in the shape of a flower. Wheels' shirt had been lifted, her askew bra revealed one of her breasts, where Adhara teethed and sucked. The roller skater's shorts had been lowered, binding around her thighs, and Adhara's hand moved slowly over the woman's pussy. The circular motion was long and languid, almost as if it were teasing her clit. Marisol rubbed her thighs together to chase away a familiar ache.

Who was she disappointing now? Mom and the ancestors, who wanted white dresses and grandchildren? Or her sister Nicole, who spoke about the pains of heteronormativity, monogamy and wished the world came out as its queer self? Who was Marisol supposed to be? She knew who she was with Vincent.

Was the late onset of sapphic horniness another manifestation of grief, or a failure to free herself from expectations?

"At least wait until I've taken my skates off."

"I like you like this." Adhara pushed Wheels against the back of the sofa. Wheels' neon-yellow, pointy fingernails gripped into the cushion. "Makes it easier to take you where I want you to go."

From this position, Marisol practically had front row seats to the feast of Wheels. After a bit of rustling and a few gasps, she took a quick glimpse of the scene. Wheels was naked now, her tiny ass propped inches away from Marisol. Adhara trailed kisses down her nipple to the soft underside of her breast. Marisol's heart thundered in her ears as she swore Adhara's predator gaze found her—looking right at her through the sweet little flower of the blanket. Marisol froze as Adhara continued to kiss down the furrows of Wheels' abs to her hot center. Closing her eyes didn't alleviate the guilt. Delicious, wet noises with breathy moans signified Adhara's expertise.

Marisol imagined the next day, telling the story to Tobias. He might take out the notepad he had tucked into his trench coat.

You're not taking notes!

You watched two women fuck.

I-I tried not to.

If I can't take notes, why are you tellin' me?

And a moment would pass where their friendship ended, and the flirtation of two almost-lovers began.

The guilt compounded, drowning out the rest of her sensations. No, Tobias was trying to be a good man now. He might even take some holier-than-thou position like, *Were they cool with you watching? You should've let them know.* As if he hadn't fucked his way through half of Shadowhaven, combining drunk dumbassery with a hound dog's indiscriminate taste.

And then she thought of why she felt guilty—him. Vincent would icily stare at her. Watch her recount the story with a pleasant turn of his mouth, but always a stare. Stare until she didn't laugh anymore. Prowl toward her until her back was against a wall. Brace his arm to pin her in. Reach into her pants dip into her underwear. *"Hm. Funny, you said? This doesn't feel like laughing."*

The Vincent of her mind would remind her how she was his and his alone. Her Vincent would ask, *What did you see?* as he'd moan in her ear.

Except grief invaded her fantasy. She could not describe the scene with this Vincent. Instead, she would cry and say, *I miss you. I miss feeling right.*

She stifled a sob.

Wheels' orgasm grew into a scream. "Fuck! Someone's here!"

"It's Marisol," Adhara said matter-of-factly, "pretending to be asleep."

"Why didn't you tell me she's here?" Wheels said with obvious clenched teeth. She rolled away and disappeared into Marisol's main bedroom.

Safe to open her eyes, Marisol peered through the blanket again. Adhara shadowed the glowing bedroom doorway. Marisol's body thrummed, sensing Adhara watching her.

Adhara laughed and wiped her mouth with the back of her hand. She closed the bedroom door, but left it slightly ajar.

And Marisol held a suspicion Adhara wanted her to watch.

18

Life Goes On

Tobias's sergeant assigned him Shadowhaven's second murder-suicide in a month. *Shit happens* was practically the city's motto, but a bank president taking a rifle and essentially ending his bloodline was a special kind of shit that happened.

Once forensics confirmed the fingerprints, ballistics matched bullets, and Tobias highlighted the spreadsheet confirming that Skipper Ecklund had bought the rifle. It was an open-and-shut case. If Sergeant Thompson removed his square head out his ass, he'd assign the case to one of the detectives who couldn't find the bottom of a paper bag. Tobias could use some of the saved time to scratch one of Shadowhaven's whodunnits off the list and earn the department a pizza party from a delighted mayor.

"You've looked more like shit lately." Sergeant Thompson plopped a thin manila folder on Tobias's desk. "I figured you could use the boost to your self-esteem, Quinlan."

Tobias scanned the file's contents, photos of the crime scene which changed the way he thought of salsa. He snapped the folder shut. To unload half the shit he saw on the job, he'd have to traumatize a therapist. Unfortunately, time was finite and insurance was shit. Therapy would have to wait for it to become convenient. "You got it, sarge."

Across the aisle in the other dead gray cubicle, Detective Burke shook his head in Tobias's direction. "You know why he gave you the case? Some taxpayers raised a stink at City Hall. They're blaming Ecklund on some serial killer. You're the only one crazy enough to take the claim seriously."

"I heard sounds in a particular order, but nothing you said made any sense."

"Your boyfriend Varian going missing? The Wellers last month and now Ecklund going berserk? People think some Robin Hood is finally getting to them. Course-correcting or some shit."

If people knew a quarter of the truth about Vincent Varian, they'd realize how far off they were. "He's not my—and course-correcting? Never took you as one of the comrades, Burke." Tobias stretched back into his office chair, flicking the folder of photographs in his hand. "Why is it when the rich commit crimes, it's a boogeyman, when I got forensic proof they bleed like the rest of us? Shit washes ashore even in the best neighborhoods because to err is human."

Burke shook his head. "Five hundred bucks says you'll have the Weller file on your desk in less than a month."

"Five hundred? You're on." He sealed the deal, shaking Burke's greasy mitt.

A surprising buzz threw him off balance in his office chair. It was his phone. He steadied himself and answered it. "Quinlan."

"Hi, this is Wendell Carp of Barton, Engel, Nunes, and Carp. This is regarding the will of Vincent Varian."

The secretary showed **Tobias** the inside of the law office. Someone had beat him there, a person hidden by the tall back of the tufted leather chair. The hider's right hand clutched the chair's arm, the rich lamp catching a pale scar. His body let go of a knot he didn't know he had twisted himself in. He slid into the chair next to Marisol. She acknowledged him with a forced simper. Her eyes seemed tired and her lips dry, but she was as beautiful as ever, as if memory never served her justice. She busied herself nibbling on a cuticle.

"Your voice mailbox is full," Tobias said.

"Sorry about that." She grabbed her phone and swiped at the screen, presumably deleting the messages clogging her inbox.

It wasn't that she hadn't picked up the phone. Tobias had put himself through torment trying to find her. "The penthouse and estate seem pretty abandoned."

"I'm back at my old apartment, staying in the extra bedroom."

"I figured. Adhara says you've been at work when I've buzzed."

Marisol shrugged.

"Except I stopped by the clinic. They said you no longer work there," Tobias said.

"I'm taking a leave of absence," she murmured.

He hadn't picked the scab completely off the festering wound he labeled Marisol Novotny. Confirming she had been avoiding him all along tore the whole thing open. "Your parents said you rarely come around."

She turned to face him, expression sunk in obvious disgust. "Are you fucking stalking me?"

He shrugged. "I'm a detective."

She pursed her lips together and faced the empty desk again.

His stating of the obvious wasn't going to win him any prizes with her, so he added, "Whatever you're going through, you don't have to go through it alone."

Shifting in her seat, she returned to attacking her cuticles.

Wendell Carp, the lawyer, burst into the room. The short, bald man settled into his desk, holding a stuffed manila folder bound together by rubber bands. "You are probably wondering why I called you here."

"Something to do with a will?"

"Yes, the Varian family has been clients of our law firm for centuries. Each generation seems to have a similar stipulation—if a Varian disappears for a length of time, draw up the paperwork. Then we contact names they have given us."

"I'm assuming we're the contacts?" Tobias asked.

"Yes. In the court of law, we usually have years before missing people are declared dead and estate matters are settled."

"He's not dead," Marisol protested.

"Indubitably, but Mr. Varian put a strict timeline in place regarding his assets. With the wreckage found, we know it's not necessarily proof of life," Wendell continued, "but he wanted to make sure certain people are cared for financially. Not just money either, the family's various properties and business ventures."

Wendell handed them pieces of paper. Tobias flipped the top fold open. He'd never seen so many zeroes in his life. His trembling hand dropped the paper.

"What happens when he comes back?" Marisol asked.

"He has outlined protocols if such an event would occur. It has happened with other Varians. They are an adventurous lot."

"If? They haven't found him yet." Marisol wadded the paper into a ball and threw it across Wendell's desk. "I don't want his money or his things. I want him back."

"Mr. Varian wants to ensure you're cared for, ma'am."

She scoffed and stormed out of the office.

Tobias wasn't an idiot. He wasn't going to turn something like this away. "What do I sign?" Wendell pointed to the electronic pad on his desk. Tobias hurried his signature with the stylus and bolted out of the office. Picking up his pace to a jog, he caught up with Marisol outside on the sidewalk.

He thought he'd have something profound to say as he gazed into those brown eyes that used to be so brilliant and full of life. But if he told her he loved her, and it killed him to watch her fade, she'd probably kick him in the balls. "Kid...I miss you." He shifted his weight, preparing to make the quick pivot after she'd tell him to fuck off.

"I miss you, too," she replied softly.

"Will you do me a favor?" With the twitch of his pinkie, he fought the urge to pull her into his arms and feel the warmth of her under his chin. "Will you go back in there and sign? Spend his money. You know he'd want you to."

She sighed and stomped back into the law firm.

When she returned outside, he asked, "Can we catch up?"

To his relief, she nodded.

They sat across from each other at the worn formica table. Grease and coffee hung in the air. A waitress brought them cups of watery coffee, not that **Tobias** minded feeling less on edge.

"What are you doing with your extra time from your leave of absence?"

"I'm studying calculus."

He spit out his coffee, catching it in the mug. "Oh, I'm sorry, you're serious."

"I've been laughed out of a few offices, asking what happens when living matter meets antimatter." She idly played with sugar, which hadn't made it into her mug.

"Why calculus?"

She held a salt shaker between her thumb and forefinger. "This is a Vincent atom. Considering mass, gravity, and friction, where do you think we'd find him in a second?"

He sputtered in confusion.

Then, she tossed it into the air, catching it before it shattered on the diner floor. "Traveled approximately four feet. My hand? The point where we can catch him. We can calculate this."

He continued to gape.

She flagged down the waitress and borrowed a pen. The napkin shredded under the ballpoint. "Give me your arm. Roll up the sleeve."

He unbuttoned his shirt at the wrist and pushed his shirt up to the elbow. He laid his arm out across the table.

"There are constants we know." She drew squiggles and letters in an organized form on his arm. The pen point occasionally tickled and then dug into his skin, leaving behind a tinge of pain. A formula etched delicately and fiercely into his flesh was the perfect metaphor to describe her.

"Plug in those values, we find him," she said, ending the formula with $= V$.

"You're becoming a mathlete."

She rolled her eyes.

"No, I like it. Smart is sexy."

She ran her thumb over the equation in a gentle graze. "Except I'm missing an exact value." Her touch smoothed over the T in the formula.

"Wouldn't be me, would it?"

She turned away, focus beyond the pies on display. "Time. The exact time when he..."

He filled in the gap in her conversation with violent pink bolts. Images sharpened inside his memory and brought with it the haunting moment of watching his best friend disappear, particle by particle.

He cleared his throat. "I should get this tattooed here."

She faced him once more and caressed his arm. The tip of her fingers danced at the crease of his elbow. "What are you doing the rest of the afternoon?"

He adjusted his hand, touching her elbow. Their grip formed into an everlasting circle. "You mean, after we get matching tattoos?" He got a smile out of her, which made all the struggle with her lately worth it.

Then his phone rang; he let it go to voicemail. A short pause, his phone rang again. It was work. Probably ballistics confirming a bullet match or the medical examiner with wiped gunpowder residue. He'd leave them hanging for a while longer.

"What are you working on?" she asked.

"You know the case with the bank president? I'm on it." A brief shudder overcame him. Flashes of the photographed murder scene played in his head. An entire family, gone. Those were the images he once hoped to erase with a shot of whiskey.

She reached across the table and threaded her fingers into his other hand. "You don't have to be okay about it. You can be a big ole weenie for me."

He gently caressed the scar bump from her once-broken hand. "Back at you." Her eyes welled with tears, but he couldn't make the pain better. Only passing time and the other ways humans numbed themselves would make it not hurt so much.

His phone rang again. "Seems like you can't ignore it," she said.

"Guess not. An open-and-shut case tearing me away from a good thing. But...my partner said they assigned me it because there's a strange theory making waves around Shadowhaven that a serial killer is coming for the rich."

"So, they put the best man on the job. You better get to work." She extricated her hand from his and pulled the sleeve of his shirt down, re-buttoning it at his wrist.

He left her at the diner, regret throbbing like a stone stuck in his shoe.

19

Divorce

One Hundred and Fifty Years After the Curse

Adhara and I stow away on a ship to Spain. The Padre had left us in America, claiming he is needed there. With only us two, I try to hold her and relive the only good time between us, but she shrugs me away. She barely speaks to me, communicating in brief statements—wondering out loud if we can make the journey without fresh water and food or warning about footsteps approaching.

The burnt but living corpse of Nando remains shackled in a crate. A few rocks of the boat upset the mindless revenant inside. I make sure to drive more nails into the thick, wooden box.

We arrive in the Port of Bilbao. I go to arrange transport to my old home. No threat of the others has touched it, according to the Vasquez family lawyer entering their second century of business. And I hope beyond hope something nasty has plagued Alvaro and

Raul in the same way Nando couldn't escape an angry mob...or their cannons or torches.

I load my furious cargo into my hired carriage. We are about to leave for my home.

Adhara says, "Wait, I see something." She breaks into a sprint, shoving her way into the crowd. Confused, I watch as a bustle of people swallow her.

She's left me.

My stomach drops as I search, strangers' faces everywhere I turn. I scream for her until my voice hurts. My driver looks me over with disgust, as if I am some madman. I pay him for his patience and keep vigil until the crowd subsides. A shadow, a rustle, excites me from my post, but none are Adhara.

Night looms, and I only have so much gold to pay and nails to keep Nando inside. My heart hurts as we pull away in darkness. She's left me, and I am now alone.

20

VEXING

Tobias smoothed a finger over the permanent crease at the top corner of his copy of *The Count of Monte Cristo*. The previous owner must've dog-eared it long ago before he had found it at the used bookstore.

In Dumas' epic tale, Mercedes had rejected the advances of Fernand and professed her love for Edmond Dantes, and her reaction vexed the villain. *Vexed* was one of those funny words no one used anymore. Then—*buzz!* Tobias had a visitor at 12:22 a.m. How vexing.

The small, childlike part of him that never stopped believing he had consumed the body and blood of his Christ once a week welcomed the impossible. Was it the Patron Saint returned from the Great Beyond? The hope of his return gave him pause.

Another *buzz!* shook him from his stupor. The Patron Saint wasn't the type to announce his arrival like a delivery driver. The masked archangel preferred to break in, enter, and lurk, emerging from the shadows right when Tobias was in the middle of a piss stream or a sip of beer. Either way, he had a whodunnit to solve and a floor to mop after the Patron Saint disappeared into the night. But alive and arriving by the front door? These were not the modus operandi for his typical night visitor, so who was it?

Buzz!

"What's up?" he said to the speaker.

A breathy alto answered, "It's me."

Marisol.

He stroked the light pen mark still on his forearm, buzzed her in, and unlatched the deadbolt. He braced his hand against the door for a moment to find his bearings. It wasn't like she hadn't visited him at all hours before, but she had a way of making him go through a cardio workout without the actual running and sweating. Was it his feelings for her putting him through the wringer? No, he had become used to guilty feelings barging in when he enjoyed the smell of her hair too much or grew weak from her smile under the Patron Saint's omniscient eye.

But the Patron Saint was dead.

His dying turned Tobias's thumping heart into a real shithead, and Tobias'd reap some sustenance from the situation like a carrion bird. If he wasn't recovering, now'd be a perfect time for a stiff drink. He scrubbed a hand through his beard and ordered his smart speaker to play the sad sack, guitar busker music louder.

He scrambled around his apartment to find the perfect casual pose. Reading? Too passive. Standing and analyzing the poster he hung up as art? Too fake as fuck. He settled for propping himself against the doorframe of his kitchen right as she opened his apartment door.

"Sorry I didn't call ahead. Did I wake you?" she asked and closed the door behind her. She latched the deadbolt, which meant her visit was for the long haul. For the rest of the night.

"Nope," he squeaked out. She definitely was running him through a secret marathon.

She took one more step inside and stumbled. He caught her. "These fucking shoes." She regained her balance by gripping his right bicep.

She was wearing a skimpy red sundress that was so short, it was generous to refer to it as a dress. She bent down to remove her sky-high, ankle-breaking shoes. The skirt of her dress moved with her and revealed the underside of her ass right where it met the crease of her thighs.

He forced his gaze upward and studied the uneven plaster job of his ceiling. Landlords always seemed to hire the shoddiest of contractors. The thought didn't cool his emerging erection. *Grandma Quinlan's floppy, raisin tits.* The unfortunate memory was just the trick. Crisis avoided, he sighed and asked, "What's that you got on?"

"A dress." She, clearly uncomfortable, hugged herself around the dress's cut-out midriff ending in a tied knot over her cleavage. It wasn't what she wore, but how she wore it. He had met women like this before, ones who put on a disguise but were not-so-secretly dying inside. Those women liked to be told they're beautiful and were grateful when their disguises fell into a heap on his floor as he took them off.

Marisol couldn't be won over so easily, at least, not without breaking his nose.

He laughed. "Oh yeah? Where's the rest of it?"

"Don't get patriarchal."

"I thought you kept me around for the occasional patriarchal snark."

"I don't *keep you around*." She wandered into his tiny living room. The wrinkle of her middle brow formed an 11. "Where did all the cinderblocks go?"

She had a right to be confused. She hadn't visited his apartment via his front door since last year. Shortly after, an interior designer and *feng shui* consultant had visited him with tape measures and plans. They delivered custom furniture, all on some "anonymous" benefactor's payroll, and now Tobias had a certifiable bachelor pad that'd turn his tchotchke-loving ex-wife green with envy. He even had those stupid pillows, which united color and design rather than propped his head.

He toyed with showing Marisol how the television disappeared into the stand, but it was a cheap party trick. His favorite addition were his bookshelves— shelves of books he read or always wanted to read, shelves of pictures of Diedre as a girl and now a young woman, shelves that showed him he had a life worth a damn so he wouldn't ever need to numb himself with whiskey or women ever again.

"It's funny how things change when you get your priorities straight," he said.

She nodded and fixated on the pattern of his new rug, tracing it with her big toe, nail shining with red polish. She started nibbling on her lower lip. The Patron Saint haunted them, even in the refuge of his apartment. She needed a comforting distraction, so Tobias thought of starting somewhere simple. "Can I get you something to drink? Water? Tea?"

Her brow furrowed further into what could be described as consternation, another one of those old-fart words no one used anymore. "Tea," she said.

He entered his galley kitchen and filled his Shadowhaven Rooks mug with tap water. He nuked the water in the microwave for a minute. The moment it dinged, he asked, "Do you want chamomile, mint, or jasmine?"

She relaxed into a smirk. "You have more than one tea flavor?"

"I recognize your shock, but I bought them for the former lady friend." Marisol squinted in further confusion. He reminded her with an eye roll. "Cesca? The yoga instructor? The one with the Kegel muscles sculpted by God?" He winced. *Bad joke.* So bad, he reversed the hard work of avoiding particular bodily responses. "What'll it be?"

She answered chamomile, and he threw the bag into the mug and handed it to her along with a small plate, which she stared at like it was written in alien code.

"For your bag, after it seeps for a couple minutes."

As soon as she set the tea bag on the plate, he took it back to the kitchen sink. She shook her head. "It's *Invasion of the Body Snatchers*."

"Will you pick your jaw off the floor, kid?"

She shrugged and began sipping. "If you weren't sleeping, what were you doing?"

"Reading."

"Reading?"

"Is there an echo in here? Yes, reading." He put on his best pompous actor impression. "It keeps the mind sharp and inspires the soul. Possessing literacy beyond Dick and Jane puts me intellectually leagues ahead of my superior officers."

"Always aiming to be the biggest asshole in the room. At least that hasn't changed." She set the mug down on the coffee table, which he promptly placed a coaster under. "Everything has really worked out for you." Her husky voice developed a crack in it.

"Not everything." He watched as her hands picked at the skirt of her dress, as if by pulling the thing, it'd grow another inch.

"Like what?"

Your boyfriend atomizing himself into oblivion, for starters. Tobias turned down the music and leaned back against a shelf. "Diedre still keeps our interactions cold and brief."

"But she's interacting. That's a big step." Marisol took a spot next to him. Her bare shoulder brushed against his arm.

Close to her, he picked up traces of her essence. She was a summer night in the city, the combination of wet concrete and a passing cloud of tobacco with a hint of lily and something else—familiar—but he couldn't place it. If he was a different kind of man, he'd lean in and smell her neck as he kissed it, just to catalogue her scent.

But as his lust crushed his temperance, he wasn't feeling like a different kind of man. He crossed his arms over his chest. "Why are you here?"

"I was out with the happy couple and needed some air."

"Adhara?"

"Yep. Probably fucking her roller-skating stripper girlfriend as we speak. My slow return to the apartment is a courtesy—to both them and my ears." She added a derisive laugh.

"Well done, her. I'd shake her terrifying clawed hand if I didn't think she'd rip my balls off with the other."

"She might go easy on you. They've been going at it so frequently, she might have carpal tunnel, even with the super-healing."

"You sound jealous."

"Of what? The roller-skating? Stripping? Carpal tunnel? Super-healing?"

"I meant the, um…" Tobias formed his fingers into a circle and gestured finger-fucking the circle with two fingers on his other hand. How would she feel with his fingers exploring her pussy? Already wet or needing gentle encouragement? He squeezed the offending fingers into a fist. The mere suggestion touched a forbidden fire.

"Who wouldn't be?" Her chest moved as she sighed, practically exposing a nipple out of the top of her "dress." She scratched the top of her foot with the perfectly red-painted toes of the other. Her voice shrunk into a whisper, "I wore a different type of mask tonight, the mask of a happy person. It's why I look so fucking ridiculous." She picked at the nail polish on her fingernails and found a weak spot, chipping it away.

"You don't look ridiculous." He nudged her with his elbow. "You look great. You always do."

She chortled. "Thank you, but you don't have to give insincere compliments just because I'm… vulnerable."

"I wasn't being insincere. I'm turning a new leaf. From here on out, I no longer spout barbs couched in the disapproving judgment of the patriarchy. You're not the first person in this city to go out in public without your pants, and frankly, we as a society need to be more accepting of the pant-challenged."

She laughed but stopped suddenly. "A man asked to leave with me. When you're recognized as a Vincent Varian leftover, people get FOMO."

A weird mix of jealousy and protectiveness slipped between his ribs. She was getting him all worked up. Vinnie with his insanely good looks, sophistication, and charm made sense, but a random barfly? "Did you… oblige?"

She scowled. "No!" Then her expression shifted. She held her face in her hands. Her long, dark hair fell over her face. "I guess..."

She was waiting for the miracle that'd never come, always longing for the Patron Saint.

"I guess I'm not in my twenties anymore," she finished.

"Indeed, we are not." He tucked a strand of her hair behind her ear, his touch lingering more than it should.

Her expression twisted as his fingers ran through her hair, skimming the shell of her ear. Her bright, anime-princess eyes met his—the kind of brown eyes people wrote songs about. Their brilliant depths continually wrecked his common sense. The memory of Grandma Quinlan's floppy, raisin tits could save him no longer.

Marisol leaped on top of him. He fell into the shelf and hit the back of his head. The force toppled objects off and onto the floor with the crash. This wasn't a kiss. She was practically eating the lips off his face. Her fingernails scratched up his sides, lifting the hem of his shirt. A pained groan escaped his throat. He might need some iodine for those scratches. She took his mouth open in agony as an invitation to jam her tongue farther into it.

This wasn't how it was supposed to be. This exact moment had played in his head a million times. How soft and warm her lush lips would be. How she'd direct him to be a good boy with a tug of his hair.

He held her by the shoulders and pushed her off. Her eyes were squeezed shut, as if she was too embarrassed to look at him. He rubbed his lips together and got a taste of her, a familiar sweetness and burn. The final scent note to a summer night. "Been drinking?" he asked.

She tipped her chin up. "I'm sorry. I didn't think I could do this without it."

His body clenched, as if it had just experienced a sucker punch. She didn't want him the same way he wanted her. He wanted something pure, like destinies fulfilled and shit. And she just needed a warm body.

"Alcohol," he licked his lips. Frenzied thoughts of pouring whiskey down her lips, breasts, thighs and drinking from them until he atomized took him over. "It could fuck up my recovery."

"I'm so sor— I didn't think—"

He straightened and adjusted his dick inside the waistband of his pants. The slight change in friction turned him into a Pavlovian dog, drooling at sucking whiskey off her toes or out of her navel. He had to pour her down the drain. "I'll hire a car to take you home."

As much as he wanted to save himself, he couldn't send her out with mere centimeters of fabric covering the good bits. "Hold on, I'll get you a shirt." Tobias darted to his bedroom and fished out a sweatshirt from his dresser drawer.

He offered it to her, and she hugged it to herself like a stuffed animal. "I hate going back to my apartment." She brought the shirt to her face, which muffled hiccuping sounds.

Tobias scratched the back of his head to conjure up a good idea, but found only a sore spot. "Maybe the driver could take you to your parents?"

Marisol snorted her obvious disgust and lowered his sweatshirt from her face, revealing not a face ruined by streaming mascara, but a blank expression of a proud woman who'd rather risk a brain aneurysm from holding everything in than cry it all out. She pulled on his old sweatshirt, which hung over her thighs and ended above her knees.

It wounded him to see her in his clothes and needing him. The devil on his shoulder told him he was overreacting. Wasn't this what he wanted? Her willing and her perfect paramour out of the picture in the most honorable way possible? She was the equivalent of a widow, for Chrissakes. Not even a year ago, if she had come to him like this, he would've torn away her dress and flimsy panties and bent her over the back of his recliner before she had a chance to take her shoes off.

But he had changed.

He picked the fallen, framed photo of eight-year-old Diedre in her soccer uniform off the floor. Though it had a crack in the glass, he placed it back in its spot on the shelf. "Call me once you're home. You can talk to me until you fall asleep. Hell, I'll even listen to you snore."

Her chin trembled as she stared at the floor. "Don't you want me?"

As long as I'm breathing. He forced himself to swallow to give himself time to think of the perfect response; the wrong one would break her. "I want what's best for us."

Her tears pooled as her eyes slanted into a scowl. "You don't know what you want." She pushed past him and picked up her shoes. "You've been following us around with your kicked-puppy eyes. If I didn't know any better, I'd think you'd rather have fucked him."

She saw through him. Through the hand gripping his shirt, the tie against his throat. Through to a night of almost and never was. Always *never was* with him.

But, no, she wasn't going to land a victory blow. Tobias had been in enough fights and couples therapy with the ex-wife to know this wasn't about him, but she wasn't getting the final jab. His balls didn't belong in a jar by her bedside. "If we're offering constructive feedback here, he never used me or made me feel like shit. Something you, Novotny, are a master of."

"Fuck you, Quinlan."

She had finally joined the secret Shadowhaven sisterhood of women who stomped out of his apartment while snapping out a *fuck you*. But he had to appreciate the irony of it all—this time a woman said it to him when he *wasn't* being a piece of shit.

"And you can keep the sweatshirt!" he shouted as she stormed down the hallway. He now had a good use for the word *vexed*.

21

By the Way

One Year Before Meeting Marisol

Tobias entered his darkened apartment. His stubble, right hand, and definitely his dick reeked of eau de sergeant's wife. Her lingering feminine tang required the sweet burn of whiskey. He didn't need to flip on the light switch. The location of his pint of whiskey had been practically memorized. How it made it from the store to his apartment without him breaking the seal was a miracle the zealous proselytized about on Sunday. *Get this man canonized!*

He climbed out his window and leaned over the railing of his fire escape. Not the most picturesque of views, a Shadowhaven alley, but cold night air had a way of cleansing him. He untwisted the cap and took a vanilla-tinted sip. The alcohol tingled his mouth and tongue as it evaporated. Soon, when the blood pumped away from his dick, the post-coital guilt would kick in. Luckily, the drinking's dizzying effect numbed him from ruminating too hard about the disasters left in his drunken libido's wake.

"You smell like pussy," a flat, gruff voice said from the dark.

Tobias jumped and lost the grip on his bottle. It shattered in the alley below. Dammit, now he was out twenty bucks. Floating eyes and a sharp jawline stuck out from the shadows. He had a visit from the Patron Saint. Though he only got a sip of his lost whiskey, he drank plenty before, which wrapped him in an invisible blanket of intoxication. "My ex-wife used to complain about my smell."

"You could at least shower." He emerged from the shadow and joined Tobias overlooking the alleyway against the railing. The Patron Saint narrowed his eyes. "But you'd rather marinate."

"You're invading my abode. Let a man live by his own rules. Besides, you now owe me a pint."

The Patron Saint rolled his eyes. Never before had Tobias experienced his night visitor so animated and unserious. His heart skipped, seeing this side of him, a reaction he attributed to the whiskey going to his head. And the blood still rushing to his dick.

"What do the streets of Shadowhaven offer tonight?" Tobias asked, his voice huskier than usual.

"Not that kind of visit. I needed...to talk to someone, and I don't...have many friends."

"I believe that."

"I'm...sorry, I'll leave." He reached to his mask and seemed to wipe something away. "I just...don't really have anyone anymore except..." The Patron Saint punched into his open palm over and over and groaned. The mysterious man was crying.

Not at all what Tobias had been expecting, which heightened his concern. Tobias stopped the Patron Saint's punching hand and placed a palm on his shoulder. "Hey man, are you okay?"

"He's gone!" The Patron Saint collapsed in his arms, wailing. Tobias held him up. The awkward embrace finally melted into a hug. Who exactly was gone? He rubbed his back and eventually found himself stroking the tie of the man's mask knotted above his nape. Against his chest, the weeping subsided until the only sound vibrating through him was the slow, steady heartbeat of his night visitor.

"Hey," Tobias whispered. He nudged the Patron Saint back to check on him. A strand of golden blond hair poked out from his mask. "I never guessed you were a blond. You're just like my ex-wife."

"Twice now I've been compared to your wife." He sniffled and laughed, but at least he had stopped crying.

"I didn't mean— Your hair, it reminds me of an angel." He clasped the piece of hair between his index and middle finger.

"I don't have room for wings in my suit."

The steady pace of the Patron Saint's heart echoed through Tobias's body and thundered in his ears. The sensation possessed Tobias. "Do you want to come inside and talk? We could have a beer."

"I don't usually drink."

"I actually don't want to drink beer." He hadn't stopped holding him, a fact he acknowledged with a nervous smile. The Patron Saint's eyes glowed like lightning. Tobias gasped, hypnotized by the wonder. A force met his mouth, warm and commanding.

The Patron Saint was kissing him.

He went rigid with surprise, but as the Patron Saint's tongue slid into his mouth, his body melted. With his languid high, he worried he might pass out. He broke the kiss to breathe, yet the Patron Saint suckled along his neck, each kiss pinging like a tiny static spark. "I've never..." he murmured.

"Never what?" The Patron Saint's lips grazed his ear.

Tobias audited his experiences: the handjob in the locker room after basketball practice, the kiss he and his roommate laughed off when the chick from biology class went down on both of them, and the hesitation he gave when the husband who busted Tobias with his wife begged to be fucked too. What made this time different? He didn't want this man to be a cheap anecdote. If anything, his partnership with the Patron Saint was the one of the few good and true things to come out of Tobias's shitstorm life.

He guided the masked man's gloved hand to his heart. How the thing battered inside his chest. "Feel how scared I am." The admission opened him like a wound. Pleasure and shame compounded into each other as if he finally stopped running and faced the ghost chasing him his whole life.

The Patron Saint extricated his hand from Tobias's and smoothed it down Tobias's stomach. His gloved fingers teased along the waistband of Tobias's jeans. The masked man drifted his hands to Tobias's back and stroked lower and traced along the furrow. The dull but tantalizing sensation tightened his balls into a needy ache. They resumed kissing, Tobias moaning loudly in the Patron Saint's mouth.

"You should be scared." The Patron Saint drew him closer, pinning Tobias's cock against the buckle of his utility belt. Between it and the fly of his jeans, the erotic friction toed the line between discomfort and delight.

Every taste of his mouth, grind of his body shed another layer until nothing existed but hope. A hope for healing each other's scars. A hope for swimming against the current together to avoid disappearing down Shadowhaven's drain. Tobias leaned his forehead against the Patron Saint's mask. "I'll be so good to you." He cupped along his jawline and grazed the fabric over his cheekbone.

The Patron Saint pushed him away and adjusted his mask. "You can't do that."

"Sorry, I'm drunk. You can leave it on. I don't care who you are just—" Tobias said while panting. "Please come inside."

"I should go." The Patron Saint patted Tobias's cheek. "You really do smell of pussy." The shadowy figure moved to the ladder of the escape, preparing to leave.

Tobias had been fine with numbing himself with booze and sex, but now he had exposed the raw nerve.

"I can shower. I'll get clean, and I'll feel so new." He wasn't begging a lover to stay, he was bargaining for his soul with God.

"Goodnight, Tobias." The Patron Saint swept his cape about himself, blending into the dark. By the time Tobias had blinked, the Patron Saint was gone.

22

What's Behind Wall Number Two?

It takes super-strength to shoulder the door of my wife's crumbling, abandoned estate open. The air inside is thick with dust. The limestone and mortar cracks from snarls of ivy growing through it.

In the mood for a project, I gather limestone and mix more mortar, not to fix my one-time home...

...but to seal Nando in the cellar wall.

He rattles and moans as I stack and mortar. Does placing Nando in a dark and mindless Hell make me a deity? Two walls deep, the noise finally stops.

Only for a new noise to replace it—the creaking of the front door and the padding of footsteps. Someone has entered.

I wipe the mortar from my hands and quickly adjust my tunic. Hope sweeps me into a rush. Adhara must've found me! I bound up the stairs toward the sound of my visitor.

"I am sorry! I am dirty from repairing a wall in my —" I'm struck by the truth. My visitor is not Adhara but a strange, old man.

"Señor, I am Florian Carp." His accent sounded Austrian. "My law firm has represented the Vasquez family for some time. I received your letter requesting a meeting. Well, here is the meeting. As for your money —"

Have I lost all the riches gained when Susanna died? A suitable punishment, possessing nothing but an estate with the living dead sealed in its walls to sustain my cursed life. How freeing, to no longer be the rich man. "It's okay if there's nothing, Señor Carp."

"Nothing, sir? The money has been left alone for generations and has grown into a mountain!" The old lawyer blinked as if I asked the question with the most obvious of answers. "Inherited wealth and compound interest, señor."

Death surrounds me but mocks me with false blessing so that I may choke on my loneliness. I can't stand another moment in my dead wife's cursed estate. "My broth— I hear long ago, my family had someone who served as a priest at a nearby parish."

"The Iglesia San Vicente Mártir[1] is nearby, señor."

"Vicente Mártir? You are a jester."

"Indeed, I am not."

"All right, Señor Carp. I'll sign your papers."

The dead are the payment for my limitless gold.

1. Church of Saint Vincent the Martyr

23

A Window into the Space-Time Continuum

The night air cut the exposed skin of her legs. **Marisol** carried her shoes, straps digging into the creases of her fingers, and walked barefoot through the city. Where? Not a clue.

The walk hurt at first. Every jagged bit of concrete, broken bit of glass stabbed into her soles. The pain chased away her emptiness. It didn't hurt so much to miss Vincent, to feel discarded by Tobias when every step challenged her to keep going. If her foot touched something wet, she prayed it was water. And eventually, the knifelike feeling of a cold, barefooted walk through Shadowhaven didn't sting so much.

When her feet numbed, the tears came on again. She didn't know what she had done to deserve this—robbed of Vincent's love, ripped from Annie's friendship, and dropped by whatever she had going on with Tobias's will-they-won't-they daddily concern. She wiped a tear with the sweatshirt sleeve.

She reached the harbor, which meant she had to turn around. Housing was in the other direction. She may have had keys to a few different places, but at the moment, none of them were home.

Walking along the harbor seemed like the better idea. At least the lights reflecting off the water offered a somewhat soothing view.

When her legs became weary, and the pain in her feet reflected the ache in her muscles, she found Saint Michael's Cathedral. Opulent towers pierced the sky. In darkness, however, the giant stained glass windows held little wonder. She walked up its steps and approached the main door.

A force possessed her to jimmy the doors, as if she were seeking refuge. She circled the church grounds until one heavy wooden door shouldered open. The thing was so warped, it was like it hadn't been opened since the turn of the century.

Inside, her feet padded against the concrete flooring. The weak glow of the candles on the altar drew her closer. The faint red light flickered from another world. The air smelled of incense, fragrant with rich oils. She knelt on the altar before the statue of the Virgin Mary, studying the details of her—the folds in her blue robe, the lily in her hand, the rosy tint to her fair skin. Her legs grew insensate, and she remained kneeling until multiple candles reached the end of their wick, dissipating into the final snake of smoke. Her eyes grew heavy. She found rest curled onto a pew. She tucked her knees into herself to keep in her body heat.

On the narrow bench, she imagined herself holding Vincent. Her knees curled right behind his. He smelled of the sweet sandalwood she had come to expect from him, but she recognized something different about him, the smell of salt in the sea air.

"I wish you were with me, my saint," she whispered to him.

"I'm trying to find you, my Stella Maris," he wept.

She had never heard his fear before. "Find me. I'm right here." Although she saw nothing but the holy ambience of the church, she reached up with her arms and ran her fingers through his hair. The silky sensation surprised her. It was as if he were right there, and yet, it wasn't the Vincent she knew. He had long hair.

"Do you feel me?" she asked. She felt him nod. "Find me," she ordered, "Please." Lying on the pew, she melted through space and time or whatever barrier had separated them. Sometimes her arms were around his waist. Other times, he held her.

The tears from her eyes echoed the tears from his. Was she hallucinating? But he felt so real and warm. He was Vincent, but not her version. Regardless of which one he was, she fell asleep begging him to find her, and as he cried, he said, "I will. I will."

A gentle nudge awoke her. **Marisol** opened her eyes to find a wide-eyed man staring at her, agog. Through weary blinks, she studied him, noticing the stiff, white collar. A priest. How long had she been asleep? Judging by the meager light pouring through the stained-glass windows, it was early morning. A few hours? The man's lip quivered until he finally spoke. "Do-do you need help?"

She sat up, shaking her head.

"I can give you the address of the women's shelter. They may have some space left."

"I don't need shelter," she said as she wiped sleep from her eyes.

"Ma'am, you're trespassing. I'll call the police," he threatened, trembling.

She scoffed. "Trespassing? What ever happened to seeking sanctuary?" Standing up, she gathered her shoes and straightened her dress and oversized sweatshirt. "Don't worry. I'm leaving. I didn't touch any of your things."

She moved through the aisle. The returning pain shot through her feet. She winced and breathed through it. Putting on her heels would most definitely not make her feel better. The stinging angered her, boiling with each knifelike step. She spun right around, "My grandma used to pray here, you asshole. Have you ever asked yourself why I don't?"

She escaped out of the giant doors at the front of the church and scurried down the steps, catching a bus in time to elude the cops if the scared, little priesty man had followed through on his threat.

One Hundred and Fifty Years After the Curse

I wake up alone in the pew, still feeling the radiant heat of my star. Was she a dream? But she had form. I'd touched her. And yet, she'd cried. Could she not forgive me?

I search for answers in the agony of the Savior on the Crucifix. No, I cannot be forgiven so easily. I turn to leave. An old man in robes startles me. He has waited in silence behind me.

"The convent offers meals and a place to rest for God's wayward children," the man says as he inches closer, using a staff to support his feeble body.

I bow my head, unable to utter a *thank you.* I lift my chin and study the old man's features. His eyes are milky white. The man is blind and unable to see my measly sign of gratitude. "Thank you, Father," I say as I pass by him.

The man grabs my arm with an unexpected amount of strength. "Come to my rectory. You seem so very weary, my son."

I freeze. My shame rises under Jesus's watch.

The old priest touches a wrinkly hand to my face. "You are forgiven."

Old, blind, what does the priest know? He hadn't been there in the swamp of my lust, greed, and wrath. Forgiveness is as far away from me as the stars. I jerk my arm away and run out of the church.

24

The Things We Do For Love

The first thing **Tobias** did when Wendell Carp gave him the keys to the Varian penthouse was wander the garage. The garage didn't feel as haunted as the empty rooms upstairs, even though it had the dead body of the Staci SUV.

A toolbox grabbed his attention. He opened it and admired how it was full of the best tools in all the sizes, even the strange ones no one ever used. Even if he hadn't accepted a giant money transfer, the toolbox would be the source of jealousy from his social circles.

Between the toolbox and the abandoned car, he got an idea.

He threw off his trench coat, dress shirt, and tie and popped the SUV's hood. Fuck, where was the battery? If it wasn't here, there was one more place to check. He opened the trunk and checked under the wheel well. *Aha!* He found the battery and disconnected it. Back under the hood, he ran his fingers over the engine control unit, finding the tabs holding the thing into place. One by one, he pulled them open and freed the unit.

In his hands, he held the one computer containing Staci which wasn't behind a steel door.

Tobias arrived at the basement, walk-out apartment. The door opened right out onto the piles of collected garbage. He needed to take his recently earned Varian cash and buy his daughter a better apartment. His fist thundered against the door as he knocked.

Diedre opened it. "What are you doing here?"

"Could you help me with something?"

She blew out a breath as if she were toying with telling him to scram. "Come in."

Heartened, Tobias stepped inside. The place was a cave. Windows had been painted over in black. Cords and wires hung from the ceiling. Tables and tables had snarled cables and broken pieces of technology. "Does your mom and Glenn know you're living like this?"

"I usually meet them at their place." She crossed her arms and popped her hip, the universal sign of taking no shit. "What do you need help with?"

Tobias handed her the engine control unit. "Someone or something put a weird something-or-other on my computer system, and I'm locked out. I was hoping you'd know how to fix it."

Diedre scoffed. "This is a car part."

"It has microchips and everything. Can't handle it?"

"I didn't say that." She popped the cover off it, which revealed the tech inside. Slowly but surely, she wired the hard drive-looking thing into a computer control tower. She turned on a monitor connected to it. Hieroglyphics poured onto the screen. Top to bottom, the thing was full of gibberish.

"You said this was yours? Funny, you don't look like Vincent Varian."

Fuck, how much should Diedre be allowed to know? "He was a close friend."

"Before or after he made like Amelia Earhart?" The clacking of the keyboard stopped. She scanned the lines of code which had revealed itself on screen. "Someone encrypted everything, files, applications, the OS."

"Can you crack it? Or counter it, or whatever people like you do?"

Her pupils moved rapidly over the nonsense. "Whoever made this was good, but not *me* good."

"That's what I like about your generation. The confidence from your parents actually believing in you."

"The encryption is a security protocol. Something tried to get in and triggered it."

Probably when Adhara messed with it.

Diedre pointed at a line of text and characters as if he were supposed to understand it. "It's constantly rewriting itself to try to predict where a cyberattack will go and build a shield around it. It kicks in when it senses something invading it. If I knew how to code this program, I'd be set for life selling it to other companies."

"Copyright law says you can wipe the dollar signs out of your eyes."

"It's pretty complex. When do you need this by?"

"No set date, but ASAP. I have a friend who is depending on this."

"I'd have to give up my jobs to decipher it." She held out her hand and wiggled her fingers. "And I don't come cheap."

Feigning a grumble, he slapped a brick of hundreds in her hand. "Don't go spending it all at once." He actually looked forward to this father/daughter time, even if he had to pay for it.

25

Rebirth

Two Hundred and Sixty Years After the Curse

Money buys a new life in France. It buys lectures at the University of Paris. I watch scientists become magicians before my very eyes, transmuting materials with reactions into all-new substances. God is a theory, not an absolute.

And as I walk the grounds of my *maison de maitre*[1] in Calais, I feel, for once, that breaking the curse is possible. From classrooms to pubs, people are more alive than ever. They demand liberty, equality, and democracy.

The woods outside my home are lush and green, with giant trees stretching toward the sky. The forest shade provides me with wonder and privacy. I can go for walks off the path, never having to reveal who or what I am. At night, they grant me the secrecy I need to become the protector. I do not need to see the stars at night. In fact, I want to remain hidden in the darkness,

1. Directly translates as "master's house" and was a style typical of the bourgeois class

for I have become something else entirely—the living, breathing form of my inner shadow.

In the daytime, however, my walks are of the relaxing variety. I slip between trees, but I stop. I hear a buzzing around me. The air possesses an energy...of being watched. I pick up my pace, using my super-powered run. I will lose my follower and barely break a sweat.

But I hear them keeping pace, the buzzing louder than ever. The hair on my neck tingles. I know this sign. Someone from the past is here. I weave behind a tree and edge around it slowly as not to make sound.

The vibrations move past me. My follower has charged ahead of me, and the buzzing fades into the distance. I hold my breath and sidle behind the next tree to make doubly sure I lost them. The woods answer me in flitting bugs and chirping birds. Breathing again, I resume my walk, but carefully.

Perhaps I am hearing things. My body may be young, but a mind of six lifetimes contains memories that are difficult to discern, and now paranoia may be an unfortunate side effect. Another step—*bam!*—I am tackled to the ground. A hand holds my head down, driving my face into the dirt.

My panicked gaze catches a cloaked figure looming over me. It sits on my back, crushing me into the earth. Its gloved hand pets down my back before it untucks my shirt. Leather meets my bare skin. The hand assesses the furrow of my back. I am prey in the clutches, pliant and accepting the inevitable wrought by teeth in my neck or into another soft spot.

The hand explores along my side until it reaches underneath me. It palms my erection. My fear recedes. In the emptiness, desire surges—twisted desire inhaling the earth chafing my face, delighting in bruises I hope never fade. I rut against the hand, the ground.

Clarity strikes me. What am I doing? Reliving the lust of the curse's fateful night. In the centuries since, carnal wickedness never silenced my solitude. A swell of fear returns, drowning me in it. I attempt to buck the mysterious force off my back, but it pins me in place. "Please," I cry.

Lips bristle along my ear. A smooth alto speaks in accented French, "Rubio, you want to be degraded because you think it will make you a good man."

"Adhara!" I roll under her. "You found me!"

Our time apart has changed her. She dresses like a man, wearing a tunic, waistcoat, and breeches. Even her hair is tied back like mine, but her honey-blond curls are worn in defined coils, shining in the sunlight. Only her stormlike eyes are the same. They spark with her power like the reactions in my chemistry lab.

"I followed the stories, a man with the face of an angel who touches the sick. The mysterious man who lives in his *maison* but hides from the world. A man known only by the name V. V." She runs her hand over the front of my face, forcing my eyes closed. She kisses each of my eyelids.

Over the years, I have cursed her for leaving me. For letting the pain of eternity cloak me in isolation. *Why?* I want to ask her. Does she understand the slow asphyxiation of my loneliness? But her kisses awaken me. I am reborn.

We make love. The ground scrapes my back as she rides me. Skin against skin, she reminds me I'm human. "You make me feel like happiness is possible," I say.

She bites the meaty part of my shoulder. Her pleasure speaks to me in her increased sighs, the way her mouth parts and accepts my fierce kisses.

In the afterglow, I hold her. She nuzzles against my bare chest. I know it's not true, but it feels like the most intimate contact she's ever given me.

"Have you seen the Padre?" she asks, speaking into my chest.

I recall a single night of wine and pleasure and the hope of company. "A fateful meeting at an inn. Eighty years ago? Then—*poof!*—gone again." My answer is playful, but like with Adhara, the Padre's leaving hurt profoundly. Better to have never seen him at all.

My hurt awakens the darkness within me, the vengeful protector. I tell her Nando is sealed inside a cellar in Spain. She toys with my chest hair, and she recounts of a story of finding Alvaro in Transylvania.

"I stuffed him in a steel box and kicked him in the ocean," she says.

Her cold vengeance warms my heart, and I hold her closer to me. "We'll find Raul in due time," I promise.

And under the shimmering leaves, I know our retribution will set our hearts free.

26

Good Trouble

Vincent's money rotted in **Marisol's** accounts. She imagined the organizations she could shower with astronomical donations or how much she'd have to spend to have a street named after her.

Yet no matter what she gave away, the balance only grew.

The rent on her apartment stayed the same, but the electric bill had become obscene. Adhara's experiments devoured power like a small reactor. Luckily, Marisol had more than a few Benjamins to burn.

To spend Vincent's fortune properly, she'd need to outsource her wealth to people far more qualified.

The roommate arrangement had its perks. The couple cooked. Otherwise, she might have forgotten to eat. Their small talk in the evening kept her sane after long, silent hours. When grief became unbearable, one of them always hugged her, a reminder she was still human.

Even so, the apartment felt emptier by the day. When Marisol asked Adhara where she'd gone, the super-powered woman shrugged. "Working."

The word stung. Adhara brought Wheels into her schemes, never her. So Marisol carried the hurt, retreating to the spare bedroom for dinner while the happy couple turned the living room into an arena of naked, ecstatic acrobatics. She tolerated the tank of fungi that took over her bathroom. Asceticism was safer than facing the ghosts in the estate or the penthouse.

That afternoon, Adhara came home early, clutching a museum brochure bright with primary colors. She slapped it across the calculus textbook in front of Marisol. According to the brochure, the Shadowhaven Museum of Art was hosting a Duguay Roquet exhibition. The brochure featured depictions of naked Pacific Islander women. In small letters, Marisol noticed, the brochure had a disclaimer, warning the artist had relationships with young teenage girls during his travels, and the damage he caused should be considered when reevaluating his paintings.

"I think it's time we take in some culture," Adhara said. "Tell me. Have you ever viewed an art gallery at night?"

Unless discovering portraits of Vincent lurking the shadowed rooms of his estate counted, she hadn't. Marisol shook her head.

"Truly brings out the beauty. It's almost as if the museum is haunted with the paintings' subjects." Adhara stared wistfully into nothing. A few more blinks and her expression softened into a smile. "Come with me. I have something for you to wear."

Adhara presented her a revamped version of her Silver Spirit costume. "You left some of these lying around." She'd repaired the Kevlar pants Vincent had ripped, her harness, and her chainmail tunic, this time a matte gray rather than shining silver. Marisol ran her fingers over the protective top. Instead of heavy metal, the links were made from a light plastic.

"The material is 3D-printed polymer. If struck with a rapidly approaching force" —Adhara swung her clawed hand against the shirt— "the material resists the impact." The strike bounced off the shirt. "And..." Adhara draped a leather domino mask with silk ties over the shoulder of the chainmail. The mask was just like the one Annie had given her, which was now locked behind a steel door.

Prickling tears formed in her eyes. Adhara was not only giving her back of a piece of Annie, but she also helped her have a piece of Vincent.

"Do you like it?" Adhara asked.

Marisol nodded.

"So, let's put it to the test. Let's have some fun."

The light rail headed to the nearest stop by the museum. To not raise suspicions on the train, **Marisol** carried her mask in her pocket. Wheels, however, had painted a domino mask in blue and pink glitter on her face. The loud popping of her gum garnered a few annoyed glares in their direction. More curious to Marisol was the small lump moving in Wheels' sleeve. Wheels fed the lump a pinch of kibble. She had taken A.J. with them on the mission.

Carrying the biggest load, Adhara foisted a large duffel bag off her shoulder, which clanked as the train slowed to a stop. What was in the bag? A tightening muscle in her stomach told Marisol not to ask. They reached the station, and she followed Adhara and Wheels, walking briskly to keep up.

The Shadowhaven Art Museum's architecture mimicked the pale stone and giant pillars of its Old World counterparts. A towering and locked wrought iron gate encircling the entire property blocked the way inside.

Adhara dropped the duffel bag, and it landed with a cacophony of items banging together. "Wait here." She leaped over the giant gate, landing on the other side gracefully, low and ready. Her gold veins gleamed in the low light. From those veins, a pulse of blue light rippled around the garden and building. Magnets—she was using magnets to disable the security system. Adhara rocketed across the yard and disappeared behind the building.

Marisol bounced into place, waiting outside the gates. Adhara returned, presumably having cased the grounds. She broke the iron stakes which had locked the gate into place. "Hurry. We have fifteen minutes before the generators kick in," Adhara stated.

Wheels slung the duffel bag over her shoulder, tottering on her skates as she adjusted her balance, and rolled inside. Marisol tied on her mask.

Instead of going to the entrance, Wheels beelined, skating along the fence's vicinity. A violent *snap!* sounded from the darkness. More figures in black moved through the garden and scurried to the museum's entrance. By the looks of it, Adhara and Wheels had recruited others to join them.

Adhara kicked the door to the museum, knocking the frame askew. She pulled the broken door off its hinges and laid it on the ground. The recruits filed through the gap; ten of them, if Marisol counted correctly. Wheels trailed behind on her skates, popping gum loudly.

Indeed, the museum at night did feel haunted. Abstract statues cast ominous shapes as the faint light from street lamps shone through the tall windows. Deep into the museum, the meager skylight provided a haze of silver light. Paintings and statues gazed empty into the shadows. Without a crowd, their footsteps reverberated through the cavernous gallery.

Security guards were nowhere to be found. Marisol's heartbeat reached tachycardia levels, not because of the potential threat of being caught but because it reminded her of Caz's returns home late at night. The first place he'd visit was the kitchen sink, always washing his hands. When he was arrested, she'd come to understand he had been cleansing blood from them. But even before then, she always knew. She asked the question in her mind, but resisted the answer.

Here she was again, reliving the fear of the reply. What had Adhara done to the security guards?

Wheels stopped and threw the duffel bag to the ground. She unzipped it and tossed out two glow sticks. They provided enough light for Marisol to see the contents of the room—the Roquet exhibit. The recruits flocked to the open duffel bag and dug out spray paint. They attacked the paintings, scribbling words: *rapist, pedophile, CSAM*. A.J. joined in, nibbling on the edges of a canvas.

One of the recruits painted with flair, as if they had experience with graffiti. Marisol walked behind the person, watching as they sprayed over the image of a girl: *victim*. The graffiti artist backed into Marisol and turned around, sliding the hoodie off their head. It was Yesenia.

Marisol stuttered as she wanted to say something. Was the girl safe here? Yesenia smiled and slid her hoodie back on, adding more precise curlicues to her artful defacement.

Adhara pulled Marisol into the center of the room and handed her a permanent marker. "You shouldn't simply look at art. You need to express how it makes you feel."

Marisol popped the top and scrawled beside the gallery's disclaimer, *Our children remember what we forgive for our amusement.*

But the graffiti wasn't enough. Adhara slashed the paintings. "Is that all you have? Words?" One of her claws popped off her hand, and Marisol caught it.

Marisol held the talon-like piece of metal, assessing the weight. Her fingertips confirmed the deadly sharpness of it. The painting of a bare-chested girl stared at her. Freshly painted graffiti bled down it, obscuring the blurred tropical trees. The subject's eyes hypnotized her. A swirl of brown and black mixed with white dashes formed the girl's sleepy gaze. Her one raised eyebrow asked, *Why?*

Marisol plunged the blade into the canvas until she hit the wall behind it. She yanked the golden blade down, ripping the painting apart. A century and a half of toxic art history died at her hands. For once, her hands held power. No more glass walls held her back. No more wondering why her love wasn't enough to keep him here to cut her down. No more letting death destroy her.

Now, she was destruction herself. She stabbed another painting and tore it. Then again. And again. Until a high-pitched ring pierced her ears. How many beautiful things had to be destroyed to suck the poison of oppression out?

A hand grasped her shoulder. The ringing stopped. "Do you realize you're screaming?" Adhara asked.

Marisol's chest heaved, her lungs burning from the exertion. She shook her head.

"When the pain becomes rage, you finally taste the power others have taken from you."

Wheels spun to a halt in the middle of the room and called out Adhara's name.

Adhara rolled her fingers one by one into a fist. "We must go."

Marisol joined the gallery vandals, who rendezvoused in the train yard. Abandoned train cars had been haphazardly strewn about, and tall grass grew in forgotten patches. They had become urban druids, gathered about a flaming garbage can to call upon the spirits of mischief. Smoke plumed above them as they passed a couple joints around, adding a potent, earthy scent to the air.

Adhara rocketed in, carrying a case of champagne. She shook a bottle of champagne and christened the recruits with the spray. The wild ruckus could start. Their joyful squeals revealed most of Adhara's helpful graffiti artists were girls. Some Marisol recognized as performers from the Pink Curtain. Perhaps friends of Wheels? The others had an uncomfortable amount of baby fat to be enjoying a drop of champagne and generous inhales of weed.

Finding Yesenia, Marisol grabbed her by the wrist, causing the teen to spill the cup of champagne she had. "You should leave. Isn't it a school night?"

Yesenia took a long sip from her cup. "Summer break. Who are you supposed to be anyway? Supermom?"

Adhara draped an arm over Marisol's shoulder. "She had more of an education tonight than any schooling. School tells you how to please, take orders, sit still. An education provokes, takes charge, shakes things up. Are you going to deprive her of that?" With her free hand, Adhara raised the joint to her lips and inhaled. She exhaled the cloud in Marisol's face.

The smoke stung the bottom of Marisol's lungs, but soon the contact high coursed through her. She had thought being good girl was going to save her, but all it did was leave her alone and rotting in her held-back rage.

Fuck being the survivor. Fuck being the daughter holding it together. Fuck being the strong one because no one would allow her to break.

The chemicals hid her doubts in a fog and killed the angels on her shoulder. The party unfolded into wild dances around the fire, spiraling her into new highs. Adhara poured a bottle of champagne over her. Marisol let it flow out of her mouth, down her chin—let it slide down her neck and drip off her breasts. It baptized her and cleansed away all the good from her. And she loved becoming the dirty girl. A dirty girl didn't worry about someone else's kid losing herself to the night. A dirty girl clenched her thighs together as Adhara spit champagne in Wheels' mouth.

A dirty girl didn't care.

27

Ah! Ça Ira!

Two Hundred and Sixty Years After the
Curse

The entire city of Paris smells like a butcher shop, blood and flesh from newly shed to varying states of decay. Disguised by a bandana, mask, and cape, I wait behind an angel statue, centimeters from the ledge of a towering plinth. The grandeur of the Port de Paris provides cover for me as I cloak myself in the night. Far below, soldiers check those leaving the city, ensuring a short escape for any aristocrat avoiding the guillotine. A horse-drawn wagon transporting coffins draws the soldiers' suspicion.

The driver's assistant opens a coffin and tosses a bag. A soldier fumbles it and leaps back. The yelling below confirms the assistant had thrown a human head. They are carrying aristocrats, yes, but only those who escaped their corporeal form.

Another dedicated soldier straightens his posture. He climbs onto the wagon and pounds on of the coffins with his fist. The soldier shouts, demanding it to be opened. The driver and his assistant exchange looks, a hesitation as good as a confession. The soldier opens the coffin's lid, and a young boy cries, "Mama!"

I take the child's yelp as my cue. I leap down, touching the ground like a thunderbolt. The soldiers stumble. *Thump!* A punch to the bridge of his nose dispatches one quite easily. Another crumples into himself the moment I kick him in the groin.

Now, muskets begin to lower. I grasp one by its barrel, pulling the soldier off balance. With a swift swing, I strike the soldier's head with the butt. One desperate soldier charges me, bayonet flashing in the torchlight. I weave out of its way. The idiot instead stabs the side of the wagon. He attempts to pull his musket stuck in the wood. I squeeze around his throat and lift him off his feet. Easily, I throw his body against the port's arch.

Time slows down. A musket's lock clicks. I fling my cape about me to throw off the soldier's aim. The gun fires. Fabric flows around me. The ball passes through my cape.

I stand unhindered. The musket-wielding soldier gulps. A hook punch to his jaw takes him out.

"Thank you, monsieur," the driver calls out.

"There will be more. Go," I say, jumping into the wagon.

We ride into the night and reach the English Channel. I help empty the coffins of their living bodies, a father, mother, and two children of the aristocracy.

The mother, kissing my gloved hands, thanks me while her daughter clings to her skirt. She asks how she can repay me.

I shrink away from the praise, my worthiness of such words a lie until my wretchedly long life ends. "Board that ship and leave," I reply tersely.

The mother's joyful weeping ceases as she seems taken aback by my brief answer. Soon, they board the ship and set off to England.

The fake coffin transporters ready the wagon to return to Paris.

"Who are you?" the driver asks.

"No one."

"I will call you an angel."

I chafe again. Any good man should protect innocent children. I bite out, "Next time, build a coffin with a dummy door. An inspector will see the corpse, and your precious cargo will go undetected."

I run until I am one with the darkness.

I arrive at my *maison* at dawn, entering through the trap door hidden in the apple orchard. The tunnel underneath leads to the cellar, a perfect place to hide my mask and cape. I enter the scullery from the cellar stairs. I meet Adhara, standing vigil. Her lithe body creates alluring shadows under her thin chemise. Her crossed-arm greeting is of the irritated variety. What half-truth can I tell her? The people I saved were humble political dissidents.

Noting the absence of my housekeeper from her morning chores, I ask, "Where's Toinon?"

"I dismissed her for the day. Told her we'd awakened your passions last night, and we needed the *maison* to ourselves."

I force a yawn. "Paris didn't have the *plumbum dulce*[1] I needed, and I've been traveling all night. Forgive me if I need a little rest before our passions resume."

"The common people dispatched their king, and you fight to preserve the aristocracy. How predictable," she says, her words oozing with venom.

I am no longer the weakling I once was, tacitly accepting every one of Adhara's bad arguments. My nostrils flare. "And the children who did nothing to deserve the blood and terror?"

"Their children become as corrupt as them! Saving one now means another boot on the neck in the future."

"What good could we be possibly fighting for if we allow the murder of children?"

She clutches my throat. No sweet squeeze like the ones before she kisses me. A constricting hold wishing it could kill me. Her eyes light with her fury. "Your dashing heroics preserve a system that starves more children than you save."

I scramble, my fingers searching for a weapon. They settle on something metal and heavy. I grab it and raise an iron pan to swing. "Unhand me!"

---

1. Sweet lead

She releases me and smiles. I catch my breath. Eyeing the pan in my hand, hanging in the potential of striking her, her wide grin delights in the violence I'm capable of. "You do have a darkness within you, Rubio."

I drop my weapon. The shame I have been escaping for almost three centuries returns. "I have to believe that grace and forgiveness changes people because I have to believe...this will end."

Her twisted glee fades as she leaves the small kitchen. "It will never end." She catches herself stumbling in the doorway.

I stare at the hand which dared to strike Adhara. The abyss continues to swallow me. Am I doomed to be here forever?

Breaking News

Overnight, an exhibit at the Shadowhaven Art Museum was vandalized by intruders. Paintings by famous French impressionist Duguay Roquet altogether valued in the millions of dollars, were ripped and graffitied, perhaps beyond repair.

Security guards at the museum claimed they had been drugged, and alarm systems had been temporarily disabled. Shadowhaven police said no security footage has been found of the incident. The suspect or suspects are still at large.

At the Grant Durant trial, the defense team raised concerning questions about the credibility of the prosecution's witness. In the day-long testimony, Juniper Starling recounted a harrowing story of her kidnapping, abuse, and sex trafficking during Durant's island bacchanals.

However, even in the prosecution's cross-examination, US Attorney Stanwycki found inconsistencies in the witness's statement. Ms. Starling testified the lapses in her memory were attributed to *forced drug use. Durant's attorneys submitted school discipline records and Ms. Starling's history of running away from home as evidence. Upon the fifth hour of testimony and cross-examination, the witness broke down into sobs, impeding her ability to coherently testify. Judge Brown ordered the court to recess for the day. No other alleged victims will testify.*

Tonight, Shadowhaven says a sad farewell to one of its families. The family members of the Clements, known for C & C Corn Starch, were found drowned off their yacht in the Pacific. Investigation is ongoing, but no foul play is suspected. Staff at their Shadowhaven home mentioned they had planned an impromptu vacation because of the rise in crime committed against pillars of the community.

brownnote6969: "It's sad really. This generation has no appreciation for culture or art."

._.artgirlie._.:"This city has had it coming for a while. Too long we've ignored the crimes of so-called great men in the name of preserving a culture. When we celebrate rapists and pedophiles, it makes me question what kind of culture we're preserving.

d.hancock: "It's obvious. The Patron Saint changed tactics and is going after the real criminals."

28

The Other Shoe

(or Roller Skate) Drops

Night still had a hold over the city because morning hadn't quite made up its mind. Yawning, **Tobias** pulled his car along the throng of emergency vehicles. He wasn't sure what the fuss was all about. A poker game had gone wrong in the back of Shaw's jewelry store—a pretty standard Shadowhaven whodunnit. He double-parked alongside a squad car, and he and his partner, Detective Burke, made their way to the crime scene.

He moved through the maze of the cars to the building's entrance, marked off by police tape. Pushing aside the yellow plastic screaming *Police Crime Scene*, he attempted to enter the store. A figure in a hazmat suit grabbed him by the shoulder. "Detective, you can't go in without a suit. We're neutralizing the acid."

"Acid?"

The figure lifted the face shield enough to speak unobstructed. "Someone rigged the sprinkler system to spray acid. Corrodes everything but plastic and some precious metals. The people showered in this stood no chance. Ate holes through the building and the water tower. We'll have to identify the victims with their driver's licenses and tooth fillings. Nothing left but sludge." He lowered his helmet and tilted his head to the side. "And poker chips."

Acid was a messy kill if someone was combining a hit and a jewel heist. The method pointed not only to a targeted murder but one having symbolic significance. The crime scene horror was the message. But what kind of a message?

Burke lowered his cell phone from his ear. "CCTV for the next few blocks is all damaged. Apart from the roof collapse, no one saw shit."

Tobias spotted movement in the alley next to the business. Someone had taken refuge in a tiny alcove. "No one or not the right one?"

In the red and blue light flashing from police cars, he made out the shape of an older man who looked like he needed a meal and a fresh pair of clothes. "I'm Detective Quinlan," Tobias called out. "You sleep here last night?"

"Maybe," the man replied with a snort.

Tobias handed him a twenty. "Care to talk?"

He pocketed the money. "Shelter is out of beds. Place down the block serves bread and soup if you ask. Sometimes I sleep here to get a good place in line."

"See anything out of the ordinary?"

The leathery-looking man shrugged. Tobias handed him another twenty. "Maintenance workers on the roof, barbecuing on the top."

Maybe the poor guy was too mentally ill to be a dependable witness, which meant Tobias was at worse than square one. "Barbecue?"

The old man pointed a crooked finger toward the roofline. "A fire under the water tower not even an hour before the roof collapse. The maintenance workers set it."

"Did you get a look at them?"

The old man held out his hand. Tobias relinquished another twenty, officially emptying his wallet. "All women. Couldn't make out their faces. They wore pylon-colored vests and hard hats."

He wasn't running to the sketch artist, but he had a start. He extended his hand, holding his contact card. "Thanks for your help, sir. Catch a bus to the Restful Inn on the highway. Give them this card. They're not the Four Seasons, but mention Tobias Quinlan, and they'll get you squared."

Tobias turned to head back toward Burke to report his findings.

The old man added, "One of them wore roller skates. Walked up and down the fire escape and moved across the roof on roller skates. I thought I was hallucinating at first."

Roller skates. Marisol had mentioned Adhara's girlfriend was a roller-skating stripper. The mess of a crime scene possibly bore Adhara's mark, especially if all the perps were women. A sour taste rose in Tobias's mouth, compelling him to reach for a numbing sip of whiskey. The last time a homicide was this close to him, he found Marisol broken at the bottom of an elevator shaft and watched as her best friend was wheeled away in a body bag.

He returned to the car. Burke asked him if the homeless man had seen anything of interest.

"No. Nothing interesting." But he scratched the back of his neck, fighting a nervous itch.

Tobias sent Burke on a mission to find any sales of the ingredients to make hydrofluoric acid. Whoever was responsible for the attack used the chemicals for the reaction caused by boiling the water supply in the tower. A little fire sent the boiling acid into the sprinkler system and rained terror on the unsuspecting poker players.

Tobias learned about the victims. Notably, the person who had access to the jewelry store after hours was the owners' son, Mortimer Shaw. Apart from being reduced to a mound of snot, he had a spotty record. A handful of years earlier, the man had been charged with assaulting a few girls and women by throwing acid on them. Scarred them up real bad. The DA dropped the charges when the evidence proved to be "circumstantial." A scan of the file, however, proved that conclusion was horseshit. They had witness testimonies, corresponding injuries on Mortimer, and a receipt to a hardware store.

Revenge for attacks on women and the miscarriage of Justice. The attack on Shaw's Jewelry was a message, all right. And Tobias had failed. He and the Patron Saint had failed Mortimer's victims, and if his hunch was correct, it took Marisol and her new best friend to balance the scales in the worst way possible.

Marisol had become like her brother—a murderer.

29

The Hangover

The afternoon sun streaked in from behind a gap in the blackout curtain. **Marisol** stumbled out of bed. The roof of her mouth felt like sticky cotton and a throbbing headache shouted at her for finishing the stupid champagne. She had overindulged, to say the least, and Adhara had carried her back from the train yard. In the zombie shuffle she took between her bedroom and the kitchen, she noticed the door to the main bedroom was open. The bed was made. Adhara and Wheels left much earlier.

The water and ibuprofen weren't doing it for her. She put on her presentable sweats and jogged to the nearby corner store. The place was a cave of three aisles and refrigerators humming their last life. Judging by the availability of ingredients, she'd make the most half-assed michelada—the best tall can of light beer available, canned tomato juice, hot sauce, and lime juice, unfortunately in the plastic lime from concentrate.

The cashier with resting grump face slowly entered the price of the products into the rickety register. She tapped on the counter to stave off the feeling of aliens hatching eggs out of her brain, ratcheted by every rattle of the receipt printer. The cashier raised a furry white eyebrow in her direction.

She returned a closed-mouth smile. "Keeping it old school, huh?"

He was unmoved. "Marisol?"

Past appearances at the convenience cave had been brief and uneventful. She contorted her face in surprise of his familiarity.

"I have something for you." He slid a folded piece of paper across the counter.

She squeezed her eyebrows tighter together. "How do you know it's for me?"

"The cloaked person said this goes to the dark-haired woman who walks around like she owns the place and seems like she can't keep her nose out of your business. But they included a cut-out from the newspaper for reference." The clerk held up a sticky note with a black and white image of her haphazardly cut out and glued to it. Vincent's arm was the only piece of him in the picture.

"Thank you?" The reaction was more to her hangover than her shock. Until the ibuprofen and beer kicked in, information was received on a delayed broadcast.

A bus stop enclave provided a close resting place where **Marisol** could prepare her hangover cure. She stabbed the can of tomato juice open and shook a healthy amount of hot sauce and lime juice into the jagged opening. Double-fisting the juice and the alcohol, she'd chase a sip of beer with the tomato-hot sauce-lime concoction. She stared at the folded paper, unable to bring herself to unfold it.

A cloaked person left this for her on the off chance she'd stop by the store. Who wore cloaks? She could only think of Vincent's capes. A childish inkling of hope gnawed at her. Had he returned? Yet here she was, drinking beer at a bus stop.

She flipped the paper open. The message was a phone number with a CALL ME written in block letters. Nothing from the handwriting seemed familiar.

She finished the last of the beer and dialed the number on her phone.

A nasally bass answered, one she swore she'd heard before. Not Vincent, though. That crumb of hope was ground to powder. "Where are you?" the voice asked.

"Bus stop, near where you left the note."

"Take the bus east. Meet me at the Cocina Familia restaurant. Come alone."

Marisol stepped off the bus and walked the few blocks to the restaurant. Inside, it was dead, as the strays from lunch service lingered. A cloaked figure with its hood shadowing its face sat at a table. She helped herself to the chair, sitting across from the figure.

A lace-gloved hand drew the hood away. The person shook out her loose, platinum blond waves. The cloaked figured had been Mijo Ray. "Good job following my jelly bean trail, Miss Casimir's sister."

"An Eastside chain? What drags us to the Disneyland of restaurants?"

"I'm wearing my worst wig, hoping no one recognizes me." She patted the top of her head with the heel of her hand and tossed a loose curl hanging over her shoulder. "Listen up. A couple nights ago, Wheels and her new girlfriend, the fangirl with the claws, walked in near closing. Wheels hadn't shown up for her shift, so Tiny was pissed. Honestly, the man was looking for an excuse to fire her ass, but it was the whole her breaking up with the Pink Curtain rather than the other way around that set him off.

"So he yells at Wheels, claiming she owes him a no-show fee. Then your friend with the manicure from Hell seized Tiny by the throat and lifted him off the ground. A woman no bigger than you lifted Tiny a foot off the ground by his neck. I thought after scaring him, she'd let him go, but she squeezed his throat tighter. Tiny was gasping for air...the way his feet kicked... I ducked behind the bar because I wasn't going to find out something myself." Mijo Ray stared ahead, her gaze focusing on nothing. "I heard his bones crunch, the bones in his neck. She killed him, and we all stood around and watched. And now his body is gone. G-O-N-E. Incinerated, at the bottom of a river, garbage dump, covered in quicklime, gone!"

Marisol's mouth tightened as she fought the pain of more loss. Tiny wasn't perfect by any means, but he had fought alongside them. "Call the police. I don't know what you want me to do."

"You know we can't call the police. We run our own community. Last year, when all hell broke loose, you and the masked guy stopped it."

Grief constricted her throat, leaving room only for a rasp. "Haven't seen the masked guy in the last couple of months." A tear escaped from between her eyelashes.

Mijo Ray gave her a long, hard look. "I worried as much." She added a sigh. "Well, I'm hitting the road, and I'm not looking back. I suggest you do the same."

"I'm not scared of Adhara." A lie. But the super-powered woman had become an ingrained belief. It challenged her understanding of one plus one if she dared to admit the fear.

"Your answer does have a way of telling on yourself. You are scared of her." Mijo Ray flitted a hand in the air. Her classic blood red manicure poked from behind the lace. "She fucked with the Shadows, and they're going to come after her. If I were you, I wouldn't want to be caught in the crossfire."

With all she had lost to the city—Caz, Annie, Vincent—what else did she have left? She'd been through a version of avoiding the worst when Caz ran with the Shadows. An eerie warmth washed over her, the kind of euphoria one had when letting go the last shred of everything. Nothing mattered. "If it's between her and the Shadows, I'd be worried for the Shadows."

Mijo Ray sucked on her teeth. "Mark my words, the weird shit from last year? She's the very same thing, and as I recall, it wasn't enough to take out a few gangsters here or there. Weird shit always wants the whole city on its knees." She stood and flicked her cloak about her neck and shoulders. "Check's on you."

Mijo Ray left.

Marisol drank a shot of tequila and chased it with a beer. How many of these would numb her heart? It would be easier to not care, because she had no idea what to do.

30

Toxic Beauty

Two Hundred Sixty Years After the Curse

Laughter echoes from my lab. I enter in a rush to find Adhara and my assistant, Françoise, shoulder to shoulder. Adhara holds a glass of a clear solution over a small fire, creating a reaction. She sets it on the counter.

"Watch me make gold," Adhara says.

Françoise leans in, watching with the rapt awe of a child. The solution cools into a magical glitter, which swirls like flecks of gold in water. The strawberry blond woman applauds. "I didn't believe you!"

"You should always believe me."

Jealousy snakes its way into me, creeping along the hairs at the back of my neck. Adhara has invaded my French life and turned it into a competition. Who is the better revolutionary, the better mind, and head of the house? If I can't prove myself, I can at least take her down a peg.

I scoff. "It's not really gold."

"Correct. It's crystallized lead," Adhara replies, unmoved.

No doubt a dent in my supplies, and a toxic one at that. "Hm."

Françoise interjects, breathless in her wonder. "Oh, but monsieur, earlier she made a violet cloud. She's a brilliant magician like you!"

"Are you finished cleaning the flasks?"

Her bright expression drops, the unfortunate victim of my surliness to extricate her from Adhara's thrall. "No, monsieur. Your wife came in with apples, requesting to experiment with amygdalin and—"

"My wife!" Adhara and I exchange glances. Whatever backstory she told Françoise was built entirely on lies. "My wife's playful nature should not be an excuse to ignore your duties."

"You're too serious, Rubio. Françoise told me your housekeeper, Toinon, hired her. Before she saw you, she thought V. V. was some old recluse, not someone so young and handsome."

Françoise blushes, and the way Adhara runs her tongue along her incisor, I know the poor woman's embarrassment is all part of Adhara's game.

"Have you ever been to a party, Françoise? Costumes, flowing champagne, and dancing?" Adhara's smile gleams with mischief.

The young woman shakes her head.

"We should hold a party, Rubio."

"Party? A bit gauche in this day and age."

"Yes, but you live far enough from the guillotines, tucked in your forest. And I think people want a break from all the blood and terror. They want to set eyes on the mysterious and handsome V. V." Adhara reaches into the pockets of her breeches and draws out a parchment. "I even have a suggested guest list."

I seize the note. "What's the catch?"

"No catch. Just people you might like to sort for your nighttime hobby—the shadow within. And Françoise must come, too."

Françoise, stuck in a submissive curtsey, lifts her head, revealing her wide-open, incredulous eyes. Adhara is weaving a web, but for whom? To win the admiration of a young French woman or to prove something to me, especially regarding my alter ego?

The nod came slowly as I resist the other more sensible option. Commanded by the admiring spark in Françoise's eyes, I say, "Very well."

"Great! There will be dancing! Rubio always likes dancing." Adhara shakes the scared woman out of her stupor and pulls her into a dance. Françoise laughs, but stifles it when my icy gaze catches her enjoying a twirl.

And Adhara's web tightens around me.

31

Blood and Flame

With tequila fresh in her bloodstream, **Marisol** didn't want to go home. She shuffled into a drugstore and wandered the aisles, lying to herself that she was browsing, but the store sold the strong stuff behind the cash register, next to the few rows of cigarettes left for the city's last smokers.

The neon chemicals of the cleaning aisle blended into the rainbow assortment of artificially scented candles. Those candles butted right against rows of the prayer candles her abuelita kept a healthy supply of. The skinny glass container with a cheap painting of Saint Michael caught her attention. The angel had his sword and shield, but the blond curls and rosy cheeks found in Renaissance paintings. If her eyes went out of focus, she could convince herself the image was Vincent.

She took the candle down from the shelf, running her thumb over Michael's face. A bottle of vodka seemed almost heretical compared to the prayer candle. She bought a lighter and a bottle of red wine—

cheap so it'd taste similar to the communion wine she drank growing up.

She had no plan as she put one foot after the other, occasionally taking long pulls from her bottle of wine. Enough chugs acted as a novocaine to her memories. Her gait became wobbly, but the direction of her journey grew more evident. Along the Southside, remnants of Shadowhaven's past lingered. Geometric track housing with abandoned yards lined the broken sidewalks. In the abandoned middle-class wilderness, a rusty cross poking above the rise of rooftops called to her.

The cross led her to a closed school, Saint Theresa's. Protected by a chain-link fence as rusty as the cross, the school resembled a blacked-out grid. She pried the particle board off a window and snuck inside.

Graffiti decorated the walls, and papers. Faded assignments or posters were strewn about the hallway along with leaves. The flashlight from her cell phone lit the murkiness inside. Her wandering stopped when she reached the chapel, which seemed to have avoided the decay of the rest of the building. Few leaves and papers rolled into the former sacred place.

Meager outside light beamed through the stain-glassed window. Marisol set her candle on the altar and lit it. Wasn't this how she found him last time? A church and lit candles?

The low flame danced in a mild draft. Wine warmed her cheeks, and she steadied herself kneeling at the altar. In her mind, she called to him. *Find me.* Her vision blurred as she leaned too hard against the rotting wood backing of the altar. The thing split, and she slipped, taking the bottle of wine with her. Glass shattered around her. A small sliver dug into her palm.

Blood dripped down her arm and dried sticky between her fingers. It didn't hurt. At least, not more than she already was hurting. She snickered at the wound. *Brought to you by another bad idea.*

The draft grew into a wild wind, and the candle flame bobbed wildly. The chapel's doors thundered shut behind her. Startled, she held her hand to her heart, which pummeled rapidly against her ribs. Ghosts haunted this place.

But only one ghost she desired to see.

32

A Lovely Convergence

Half of Paris's high society comes to my Calais *maison*, pretending 1789 never occurred. Meeting the mysterious V. V. astounds them. They claim I resemble the angel who goes to the quarantined parts of the city to heal the diseased. The threat of death brings out their decadence. Drinking and dancing, their lives burn like a meteor in the atmosphere, growing brighter and brighter until nothing is left.

We follow suit in our opulence. Adhara wears an elaborate, cornflower blue dress with white lace trim and fine golden stitching. Her mask is similarly adorned, but from behind the eye holes, her overcast irises storm with the power coursing through them. Her rich brown skin has been powdered and painted in pinks and reds. She has styled her honey-blond hair into shining ringlets and pinned them in elaborate coils.

I match her with my waistcoat, breeches, and mask, but I do not match her energy. She and Françoise dance in dizzying, rotating patterns, hypnotizing others into their chaotic movement. Françoise is dressed more simply, gray brocade dress and a black domino mask. Together, the women are entropy. Adhara jumps into the men's circle to swing Françoise by her waist, both laughing. Yet when I blink, Françoise has dark hair, cascading in waves to the middle of her back, and her dress shines silver in the low candlelight.

I know this face. And I know she is from my future. She is the voice of the star, the one who embraced me in a pew in Spain. But no, I know more, as the barrier of space and time fades. Effect becomes cause, and I know she is my spirit, my guide. She is Marisol.

But it can't be. I haven't met her yet. I blink the lie away. No, the woman is Françoise with pinned-up, Venetian-blond hair and fair skin powdered and rouged to seem all the more delicious. And I want a taste. I slip in among the dancers, waiting for my moment to pounce. A few bows, circles, and claps, and I snatch Françoise away from Adhara.

Her sparkling smile ceases, as her lips part in awe. Breathing deeply, her breasts rise above her teasing lace trim. Desire commands her every pulse. I close my eyes and hold Marisol. Adhara grabs her again. And in front of the whole party, we break the rules of the dance and fight over our partner.

People leave the dance floor and recede into the shadows—to watch us clapping, kicking, and spinning. My guests are a Greek chorus behind grotesque masks, which mean the gods await to dole out their judgment.

We find in our push and pull a new dance and a new pattern. We work together as a trio, burning brighter than any fire in the sky. Out of breath, Françoise breaks the bond and helps herself to a glass of champagne. She raises the wide cup by the stem. Adhara grips her hand, crushing the glass between her and Françoise's palm. Blood oozes from their wounds.

But the injury only draws Françoise further into Adhara's spell. I bet the French woman wonders why her hand still bleeds but Adhara's doesn't. Why the powerful woman's eyes shine in the dark. Why lightning follows them on a night of the hunt such as this one.

Adhara kisses the slight gash, sucking the glass out of Françoise's hand. "No champagne, mon cherie. Do not numb your sensations. I want you to feel everything," Adhara croons into Françoise's ear.

Our dancing continues into the long hallway, away from the crowd and the candlelight. The movement becomes something else entirely when I pin the young woman against the wall and kiss her, my tongue breaching her mouth as she gasps. Her mouth tastes metallic, the blood of her and Adhara. Her body melts in my hands, becoming pliable and needy. I have beaten Adhara in this game, achieving the first kiss. The fact stokes my lust.

Françoise pushes me away. "Monsieur V! You wife!" Her blue eyes are wide, reflecting the supernatural glow of mine.

Adhara closes in on the other side of the woman. "It's okay, *mademoiselle*. Let the passion lead you."

Adhara teases her fingers along the curve of the French woman's cleavage. She loosens the laces of Françoise's gown and unties her stays. "Let Monsieur show you what a gifted mouth he has."

I bow my head down. Françoise's heart beats rapidly in my palm, and I lift her breast to my mouth. I flicker my tongue against her chemise-covered nipple, which furls into a succulent point under the wet linen.

Adhara's gray eyes, too, glow in the dark. "Don't close your eyes. I want you to look in mine and tell me how he makes you feel."

"Dizzy, like my heart is going to beat out of my chest," Françoise says, panting.

I suck the hardened nipple and take more of the thin fabric and her breast into my mouth.

"Hot," Françoise moans.

"Where?" Adhara asks.

"My skin."

"Just your skin?" She trails her finger along the assistant's neck and exposed shoulder.

I temper my ravenous laving into teasing. The pointed tip of my tongue brushes against her sensitive nipple.

Françoise swallows and replies, "Between my legs."

And further into sin, I draw her. I close my eyes and bite down on her furled point. She cries out, but Adhara muffles her scream with a kiss.

Françoise's voice changes. Instead of sweet, it becomes raspy and alto. *"I knew I'd find you."*

My eyes open. She has become Marisol once more. "*How?*"

"*I felt you once before. Communion brings you home to me.*"

I am only speaking to her in my mind. "*I'm in the middle of the last time Adhara and I were happy together. My home in Calais. Where are you?*"

"*I'm in an abandoned chapel in the southeast side of the city. You've been gone for two months. Sometimes I feel like the grief will kill me.*"

I draw her into my chest. "*But I'm here now.*"

"*Can you come home with me?*" Marisol asks.

Surrounded in the liminal abyss, I lift my hand to feel Marisol's face. Instead, I feel Françoise's face. I graze her lips with my fingertips. A pink glow emits from my hands and dusts along her full mouth.

Marisol covers my hand with hers, and a halo of magenta light outlines her fingers. "*I feel you. It's like the gentle touch when you wake me, but when I open my eyes, you're not here.*"

Marisol's mouth swells from Adhara's greedy kisses. I can do better. With a gentle tug at her chin, I direct her mouth to meet mine. I slide my tongue past her lips and spell prayers on hers. "*Do you feel that?*" I ask.

Marisol moans, her voice melds with Françoise's. "*I do.*"

"*Then become one with my memory.*"

She breaks away from the kiss. "*Can I touch you the way I want to, or am I a passenger in this woman's vessel?*"

"*I don't know.*"

She holds my painted face in her hands and caresses my lips with her thumb, surely smearing my lipstick along my jawline. "*I left my mark on you,*" she says.

I gently suck along her neck. She catches her breath, and another mouth meets hers.

"*She feels different than you. Like light electrocution.*"

"*I think you're feeling the barrier between us. She is different because you know how I feel from your memory. For you, she's nothing but energy. Do you like the way it feels?*" I move my mouth along her bare shoulder.

"*Yes.*"

"*Then feel everything, my spirit.*"

We stumble the final stretch of the hallway to the bedroom, pulling and loosening. The door closes, and I rip the rest of the gown from Marisol's body, leaving her only in the wet chemise. I toss my waistcoat and cravat aside.

In the real memory, Françoise shivers, watching us undress. I light my fireplace to comfort her. Merging with Marisol, however, the young woman's tremulous hesitation becomes Marisol's unwavering confidence in the wicked aura of the firelight. She begins to slide her mask off.

I tighten the ribbons at the back of her head. "No, leave it on."

She smiles and kisses me, mask to mask, a symbol of souls meeting and understanding. Her love cocoons me in her steadfast devotion and acceptance.

I turn her to face away from me to present her to Adhara. My cock, straining in my breeches, nestles in the notch under her ass. "I can feel how warm and ready you are. Do you feel me?" I thrust my hips once, practically fucking her through the chemise's fabric.

"Oui, monsieur," Marisol answers in a sing-song.

"She didn't answer me."

"I sense traces of her memory—what she was thinking, what she felt. Françoise was scared of you. She didn't know what you were but knew you were different. She never understood her desire for you both."

I stroke down the back of her arms, ending at her fingers, where I entwine mine with hers. As if she were my doll, I direct her arms to a T. "Feel how warm she is."

Adhara slowly steps out from behind her changing screen, wearing only her mask and white stockings tied coquettishly with blue ribbon above her knees. Her face is a secret, but her naked body, strong with compact muscles, holds no secrets, exposed in the orange light.

I kick Marisol's legs apart. Adhara approaches until her dark nipples bristle against the fabric of the chemise. Adhara reaches under Marisol's hem of the billowy linen. "Right here?"

"Oh fuck!" Marisol cries out. She writhes, finding me a wall forbidding the escape from the sensation. I keep her arms firmly in place as Adhara glides her touch higher.

"*What is it?*" I ask.

"*It's like static pings.*"

"There you are," Adhara whispers as she makes delicious wet noises—fingers delving into my beloved's dripping cunt.

Marisol rocks into me with the same rhythm as Adhara's hand moves.

"Feel everything, mon cherie," I breathe into her neck. "I like watching what she does to you."

Marisol's squirming ceases, and Adhara raises her working hand. Firelight glistens off her fingers, which she smears over Marisol's lips. "How do you taste?"

She hums, rubbing her lips together. "Like iron and salt and warm apples."

"Sweet and savory, my favorite flavors. Shall I have a taste?" Adhara kneels, burying her face at the apex of Marisol's thighs.

Marisol's forehead creases as she twists. I guide her arms behind my neck. Pulling down her chemise's ruffle, I free her breasts and take in the sight of her wine-colored nipples. I knead her generous curves and pinch the peaks. She arches her body, canting her hips closer to Adhara's mouth.

Marisol's eyelids flutter and her mouth parts as pleasure takes hold. It's glorious watching the shifts in her ecstasy. I've missed her subtle changes as we've made love, but now I am blessed to enjoy her at a different angle. It's like falling in love all over again. Sharing her bears witness to the beautiful bliss we create. It's not a dream. It's magic. And it's real.

Her legs give out, and Adhara hooks them over her shoulders. Between Adhara and me, Marisol is stretched out like a willing sacrifice. An ode to her plays in the slippery sounds of Adhara's hunger and Marisol's wet satisfaction.

"I want to watch you like you watch me," Marisol says.

Adhara stands, her super-healing erasing the divots in her knees. She lifts the chemise off Marisol's body and gives Marisol's ass a playful squeeze. Both dive onto the bed, giggling. The laughter melts into sweet hums as they kiss and smile.

Marisol is an enchantress. How else can I explain the way she makes memories better? Smiles are wider, orgasmic moans louder. What else does she have in store for me? *"How may I please you?"*

"Show me how you make her come."

"She hated me at this point. The rest of the night, I made love to Françoise."

"Are you telling me you can't?"

She dares me to prove my mettle and warn me of the decadent punishment she has in store if I fail. The memory continues to change as my arousal bleeds through my pants. Past me has more control. Yet reliving it, harder and tighter, I already seek release.

I crawl over Adhara, and her lips form a line of concern, as if she knows I am straying from memory's script. My knuckle brushes against a shining, coiled tendril, which has escaped her updo. "More than 200 years, and we were always chasing the night we touched the stars." My ancient lover nods. I hadn't perceived her as this vulnerable since the morning after we'd drank from the Fountain. Despite Adhara's ferocity since, she continually sought love and affection —just not from me. This hopeful part of her still believes in Justice and breaking the curse.

Marisol, to my right, runs her fingers through my hair, freeing most from the tie at the back. Her fingers linger at my ends, presumably assessing the length of the longer hair of my past self.

Her pupils eclipse her kind brown eyes, turning her into a dark and powerful creature. "*I'm your star. And I'm telling you to make her come.*" She props her head on her hand, angling to have a better view of Adhara's face. "*I need to know vengeance didn't numb her.*"

Taking her inside this memory is more than indulgence and seduction. Marisol's touches seem somber as she caresses Adhara's jawline. She lowers herself to meet Adhara's lips and kisses her gently, almost solemnly.

It dawns on me how Marisol must witness Adhara as guileless and openhearted, because Marisol needs to know after all her grief, she herself is still capable of these feelings. Marisol tips her chin in my direction, inviting me to feast.

I teethe Adhara's nipples and nibble along the undersides of her small breasts. She claws at the back of my head, holding my body to hers. "Rubio. My Rubio."

With my tongue and teeth, I lavish her abdomen with voracious attention, licking into her shallow belly button. Adhara hooks her stockinged legs over my shoulders and raises her hips toward my mouth. We'd been equals as super-humans, but as her body arches through the tantalizing massage of her labia, I'd finally found the way to best her.

"A sight to behold." Marisol tenderly sucks Adhara's breast, taking the immortal woman's areola into her mouth before dragging her lower lip along the tight nipple.

Adhara gasps. Marisol bites on her lower lip and hums, relishing in the desperate sounds she conjures out of Adhara. Adhara and I are the super-powered immortals, but it is Marisol who is in control. Sharing how easily she weakens another like me compounds my bliss. I home in on Adhara's clit, teasing the swollen bud with my mouth and burying my masked nose into her soft curls. I lap fervently, tasting her slick juices.

Marisol meets Adhara's surprised mouth with more kisses, muffling Adhara's erotic coos. "Is he good?" Marisol asks.

"Yes," Adhara hisses.

"Did you hear that, my saint? You're good."

Every time she calls me good, I rut into the mattress. My cock strains in my breeches, the tip caught between my stomach and the waistband. The movement threatens to throw me over the edge. Adhara glides her calves down my back. She grinds into my masked face. Her body bucks off the bed, and she seizes.

My thrusts into the mattress match her contortions. One more movement and I'll release on my stomach. A sharp yank of the hair at my nape pulls me off Adhara's pulsing quim. The pain edges my pleasure back from ascending into euphoria.

"Are you really going to lose it, humping a mattress like a dog?" Marisol seethes.

I grunt and shake my head, but I want everything, my punishment and reward.

Adhara laughs. The throaty sound cuts into me deliciously, to be insulted and mocked. My cock twitches, screaming for the friction.

"Don't you dare waste a drop. It's all for me," Marisol scolds.

The women pull me further onto the bed and shove me onto my back. Working together, they peel my breeches and stockings off, freeing me from the last shred of restraint. We kiss, sharing each other's lips and tongues. I move my arms to embrace my lovers, but they have tied me to the headboard using my stockings. The tie is tight enough to dig into my wrists. I give my bindings a super-powered yank, but they don't budge. Adhara must've tied them.

Marisol straddles over me and sinks down centimeter by centimeter until her hips meet mine. Sweet agony opens her mouth as she adjusts to me. Adhara steals a kiss from her while massaging her throat. Marisol's hips begin to pump me. As soon as she braces her hands on my thighs, she moves wildly, lengthening each pump with frenzied rocking. Adhara invades Marisol's mouth with her tongue, stroking her clit in the same wild rhythm.

"All for me," Marisol breathes.

She clenches around me. The pulsing of her channel works me in as vigorous rhythm as her riding me. So much squeezing and twisting, her climax clenches me. I inhale and tear myself from my bindings. More pumping and pulsing builds at the base of my spine. Arms freed, I hug her body still as I drive my release deep inside. A halo of pink particles surrounds us, as if breaking the barrier between space and time turn us into pure energy. I am no longer solid form but bouncing atoms—life at its most basic state.

"So weak," Marisol taunts, breathless. "I'll have to feed it back to you. Nurse you to bring you back to life." She crawls up my body and smothers my face with her cunt.

I taste her; the sweet gives way to salty and metallic. My cum, she is filling my mouth with my cum. All sensations are pronounced with her. Her loving act, disguised as degradation, grounds me. I am not a lost entity in space and time. I am hers.

She slides off my face. Adhara helps her remove the remnants of my stockings from my wrists, but Marisol kisses the burning indentations from the tight tie until they fade into nothing.

"You missed a spot." She playfully licks the corner of my mouth, cleaning the last of our mess.

One by one, we take off our masks. The effervescence of before simmers down, much like the dying embers flickering in the fireplace. Marisol lies bracketed between us super-humans. A thunderstorm has arrived. Lightning flashes in the window. The drums of thunder follow it and fade into the rain tapping against the glass.

Marisol curls closer into me, resting her ear against my chest. In the sobering free fall, Marisol murmurs, *"You helped me forget how much I'm hurting."*

I dare to pull her closer, but I cannot. Her body already meets mine. The attempt highlights the faint pink atomic prophylactic between us. I inhale the scent of her hair, but she is beginning to smell like Françoise, less like sweet, woodsy musk and more like sun-ripened strawberries. The ritual's magic, which broke us through to each other, is dwindling.

"My hand here throbs. I cut it on a wine bottle."

I bring her hand to my lips and suck on the wound, Françoise's blood but Marisol's cut. I tie my shredded stocking around her hand, finding one more good use for the silk, hoping to provide a semblance of comfort to her.

"For what it's worth, I liked sharing you, even if it was to memory ghosts," she says as her body tenses.

I sense her need for reassurance. *"I liked it, too."*

She presses her hand into my skin. *"Anything else you'd like to do?"*

"I only wish more love for you. It's what you deserve."

"Don't you deserve that love too?"

I chuckle, but my forced mirth fades as soon as it arrives. Stuck in the prison of time and space seems like my rightful place. *"More love for the both of us? A tall order, like true Justice releasing me from a curse."*

"I'd like to think it's possible." She sighs, growing sleepy or falling deeper into thought. *"It kind of feels like you're telling me to move on."*

"Maybe I am."

"Why did you leave?" Her voice cracks.

The night I entered the collider, messages of my worthlessness and how much I needed to disappear had commanded my every thought. Usually, when these thoughts attempt to take over, I can talk them down or allow a distraction to prevent it. Marisol's presence in my life had dulled the horrible ideas, but the will to destroy myself had won, despite all the sound reasons I'd had to keep going. *"I became addicted to the idea of dying."*

Her breath stutters. She is crying. *"Will we be like this until I die? Long-distance phone calls with prayer candles and holy grounds?"*

I stroke her shoulder. *"Let's hope not."*

The wind picks up outside; branches scrape the window. As suddenly as Françoise had become Marisol, she becomes Françoise once more.

Marisol has left my memory.

33

Directionless

Marisol opened her eyes. Smoke trailed from the burnt wick. The candle had been blown out. Parting from Vincent was like violently awaking from a dream. The open wound on her hand ached. The pleasure turning into unbearable pain inflamed her anger. She held the cheap drugstore candle that only superstitious fools believed possessed any power.

She spotted the crucifix hanging askew above the altar. A sneeze might knock it to the ground. Through the haze of darkness, she made out the pained expression of Jesus. Tobias had been right. Self-destruction overtook Vincent, drowning out the good he had to live for. And there was no saving him. She threw the candle at it, but it missed the ceramic martyred god, crashing in the chapel's unseen depths.

"You could've let me say goodbye," she shouted. The room's echo mocked how truly alone she was.

Then she started her walk home.

Marisol wriggled out of her T-shirt beneath her hoodie and wrapped the fabric around her injured hand. Her route wound through a few blocks of bars and clubs. Music's thunderous bass pounded into the streets. People staggered from doorways or huddled along on curbs, faces lit by their phones, which promised someone a ride home. The air hung thick with beer, fried food, and cheap perfume.

She passed a metal trash can overflowing with fast food wrappers. Something on top pulled her into a stop. Someone had ditched today's newspaper to the trash, face-up to the sky. The headline read *TOUGH DAY AT DURANT TRIAL.* Beneath it, a full-color courtroom sketch showed a girl on the stand, her face hidden by her hands.

Marisol pulled the newspaper free and unfolded it. The girl was Juniper Starling, the teenager she had rescued from Durant's compound. Juniper had testified against him and recounted her abuse only to be treated like the criminal instead. Her mouth was drawn in permanent anguish. Her roughly penciled hands shielded her from the judgmental stares of those who were too easily swayed by the same ole claims. Juniper was a disruption, a nuisance, a whore. The sketch echoed the museum paintings, shadows as dark as the exploited child's eyes, reaching through to Marisol more than a hundred years later. Juniper and the girl's pain said more about the ones who watched and did nothing. And Marisol was one of the watchers.

The "right way to Justice" Tobias preached had turned victims' dignity into collateral. Their peace was sacrificed to preserve the charade of judicial fairness.

The only way to honor the survivors was to destroy the system that had made their suffering possible.

Adhara had been right. When Marisol's pain finally hardened into rage, she'd have a taste of the power taken from her, from them, from all the girls. She'd watch no more. Marisol would be the claw, and anything in her path, the canvas.

She tore the paper into shreds until a breeze swept them into the night.

Violent motion across the street snatched her attention. A man and a woman argued in the half-lit parking lot. He held something above his head while she reached for it, frantic.

"Give me my phone!"

"What else you hiding, you disgusting skank?" he yelled, shoving her so hard she hit the ground.

Marisol had seen enough. She didn't have her mask, so she improvised. The bloodied T-shirt became a makeshift gaiter covering her mouth and nose. She pulled her hood up, cracked her knuckles, and sprinted.

Marisol tackled with full force, slamming both her and the man onto the pavement. The phone flew out of his hand, but the tackle didn't satisfy her wrath. Who else had he hurt? Who else *would* he hurt? She held back her first punch, a test to see how well her anger consumed her. The second landed on the bridge of his nose. The crack of it shot through her like lightning, splitting her own knuckle open.

The man screamed, but Marisol didn't stop, because he had to pay. Each vicious strike blurred into the next until her hands went numb and the sound beneath them became wet. When she finally rolled off him, she was out of breath. Her hands were slick with blood. Hers? His? She couldn't tell. *So much for bloodborne pathogen training.* She punctuated her thought with a bitter laugh.

The phone lay near the man's open hand. Marisol picked it up and offered it to the woman cowering between cars. Her shadow loomed over the woman. All that mess and the rescued wasn't going to take it? Marisol tossed the phone toward her.

"Ayo! It's the Patron Saint!" someone shouted. A group of drunks had gathered. Their phones aimed to record.

Marisol bolted. She ditched the T-shirt a few blocks later, the hoodie a few blocks after that. In her sports bra and loose pants, she slipped into a crowd of scantily clad women leaving the club. Only her hands betrayed her, raw, stinging, and red. She shoved them into her pockets, the fabric bristling her skin. The pain was the price of saving someone.

Marisol went to bed with open wounds. By morning, her sheets looked like a crime scene. She stripped the bed and rinsed the stains in the kitchen sink. The water ran red, then pink, the same shades Caz's hands turned after a night of enforcing.

"I've found soaking in salt water works best."

Marisol jumped. Adhara stood behind her, gray eyes cool, expression unreadable.

"Thanks for the tip." Marisol shut off the tap but didn't turn around.

"Your hands." Adhara stepped closer, taking Marisol's battered ones. "What happened?"

"Cut them on glass," Marisol said, but her resolve gave up. A cry broke free from her resisting it. "And I beat the shit out of someone."

Adhara didn't flinch. She guided Marisol to the couch, fetched the first aid kit, and knelt beside her. "Did he deserve it?"

"Maybe." He'd shoved the woman and stolen her phone, but after a night's rest and the ache in her hands, her righteousness had cooled to doubt.

Adhara cleaned the wounds with gentle precision. "They use our morality against us," she stated calmly. "They teach peace so we'll accept the pain of our oppression. And when we return even a fraction of it, they sermonize about forgiveness just to preserve their power."

She taped the gauze, wrapped each finger, and tied off the bandage.

"What if I'm like my brother?" The question came out as a whimper, as her worst fear was given voice.

Adhara brushed a lock of hair behind Marisol's ear and cupped her cheek. Her thumb smoothed a tear away. "You were forged in the same fire," she said, "but he killed to uphold fear. You fight to end it like a soldier of God, purging the world of its wickedness. You're not him."

"What if I make a mistake?"

"There are no mistakes when the goal is Justice."

In the warmth of Adhara's care and understanding, the emptiness that had consumed Marisol seemed to fall away. Adhara was everything—nurturer, lover, friend. Marisol leaned her cheek into the ancient woman's hand, inviting more of her assuring caresses. Adhara's touch wasn't the electric tingles of last night. It was flesh and heat, shifting the memory of Adhara's mouth and fingers from an abstract to something alive.

"You've missed a lot of fun the last couple nights," Adhara crooned.

Marisol closed her eyes and pressed her lips to Adhara's palm. "I'm ready for more."

Something stirred at the doorway. Wheels stood there, silent. Her gaze flicked between the two women before she turned and disappeared into the bedroom. The door slammed behind her.

Adhara sighed and gathered the scraps of gauze. "I should talk to her."

Marisol nodded. Three didn't seem like a sacred number when it only reminded her that she was alone.

The couple had left the apartment. **Marisol** never saw them leave. Without Adhara joining her for a hunt, she left to stalk the night alone.

34

Catching Strays

Neighbors had reported screaming and the sound of a struggle, a prelude to Shadowhaven's newest crime scene. Boyfriend stabbed his girlfriend and then slit his own throat. Their blood pooled into a wet stain on the apartment below's ceiling.

Tobias took notes while scanning the one-bedroom apartment. An outline of the bodies laid on the small patch of linoleum flooring in the tiny kitchen. The murder weapon of choice was a kitchen knife. He spotted the knife block and wrote it down. A dining chair had been upturned in the struggle. Judging by the state of the place, the boyfriend had probably chased her.

In contrast to the chaos, the walls of the small apartment were full of photos of them—hugging, kissing, smiling, doing what happy lovers did. Except it wasn't Tobias's first rodeo with an apparent happy couple ending up a forensic marker.

Detective Burke walked gingerly through the police tape at the apartment's entrance. He stood with his hands on his hips, hiking the vent of his blazer up, which revealed his piss-poor job of tucking in his striped dress shirt.

"When you stand like that, you got something to say." Tobias made note of the sign of struggle.

"Talked to the nice lady next door. They were planning to get married as soon as he quit his catering job. She said she had just seen them in the hallway. They seemed perfectly happy until a few minutes later, screams and—" Burke mimed his thumb going across his throat.

"I've heard that one before."

Burke squatted down to be nearer to the level of the bodies' outlines. "I wonder what made the sorry motherfucker snap."

"But they're not called whydunnits." Tobias murmured as he wrote down that the perp's work clothes were hung up on the closet door, a crisp, white shirt and clip-on bow tie looped through the collar.

He carefully stepped through the bedroom. Nothing else seemed amiss. He ducked his head inside the bathroom right off the bedroom. Nothing again. Except...a brand-new prescription box. Intriguing. Was this the motive? Sudden murderous impulses brought upon by pharmaceuticals?

He wiggled his hands into a pair of latex gloves, and he picked up the box to read. It was a cream for a rash. Freaking athlete's foot. The killer had a prescription for athlete's foot! None of the side effects warned improper use led to becoming stab-happy with the nearest knife. He set the cream down. At least the killer died itchy.

Tobias recalled a case reaching a mistrial on an account of a half-eaten sandwich not submitted into evidence. Leaving no stone unturned, he put the prescription in an evidence baggie, as if jock itch was going to take the stand.

Burke plopped a newspaper on **Tobias's** desk, interrupting Tobias's finishing his report on the killer caterer. The headline read: CITY MOURNS CORN STARCH MAGNATE.

"I wasn't the type to make gravy." Tobias shrugged and continued typing.

"It's spooky shit, Quinlan."

Tobias read the names of the deceased. *Hogarth Clement*. The name rang with a distinct familiarity—strange, considering he never bought a single box of corn starch. But something itched about it. Maybe he's contracted the caterer's athlete's foot? He hit *Save As* on the report and scanned the names of all the recent files he'd worked on.

His breath stopped. His cursor floated over *vvpartylist.xl* He clicked it open. The list contained the names of the people who attended Vincent's collider party. The names which had to be cross-checked with attendees of Grant Durant's soirees. With the way the trial was going, the Feds probably had done jack and shit with the info.

He scrolled to the name *Hogarth Clement*.

His eye twitched as he moved to another predictable spot on the list: *Skipper Ecklund.* The recently passed rich attending Vincent's shindig had to be a coincidence. The data presented hadn't reached the level of spooky shit. At least, not yet. Shot in the dark, he entered the caterer's name, *Kyle Roberts.* He had a match, notable, but not enough to tie red yarn between thumbtacks yet. He wasn't the only Kyle Roberts at the ball. Kyle K. Roberts, a tech bro who made a crappy, earlier version of an app and sold it to the better company had been in attendance. Kyle J. Roberts was the caterer, but the points weren't connecting just yet. He tapped the arrow to a different spot in the list: *Roark Weller.*

He got on the phone line with Records. "Hi Bev, could you send up the Ecklund file?" Adjusting in his seat, he fidgeted his wallet from his back pocket, counting the bills. "And the Weller one?"

Burke burst with laughter. Tobias hung up the phone. He held the bills up between his fingers. "You win, asshole. But while I'm looking at files, I want you to make a couple of phone calls. One, get a hold of Kyle K. Roberts's people. For his safety, tell him to stay in one of his vacation homes—*alone.* Next, confirm what catering company our murderer worked for. I have a hunch he worked the Varian ball a few months ago."

"More spooky shit?"

"You bet."

Tobias held the cap of the highlighter between his teeth as he read through the Weller and Ecklund files. He struck a yellow line through suspicious similarities between the police's records and Vincent's information gathering. Both had attended the last Varian ball, cellular data and airport logs pointed to partying with Grant Durant, and their autopsies noted the bodies showed signs of a fungal rash. Thank God he baggied everything at the Kyle Roberts scene. When he received a text from Burke confirming that yes, their killer caterer had worked the Varian ball, the similarities among the cases had to be more than mere coincidences.

Tobias wracked his brain, thinking of anything suspicious he noticed at the ball. His mind kept focusing on a few notable items—Marisol's bare hip and the nude painting of Vincent. The knot of his necktie echoed the secure bow tie at his throat that night. Everything else passed as a blur. Fuck, why had his weaknesses distracted him?

He focused on what he could control. He'd get on the phone with the Coast Guard and ask them to send over anything about the drowned Clements. But first, he had to race to the medical examiner before she sewed the caterer up and shoved the unlucky guy into a fridge.

A surprise to no one, the path to the morgue was creepy. Built to be indestructible and full of asbestos, sallow brick walls lined the chartreuse-tinted concrete floors. The sickly ambience of the humming fluorescent lights matched the chemical smell of formaldehyde and dead bodies.

In this cave, Dr. Bracken was in the middle of circular sawing off the caterer's cranium. **Tobias** held his hands over his ears as the shrill whir of saw teeth met skull.

Dr. Bracken shut the saw off and set it aside. "Hello, Detective Quinlan. What can I help with today?"

One look at the cranium turned bowl and the uncovered squiggly brain, Tobias noted he wasn't eating microwave ramen soon. "Any information you can tell me about our dearly departed?"

She plucked the brain from the body and set it on a scale with a meaty plop. "The brain weighs more than average. You know who else had that?"

Tobias shook his head.

"Skipper Ecklund and Roark Weller."

"With all the stone cold ones you deal with, I'm surprised you remember."

"I'll show you why I remember." She clacked the end of some tweezers together and plunged the narrow tools through the brain curlicues. Slowly, she pulled out a white film with flimsy follicles, which looked like a jellyfish.

"What on God's green earth?"

"Fungus. Might explain the sudden behavior change."

He scratched the back of his neck. "How did it get in there?"

"Ingested. Probably something they ate or drank. I found growths like these all the way in the small intestine. The spindly looking things, however, brain only."

His itch intensified. What had he eaten or drank during Varian's ball? "Other than a change in behavior, would there be any symptoms?"

"Judging by their medical records, all presented a fungal skin rash and a low-grade fever. Hotter conditions cause rapid growth."

The information released a slight clench in his butt cheeks. He had no rash or fever. One last muscle held onto a worry. "Would that thing grow in someone, uh, asymptomatically?"

"The fungus needs the body temperature to rise to spread in the body. If a human is presenting healthy, chances are, they haven't contracted it."

He breathed a sigh of relief. He wasn't infected. "Thank you, doc."

The puzzle pieces were coming together, but he wasn't sure of what picture they were forming.

Tobias plopped in front of his desk. The fungus connected everything, and not because it had weird jellyfish tendrils. Something strange had happened at the Varian ball, and he was going to prove it.

"I wouldn't get comfortable if I were you." Burke dropped his yellow notepad across Tobias's keyboard. "Called the caterer. I mentioned the Varian ball, and it's as if I was his therapist. He suspected our throat-slicer was taking alcohol from him and wondered if I could help him with posthumous charges. When I asked about other strange things, he ranted about a new insubordinate employee who disappeared before finishing the shift. And he sent me the hiring file." Burke handed him the printed paper. "One look at the license, and it's obviously fake."

The name on the license was Jane Doe, but the picture Tobias recognized immediately—Adhara.

With the dead bodies piling up, especially those of Varian-ball attendees, he needed to see one person: Marisol.

35

FEMME FATALE

Tonight, she hunted, but not for her prey. Dressed as the **Silver Spirit**, she had become another of the city's lost souls with her hood up and shoulders hunched forward.

In this state, Marisol bought another prayer candle from the drugstore and walked, combing the streets for a sacred sign. She roamed, but found direction when the Shadowhaven City Cemetery and its rolling knolls of twisted gravestones called to her.

She took cover in the recessed entrance of a mausoleum. Lighting the candle, she closed her eyes and waited.

And nothing.

No gusts of wind or sweeping magic. Closing her eyes meant she only saw the inside of her eyelids. The sacred power of the mausoleum called to her the way the church did and the way the chapel had. And she had communion of air and fire. What didn't complete the spell? Why couldn't she find him?

He had told to her to move on and that she deserved love. And now she had to prepare herself to let go.

She took a deep breath and her phone buzzed. *Tobias.* Flicking the notification away, she returned to wearing a hole in space and time.

Another buzz.

What the fuck did he want?

I'm home. Come see me. It's urgent.

He emphasized the importance of the message.

Please.

Fine. He needed to see her? She sent a *k*.

If a Communion of bodies brought her to him during his time, maybe she could do the same in hers. She was going to play.

Tobias sat in the dark, looking at the *k* she sent. The questions from earlier became shouts. Were there limits to forgiveness?

Is Marisol a murderer?

A shadow moved on the fire escape. He opened the window and saw her, mask and all.

"You're wearing more clothes than the last time we met this way," she said.

He pulled himself out onto the escape. "We don't have to meet this way. I'd let you in the front."

She circled around him, slowly and methodically. "Come now, Quinlan. I thought you always wanted me to enter your back door." Her touch lingered along the back seam of his jeans, teasing at his hidden center. There it arrived, the twitch, the wickedness he wanted to lose himself to.

"As much as I'll acknowledge I walked into that one, my needing to see you is all business and no pleasure."

She smoothed her hand over the groove in his back and along his right shoulder, completing her dance around him. "No pleasure?" With a lift of her chin, her breath grazed his jawline.

He held his ground, resisting the magnetic pull of her full lips. "You can tell me about your recent whereabouts."

"Bringing a couple gods to their knees." She licked the edge of his jaw. "Want a demonstration?"

His knees threatened to give out as if his body desired to serve her. No, she wasn't going to win him through temptation. Games such as these cheapened his feelings. Gripping her biceps on either side, he steadied himself. "It's serious, kid. Tell me, and whatever trouble you wind up in, I'll try to get you out."

"Do I look like I need help?" She hooked her foot behind his, shoving him sharply. He fell backward. The metal grates provided a poor cushion for his fall. He gasped in an attempt to catch the wind knocked from his lungs. She crawled on top of him and straddled his hips, her apex pressing right into his cock. His zippered fly dug painfully into his sensitive skin. Pain bloomed into exhilaration as she undulated lavishly against him. "The only trouble I get into is the good kind." Her grinding picked up speed, and she moaned. The sweet sound moved him from hard to his dick practically weeping.

He squeezed her hips to stop her, but the embrace deepened the luxuriating roll over him. The heightening desire tightened him into a rasp. "Is this what you want? To make a mess of me?"

"I know you want it messy, Quinlan. You want me warm and used, my thighs slick with him. You never made a move when you had a chance because you want him all over me." She sat up and ran her hands over her armored tits, pushing them together as she pumped away. He stopped resisting and guided her movements. "I have the power to bring him here. I can give you what you want. Make you my bad boy."

She was hiding from him, putting on a performance. Something had scared her and molded her into a madwoman. If he lost himself to her like this, it wouldn't be love.

He rolled on top of her and pinned her arms above her head. She laughed, loud enough to echo among the buildings. Her hands were bandaged. Chemical? Sign of a struggle? Neither boded well. "Bodies are piling up, kid, and everything points to Adhara. Were you with her when she rigged a water tower with acid and turned a group of poker players into goop?"

"No!"

"Don't lie to me. A woman like her can't go to a traditional prison, so they're going to shitcan any mortal they can place at the scene." Tobias lifted his knee, nudging her legs wider around him. She bit her lip as his thrusting dragged across her sweet center. "Including you."

Her writhing and moaning ceased. The eyes behind her mask grew big.

He stopped, besting her. A smirk from within arose. "I guess you got what you were lookin' for. You're fucked."

She attempted to escape the hold, her legs kicking and pushing to no avail. "Get off me. Get off me!"

"Gladly." He pushed himself onto his haunches, making space for her to stand up.

She bolted to the ladder, keeping her back to him. "You're upset because she's changed things."

"I'm upset because your hands are hurt. What did you do?"

She crossed her arms, stuffing her incriminating mitts into the crease of her armpits. "It's nothing."

"Would he want you chasing danger around like you have?" It was good to lay on the guilt. That's how Ma Quinlan got her confessions.

She flinched as if taking a blow to the stomach. The magic fucking words: *what would Vincent do?*

"Don't go back to your apartment, kid. Take your money and leave town for a while. Things are escalating around here, and you don't want to—"

"I have no one," she whispered.

He picked himself up off the landing and straightened. "Not true."

She turned her face so that her watery gaze met his.

Protecting her and being on the right side of the law pulled him in two, but his love for her would make him choose. "Whatever you did, I'll try to help you. I'm not putting you in any bracelets, but you have to listen to me."

She hit the side of the ladder, and the gears released it until its final rung hovered a healthy drop above the ground. The rubber of her boots scraped down the ladder as she slid past the rungs. She landed on the ground below and sprinted out of the alley.

How could he save her when she didn't want to be saved?

36

Grown Ups Are Liars

Marisol was deep into a physics textbook. Too deep. She had two missed calls from the clinic. Didn't they remember she quit? On the third attempt, it was up to her to remind them. "Marisol, I no longer work there," she greeted in a sing-song.

"There's a patient demanding to talk to you. I've told her you're no longer here, but she threw a pile of STI brochures at another nurse. I don't want to get the cops involved if I don't have to. Can you talk her down? A Yesenia Lopez?"

Marisol had last seen the girl slurping bubbly in the train yard. The girl looked up to her, and what had happened? Marisol abandoned her post at the clinic and messily lost herself in too much intoxication. She tilted her head from side to side, until she heard the satisfying click of her neck. "Tell her I'll be there in ten minutes."

Yesenia sat hunched over on the treatment table. Her eyes were red from crying. The evidence of her tantrum remained, a pile of brochures scattered on the shining tile floor.

Marisol sighed, crossing her arms. The girl being an asshole to former coworkers scabbed her bleeding heart over. "Tell me why I'm here."

"Forget it."

"We're not going to forget it. I had a nurse seconds away from calling the cops on you."

"I'm in distress, and you want to involve the five-o. You know what? Kiss my whole ass." She headed to the door, wiping her eyes.

Marisol put her hand on the door. No, she wasn't going to make a scene and an exit while she rubbed her eyes raw from crying. "Tell me."

"Guillermo's grandma called me. Said he hopped a bus to get back to the city. She begged me to talk him out of it, so I got a hold of him." Yesenia's lip quivered. "The Shadows are after *her* and anyone associated with her. I told Guillermo I'd hung out with her that night, when we destroyed the paintings of the pedo artist. He said I shouldn't have told him. He has to prove himself to the Shadows. He can only protect me so much." She broke into a full-blown sob. "I thought you'd know what to do—to call on the Patron Saint."

The Adhara situation verged on spiraling out of her control, an outcome Mijo Ray had warned her about earlier. What could she do against a gang hell-bent on making a name for themselves with vengeance? When a stubborn force met an indestructible one? She swallowed back the bile of her unease, resisting with clenched fists.

Truth was, the Shadows exploited women, and Adhara carved a line in the sand. A line which said *no more. Enough.* Good for the super-powered woman for turning their murderous control over the Westside against them!

"The Patron Saint doesn't exist anymore." She only had him a couple times. As much as she called for him again with ritual, he had only returned silence. He wasn't coming back. Self-destruction won, and the pain of it came out in a tongue-lashing. "Tell your boyfriend to bring it. The Shadows will regret every moment they crossed her—just like Tiny did. Guillermo can't protect you? He'll need you to protect him! And while you're at it, ditch your piece of shit boyfriend!"

"Fuck you!" Yesenia buried her face in her hands.

Marisol's arms twitched, wanting to hug the scared and angry girl, but she kept them still. She couldn't offer the girl comfort. She couldn't save the day. Everything good around her had been destroyed.

With another sniffle, Yesenia's face went blank, and she left the treatment room.

The city created a lot of scared and angry girls. It was the Shadowhaven way, and Marisol couldn't do anything about it.

37

Rolled into a Corner

Tobias was sure Adhara had done something at the ball. Although appearances suggested otherwise, she was a Goliath and he, David. His safest way of getting to the deadly immortal would be the girlfriend who preferred scooting around on wheels. To find her, though, proved to be tricky. The storage shed Adhara had occupied earlier, using the same Jane Doe license, had canceled its lease, and the only person going in and out of Marisol's apartment lately was Marisol.

His surest bet to find her was at the roller skater's place of employment. His butt went numb watching the entrance of the Pink Curtain. At this point in the day, the club was usually open for a lunch buffet, but the neon signs had been shut off. Yet, young women had gone in and out of the place using the front entrance. A private party, perhaps?

He couldn't have Burke spy on the club's back entrance. His partner would become too suspicious of Tobias's interest in the Pink Curtain's women and connect the dots to the new lodger at the Restful Inn.

The fewer knowledgeable eyes he had on this project, the likelier he could keep normally-powered people from approaching Adhara and risking their lives. His exception was a couple numbskulls from narcotics who were eager for a promotion. He ordered them to monitor the club's goings-on at the alley entrance. To Dipshit and Shitdip, they were monitoring Tiny and his underlings for drug activity. Detailed logs, Tobias claimed, sealed the cracks in the DA's cases.

But no dancer on wheels. The narcs reported some women entering or leaving, but none matched the description of Adhara's moll—rail-thin, pigtails, noticeable scars on her torso and face, and most importantly, roller skates. Surprisingly, no Shadows had come or gone either.

No offense meant to the fairer sex, but where had the men gone?

Like rolling Yahtzee, a supermodel-tall woman with hair in two neon-purple buns rolled out of the club entrance. She wore a cropped baseball tee, shredded black shorts, and knee-high socks with stripes at the edge. From carefully studying her in the rearview mirror, it was hard to tell if the pink on her face were scars or makeup. She glided down the block, popping bubblegum. He trailed behind her in his car. If Adhara showed up, he'd be reduced to a puddle of vomit with human organ chunks like the jewelry store poker players.

She spun around a bus stop sign until twirling into a sudden halt. Not the smartest maneuver, but he pulled his steering wheel left and immediately U-turned into the opposite lane. Tire squeals and *fuck yous* greeted him as he straightened into the bus lane.

He popped out of his car. "Selu Williams?"

Wheels looked up, an automatic response to her government name.

He stepped up on the curb, unveiling his badge. "I need to talk to you."

And—shit—she was off. He chased after her, knowing in a few more glides, she'd be scot-free. She checked over her shoulder. Perhaps to confirm her victory? Congrats, you out-skated a middle-aged man with a crick in his left knee.

Bang! The United States Postal Service came to his aid. She bounced off a mailbox and crashed to the sidewalk.

Breathless, he lumbered toward her. She wriggled in obvious pain, like the time toddler Diedre touched the stove after he told her not to. "C'mon, I got a first aid kit in the trunk of my car."

She grunted and nodded, reaching up to him with her non-busted arm. With a gentle pull, he steadied her to her feet.

Beep! The door of the city bus opened. "Move your car, you bozo!" the driver called out.

Ah, the Shadowhaven community he protected and served reared its bountiful gratitude.

The medical office of **Tobias Quinlan** was the passenger seat in a nearby parking ramp. She sat, door open and legs extended on the pavement. He helped her apply iodine to her skinned elbow, fanning it as it stung, and bandaged it. A few bends of her arm confirmed to his layman brain she hadn't broken anything, though it would've taken wild horses to drag her to a hospital if she had. He gave the ice pack a crack and handed it to her. She held it to the back of her head. No words had passed since he scraped her off a Westside sidewalk.

"I'm going to be frank with you. I could take you down to the precinct in a shiny set of bracelets with what I know."

She twitched, as if she was ready to bolt again.

"I also know a bit about Mr. Shaw, who's been turned into sludge. He hurt women—girls." His jaw ticked. If the now-goo had even attempted any of his shit with Diedre, it'd be the sole of Tobias's boot pounding him into snot and not a chemical reaction raining down. "I'd want him to pay too, but you got sloppy. Adhara may have cleaned the surveillance footage for twenty miles, but you didn't count on those living in the shadows and what they'd see. The theatricality homed me in on Adhara, but when they said someone glided across the roof as if they were on wheels, I knew who to look for."

Her focus seemed distant, the dead-eyed stare of someone who saw too much shit. He'd seen it before in his interrogation rooms—the hopeless victim. "What are you going to do to me?" she asked.

"Up to you." Tobias dug into the front of his coat, where he'd fit a small brick of cash courtesy of his Varian funds. He set it on the dashboard between them. "There's more where this came from. You get out of here and make yourself a life far from the city. If you keep your end of the bargain, I can guarantee you won't see the inside of a cell or have to spend the rest of your life looking over your shoulder."

She sat forward, practically salivating at the sight of all those Benjamins. "If I don't leave?"

"You'll be Adhara's patsy, and you won't see the outside of a prison until you're an old lady. If you survive it." Quite the decision she had to make—true love forever or cash-sweetened freedom.

Her scowl told him to go fuck himself. "She can look after me better than some man's money can."

He reached to take his cash back. "Very well."

She halted his hand and dug her teeth into her lower lip. "Can I take my mouse?" she asked.

Mouse? The rabid little thing that tried to eat his big toe last year? How easily he had forgotten it had become Adhara's adopted kid. He'd sweeten the pot, if he wasn't already handing off a small brick of hundreds. "That unholy thing? Be my guest."

"A.J.'s adorable!"

There were plenty of adjectives in the English language to describe the little monster. *Adorable* wasn't one of them. "How'd you do it? Getting the little critter to eat out of your hand?"

"She did it by feeding it fungus and using it to take over its brain waves with a computer. It was cool, watching how she could use mushrooms and computer code to control its mind."

The vinyl of the steering wheel creaked as he gave it a strong squeeze. *Mind control.* How the fuck had Adhara gotten all those people to go berserk? She fed them fungus that made a home in their brains and typed orders for them to follow. And if she could do it to A.J., she could do it to someone more formidable.

Like Vincent.

How had she fed it to all of them? The caterer's boss wanted to nail him for stealing alcohol. Adhara posed as a caterer and tainted the alcohol. Tobias and Marisol had been safe because they didn't drink. But as for Vincent—Tobias had ordered the drink that sealed Vincent's fate.

Wheels grabbed the cash on the dashboard and bolted out of the passenger seat. The damn roller skater took advantage of his case-cracking stupor. She zoomed through the parking ramp and out onto the sidewalk.

God. Dammit. The car engine couldn't start fast enough. The tires squealed as he sped after her. But one missed turn, and he lost sight of her. He circled the blocks, searching for her, and found blaring sirens and blue-red lights instead.

Dipshit and Shitdip from narcotics had nabbed her just as he asked, putting her in bracelets for not following a lawful command and a bullshit resisting arrest. Instead of getting a ticket out of here, she was in the back of a squad car. He sighed. She had made her choice.

Tobias only had one suggestion, to lock her up in County and not the city's jail. His lie was that it was to protect her from the Shadows finding her.

But Adhara posed the real danger. The more distance he could put between Wheels and Adhara while Wheels was locked up, the safer they'd all be.

Well, *safe* on a relative scale. Mind control, murder, and the girlfriend arrested? Everything was weaving into a giant tangle. He trusted one person to unravel this whole thing, and she was clacking away on the computer in her basement apartment. As he started his car, his stomach knotted.

Adhara's fire was already breaking containment. How long would it take before the flames consumed them all?

Breaking News

C harges of kidnapping, trafficking, and rape were dropped today against Congressional candidate Grant Durant. Federal prosecutor Penelope Stanwycki argued that once the defense presented their case and poked holes in key witness testimonies, it was unconscionable to pursue the case any further. Legal critics argue that evidence suppression gave Durant the opportunity to escape responsibility on a legal technicality. Law professor Rachel Ryan said that the prosecution barely had a chance to build a case against Durant. "Insisting on a speedy trial tipped the scales in his favor. If the swamped prosecution had only weeks to collect flight logs, guest lists, and cell phones records, they're bound to come up short."

In other news: Are you entering a military zone or one of Shadowhaven's gated communities? It's hard to tell as many of Shadowhaven's elite families hire the private paramilitary group, Shepherd's Watch. Neighborhoods once noted for their opulence swarm with mysterious mask-wearing individuals shrouded in tactical gear. An anonymous source said the protection is necessary after the uptick in strange deaths targeting wealthy families. Quote, "The deaths started with Vincent Varian. Who will be the last?" End quote. Some critics argue the excessive protection is unnecessary, since many of the deaths have been committed by the very class of people they're protecting.

YesiLo11: "We know what he did to those girls. They were my friends. If the system doesn't work for us, it's time to crush the system."

xavierblorelifecoach: "Justice is one thing, but these kind of girls don't stop until someone is ruined. What is their part in all of this?"

ladyvanguard: "I heard they didn't consider video evidence of the crime. How can they claim justice was served?"

On the Precipice

The candle's flame dimmed, hovering over the thick puddle of melted wax. How long had **Marisol** laid here like this, hypnotized by her lit prayer candle?

Waiting for her prayer to be answered?

A crash from her living room snapped her into focus. Opening her bedroom door a crack, she glimpsed Adhara stomping the perimeter of the living room, throwing random computer parts. A keyboard shattered against the wall, and its letters fell like plastic confetti. The resulting chunk in the plaster ate up more of Marisol's security deposit, leaving it next to zero. Before Adhara, she could've counted on the whole thing returning to her.

"Hey!" Marisol shouted before Adhara julienned a computer tower.

Adhara stopped so suddenly, her exoskeleton hummed. "Wheels is missing."

Missing? Was she kidnapped? Her stomach clenched as if she were expecting a sudden strike of a fist. If Yesenia's worries were true, would the Shadows hurt the roller skater? "What happened?"

"Without a word. I—" Adhara flopped her arms in the air as if they'd find the answer hiding in it.

Marisol blew her candles out and edged out of her bedroom. "Want to talk about it?"

A gleam entered Adhara's eye. "Are you afraid of me?"

The question caught her off guard, and she had moments to answer. *Sometimes,* she wanted to say. The person Mijo Ray and Tobias painted was terrifying, and Marisol had only peeks into the scary side of Adhara— the power she helped unleashed as they tore up the museum or the slashes she made out of the 86ers. But Marisol had also seen another side of her—the utter awe in her face as Wheels danced, the tenderness she still held for Vincent from deep inside another woman's memory, or the savior who patched her torn hands.

Marisol shook her head.

"I think I scared Wheels."

Marisol saw an opportunity to touch greater power and darker secrets. Namely, had she killed those people? "You don't scare me."

Adhara closed her eyes and audibly breathed through her nose. "Do you feel the charge in the air?"

The apartment felt the same, cramped and wired ever since Adhara had taken it over. And now messier after Adhara's shit fit. But no charge.

"Something big is coming, which will change the city forever. And it feels..." Adhara raked her teeth over her lower lip. Her carotid pulse twitched a soft spot in her neck.

The dangerous lure of her night with Adhara and Vincent rang through Marisol's body. Memories of touches and kisses turned static prickled over her skin. "Electric," she said.

Adhara opened her eyes, her gaze like x-ray vision into Marisol's soul. "Let's go dancing. We always danced before a revolution."

"Novel idea." And so Marisol rode the edge, teetering along danger. What would happen if she jumped?

Maybe she would fly.

Diedre handed **Tobias** a souped-up burner phone. "I uploaded a program to this device." She untangled a cord from the nest of them on her desk. "Using this, you can introduce it into the Staci system to counteract the security measure blocking you. Since it's fighting a program continually generating code to protect itself, it will take at least twenty-four hours to restore the entire system back to how you found it."

She showed him how to connect the phone to any hard drive. Like the good teacher she was, she loomed over him with hands on her hips, expecting him to demonstrate a successful attempt at securing and soldering wires to an even more fragile microchip. His callused paw fumbled the tweezers. Dammit, why did she think he could do this?

Diedre possessed a level of patience modeled only by her mother. "Don't let your nerves control you. Take deep breaths."

Hard to pour his concentration into a microscopic twist of the wire when he sensed her watching him. He tossed the tool in the middle of the table. "What?"

"A lot is hiding behind military-grade encryption, but I helped myself to some of the data." She waggled her eyebrows. The kid knew something.

He shifted in his chair. How many more lies would he need to tell his daughter? "And?"

"Have you ever heard the theory that the universe has been slowly falling apart after some important person died or event occurred? One dead pop star a decade ago or one apocalypse-level computer glitch thirty years past actually ended the world, and we've been unravelling ever since?"

The bizarre segue. He'd keep criminals he interrogated on their toes by telling a strange story. The strategy kept them from predicting where he'd go next in his questioning. Funny how the skill seemed genetic. "No. Enlighten me."

"Something important happened April 3 this year at 12:47:53 A.M. I cross-checked it with strange reports. It turns out Shadowhaven had a surge in the electrical grid around then. The very one Vincent Varian recently promised to power himself with his collider. A week later, he's missing. Important event. Important person."

"You're more like me than I thought. What do you know, Deeds?"

"It doesn't really matter what I learned about Vincent Varian. It does matter to know electrons travel at different speeds. Charging can increase an electron's speed; crashing into atoms slows them down. Something lost at such a level would be improbable to retrieve."

He swallowed. Truth's sting had a way of hurting more when it came from his wide-eyed progeny. "So, what's the point in trying?"

"When someone I loved seemed improbably lost, I nearly gave up." She buttoned her mouth to one side. Sighing, she continued, "But I'm glad I didn't."

"Oh." Warmth echoed from his heart. She was speaking about him, right? He had to make sure. "Don't tell me it will take twenty-one years to find him."

"The collider opens the door, but something has to be a beacon to guide them through it. Science meets seance." She laughed at her own joke.

So, he should start the collider and shine his high beams? Something was better than nothing. He drew his notepad from his shirt pocket. Could this be Marisol's elusive *T?* "What was that date and time again?"

"April 3 at 12:47:53 A.M. You still haven't soldered the wire correctly." She arched a single eyebrow.

"Yeah, yeah, yeah." He tucked his notepad back in his pocket. A breath bottled inside his chest and steadied his hand. He picked up the tweezers and completed the connection. Voila! The program on his phone began speaking to Diedre's hard drive.

Hope lay on the horizon, Staci rebooted, Vincent returned, and Marisol—he'd get his Marisol back. Well, not his, but last year's hope that had saved them all would reappear. And they'd be happy. And he'd watch as they smiled and loved each other. It wouldn't be perfect, but it would be enough for him. "Thank you."

"This is the point in the transaction where I ask, is there anything else I can do for you?"

His mind flashed to crime scene photos and jellyfish pulled from people's brain matter. He had an Adhara problem in need of addressing. "Rolling the dice here, but what do you know about computers, fungus, and mind control?"

Diedre scoffed. Of course he sounded ridiculous.

"Listen, I know it sounds something straight out of a sci-fi—"

"No, it's..."

He stood to dig out his wallet. "How much do I have to pay?"

"You don't have to pay me!"

He stilled. Color him confused. Since when did Diedre turn down money—his money?

"Is the mind control wired or wireless?"

"Wireless."

"Short range or longer?"

The Clements went kablooey across the continent. "Longer."

"Damn." Her mouth pressed into a flat line as she rubbed her chin. "Are the commands local?"

Wheels explained that Adhara had used a computer in Marisol's apartment to change the rabid mouse. "I think so?"

Diedre sighed as she seemed to scan the contents of her tech jungle. She ducked through wires and bounded to a filing cabinet. The drawer opened with a grunt and an ungreased squeal. Tossing random video game controllers, she rummaged through the contents, settling on what looked like a remote duct-taped to a handheld transistor radio. "Computer control over fungus is a relatively new innovation, but it relies on good, old-fashioned radio waves to translate code to mushroom language. This device can home in on the communication channel and temporarily scramble it. It has the same power as a local radio station, so if the commands need to cross the county line, you're SOL."

She passed the contraption to him and fidgeted with its buttons. "Turn the knob until you hear a frequency sounding like fairies screaming and push this button. The scramble will probably buy you enough time to subdue the controlled entity. Unfortunately, anything more powerful will get nasty attention from your buddies in the federal government. Anything else?"

He smiled proudly and inched his way to the exit. "Stay out of trouble?"

"No guarantees."

Noncommittal sass, oh, how his genes reared their ugly head. "Your mom and Glenn would appreciate it."

She rolled her eyes as she unlatched her front door locks. "I'll see what I can do." She opened the door with an exaggerated jerk.

He stood inside the frame, ducking his head. Other words called to him, the kind fathers said to their grown daughters.

I've never been prouder.

Take no shit.

I love you.

Instead, he stepped outside and gave her a nod. The door slammed behind him with a familiar, furious thud which had ended more than a few of his relationships. He lingered, waiting for the bravery to knock on the door and tell Diedre the things he left unsaid. The snick of the locks barring his reentry confirmed the moment was over.

Tobias walked up to the street. He was going to get his friends back.

39

Bad Apples

Two Hundred and Sixty Years After the Curse

Adhara kisses the top of Françoise's hand and disappears behind her changing screen.

I finish sewing the tear in Françoise's dress and help her back into it. She fixes her gaze downward as I tie the last bow. "Tomorrow, Toinon will want me to help clean up, but I know you are low on certain supplies. I could...I could isolate the ore into the powder you like?"

I sense the embarrassment. I take her hands in mine, and she blushes again. "Françoise, you make my wife—us—happy. I'll help Toinon with the extra cleaning up. Even if I have *la gueule de bois*[1]."

She laughs. "Monsieur, we did not drink tonight."

"Let's change that. Bring us some champagne, please?"

1. Hangover

She curtseys and leaves the room. From down the hallway, I hear the party dying down. The uproarious laughter has become murmuring conversation. Music has dwindled to a few plucks of the strings. Adhara emerges from the partition she changed behind, dressed in her simple breeches, waistcoat, and tunic—not the outfit of someone returning to a party like Françoise or going to bed like me.

I tense from my emerging misgivings. "Going somewhere?"

Before she answers, a scream from the ballroom curdles my blood. I race toward it. A handful of people flee. Musicians, by the look of them. I sprint to the room.

The bodies of our guests lie on the floor and slump in chairs. Françoise stands in the middle of it all, still screaming. I check one body's pulse. Dead. Another and another. Dead, dead, dead. All the guests are dead. I shudder and wipe my hand on my silk robe, cleaning an invisible bloodstain.

"You're a monster! A monster!" Françoise runs out of the *maison* and into the night. Her cries of *monsters* echo from the woods.

Adhara approaches from behind me. She saunters toward the carnage, far too calm for a woman witnessing a ballroom of dead bodies to have no hand in it. Disgust arrives in an overwhelming, warbling nausea. I pinch my lips together and swallow. "What have you done?"

"Cyanide. I made it from the apples in your orchard. Put it in the champagne, and those blue-blooded pigs chugged it down. I'm surprised they lasted as long as they did."

"A young woman screaming in the night? A mob will be here."

"Demanding justice for what? The hero who freed them from having one more of those shameless swillers walk by them holding a cloth to their nose, seeing through them while they luxuriate in their gluttony, and the others starve?!"

I do not argue with her. There is no time to. Adhara's mess will hang on me, dragging me into Hell. To escape it, I must start anew. I hoist one of the bodies on my shoulder and move it to my bed. I dress it in my robe and replace its jewelry with a few key items. V. V. as the world knows him, is dead.

I change into my other self, wearing the colors of the night. Ready to blend into nothing, to disappear.

Adhara sits, her proud chin lifted, among the bodies.

"You should go. Mobs can do lots of damage to us. Think of Nando."

"There will be no mob. I'll be hailed a hero. You'll see."

I flee into the night, where the forest swallows me. Here, no stars guide me, and I am lost again.

40

Girls Night Out

The dance club rumbled with techno music, mimicking the pulsing in **Tobias's** veins. The blue and gray shadows intermittently lit with flashes of strobe light. A head taller above the crowd, he scanned the place, his back to the bar. He'd recognized the club's cheeseball lighting when he texted Marisol a *Where you at?* and received a photo of her middle finger in response. A vial of sedative he "borrowed" from the evidence room poked his thigh from inside his pocket.

A cloud of smoke rose above the dancers. Someone was smoking. That was when he saw her—eyes closed, swaying alone to the music. Adhara prowled to her and seemed to awake her with her gold claw dragging across her cheek. Marisol opened her eyes and hugged loose arms around Adhara's neck.

The way she flailed, he recognized the floppy movement from his past. She was drunk.

They danced into a spotlight on the dance floor, writhing together.

Adhara ran her clawed hand through Marisol's hair, drawing it back and exposing her neck. The tipped finger traced along the soft spot between Marisol's tendon and voice box. Marisol's mouth parted as if she were surrendering to a vampire. And she was.

Marisol seemed to bite Adhara's wrist. Then, she arched back, facing the ceiling, Adhara's grip around her waist the only thing keeping her from falling. Smoke rolled out of her mouth as she exhaled. Her body completely acquiesced, Adhara dragged her claw across Marisol's lower lip, throat, across her sternum, and teased the shadow of her cleavage before pulling her body upright.

Half the men watched them, salivating, as if they became vultures following the women into a desert, waiting for one to collapse. Tobias clenched his jaw to stave his protective rage. Marisol was the easy prey.

Adhara and Marisol danced, moving away from the spotlight. However, in a new place on the dance floor, a blue light highlighted glitter around Marisol's eyes.

Not glitter, but tears.

Marisol staggered out of Adhara's embrace and shoved her way through the dancers. Off balance, she caught herself on the ledge of the bar. Her watchers prowled closer to her.

"Tequila," she ordered. She shot it as soon as the drink arrived.

"You're not safe," he warned.

"You following me?"

"I am tonight."

"Not wise for someone who's recovering." She dangled the shot glass between her thumb and forefinger. The bartender took the cue and gave her another shot.

Tobias kept his cool. Otherwise, he'd mistake Marisol for being a spiteful shithead and not pretending to be one. "Your dancing is attracting a lot of onlookers."

Marisol snorted. "Yeah, probably with their dick in the other hand."

He studied the watchers again. In a different angle of the light, they seemed like they wanted to murder her more than fuck her. The way they carried themselves, he had seen it before as undercover cops prepared for a takedown. But something about them said they weren't cops. What did these not-cops want from Marisol? "I wouldn't be so sure."

"Hey!" Marisol yelled to one of her vultures. "It's rude to stare!" The watcher slunk away into the shadows. Obviously proud of herself, she forced a laugh.

"Vincent didn't kill himself."

The drunken smirk disappeared from her face. "Psh!" She flipped him off, took two steps, and fell. He caught her by her upper arm before she met the floor. In his arms, she couldn't hide the tears. They streamed from her eyes.

"She infected them with fungi at the ball a few months back and programmed the mushrooms with orders. You've seen it with your own eyes with the mouse. She used it to get the other billionaires, and she used it to get him."

Marisol eyed the dance floor. Adhara watched her from the distance, occasionally bobbing to the music. "How?" Marisol asked.

"My daughter cracked the code. Thank God she has her mother's brains. We can get Staci back online." He took a deep breath. "And we can get him back. *T*, the constant you needed? It's right here." He handed her the slip of paper with the date and time.

She pocketed it and hiccuped.

"Leave with me, kid. You're not in a good way right now."

Her watery eyes widened into something wild and angry. "All that time, no one believed me." The anger turned into laughter. "I was the crazy widow, and you—you abandoned me."

"I didn't think I could stay then." Leaving her because of his weakness squeezed at his heart. His soul had been saved as he conquered addiction, but he left Marisol behind, falling further into her despair. "But I will now."

Her sweet brown eyes peered through the space in her hair. "You're trying to separate me from the one person who stuck by me."

"You mean your enabler."

"Fuck you." She extricated her arm from his grip and gave him a shove. Free from him, she returned to the bar and ordered another drink.

He couldn't watch her destroy herself anymore.

The bartender poured the shot, and Tobias snagged it and threw it to the ground. Club patrons reeled back as broken glass sprayed at their ankles.

He wrapped his arms around her waist and used his strength to push her through the crowd. He pinned her against a pillar. She was too stunned to resist. He took the opportunity and jammed the vial and case in the front pocket of her pants. "Sedative. For protection against her."

A metallic hand clamped at his neck. The swift clench punched his breath out. He gulped and gagged for air.

Glowing, overcast eyes looked up at him. "Typical man. How many times does she have to tell you no to get you to leave her alone?"

"Adhara! Stop! You'll kill him!"

Adhara dropped him. On his hands and knees, he gasped for air. Security scurried in from the crowd and lifted him up by his arms. He looked to Marisol, pleading for her to leave with him.

But she shook her head and whispered, "She'll kill you."

Security dragged him a few feet before he caught his breath. He forcefully wiggled from them and raised his hands up as a peace offering. "Relax, I'm police."

"The weird boyfriends always are. Do yourself a favor, and stay the fuck out of here." One more shove, and he was outside the club in the alleyway.

He flicked the collar of his trench coat up. Diedre had given him a chance to make things right, and he was going to start before it was too late.

A catlike grin moved Adhara's lips. Her gaze tracked their audience, wannabes who were shit at seeming like natural clubgoers. Something about the way they couldn't even tap their fingers to the beat.

"Come," Adhara said. "I know a way we can lose them."

Marisol followed her to the bathroom. Here, Adhara kicked open a window leading out to the alley. Women primping in the mirror froze with puzzled frowns. What the fuck were two women doing destroying the window and leaving, they must've wondered. Marisol and Adhara stepped out into the alley.

"Wait here," Adhara ordered. "I'll get a ride to throw off our trackers."

Marisol ducked behind a dumpster. A stretch of time passed, which Marisol measured in the song changes muffled by the wall. Forever seemed to have passed since Adhara said she was getting a ride.

The sedative burned inside her pocket. Tobias couldn't have been telling the truth. They couldn't bring Vincent back. Because as much as she fought for him, no one could bring back the dead. Not Caz's victims. Not Abuelita. Not Annie.

A red sports car arrived, engine roaring. Adhara, in the driver's seat, opened the passenger door. "Get in." She had also suited up in her armor.

"Is this yours?" Marisol wasn't sure why she asked. She knew the answer.

"It is now."

Marisol lowered herself into the car. The moment she shut the door, Adhara sped away, weaving the car through the street. She braked suddenly, and Marisol braced against the dashboard. Laughing, Marisol said, "You drive like that, I'll puke all over the interior."

"Take a look in the back."

Spread out across the backseat was her domino mask, Kevlar pants, and trusty 3D-printed, hooded chainmail shirt.

"This world is ours," Adhara said.

Marisol crawled into the backseat and awkwardly wiggled into her uniform. The sedative Tobias tucked into her pocket, she moved into her Kevlar pants. She held on to her mask as she moved up to the front again.

They pulled up to a red light. Another car crept next to the driver's side. The passengers rolled down the windows.

"Yo, Mare," a man called out. Funny, *Mare* was the name the Shadows called her.

Oh shit, the Shadows!

Gun muzzles emerged from the other side of the lowered windows.

"Run, Marisol!" A much younger man screamed. Was it...Guillermo?

Marisol hit the floor.

A tennis-sized ball rolled out of Adhara's exoskeleton and into her palm. She flicked a pin with her thumb and tossed it into the other car.

The vehicle's occupants scrambled out of the car onto the street. The light turned green. Adhara revved the car and sped away. Marisol turned to look outside the rear window. *Boom*! The Shadows' car blew sky-high in an explosive cloud of fire and smoke. Shock waves rattled the sports car. Silhouettes of crawling Shadows contrasted against the flames.

Those who sought to harm her or Adhara would pay. Marisol laughed. "That was...awesome!"

"I can give you everything the world offers." Adhara held out her hand. The gold exoskeleton shimmered in the low light. "You'll follow me to the depths, won't you?"

Marisol nuzzled her cheek into Adhara's metallic palm. She sucked on one of the gold tubes, a vaporizer for weed. Marisol's lungs burned as she held in her breath. When she finally released the potent cloud, her high dropped her down a well. The lights, music, Adhara, all experienced from the bottom. Far away. Limbs heavy. Numb.

It felt glorious.

Adhara returned to controlling the steering wheel. Her foot slammed the accelerator, and the city sped by them in streaks.

Marisol rolled down the passenger side window. The wind whipped her hair around, another layer to disappear into. "I want air." She stuck her head out. The cool summer air washed over her skin. The car picked up speed. Marisol edged more of herself outside the window, the lure of danger calling to her.

"We can face anything!" Adhara shouted over the rumbling speed.

Marisol slid halfway out the window, arms flailed out. The ends of her hair skidded across the pavement. The only thing keeping her in the car was Fate itself. In her head, she heard Vincent. *If you're lost, I'll find you.*

Adhara spun the car 180 degrees. Tires screeched. Rubber burned. Marisol's heartbeat thundered in her ears. Centimeters from becoming a splatter mark on the pavement, a claw pulled at her chainmail and yanked her inside. "I got you," Adhara called after her.

Adrenaline coursed through Marisol's veins. And she laughed again.

In the rearview mirror, Marisol noticed another car following them. Did Adhara have more explosions up her sleeve? "We still have a tail."

Adhara's eyes glinted. "They will take care of themselves."

She rolled the car window's back up and slowed her driving to a crawl as they entered a gated community. The guard at the entrance waved them through. The car belonged here. Whose car was it? Adhara stopped in front of a driveway protected by a giant stone wall and a wrought-iron gate.

"Stay right here."

Marisol watched as the super-powered woman pushed buttons, and the gate slid open. Adhara reentered the car and pulled it into the driveway, and the iron bars shut behind them. They approached a mansion but entered a giant garage, pulling alongside a couple more cars and motorcycles. "I think you can enjoy your present now."

"Give it to me."

"Follow me."

Marisol put her mask on and walked to the tiny trunk of the car. She rubbed the top of her thigh, checking where the vial and syringe case rested in her pocket. With a push of a button, Adhara opened the car trunk. Scrunched into the fetal position was Grant Durant. She lifted him out and propped him up on his knees. A cloth gag muffled his screams, and his wrists were bound behind him.

The shock seized Marisol, freezing her into place. "What's going on?"

Adhara reached into the trunk and drew out her curved sword. "You want Justice. I can give you Justice." She twirled the weapon in the air until the handle pointed at Marisol, and the blade faced Adhara.

Marisol floated her hand over the hilt. Justice had eluded Grant Durant. He systematically hurt those girls and remained protected behind his money and power. If anyone deserved the Fate about to be bestowed, it was him. She gripped the hilt with both hands and raised the blade in the air.

Her Justice was righteous, she told herself, as the memory of Caz washing his bloodied hands in the family's kitchen returned to her. Fear had paralyzed her then, as it did now. As it had when Annie's lifeless hand stretched out into her view, blood trailing around her. Her bandaged hands shook as the memory of Vincent stopping her in the street as she beat Grant's teeth out and ached as they relived turning the random man into a pulp. *If you're lost, I'll find you.*

The sword fell from her hands and clanged on the ground.

"Weakling. You lack the courage of your convictions." Adhara stepped into Marisol, pushing against her chest. She looked down at her, sneering.

Marisol swallowed and lifted her chin. "I'm not a murderer."

Grant tongued the cloth of his mouth, pushing it past his chin. "Stupid bitches. I got Shepherd's Watch protecting me. You're fucked. If you let me go now, I'll promise when they find your bodies, they'll be able to tell you apart from canned spaghetti."

Adhara kicked her sword up into her hand. She raised the blade. Marisol popped the syringe cap and held the needle to Adhara's neck. "I can't let you do that," Marisol said.

A side door pounded, and Marisol hadn't yet plunged the liquid into Adhara's artery.

Adhara crushed the syringe in her fist and threw Marisol—*thunk!*—into the side of the sports car. Pain wracked her body. Where was it coming from? A few movements of her limbs confirmed she'd dislocated her shoulder.

The garage door rattled, another throng attempting to get in. A pulse echoed from Adhara's exoskeleton, and the garage remained firmly shut.

The side door split open behind them. Shadows poured in, holding automatic rifles. Their guns clicked in unison as they aimed to fire at them. Flight took hold. Marisol dragged herself to the protection of the wheel well, to put as much car between them and their rifles. Her dislocated shoulder's pain stabbed into her like a knife. She braced for the bullets, but the hinged door between the garage entrances swung open.

Shepherd's Watch swarmed in, scattering in front of the closed garage doors. They aimed, mirror opposite of the Shadows. Marisol hit the floor. The crack of gunfire assaulted her ears. From her stance peering under the car's undercarriage, she could see the unarmored Shadows hit the ground, bodies ripped by bullets.

The gunfire died down. Adhara exploited the pause in action to shoot flames from the tubing in her arm, forcing the soldiers back. "They'll have to pry you from my hands," Adhara shouted, dragging Grant Durant by the collar of his shirt. Clear fluid shot out of her wrist. A quick flick of the lighter at the end of her claws, and a wall burst aflame, creating a barrier between them and the paramilitary group.

"I'll tell them not to shoot you if you get me out of here alive," Grant shrieked over the fire's roar.

"Alive?" Adhara bent down. "I'm already dead." She kicked him to the ground, stood on his back, and swung the blade down on his neck.

Marisol flinched as the blade scraped against the floor.

"Shoot!" one of the black-clad soldiers shouted. Gunfire sliced through the air. A hail of bullets attacked Adhara and pinged off the sports car.

Marisol ducked. "Adhara! Help!"

Grant Durant's dead body lay in a lump on the ground. A puddle of blood between his neck and severed head reflected the rising flames. Adhara spun her blade, bullets ricocheting off it. A few bounced back and took out some of the paramilitary. The super-powered woman leaped through the wall of fire and cut through the guards. She sheathed her sword at her back and wrenched a rifle from one man's hands. Her ankle rockets launched her toward the rafters above. Taking the higher ground, she opened fire.

Another round of bullets whipped through the air. Adhara emptied the rifle in their direction and ditched the spent weapon. She balanced along the beams to a window at the roofline.

Marisol cowered as the fire's smoke stung the depths of her lungs. "Help!"

"I gave you a chance to prove you're worthy. You have disappointed me."

Marisol leaned her head back against the dented car. The truth could no longer be skewed by her sadness. She had let so many people down—Tobias,

Yesenia, and now Adhara. Who could accept and forgive her now?

"If you make it out alive, we can talk." Adhara shattered the glass and jumped out.

As the flames rose around her and more of Shepherd's Watch blocked the exit, Marisol prayed for a way out.

Because prayer was all she had left.

41

Synergy

Tobias ran to the shuttered underground lair of the Patron Saint. He wired Diedre's smart phone to the keypad entry to the lair just as she showed him.

The smart phone's screen flooded with *1*'s and *0*'s. "C'mon, Diedre, don't let me down." He bounced in place as if he needed to piss.

The doors opened. He expected the underground hideout to light up, but it was stuck in the dark. He looked at the screen of the smart phone, which read *1% system rebooted.* Luckily, he brought a crowbar and a flashlight with him. The collection of random items in his car trunk had proven to be heaven-sent.

Within the depths of the underground lair, he broke into the storage drawers typically computer-operated by Staci. What did he need to take out someone like Adhara? He held the flashlight with his teeth and pried open the drawer of the tranquilizer. Damn. Nothing there would knock Adhara out, but the drawer had ten vials of the healing serum. He could level the playing field between Adhara and him if he juiced on the whole lot of them. What else?

He jimmied open the armor to get a Kevlar vest and whatever else he had used last year, but he lost his grip, and the sharper end of the crowbar sliced his hand open. He squeezed his hand shut, letting the blood trickle down his wrist. A little electric sizzle could seal the wound shut. Opening the drawer of weaponry, he drew out a handy-dandy cattle prod. He held the prod between his chin and wounded hand and set it to its lowest setting. *Here goes nothing.*

Zzzt! Tobias squirmed in the dark, moaning. God, he hoped the surge didn't fuck up his heart. Adjusting the flashlight, he saw that his hand looked like absolute shit, but at least he had barbecued the wound shut.

He double-checked the progress on the smart phone. Two percent freaking rebooted. It was going to be a long weekend.

In the void, **Vincent** smelled smoke and blood. Marisol was calling to him. He rushed to the source to see her in a garage, injured, and surrounded by flames. He knocked on the wall of the void, hoping to find a weak spot. How could he save her from here?

Another sacrifice of blood and smoke wafted toward him. He ran to it. It was Tobias, wandering the hideout in the dark. He reached through the barrier. The magenta layer wrapped about his body. His hand tingled as if it were asleep. He grabbed Tobias by his watch and tapped *SOS*, not the real distress call but the way he had told Marisol he loved her, using the light-up function. Nothing happened. Tobias flicked him away like a mosquito bite. Vincent tried again. *SOS. I love you.*

The watch on Tobias's wrist glowed faintly and petered out. Tobias stopped and looked at it.

Yes! Vincent had gotten his attention. He stretched out his arms, both hands reaching for the watch. *I love you. Save her, Tobias. Please, save her.*

The watch lit up. Finally, Vincent manipulated the glow to communicate *SOS*.

"Marisol," Tobias said. "Where are you?"

He could barely send the message that would drag him across the city to find her. Vincent searched for another way to communicate. The motorcycle!

He focused his energy, surrounding the machine with the power sourced by the friction between him and the void's wall. Heat vibrated from him in waves. The engine of the cycle turned on, glowing pink rather than its telltale blue. No Staci yet. The system was still rebooting.

Tobias boarded the motorcycle. "Staci?"

Vincent closed his eyes to bring the timeline to him. He relived their memory of the kiss on the fire escape, fueled by grief and whiskey. Three years ago, he was kissing Tobias. Now, the sensation was his thumb over Tobias's lips.

"Vincent, it's you," Tobias called out in the dark. "Do you see where she is?"

Vincent hugged his arms around Tobias, drawing him further into their shared memories.

In their trance, they re-experienced the night Tobias told him to go to Marisol over a year ago. Vincent remembered it as the night he and Marisol made love for the first time.

The Week of Meeting Marisol

Effect and cause. Tobias, gray and grizzled, drinks a beer and looks out at the lights of the alleyway. He hasn't taken the serum yet, which chases away the silver in his hair. While he is distracted, I fog over the window to the fire escape and write an address from the future.

As if following a script, my past self takes over. "Is she safe?" I call out from the dark recesses of the fire escape.

Tobias, leaning against the ledge, drops his newly opened beer. The bottle shatters in the alleyway below. "Jesus Christ! This is, like, the third beer you owe me."

"Is she?"

"Yeah, she's safe." Tobias sighs. "I thought we had a moment, her and me. But she's looking out that window of her apartment, and I knew what she felt."

"Knew?"

"Because I feel it too—looking to the night for an angel to come. You're my angel, but you know that." His glazed-over eyes become watery.

I adjust my mask. I have understood our past incorrectly. The night of our kiss had been fueled by my despair. I hadn't pursued the moment any further, but Tobias's kiss wasn't hopelessness. It was a promise.

My gloved hand slides closer to Tobias's.

But the past follows a script. Tobias lets go of the railing and crosses his arms—guarding his heart. "Go to her. I'm a wretch, lucky to breathe the same air as her. I'm doomed to wrestle angels and lose."

I nod, and the Patron Saint's steely resolve courses through me. I slip into the shadows and disappear. Yet, I stop. I watch Tobias from the depths of the night.

He turns away from the ledge and pinches the bridge of his nose. He drops his hand. He sees the message, which hadn't been there the first time, but with information he'd carry into the future—the address of Grant Durant's home.

Tobias pulled the knit ski mask down from his forehead and rode the motorcycle out of the lair and into the night. The lair's garage door shut behind him— Staci was slowly returning back to her normal self. The speed whipped his trench coat behind him. "26 Heights Drive. A garage. Let's get our girl."

The fire choked the air from the garage, but the flames kept the Shepherd's Watch men at bay. Die from burning or the bullet? Which would be better?

From the ground, **Marisol** grabbed the handle and opened the driver's side door of the sports car. It might give her enough coverage to make it to an exit, maybe crush of few of those soldiers under the wheels.

She crawled inside. A few bullets pinged off the car's body. The threat kept her head down below the dash. Sidling her feet to the pedals, she pressed the brake and started the car. She pulled the car into gear, and the tires squealed as it bolted in a random direction beyond the ring of fire.

Crunch! The front end hit a vintage roadster. Bullets zinged through the glass, creating fractals. Not close enough to an exit, and definitely not enough gunfire cover. She yanked the gearshift into reverse and hit the accelerator. The car crossed back into the ring of fire. This time, Marisol turned the wheel from her place crouching below—anything to shift directions. Another shift of the gears and a slam of the accelerator, and the car hood knocked a soldier into the flames. Except the rest gathered and aimed at her back window, shooting it out. She adjusted the gearshift to reverse. No traction. The flames had melted the tires down to the rims. Smoke began to fill the inside of the car. The fumes stung as she inhaled. If she breathed more of it in, she'd pass out. But the gunfire, shredding the car open like a tin can, kept her inside. At least if they shot out the windows, she'd have more breathing room. In every cloud, a silver lining?

The paramilitary stopped to reload. Marisol kicked open the car door and crawled to her feet. She ran to the only unprotected exit, scrambling over the bodies of the fallen Shadows.

A motorcycle exploded, sending shrapnel her way and blocking the exit. She spun to sprint to another exit, only to face an aimed rifle barrel.

She raised her hands in surrender. "Don't shoot!"

The garage opened partway. A motorcycle sped in. Tobias skidded to a halt, aimed his cattle prod, and took out the soldier with an electric blast. *Pow! Pow! Pow!* The blue rays paralyzed guard after guard.

"Get on, kid!"

Marisol ran to her rescuer and mounted the motorcycle. He revved the engine to speed their way out and down the driveway. Only at the gate, more of the Shepherd's Watch surrounded them, guns raised.

"Shit," Tobias said.

She closed her eyes, bracing for the end. *Click, click, click.* Where were the bullets? The guns! They hadn't shot at them.

A familiar, soothing feeling washed over her, cooling her burns. "Vincent?" she asked the ether.

Tobias shot another blast, ensuring a wide enough hole in the group to escape. The motorcycle accelerated past the paramilitary men to freedom.

"Who the fuck were those guys?"

"Shepherd's Watch protecting Grant Durant. Adhara must've got by them to kidnap him. She killed him and left—" She should've listened. Tobias tried to save her, but she hadn't listened. She hugged around Tobias tighter as he drove through the night. Her embrace begged for his forgiveness.

Sirens blared in the distance, coming to quell the fire reaching toward the sky.

Oпe Good Thing

Tobias drove them past the city limits, where lighting was sparse and trees lined the highway.

"Where are we going?" Marisol asked. The first words she had spoken since speeding out of the gated neighborhood and fleeing the garage engulfed in flame.

"A little up ahead!" he shouted over the whipping speed and loud hum of the engine.

They arrived at an old farmhouse with a rickety barn, leaning to one side. Tobias pushed the motorcycle into some overgrown bushes and pocketed the scrambler, and then the vials of serum he had stored under the seat. Ascending the dry-rotted steps of the house, he spotted a plastic, weathered frog statue. Inside it was a key to the front door.

"My partner's house. He's fixing up the place for retirement. By the looks of it, he seems to be escaping here to drink beers and not much else."

Marisol hugged herself and nodded.

"She can't find us here," he assured.

He opened the crooked hinged screen, unlocked the front door, and shouldered it open. He reached for a light switch on the wall and gave it a flick. The foyer's light fizzled on. The glass enclosure around the dim bulb was full of dead bugs. Not a lick of furniture except for a couple of upturned buckets and a stack of crushed beer cans. He emptied the deep pocket of his trench coat and set the cattle prod near the front door, which he immediately locked.

The strangely shaped fungus scrambler weighed heavy in his hand.

"Scrambler," he explained. "It messes with the signals Adhara sends to mind control mushrooms." He turned it on. Static whispered over the receiver. "No weird singing. We're clear." A twist of the dial clicked the contraption off.

"So, you're saying I acted like a fool all on my own?" She added a quiet chuckle, almost rueful in its weakness.

He lifted his ski mask from his face and shook his head. If only interfering fungi were to blame for all his mistakes. His shoulder throbbed, a reminder of his waning adrenaline. He threw his trench coat to the floor and ripped off his Kevlar vest with a satisfying tear of Velcro. Sure enough, on his left side, a puncture in the material and a flattened round.

"I took a hit." He rubbed his shoulder and the sore spot. Someday, death coming in just a fraction of an inch from his heart might cut him down. Tonight, though, it was simple. They were alive. He whipped his Henley shirt off, taking his undershirt with it, and glimpsed the angry welt on his pectoral. "That'll smart in the morning." The serum tempted him from his coat pocket, but he wanted to handle the pain the right way, to prove to himself he wasn't an addict. "Help me go look for some first aid, why don't you?"

She searched through the cabinets in the empty kitchen. Tobias checked the bathroom. Nothing. Upstairs, he found a bed adorned in rumpled, threadbare sheets and an army-green wool blanket. Great, and a single flat pillow. On the bright side, at least it was a double.

He scoured the cabinets in the upstairs bathroom. Nothing there either.

Marisol stood in the kitchen, holding up a first aid kit. "This was under the sink."

He opened it up on the counter. The kit contained crusty bandages, half a tube of antibiotic ointment, and a couple of packets of ibuprofen. He popped a few of the painkillers. "Want any of the good stuff?"

She shook her head while making a lousy attempt at lifting the edge of her chainmail. The little movement caused her to groan. "My shoulder's dislocated."

"Jesus, kid, why didn't you say something?" He picked her up, set her on the counter, and lifted the chainmail off her with ease. Hot from the fire, a chain link pattern had been seared into her skin.

"I don't know. I thought feeling like shit was fitting with how sorry I am."

He placed the hand of her dislocated shoulder on his opposite one. She bent her elbow a bit, and he gripped the crook for leverage. With his other hand, he gently pushed her upper arm. "Suffering doesn't make you better. It just fucks you up."

Pop! Her shoulder adjusted back into place. She squeezed her eyes shut and grunted as the pain took over. Her heels kicked at the lower cabinets. Her breath steadied, and she began rotating her arm in the socket. Her eyes opened right into his. "Thanks."

He wanted so much to kiss her then. Because they were alive. Because for once, she wasn't looking right at him and seeing someone else. But the matter of Vincent. Tobias cleared his throat.

"Staci is taking a while to reboot. In about a day or so, her entire system will be back online. We can hide here until then. By the end of the weekend, we can get Vinnie back."

Her mouth curled into a weak smile, obviously haggard from her injuries. Nothing in the first aid kit comprehensively fixed the pain she was in. Except... "I have more of Vinnie's healing serum. You'll feel a lot better."

"I'll take it if you do."

Her raspy alto flayed him open. He couldn't hide from her anymore. "I've been taking it. Stole a handful a while back. I didn't beat my addiction. I replaced it." He bowed his head, overtaken by the weight of his shame.

"Oh." She cupped her hand against his jawline. "It's a cycle, isn't it? Sometimes you'll carry me. Sometimes I'll carry you." Directing his head upward, she look straight into his eyes. "Sometimes we'll carry each other."

A weight lifted, and he stood straighter. He wasn't a cheating liar anymore. "You've been pulling more than your own weight for years. Lean on me all you need."

She unbuckled her harness and unzipped her pants. A few wiggles, and she inched her waistband down to expose her hip. "Do it."

He prepared the serum. As he hovered the needle over her hip, he noticed how her long eyelashes cast a shadow along her cheekbones. She was so fucking beautiful, it hurt to look at her. He pierced through her skin to the muscle and pushed the plunger down.

At first, she closed her eyes and bit on her lower lip. Her muted hum sent his blood flow in a regrettable direction. Lolling her head back, she exposed her throat, muscles twitching as she rolled through her climax. He cradled her head so it wouldn't knock against the cabinets. She pressed into his chest, her breath warm over the bruise above his heart.

Without a word, he took her hands, one after the other, and unwrapped the ragged tape and gauze from them. Her skin was smooth now and soft, no longer callused like a warrior's. Whatever she had done to hurt herself no longer mattered. Now was her fresh start.

Her eyes fluttered open. They were clear, no longer bloodshot or drowning.

"What?" he asked quietly, still holding her hand.

Her fingers found his forearm and followed it upward. When she reached the tender welt above his heart, she lingered, tracing a circle that made his breath catch. Her touch wandered to the pendant at his chest. "What's this?"

"The shield of Saint Michael. Diedre gave it to me when she was little. More likely, her mom bought it for me. But when she told me it was to keep Dad safe, I sort of thought the girl enchanted it with some good juju." Their fingers met, twirling the shield between them. "What do you think of the plan?" He whispered, afraid it'd break the quiet.

Her smile grew warmer. "He was there at Durant's. The fire and blood brought him. Did you feel it? He jammed those guns so we could escape."

Magic weaved about him, shimmering inside his chest. It was the same sacred feeling he remembered when a hymn hit right during Mass. Like everything standing on end and finally listening to Heaven. "He told me where to find you."

Her hands traced from his chest to his neck. "I used to think I was a piece of shit for loving him and having feelings for you."

The gunfire must've put a ring in his ears. He hadn't heard her right. "What's that you said?"

"I thought it somehow made my feelings unworthy, but he's been bringing us together from the very beginning. Don't you feel it?"

Her assuring alto pulled at his chest. There weren't secrets and shame among them, but something so strange and beautiful. His sinuses stung. "I do." He held her chin. "I always have. Just thought I was a freak for thinking it. I never thought you—" He took in a breath and kissed her. Not one of their awkward tight-mouthed kisses. No, he sucked on her lower lip, which had been begging for his mouth since he met her.

They'd been fighting the inevitable since the moment they met, and coincidence worked to pull them apart. Not today. She moaned into his mouth, which he took as an invitation to slide his tongue between her lips, as gentle as if he were writing scripture with it. She gripped the solid muscle of his bicep and circled her tongue against his. With her encouragement, he released the beast. He hooked his fingers into the belt loop of her pants and yanked her closer, tightening the space between them. She hooked her legs around him and rolled her hips, riding his erection into rock hard. His teeth knocked into hers, a beautiful accident, when they were smiling so widely.

He came up for air. "There's a bed upstairs." No more nervous stammering and avoiding. He pressed his erection into her thigh so she knew exactly what he wanted to do with her.

She flashed a teasing smile, her lips swollen from his mouth and beard. "Want to make a mess of it?"

"You read my mind."

They struggled walking up the stairs of the farmhouse, kissing and grabbing at each other while they moved. A few stumbles, and they were going to end up unabashedly going at it on the landing, risking a splinter here if they weren't careful.

They finagled their way into the entrance of the bedroom. **Tobias** pinned Marisol against the doorframe, growled, and smacked her ass, possessively cupping a cheek in his giant hand. They staggered inside. He kicked the door shut and hugged her from behind. His hands moved from her hips to her breasts, caressing them over her shirt. His thumb circled over one nipple while his hand kneaded the other breast. "Let's get you to bed?" he breathed into her ear.

They kicked off their shoes, kissed, groped. Tobias spun her to face him and pushed her on the bed. Her princess-like eyes gazed up at him—open and full of wonder. They were the eyes he'd fallen in love with before he knew what love was. In this simple state, so much of her resembled home to him. Every kiss or touch needed *finally*. He kissed her like she'd slake his thirst, finally. Groped her like they belonged to each other, finally.

The mattress bent under their weight as she stretched across it and he hovered over her. He peeled the Kevlar pants off her until she rested her bare feet on his shoulder. The graceful shape of her foot, he couldn't help but kiss the top of it. The kiss grew into a suckle as he ran his hands down her legs to the scalloped band of her panties.

"Do you have a condom?" she asked.

He crawled on top of her and toyed with strands of her hair. "Didn't think I'd be needing them."

She leaned her forehead against his and caught her breath between their kisses. "Maybe your partner has a stash around here."

Another kiss of hers landed on his teeth as he held back a laugh. "Did you see the first aid kit? Wishful thinking."

Her fingertip circled the buckle of his belt. "We don't have to have one." She began to ease the leather through the metal.

Every one of her tugs and unbuttons sent him from the agony of restraint to the agony of release. "You want to be a good Catholic?"

"It wouldn't be so bad, though. You, me, and a perfect mistake." She slowly lowered his zipper and planted a suckling kiss on his chest.

Such a future gutted him. He never thought he'd have a moment like this again. A chance to be new, possessing a hope so profound, the godforsaken world felt right. The pure kind of love from her devastated more than any bullet. "Let's save the world first."

"We'll make it a perfect place for our bab—"

He ravaged her mouth with his, overcome with the need to mark her, to feel the squeeze of her as he came deep inside. From this angle, his cock slid across her panties, held back by a thin layer of cotton. The facsimile of driving penetration made him ache for it. He could surrender himself to bare and unprotected. His rapid and wild thrusts would render her senseless. Her thighs would drip with him and their bodies commune—seed and womb, matter and spirit, earth and heaven. They had so much work to do to make a world good enough. Good enough for her. And Diedre. And the growing family of hormone-fueled dreams.

"We could always do other things," he said.

"Yeah?" She sat up on her knees and pushed him two steps from the end of the bed.

Her eyes darkened, as if she became possessed by someone or something else, conjuring delicious wickedness which opened her body to him. Her gaze moved to the glistening head above his open fly. "Get it out and show me how you touch yourself when you think of me."

He gulped then laughed.

"You're not shy, are you?"

"Around you? Maybe a little."

She smoothed a hand from his stomach, over his chest. High on her knees, she reached up so her thumb and index finger formed a V against his throat. She massaged along the tendons in his neck, squeezing and releasing. The sensation held him captive, as if everything he had tried to hide—to be ashamed of—could be read so easily by her. The pulsing ache of being hers, the way she'd collar him and lead around. To have this much wanting on the precipice of indulgence, it overwhelmed him to the point of stillness.

She crooned, "I'll show you how I do it when I think of you." She freed one breast from under her shirt and pinched her tight, burgundy-colored nipple.

He watched her, encouraged by the essence of Vincent lingering here. Images of him kissing the side of her gasping mouth. Of his deft fingers plucking her nipple tight.

"His beautiful lips would glance over me, and I'd want to be rubbed raw from your stubble. He'd tease with a light touch of his hand, and you'd work me with your roughness and force." She cooed and writhed, enjoying the circle and dip of her hand.

"Fuck," Tobias breathed. He took his cock out and stroked it. It was already flushed and shining slick with his pleasure.

Marisol propped herself up on an elbow and studied him. "That's it."

He picked up the pace. His breathing intensified, his skin flushed. Faster and faster. His eyes closed, feeling the magnetic draw of being watched. By her. By him. A moment from release.

"Stop," she ordered.

He stopped and sighed. The denial wounded him, but he wanted to be under her direction. To be her good boy.

"Don't you want to come on these tits?" She pushed her undershirt above her breasts and squeezed them together. Fuck, they were round, luscious, and more than a handful. Her loving would cleanse him by fire, and he'd be worthy enough to mark her.

She reached out and ran a finger along his shaft, smearing the liquid leaking from his tip. "Or would you rather come in my mouth?" She licked and sucked his arousal from her finger.

He was so close to breaking apart from her teasing. The promise of rewarding him for a job well done with her cheeks hollowed and his semen running down her throat drew his balls tight. When her finger popped out of her mouth, it was too much. He bit his lip, hard, and nodded. The promise hurt more than the bruise over his heart.

"Then be a good boy and kiss my feet." She untucked her legs from beneath her and extended them with pointed feet.

Compelled by the need to serve, he took one foot in his hand and dragged his lower lip across the underside of a baby toe, suckling on the tip.

"That's the best you can do?" she taunted.

He opened his mouth and sucked in her toes, tracing the lines of each one with the tip of his tongue. Where one foot was sucked, the other was licked. Each sloppy wet flicker of his tongue elicited a gasp or a moan, whipping him into frenzy.

He rose to his knees on the bed, grinding into the cotton barrier at the apex of her thighs. "I want to make you feel the way you make me feel. Let me show you how good I am." He trembled as if he were approaching God.

"Be a good boy then."

He pulled her panties down her legs and gave each foot one last succulent kiss as he slid them off. He bent over her, encouraging the parting of her thighs with trailing kisses. With his destination unobstructed, he buried his devouring mouth and prodding nose into her. The sweet taste of her was like drinking heaven.

She nudged him with her thigh. "I'll only let you eat me out if I can sit on your face."

He laughed and lay down next to her. He threw the measly pillow out from under him, lying flat. He held out his arms in a T shape. "Well?"

She sat on his chest, and her thighs bracketed his face. He grasped her hips and pulled her toward him, smothering himself in her intimate heat. He massaged a flat tongue against her mound, and when she sighed, he sucked hard on her clit. Her body melted into him with his soft kisses and licks. His tongue explored deeper, and she rocked her hips. Her rhythm wilder and wilder, her insides pulsed around him as she rode. Each delicious drop of her fed his own pleasure. He hummed to send more vibrations through her. She leaned forward, catching herself on the wall. With his nose dragging, tongue thrusting, he was showing what a good boy he could be. She pushed down against his mouth. Her sex was his oxygen. He didn't need to breathe air—just live off her cries and cum, which he wrung out from her. She fell limp, curled over his face and chest.

He lifted her off and pushed himself up to his knees. "I could come just tasting you."

She took him in her fist and stroked. "Me too." Then she licked his sensitive tip. He shuddered. She sucked, taking him farther into her mouth, caressing what couldn't fit into her wet fist. He whimpered, prey under his lioness' control.

He gathered her hair in his hand, and her eyes dared him to admit defeat. The moment his gaze met hers, he was destroyed. The back of her throat clenched his sensitive head. With her eyes searing into him, he came in hot spurts. Every pulsing release shook his body.

Before she could swallow everything he gave her, he pulled her up into a kiss. Saliva to saliva, tongue to tongue, their tastes combined. Salt, bitter, and a hint of sweet. Up on their knees holding each other, they appeared in prayer.

Then he broke the kiss and hugged her, resting his cheek on top of her head. "No one makes me feel the way you do. You make me so good."

"I know. You're my good boy."

He continued to hold her. If things went to plan, they were on the eve of Vinnie's return. In their perfect couple, there'd be no room for Tobias. So, he tightened his embrace and swore tonight would be enough.

43

The Dying Sickness

I do not leave France immediately, choosing to follow news of Adhara's fate. To my surprise, authorities arrest her peacefully. She did not fight them. Is she resigned or repentant?

She is due to face the guillotine. Why doesn't she use her superhuman strength to escape? We can't die, but we can become something else, prisoners in our rotting bodies. I confront the sorrow of dragging a mindless Adhara throughout eternity with me. My worry compels me to break into her prison to free her. The rough stones of the building are coated in the sludge of time and miasma of sewage.

I find her in her cell, sitting with her legs tucked into her chest. Her curls have lost their shine.

"I'm here to save you."

She snorts. "From what?"

"You're not going to see the conclusion of this charade!"

She says almost dreamily, "When the mortals write about the monsters they've created, they emphasize the head. None of us tried decapitation when we've fallen into our dying sickness. Maybe I'll finally be released." She stands up and tiptoes closer to the bars. "What have you tried, when the wish for death consumes you?"

A tear escapes my eye. The final mask slips—the quiet suffering of the ultimate pain we desire to inflict upon ourselves. "The more I long for it, the more I become my shadow. He gives me the strength to do what's right."

"Hm." She nods. Her hands clutch the bars. "Do you know why I found you after all these years?"

I shake my head, but I want her answer to be like mine. I had been robbed of affection and she, once upon a time, gave it to me without question. Though we argue, being with her on our bright days took away the pain of my eternity.

"I felt so alive when I imprisoned Alvaro, knowing his ever-after was going to be as sunless and void as his heart. It felt right. Don't you see, Rubio? Our doom will set us free. I came here to seal you in steel and plunge you into endless darkness. I found you to watch the life drain from you."

I step back from the cell bars. Stunned as our time together came into focus like a final adjustment of a microscope. We were fellow passengers suffering through our miserable circumstance—lovers, yes, but never friends. We went through the motions of companionship, but never understood each other. I had wanted love. She had wanted freedom.

"But you live in a dark box of your own making. You don't need me to place you in one. Now go."

And I leave her. I board the first ship to America.

44

Entropy

obias's phone vibrated off the bucket-turned-nightstand and crashed to the floor. He picked it up. The caller? Work. Typical for his sergeant to come between him and a good thing. He answered, "Quinlan. This better be good."

"Bring your ass down here. We need you." Had to give Sergeant credit. He knew how to prime the pump.

His superior officer sounded pissed. Maybe they found the mess Adhara left behind of Grant Durant and Shepherd's Watch. Better play stupid. "Another blue blood go ballistic?"

Marisol stirred awake, making low groaning noises. Her hair curtain parted to reveal a coyly gleaming eye. He watched reverently, combing her wavy strands aside with the other hand.

"I can explain in detail when you get here," the sergeant said.

"Playing mysterious, are we?" He could give a good God fuck what the sergeant said. She was the kind of beautiful which made him want to live in bed with her. "What if I told you I was out of the country?"

"I'll see you in a half hour."

He sighed. It wouldn't be all bad. The sergeant was most likely referring to the mess at Durant's. He'd show up and play dumb. When the opportunity presented itself, he'd volunteer to check something in records and sneak away to drive back to the farmhouse with some much-needed supplies. "You got it, boss."

Tobias got up and put on his pants.

"What is it?" Marisol asked, raspy from sleep but utterly sexy.

"Work. I have to go in, and my sergeant doesn't accept *tied up by beautiful woman* as a decent enough excuse." He found his socks and boots, shoving his feet inside. "Figured I'd make an appearance and half-ass it, for once. I'll be back before you know it. Serum's in the fridge, and you can help yourself to the canned food. We got pie filling."

She rolled her eyes. "Yum."

"I'll come bearing gifts. Decent food, change of clothes, and other things to help pass the time until Staci reboots and..." He shrugged, daring not to utter about Vincent's return. Last night gave the both of them an end to their most recent misery. But was this the last day where she'd be his and his alone?

"After last night, I'm hoping to be delightfully bored. Does your partner keep any books around?"

"You might find a twenty-year-old phone book."

She performed a comedic groan and crawled to the edge of the bed, her dark hair wavy and lush from the friction of sleeping. Her golden-brown shoulder slipped out of the neck of his undershirt. She was so gorgeous this way. "I'm bad at being the girlfriend who waits at home for her hero to return. Alas, I have a type." She wrapped her fingers around his Saint Michael's shield pendant and gently pulled his necklace. He bent down to meet her in a kiss.

Tobias rode the motorcycle into the city. Its power center glowed blue, which meant Staci was returning online. He weaved through the streets and noticed crowds of people heading in the same direction as his precinct. They carried signs. *Protect Our Girls. Rich or poor: One law.* From the center of Justice Square, a megaphone's static blared. People gathered into a protest in between the precinct and the courthouse. Was this what the sergeant called him in for? What was Tobias going to do? Flick the collar of his trench coat at them?

He stopped and listened to the leader on the megaphone, a college-aged woman. The megaphone clicked. "Last night, files of multiple crimes committed by Grant Durant were shared. These have been ignored by prosecutors like Penelope Stanwycki. Prosecutors who demonized victims as runaways, addicts, and liars. If our system doesn't protect the innocent and punish the guilty, there is no point in continuing something that doesn't work for us. The rich are no different than us. They do not answer to another set of laws. One law!"

The gathering crowd chanted and cheered.

Tobias's stomach dropped. The files documenting Grant Durant's abuse? Those were Vincent's files. The only other person who had access to them was Marisol. If the people knew about their contents, despite the efforts of slimy defense attorneys to bury them, the city would be lucky if it only wound up with a throng of angry people peacefully protesting. Except the queasy feeling told him something bigger loomed.

He carefully rode through the crowd as he headed for the precinct's underground parking ramp. Whatever work had in store for him, Tobias sensed it was going to be a doozy.

Tobias emerged from the locker room, sporting the cheap dress shirt and tie he kept as backup in his locker. Sergeant Thompson sat on Tobias's desk reading a newspaper, his legs dangling over the edge, bouncing with giddy excitement. The headline read FIRE AT DURANT HOME. Fire was the least of Tobias's concerns when he'd been there last night, but if that was the headline, it meant no one found his headless body yet. Or the bodies of the Shadows. Or of the Shepherd's Watch soldiers. Who had scrubbed the scene? Who would be powerful enough to feed a gigantic lie to the official channels?

Fuck it. At least he didn't have to fake his way through a homicide scene this morning.

Tobias carefully hung his trench coat off the nearby coat rack. The cattle prod clanked a little too loudly against the wood stand. He forced a smile, fake enough to scare his boss off his desk. "This better be good."

"No hello or good morning?" Sergeant Thompson laughed.

Crossed arms over Tobias's chest counteracted the mirth exuding from Thompson, a solid wall of *fuck you* in zero words. He didn't like coming in on his day off, especially when he had the world's best woman waiting for him.

"All right, the Commissioner wanted all hands on deck as people get feisty out there."

Tobias wrinkled his nose. "I'm a detective. I'm not exactly the type to send a pepper spray canister into a crowd because the people in charge don't like what a bunch of kids have to say."

"Don't worry. If they keep their cool, you'll sit on your ass."

Marisol dusted off the top of the box television. Adjusting the rabbit ears at least crackled the hushing static. A few more adjustments and the screen showed a fuzzy, old Zorro movie. Sure, the film seemed like it was passing through an ailing microwave and chock full of commercial breaks, but it'd pass the time before Tobias came back. The growl from her stomach directed her to the kitchen pantry.

One look at the cans sprinkled in rust and she sneered at choking down some decade-old Vienna sausages. More growls however, had her reaching for the can of peaches. The television blared the wonders of the air fryer from the other room as she strained to open the can with a rudimentary can opener. She'd slurped one wedge into her mouth when the victorious trumpets of an action scene broke into a news theme.

"Demonstrators gather inside Shadowhaven's Justice Square over the recent outcome of the Grant Durant trial. Prosecutors agreed to drop charges after a witness gave inconsistent testimony and others refused to testify against the Congressional candidate. One of the organizers says their demonstration is due to footage of Durant's crimes, including those of other prominent figures, which had been uploaded by an anonymous source to multiple websites."

The files! Adhara had probably shared the files when the court case went belly-up. She had said a change was in the air. Dammit, she must've meant releasing the footage of Durant's crimes. Marisol ran from the kitchen to the sparse living room.

"Expect delays in traffic near Justice Square. We'll keep you updated on any developments."

As soon as she gulped down another slice, the news footage broke in again. More demonstrators were joining the crowd. Four large, cloaked figures dragged a giant flatbed. Standing on it rode two smaller but shrouded people. The figures shambled through the crowd, who gawked as the flatbed creaked by. Their dragging ceased as it reached its position between the curated landscape of the square and the police precinct stairs. One of the shrouded people standing on the flatbed doffed their cloak. Sunlight glinted off their golden armor. Adhara!

Marisol ran to her phone to warn Tobias, but it was dead. She suited up, putting on her chainmail and Kevlar.

She rushed out of the house and kicked the door to the rickety garage open. Fuck, it didn't have a car. However, a crowbar hung off a rusty nail. That might come in handy, the way crowbars against insurmountable forces did. Except she wasn't a crowbar against a train track. She hooked the crowbar on her harness next to the scrambler Tobias had abandoned on the kitchen counter.

The serum was the last thing she grabbed. The winning edge it promised called to her. She injected one of the vials and suppressed the wave of euphoria with a held breath and a grunt. As ready as she'd ever be, she ran to the main road, carrying the rest of the serum in an old plastic grocery bag.

News of the unofficial parade float buzzed through the precinct, reporting that it was dragged through the streets led by members of the Illuminati. **Tobias** pushed his way outside, watching the strange pageant from the stairs. The oddity froze the rest of the demonstrators in quizzical silence. The sight must've sown enough unease, because a handful of officers in riot gear lined up at the base of the stairs.

The Illuminati member riding the platform flung its shroud off. Motherfucking Adhara. Tobias staggered down a few steps in awe. Common sense told him to run inside the precinct and blockade the door to the Homicide department, but she was a burning building he'd walk right back into.

Adhara held out her clawed hand to the speaker Tobias heard earlier. The woman crept to the platform, gingerly handing Adhara the megaphone. The girl's shoulders met her ears as she eased her way back to where she had been standing.

Adhara lifted the megaphone. "We are here because our justice system failed us—continues to fail us. Even as the rich kill their own as if a god were handing down retribution. The law protected those in power and punished the victims."

A few crowd members cheered.

"We softened, thinking shame and appealing to their sense of morality would protect us. But these people have no shame, recording their crimes and telling us to deny what our own eyes see. These people have no morals. The only thing that works?" She paused, her gaze moved over the crowd. A breeze stirred her braids but didn't flutter her composure. The crowd stepped forward, faces upturned like devoted congregants. She wet her lips, and the megaphone clicked sharply. "Fear. The rich and powerful need to be afraid of us again."

The rest of the crowd joined in the roaring enthusiasm, whooping and clapping. Tobias swallowed back his rising dread. As right as she was, these people didn't know their gleeful support sealed them into her devil's bargain.

From the cloak pooled at her feet, she drew something the size of a bowling ball. She held it like someone plucking an onion from a garden. Bloody and frozen in a grotesque face, she held up the head of Grant Durant by his hair.

Some in the crowd gasped. Others wondered among each other if the head was real or a prop. Tobias knew. Too well, he knew how studying the gory face of death emptied him little by little. He pivoted slightly, readying to duck into the safety inside, and yet, he had to watch the scene unfold.

"I hold the head of Grant Durant. He, who raped girls for his own sense of power. He, who trafficked them so others like him could use their bodies for their gratification. It wasn't enough for these people to be wealthy. They got off on the suffering they caused. Look at his head. This is the brutal end the lawless elite class must face to restore Justice!" She punted the head into the gathering crowd.

One person in the crowd shouted, "It's real!" A small group scattered away from the square.

Another laughed and said, "A Halloween prop!"

The murmuring speculation rose to a frenzy. More who appropriately panicked peeled away from the throng. The roaring reached its peak, and Adhara pulled the cloak off the other figure standing with her on the platform. US Attorney Penelope Stanwycki sat tied and gagged. The crowd responded with a chorus of gasps.

The officers who lined up at the bottom of the stairs moved in a phalanx toward the wheeled stage.

"Penelope Stanwycki, you buried the evidence of these rapists' crimes on a technicality," Adhara shouted into the megaphone.

The crowd booed. Dread curdled in Tobias's stomach.

"You humiliated victims, putting them on the stand so they could be viciously accused of being liars or sluts when they are traumatized girls."

Rage seethed from the crowd. A person shouted, "Kill her!"

"You let a rapist, kidnapper, and trafficker go free. Your corruption is a cancer. And you must be cut out."

Tobias watched impotently as the tied woman wailed. The crowd, frothing at the mouth demanding her death, compounded the terror etched on her face. Adhara unsheathed her sword and raised it high. A plainclothes officer—the walking hard-on Franchetti—shoved his way from the center of the crowd with his gun raised.

Tobias ran down the stairs, hitting the wall of riot police. He tried to wedge himself by the giant shields, but he couldn't break through. "Adhara!" he screamed.

She lowered her sword. He screamed her name again, and finally, her gaze found him over the chaos. "Your issue is with me. You don't need to bring anyone else into this!"

"Our hero." Adhara bowed halfheartedly with her head still raised. "She trusted you, and look what it's gotten for this city." Her body sank for a moment, heaving as she caught her breath. The sword at her side kissed the ground of the platform. "I should thank you. If not for the chaos, for cracking the computer code, this would never have happened. I accessed all sorts of goodies."

She had been to Varian's hideout after him. What did she access? The weight on his chest compounded. But whatever she had planned, people weren't going to needlessly suffer for it—not any more than they already had. Hoarsely, he called out, "Your beef is with me, yes. I didn't do enough when I had the chance. I never do. But if you drop the sword and let her go, we can talk about it. I'll even tell you where you can find Wheels."

Her breathing slowed, and she stared ahead at him, eyes watering.

"Drop the weapon!" Franchetti shouted. The crowd retreated behind him but congregated at the riot police, who pinned the demonstrators between their shields and Adhara's stage, bottlenecking them as they fled.

Tobias clawed again through the sea of people, making no headway. The buildup of people pushed against him. Every inch of progress toward the stage was counteracted as more and more people were crowded before the precinct.

"Don't shoot!" His vocal cords burned from their overuse. Nauseating realization blotted all sound from his ears. In slow motion, he watched Adhara raise her sword again. Franchetti fired his gun three times. Adhara flailed back and dropped to the ground.

And still, everything moved slowly. People had to be screaming. Yet he heard nothing but the sound of his own breathing. People stampeded toward the courthouse. Armed officers shoved and clubbed the frightened demonstrators away from the precinct's stairs.

Adhara's sword rolled out of her hands. Was she playing dead? Or was she—?

The super-powered woman reached up, fingers wiggling feebly as if asking for help. Her clawed fingertips sliced Penelope Stanwycki's throat, who slumped over dead. Franchetti stood dumbfounded.

The four cloaked figures, stock still among the chaos, tore away their cloaks. One he recognized, the skull-like, sunken face with douche bro slicked back hair. The soulless eyes he looked into when he was beat within an inch of his life last year. Stone motherfucking Ruthven, also known as the Bloodsucker. The other three seemed to be in varying state of decay—charred human barbecue with a hole in its chest, a man made of more deforming scar tissue than flesh, and a walking water-bloated corpse.

Tobias ping-ponged among the scattering, frantic crowd, bursting through a break in the bottleneck. He focused his sight on Franchetti, staring into the monstrous form of the scarred creature. Franchetti's expression, gaped in horror, had yet to understand the monster's immortality. The only way to make it on the other side of one of these things was to run. *Run,* Tobias hesitated to form on his lips. The screaming reentered his hearing, overriding his fear. But the scarred creature's gnarled hand clutched Franchetti's gun and hand, crunching both in its paw. Pained howls pierced the air.

"Run!" Tobias yelled.

Franchetti didn't move. The monster punched him with the full force of its super-power. Franchetti's lifeless body landed on the ground with a thud. Tobias spun, running in the other direction, clambering for refuge inside the precinct.

When he reached the stairs, he looked back toward Adhara. She stood, smearing the fallen attorney's blood on her face with the back of her hand. Pointing the tip of her sword in the direction of the precinct, she gritted out, "Kill the pigs!" Her eyes grew wide, lit with the fire of vengeance.

Marisol held out her thumb as she charged down the shoulder of the highway. Cars zoomed by her, gnawing away at her hope of returning to the city in time to stop Adhara's inevitable ruckus. A semi truck roared by her, kicking up small debris. It pulled onto the shoulder and honked as it stopped. *Fuck yes!*

She ran to the cab and pulled open the door. "Can you take me to Justice Square in Shadowhaven?"

The truck driver, sporting a beat-up ball cap and a face of thick stubble, retorted, "You obviously haven't heard the news."

Shit had to have hit a gaggle of fans since Adhara showed up on live television. She sighed. "Is it possible to take me into the city? You can get me as close to Justice Square as you're comfortable."

The driver stared ahead at the road as he considered. The longer he blinked, the more a timely arrival in Shadowhaven seemed like a far-off dream. With one more rub of his stubble, he answered, "Deal."

Marisol tossed the bag of serum into the seat and jumped up into the cab. The news on the radio reported a sword-wielding woman and four burly men in special effects makeup were attacking people.

As she ran her finger over the edge of her domino mask in her pocket, she prayed for another miracle.

45

Pyrrhic Victory

Tobias slammed the door to the homicide department behind him, muffling the screams on the other side. Blood splattered across the door's frosted glass window. He breathed in. What did he need to do next? His hammering pulse eclipsed the answer.

Burke dragged a metal filing cabinet in front of the door and bent down, hands braced at his knees, out of breath. "I thought those motherfuckers were supposed to go down with a bullet in the head."

The door rattled behind them but barely budged under the weight of the cabinet. "These are a different motherfucker entirely." He unsheathed his cattle prod. "Does the evidence room still contain the mountain of heroin the 86ers tried to deal?"

Burke shook his head and wiped the sweat off his forehead with a hanky. "A little early for a party, don't you think, Quinlan?"

"Not for me. You inject one of those zombies with enough heroin to take out an elephant—and I'm not speaking in hyperbole—we might have a chance at locking them up. I'd also suggest getting your hands on thirty zip ties per deathless freak. Fifteen at the wrist, the other fifteen at the ankles. That's 150, if you need a calculator."

His partner replied with a snort. "More Shadowhaven spooky shit you seem to have special knowledge of?"

"You bet." Tobias twirled the cattle prod in his hand. "Let's take the back stairs."

The driver dropped **Marisol** off six blocks from Justice Square. After thanking the driver, she jumped out of the cab, adjusted her domino mask, clenched the crowbar in her fist, and ran. The bag of serum hanging off her harness smacked against her hip. Far enough from the square, the streets had become a ghost town. But still she ran, lifting her knees and reaching the full extension of her stride. She beat a rapid rhythm against the pavement.

A smattering of frightened people breezed past her. Running upstream? Her lip quivered as fear spiraled from her tensing muscles. She refocused, syncing her breath to her striking feet. Eerie clouds of tear gas floated above the road as she approached Justice Square. Swallowing and blinking away the burning sensation, she skidded to halt to assess the damage. Debris, blood spatters, and bodies marked the path of Adhara and the Others, ending at the entrance of the police precinct. Screams and gunfire echoed from its opened main doors. Obviously, she'd have to find another way into the building.

She beelined toward the back. The main floor had become a meat grinder. If she stood a chance against five super-powered immortals, a sneak attack was her best bet. But how? Marked entrances were out of the question. She focused on a superficial balcony built around a window. Its proximity to a streetlight might be to her advantage. The climb up would exhaust her. If she was going to have any chance against Adhara, she needed all the strength she could muster.

And she had a grocery bag of liquid courage. She untied the bag and peered inside. Eight vials. If one vial was like having a full night's rest and a sensible breakfast, with unfortunate orgasmic side effect, a larger dose could be what the doctor ordered...or nurse. She leaned into the lamppost and prepared a syringe, filling it to its final line of measurement. Inching down the band of her pants, she exposed the upper part of her hip muscle. She stabbed in the needle, the serum expanding into a sizzling web over her body.

The serum didn't arrive in waves like the last time she took it. It flexed her every muscle, pumped inside every vein, and chugged her heart along with a sickening speed. Tears streamed from her eyes. Each tear shed seemed to scrape a layer of gray wash from the world. The noise from inside the precinct chattered in her ears. Sight was loud. Sound was bold. No euphoria this time, but madness. It escaped from her mouth in a scream.

She shinnied up the streetlight with the ease of walking across the living room. At the top, she pushed herself off, catching the balcony's edge under her arms. Swinging her leg over, she landed on the foot-width of balcony before the office window. She unhooked the crowbar from her harness and shattered the window in one fell swoop. Super serum, making yesterday's improbable feats into today's small tasks.

She jumped inside an empty office. Scattered papers and an upturned office chair—this person left in a hurry. Pressing herself against the wall, she inched cautiously toward the exit. Kicking the door open, she entered the hallway, carefully moving with her crowbar raised.

An officer burst into the hallway with both arms extended, elbows locked, pointing his gun. *Bam!* He fired the gun. Marisol's drug-enhanced perception slowed the bullet down. It grazed along the plastic links of her hood, buzzing like an annoying insect. Marisol dropped to the ground. "Dumbass, I'm here to help!"

"Drop your weapon," he shrieked, as a tremor overtook his hand. Sweat beaded on his upper lip. Fearful and deadly formed into a dangerous combination.

Marisol squeezed the crowbar tighter and took a step forward. Officer Scared Shitless didn't pull the trigger yet, which gave her an idea, a shoot-for-the-moon gamble of an idea. "Your gun won't hurt me."

He blinked, looking as if he was resisting the urge to cry.

She took another step forward. "But I won't hurt you if you don't act a fool. You saw what happened to those who dared to try us."

His mouth flexed into a pained grimace as he sniffled. He nodded but didn't lower the gun.

Shuffling closer, Marisol hadn't just overshot the moon, she practically had entered a different galaxy. The gun hovered almost an inch from her chest, aimed at her sternum. "You want to come home tonight, right? So you go into one of those offices, barricade the door, and you don't come out until...until—" Who did the police rely on in an emergency, anyway? "Until the fire department comes. And if you can, you get on that little walkie talkie of yours and convince your buddies to do the same thing. Otherwise, you'll end up ground beef like the other people who refused to listen."

The floodgates opened, and the officer was in a full-blown sob. Unpredictable, which didn't bode well for this gamble landing.

"What are you waiting for?"

He finally lowered the gun and dashed into an office, closing the door behind him. The lock snicked, and soon the scrape of moving furniture followed. She collapsed in herself, releasing the breath she definitely knew she was holding. Her body fallaciously believed lungs filled to capacity would've totally handled a bullet at point-blank range.

She shifted the crowbar in her grip and wielded it like a baseball bat before heading upstairs.

Tobias, the Pied Piper of terrified adults, led the Homicide department with his cattle prod. They made their way to the back stairwell.

The exit door swung open. Adhara stood on the other side. "Thought I smelled bacon," she growled.

"Go back up! Run!" Tobias ordered as he spread his arms from rail to rail in attempt to shield his coworkers. Some whimpered as Adhara swatted the air with her sword. "Quit crying and run!" Others stumbled as they attempted to change direction up the stairs. Tobias turned to Burke. "You have to get to the evidence room! Climb down if you have to."

"You've survived my pets. How impressive," she taunted as her sword whipped in half circles.

"You made your point, Adhara. Leave the rest of us alone. We're good people." He tripped upward onto his backside, lying flat on the landing.

Adhara lifted his chin with the edge of her sword and squatted down to his level. The cool metal contrasted with the lukewarm sensation of drying blood. "You know what happens when there's one bad apple, don't you?"

He swallowed, feeling the blade's scrape along his Adam's apple. The cattle prod grew warm in his sweaty grip. He couldn't take her out, but he could buy himself time before the inevitable. Raising the prod, he lined its charged end against the metal plate over her chest. "Remind me." The charge knocked her back a foot.

But he might as well have attacked her with mosquitos. She shrugged off the pulse. "We cut out the corruption."

Whoosh! The sword swung down, slicing through his right arm.

Shock came first. He looked at his arm, the entire thing from below his elbow, on the floor. Finally, the pain came, dizzying and all-consuming.

Marisol froze on the landing of the eighth floor, home of the Homicide department. Yelps and squelches around the corner staked her down in place. Super-powered creatures wrecking shop on Adhara's orders? Sounded a lot like mind control.

She unclipped the scrambler from her harness and turned the knob. With a few adjustments, it locked in on shrieks sounding like a throng of cartoon chipmunks. *All right, fungus fuckers, time to get fucked up.* She smashed the button, delivering the quiet scrambling signal. Wet carnage and its accompanying screams cut to silence. The sudden shift wasn't exactly comforting.

She sidled into the main hallway. Bodies were strewn about and nothing moved, which meant Adhara was closer. She had to stop her. Blood's metallic smell hung in the air. Marisol scanned over the bodies, nausea beginning to overwhelm her. *Please don't be him.* But no familiar broad shoulders in a trench coat. He had to be alive.

She tiptoed but slipped in a puddle of blood, steadying near a body she recognized. It lay flat like a pancake. Not Tobias, thank God. Morbid curiosity overtook her, and she bent down to see. It was the freaking Bloodsucker, last year's scourge of Shadowhaven. She eased by him and gave his unconscious body a kick. "That's for Annie, you shit." It twitched, unconscious but not lifeless. The scrambler might have worked.

Turning a corner, she found the door to the Homicide department, decorated with blood splatter. Thankfully from the outside. Marisol rammed the door with her shoulder. Damn, something barricaded the door. A swing of the crowbar into the door's frosted glass cracked it into a spiderweb. She dug the clawed end of the bar into the opening. A few more targeted strikes, and she crawled inside, finding herself on top of a metal filing cabinet.

A group of detectives recoiled from her. One with a bulldog build looked a little like Tobias's colorful descriptions of his partner.

"Tobias, is he here?" Marisol asked.

"He was right behind us at the back staircase," the bulldog-ish man answered.

She jumped down from the cabinet and sprinted toward the door.

"Wait!" he called after her.

But she persisted. The serum's power fortified her muscles, linking the fibers into an unbreakable chain. Her rage escaped from her mouth in a banshee scream as she kicked open the door to the back stairs.

She found Adhara standing above Tobias on the landing below, sword raised to strike. Curled on the ground, he held he cradled his bloody elbow against his stomach. His right arm lay beside him, severed.

Adhara had hurt him. Adhara hurt the man she loved.

She would pay.

"Get away from him, you bitch!"

Adhara lowered the sword and laughed, deep and throaty. "Ah, the masked hero!" She used the jets at her ankles to fly up the stairs, meeting Marisol eye to eye.

"I spent the last few months in Hell because of you. Tell me why I shouldn't break your face."

"A puny mortal like you can't—"

Marisol struck Adhara across the face with the crowbar, landing with a crunch and ping. Adhara reeled back, blood trickling from her nose. A prideful grin pulled at the corners of her mouth. Guess a mortal could make a god bleed. "Oops, left a scratch."

Adhara's laugh grew from throaty to hysterical. "There she is! There's the killer. Come now, do it again. Make it sexy."

Marisol swung the crowbar again but missed. Adhara met her in a bear hug and tackled her through the exit door into the Homicide department. Breath knocked from her lungs, Marisol choked on her own gasps. But Adhara jumped to her feet, sword raised. She plunged it down, but Marisol rolled out of its way. Adhara stabbed through the floor. Her sword stuck, and she struggled to yank it out. Marisol took the opening to kick Adhara in the chest. Adhara flailed back, but regained her footing and dug her clawed hands into Marisol's armored shoulders. The super-powered woman threw Marisol into an office partition. Her body broke a hole through it. The force knocked her crowbar from her grip.

Marisol stood, feeling her body click into place, bruises and broken bones a temporary inconvenience under the thrall of the serum. Sword freed, Adhara sliced the air, stalking nearer to Marisol. Marisol pulled a metal desk drawer out and flung files and papers everywhere. The tank-like drawer blocked Adhara's strikes. Sparks flew, the sword driving deeper and deeper into the metal as Adhara leaned all her weight into the sword. Marisol's muscles burned as she held the desk drawer like a shield. Her biceps shook, fighting the pressure. Yet the fury of the serum kept her in play.

In boxing, when an opponent threw too much weight behind a punch, they risked an even greater punch to the face. Marisol kicked Adhara in the gut, forcing her off balance. Collapsed over from the kick, Adhara exposed the back of her neck, where her metal spine met the base of her skull. Marisol brought a corner of the desk drawer down on it, flattening Adhara to the floor.

Marisol shuffled back. Adhara's left shoulder slumped and her breathing strained. The minor damage to her exoskeleton struck an interesting blow. If Marisol could hurt more of the golden spine, Adhara could be injured enough to be taken into frozen custody.

Adhara's body loudly whirred and wheezed as she wildly punched. Walls, desks, glass partitions caved into nasty divots or burst into dust under Adhara's unbridled strength. With her acute senses, Marisol parried and ducked to avoid the clawed hand's destruction. Flying particles cut into her cheek, but the sudden stings flitted away like magic.

Marisol blinked away the jagged debris. A flash of gold flew toward her. She stumbled back. The claw struck her mouth, and her jaw went slack. Blood poured over her tongue. Disoriented, Marisol staggered, feet slipping on the mound of broken things. Her body became weightless. She was being lifted.

Crack! The force of her broke a desk in half. She lay there, hit by what seemed a concrete wall of pain stealing any breath she had away. Bruising, bleeding, everything. The throb reached a gut-curdling peak before subsiding thanks to the serum in her system.

Just within her reach lay the crowbar. All she needed to do was inch her fingers closer. A metal-capped heel dug into her forearm. Marisol squirmed to fight off the crushing weight snapping her arm, yet the heel pinned her in place.

"I commend you for putting up a fight, but I'm just a cat playing with my meal." Adhara clacked her gold claws together. "I won't kill you yet. You have to see the totality of my vision."

Adhara cackled, and the lights overhead buzzed on and off. "Ah, the particle accelerator. Everything is going as planned."

Adhara's gaze shifted to the pulsing lights. She released the pressure on Marisol's arm. "Is it irony? You and your boyfriend's desire to bring him back will end everything. You thought love would save the world, but your blind devotion will destroy it."

Marisol cradled her arm, scooting herself up to sitting. It crackled as it moved back into place. "Lemme guess, Tobias rebooted the system, and you accessed the accelerator."

"And with a few flourishes to the code, it's going to produce enough antimatter to rip a hole through existence. That's the only way to end the curse, the only way to bring about the balancing of Justice—to end existence."

The lights were already flickering. There'd be no way to reverse the accelerator's activation, but a rebooted Staci might work to her favor. Marisol had five minutes to shift events in her direction. "There're good things, Adhara. I've seen you love. I've seen your happiness. What about Wheels? Françoise? You shouldn't destroy them or their memory."

Adhara's anger smoothed over, as if lost in a memory, the kind of momentary glitch Marisol had recognized in Vincent. The distraction worked to Marisol's advantage. She grabbed the crowbar.

And swung. The clawed end wedged under Adhara's golden spine. Dad's advice echoed through Marisol's mind. *Swing good.* She wrenched the crowbar away, prying the metal from Adhara's back with a squelch. Another yank and the entire thing ripped away like a shiny, gold bandage dripping with bio-fluid.

Adhara collapsed to the ground screaming until the bio-fluid drained from her body, and her voice became a husk. She shriveled into a crooked mummy, her flesh shrink-wrapped to her bones.

The adrenaline pumping in Marisol's veins shook her body. Adhara was over. Now she had to save existence.

Crash! Marisol jumped at the noise. Tobias, pale and sweaty, staggered into the room. His belt had been wrapped tightly at the top of his bloody arm. He took one look at Adhara and exclaimed, "Holy shit! What'd you do?"

Relief chased after her fright. "Took care of things." With a newfound focus, Marisol bent down to pick up the rocket system fallen off Adhara's shriveled body. Flying to the collider might be the best bet to shut it down. She strapped the pack to her back and shoved her legs into the jets. "Rebooting Staci opened the system up to manipulation. She's activated the collider to produce enough antimatter to destroy the world."

"Pyrrhic victory," he said, smiling, dizzy and weak.

If she didn't need to save existence, she'd hold him, race him to the nearest first responder, and stroke the hair matted by sweat on his forehead. She turned an office chair back up onto its wheels and directed Tobias into it. Tightening the belt used as a tourniquet, she attempted to slow down his bleeding.

"I can stop it." She met his clammy lips in a kiss.

The department door flung wide. All four of the revenants marched in, eyes rolled inside their skulls as if in a trance.

"What the fuck now?" Tobias grunted.

Marisol searched her harness, but the scrambler must've fallen off her during the fight.

The revenants ripped off another layer. The Bloodsucker opened his dress shirt. The scarred one tore off his threadbare top. The burnt skeleton reached inside its chest hole. The water-bloated corpse tore away the goopy flesh at its stomach. Hiding underneath were grenades. Mummified Adhara rattled out what sounded like a laugh.

Marisol's stomach tightened. "We have to get out of here. Fast."

Tobias stood and kicked the office chair into a window, shattering it. The drop down would break them, if Tobias survived the jump at all.

"Get on my back. I can carry you," Marisol said. She gave the rockets at her ankles a test, awkwardly lifting herself off the ground.

He stepped away from the ledge. "You carry me, we'll go splat."

"We have to try." Her voice broke, as if her body understood what he was saying before her brain did.

He ripped his necklace chain and forced the shield of Saint Michael into her hand. "Go save the day."

Panic at the inevitable shook her body. She hiccuped out, "But I love you, I can't lose..." Clinging to him, she stopped herself collapsing from tears.

"Right back at ya." He wiped the tear from her face with his thumb. "Bring him back and love him the way we never got to."

A million protests vibrated her lips, if she had the strength to utter them. He gave her a sweet kiss. She disappeared into the gentleness of his mouth, and the soft sensation of his beard. He was home to her, rough and grounding and unafraid of the truth.

But gripping her by her chainmail, he tossed her out the window. She flailed until she kicked in the rockets and jetted to the rooftop across the street.

The eighth floor burst into a cloud of dust, exploding behind her.

It's funny what goes through your head near the end. I remember winning yards and yards of tickets playing Skee-Ball and coming back home with a ridiculously huge stuffed bear and ropes of red licorice. I remember the healing power of listening to music from my stereo as a teenager. Kissing Sarah Murphy in the back row of the movie theatre, and the sweet little sighs she made when she let me touch her boob. The fear and excitement I felt when Laura showed me the positive pregnancy test. Holding Diedre in my arms as she cried for the first time. Watching Diedre on Christmas open gifts and believe in Santa with breathless joy. Diedre hitting a double at a softball game. Singing in choir. Graduating high school. She was always the reason why I wanted to help the city.

I'm sorry, Diedre, for losing my way.

I remember Vinnie. The night we survived a hail of bullets and arrested a third of the Mafia. The way his kiss awakened me and destroyed me all at once. The way he helped me believe in miracles.

And Marisol. The look of love she had for me when she thought I was the Patron Saint. Her belief in me to recover. Her eyes filling with tears, begging me to stay. I wish I could. Because I see so much more. Feeling a baby kick through her pregnant belly. I know the child is ours. And she's so happy. I rub her feet as she leans back into Vincent, saved from the beyond. We'd have been so perfect, the three of us becoming four. So perfect. I wish I had more time to realize that when I was alive.

I make the Sign of the Cross.

The end comes in a white-hot flash bang.

46

The Journey Home

Marisol picked herself up off the rooftop. Her lungs were full, unable to take in a complete breath. Tobias was gone. She was alone. Again. Giving up, however, wasn't an option.

Launching herself off the rooftop, she flew over the city. She shot through the sky, and details became streaks of light. Her senses in overdrive blurred the city in a kaleidoscope of boisterous colors. Unable to trust her sight, she closed her eyes. Faith guided her to the collider, a line of the dead reaching out to her— Abuelita, Annie, and other departed souls building with their incorporeal bodies a net to catch and save the future.

She blasted through the doors of the Varian Energy and Particle Physics Center and opened her eyes. Adhara had started the accelerator with its maintenance latch open. Magenta balls of energy burst around the room, flying faster and faster and breaking into miniature swirling galaxies. The unleashed energy burnt her skin. The serum fresh in her veins fought against the damage. Her skin stung, stuck in a perpetual state of peeling.

Through gritted teeth to stave off the sting, she shouted the formula she once drew on Tobias's forearm, T being the date and time his daughter had given him. With the new information, Staci hummed louder, and the galaxies spun in a different direction. But the shift didn't bring the change she had hoped for.

She slammed her hand against the computer mainframe. Her last hope was seeking answers from a higher power. "I got this far!" she screamed, her request verged on desperate sobbing. The prayer became a plea as she beat her hand against the control panel. "What the fuck do I do? How do I—"

Memories answered her—the prayers of her Abuelita who lit candles for the dead, and the transubstantiation of the blood and flesh of her First Communion. How miracles touched Earth, weakening the walls between the mortals and divine. She sliced her hand open with Adhara's claws and lit a fire in her hand with the flamethrower built within. *"Ven a mi, Vicente. Encuéntrame, mi amor."*

The sound of her heartbeat overwhelmed her ears. Her chest tightened. The wallop floored her. Fuck, she'd die here, wouldn't she? She rubbed her chest and shouted, *"Corre, se lo pido."*

He better save the world after she died.

At least one of them deserved a happy ending.

Two Hundred Sixty-One Years After the Curse

I step off the boat, eyes adjusting to the bright daytime. The only star in the sky is the sun. My powers do not ameliorate the burning taste of the sea air in my throat, so I stagger from the beach in search of fresh water. I wander the wilderness, no human or creature in sight. A worry rises within me. What if I came upon the cursed and starless land again?

The sun dips below the eaves as I journey further inland. My thirst threatens to turn my all-powerful muscles brittle. I stumble, wanting to cry out but barely able to utter. My laughing comes out in cruel snorts. How ironic to be surrounded by the lush greenery but have no water!

Stars poke holes in the deep blue firmament. I collapse, acquiescing to the woods surrounding me in their oppressive darkness and serving as a far greater steel box than whatever Adhara could seal me in. On my back, I watch the stars. I have been afraid of them for so long, the light they could cast at night. What crimes of mine did they see? What judgment will they bestow upon me? I had turned away from them in France, thinking through my experiments, I could bring the voice to me in unstable reactions and logical alchemy. Cut down again, I humble myself. I talk to them as I had in Spain. *Forgive me. Help me. Guide me.*

And then a beam of light shines through the trees, warming my face. Awe melts away my exhaustion and doubt. It quenches my thirst and provides balm to my wounds. I follow the path, the light growing brighter and hotter. Closer, I hear the voice, louder and clearer than I ever had before. *"Ven a mi, Vicente. Encuéntrame, mi amor."*

In the blinding clearing, I see her, my star. She reaches her hand out to me.

Time collapses in on itself.

I am Vicente Vasquez. She is my star. I am Vincent Varian. She is Marisol. She calls to me from my home in the blood and smoke of Susanna and our baby's passing. She offers me a tissue at the pinnacle of my grief in Shadowhaven. She heals my wound in an abandoned treatment room in the hospital I build. She orders me to crawl to her in my rotting American palace. She is the face that haunts me. She is the reason I create my new life here in Shadowhaven. She is the vision captured in a painting. I know her before I meet her, my Marisol, my spirit. *"Corre, se lo pido,"* she cries.

I run. *"¡Ya voy, mi estrella!*[1]*"*

Vincent crossed into the collider. He held out his hand and the magenta light streamed into his fingers, absorbing all the matter. Energy swelled inside his body, awakening a new power—atoms rearranging, creating, splitting, destroying. With a flick of his fingers, he closed the latch.

"Welcome back, Mr. Varian," Staci greeted.

1. I'm coming, my star!

He found Marisol on the floor and teleported to her, scooping her near-lifeless body in his arms. Unlocking atoms revealed the secrets of the universe to him. As he held his dying beloved, the human need to worry fell away. He knew. He touched his hand to her chest. Atoms formed into the silver cross necklace she had once given him. But it wasn't enough. Charging the atoms around him, he defibrillated her heart. Her eyes opened.

"You found me," she whispered.

"You found me." He kissed her until the air came alive with static electricity. The power lifted them off the floor and away.

Breaking News

Shadowhaven grieves in the harrowing aftermath of an unknown terrorist group's attack on Police Precinct Four. Unidentified individuals assailed citizens and officers alike with swords, and explosives which destroyed one floor of the precinct. Authorities currently estimate twenty-seven fatalities, including controversial Congressional candidate Grant Durant, US Attorney Penelope Stanwycki, and Shadowhaven police Sergeant Sylvester Thompson. Investigators claimed all the terrorists died in the attack. At least a hundred demonstrators and police officers were injured.

The proposed motive of the attack was anger over the mishandling of the Durant trial after footage had been found uploaded to various websites, which not only recorded alleged crimes committed by Durant but also by many members of Shadowhaven's elite families, including Roark Weller, Skipper Ecklund, and Hogarth Clement. Some claim the Bloodsucker terrorist group, responsible for last year's attack at the Rooks' basketball game and the Varian Family and Research Hospital, planned this attack. Updates are ongoing. On a related note, investigators are reviewing the individuals in Durant footage and shared that "confessions already are pouring in."

A surprising volunteer joined search and rescue efforts. Vincent Varian arrived in Shadowhaven to help those in need, visit hospitalized victims, and listen to grieving families.

We asked him about surviving his plane crash. Varian replied, "Before waking up in the coma in a private residence on the island of La Plata Pez, I remember flying into adverse weather. I am grateful for the care I received, and I am lucky to be alive. I wish the miracle of my recovery on all those coping with this heinous attack."

Grant Durant's estate is headed back to court. Wendell Carp of the law firm Barton, Engel, Nunes, and Carp submitted a civil lawsuit on behalf of Juniper Starling and other girls who claimed the late Congressional candidate had abused them. Mr. Carp warned similar suits are on the horizon as more associates of Durant turn themselves in. When asked if the lawsuit was unnecessarily cruel given the involved party's recent death, Mr. Carp said, "Though Durant's death is unfortunate, the ideal time for Justice is sooner rather than later."

godspatriot: Watch out! The government secretly tainted crates of alcohol to slowly introduce its mind control program. We need Shepherd's Watch to protect all of us. Wake up, sheeple!

cloudseeder28: Official channels claim they were terrorists, but eyewitnesses claimed they were zombies. The end is nigh!

fakedmoonlander: Vincent Varian actually died in the plane crash. What returned to Shadowhaven is not him.

47

Ever Before and Ever After

Heaven sure had a lot of beeps and decompression hisses. At least the angel dressed in white was beautiful.

"You look like shit," she said.

Huh, not what **Tobias** had expected from winged messengers escorting him to the afterlife. He had to crane his head farther than expected, unable to see out of his right eye. Cords for an IV drip and oxygen connected to him. He wasn't in Heaven. He was in a hospital room. And the angel? Marisol in a hospital gown.

"Hey," he said, barely over a croak. Waking up, he noticed her hospital bracelet. "What do they have you in here for?"

"Arrhythmia. The serum sent my heart into overdrive, so they shocked me into a regular heartbeat. Now, I'm waiting to get the clear to go home with a heart monitor. Under orders to reduce stress."

What could be more stressful than vigilante crime-fighting? Battered and bruised, they faced an end of an era. "Early retirement." He forced a sad chuckle. An itch formed on his right hand. Reaching to scratch it, he touched the bed. The unexpected empty space reminded him—he'd lost his hand.

He performed a quick scan of his body and jerked up. No right hand, right eye, or left leg. "Early fucking retirement!"

She shushed him and stroked his upper arm. Her touch ended on the gauze over the healing stump. "Vincent found you in the rubble. The explosion..." Tears formed in her eyes as she tenderly ran her fingers through his hair.

The hand, he'd lost to Adhara, but the rest had been torn from him in the explosion. Vincent found him? That meant—

"Y-You brought him back," Tobias said.

"Indeed," Vincent's sonorous voice sounded.

Tobias snapped his limited focus to him—Vincent Varian, casually suave in a T-shirt, cardigan, and jeans. His golden blond hair had been effortlessly styled in short, messy waves. Tobias's confusion softened. He was safe and surrounded by two angels.

His excitement fell, because angels tended to deliver difficult messages, and both of them avoided looking him in the good eye as the silence grew. They needed to share bad news. And it wasn't *your new body has a lot of physical therapy ahead of it.*

"We need to talk," she said, breaking the silence yet somehow pulling the tension tighter.

Judging by Vincent's squirm, it was about Tobias and Marisol's naked fun time. "Being in the void, I know things changed among us."

Marisol's face started to cave into a cry. If he could help it, Tobias never wanted to see her that way. "Listen, we've had a strange start—all three of us. You thought I was him once, and I caught feelings. And with your grief and all, things got a little steamy when he was gone. But I know my place, and I would never dream of coming between you two. You're together— just as it should be." He hiccuped over the last words, resisting his disappointment.

Marisol and Vincent locked eyes and exhaled, Tobias's loss giving them their much-needed relief. Unlike the last time Tobias bowed out gracefully, he had a taste of what he was letting go. His heart ached more than his maimed body.

"I meant to say, traveling through the void, I experienced memories differently." Vincent clapped his hand atop Tobias's good one. "I may have missed some signals." A magenta vibration traveled up Tobias's arm, ending on his lips—the same sensation as their kiss. In the electric flash of memory, another image emerged, Tobias's hand moving away from Vincent's because of his hurt, fear, and doubt. But his touch shared another memory—Vincent's fingers intertwining with Tobias's in a moment of euphoria.

The memory hadn't happened. It was a promise.

Vincent continued, "But I won't be missing any more."

The assurance lulled Tobias into a calm. "I won't either."

Marisol's face pinched together, obviously not catching the moment between Tobias and Vincent. "My mom and dad might shit their pants, but maybe we started strangely because we're supposed to be together." She joined Vincent on the left side of the bed, dragging her IV drip behind her. "I need your kindness and understanding. The way you indulge me—it gives me flight." She kissed him quickly and then held Tobias's hand. "And you, you don't give up on me, and I need the way you ground me. It helps me be a better person." Lifting Tobias's hand to her face, she kissed the inside of his wrist and nuzzled her cheek inside his palm. "So how about it? Let me love you? The both of you? And we'll figure out the logistics later?"

Vincent blinked and nodded. She smiled and kissed him again. Parting to take a breath, she turned to Tobias, her eyes widened with anticipation of his answer.

Silly, really, her fear. He knew the answer before she asked.

"Okay."

She sniffled and leaned over the bed railing, allowing him a chaste kiss.

Tobias rested back on the gurney. He and Vincent shared a glance. One where his sharp blue irises lit from within and flickered pink, a glint of rich boy mischief championing three bodies merging in a wet glide. Their gasps. Skin brushing against another's skin.

Marisol narrowed her eyes with mocking exaggeration. "Don't get so excited. I'm bad at multitasking."

Tobias cleared his throat.

Vincent said, "I didn't say anything."

The door to the treatment room swung open. Diedre burst into the room. "Dad!"

Tobias's surprise tugged at the bandage over his missing eye. "Deeds! What are you doing here?"

She halted in the entrance and rolled her eyes so hard, her head swiveled. "I'm your emergency contact."

"Oh."

Marisol and Vincent tiptoed toward the door. Marisol mouthed, "We'll leave you alone."

Diedre sprang from the spot and hugged the breath out of him. The force of her embrace would've tackled him if he wasn't already lying down. "When I heard about mass casualties, I assumed the worst." She relaxed in his arm and pulled away, revealing her streaming tears.

Tobias wiped one away with the back of his hand. "You haven't called me that in a while—Dad."

Diedre hiccuped and sniffled. "I'm trying it out, seeing if it fits."

He had no smartass-isms left in him. They shared a soda and a slab of Jell-O.

Once he got out of the hospital, he'd give his daughter the world.

In the basement hideout of the Patron Saint, Marisol checked on mummified Adhara. Skin shriveled tight, spine severed, the once powerful woman lay in a gurney. Pity tinged the persistent fury **Marisol** still felt —the choking betrayal, the agonizing need for Justice. Holding those emotions back, Marisol crossed her arms, but tears burned her eyes.

"You were right about sharing the files with the public. Shadowhaven's unofficial grand jury is taking care of those who were Grant Durant's frequent visitors. Feds are running themselves ragged to outrun the scathing rebuke of the people. Even a good lawyer can't cover up their crimes. Blink if you understand what I said to you. That I know you were right."

Adhara blinked slowly. Her dried skin struggled to cover her sunken eyes.

Marisol wheeled an IV bag and its stand as well as a standing desk with a computer close to Adhara's gurney. "This program tracks the movement of your pupils. Look at a letter, and it will spell out your words."

Marisol sighed, hunkering down as if preparing for the confession she had avoided since shutting out the Church. "When my best friend was taken away from me, I thought the darkness and loneliness in her wake were going to consume me. Meeting you, I thought you were the friend who understood that part of me. I wanted you to be my best friend."

She meditated on Annie and the collapsing silence after her murder. Her chin trembled from the grief. "I wanted to love you, but I will never understand the fathoms of your pain. Vincent's men stole your world, but your vengeance almost ended every single person I care about. After the losses I've experienced, I wonder if I'll ever forgive you."

The cold cadence of the computer replied, "Will...you...freeze...me...like...the...Others?"

"Vincent's new powers cast them into the abyss. No one will be able to weaponize them, because no one will be able to find them."

"Will...he...?"

"No. I want you to experience the world the future builds. Someday we will have a just world, and I plan to bear witness to the day you'll have peace in your soul." She may have experienced most of Adhara's peaceful side the night she zapped into the body of the French woman, but the laugher from their night together still echoed in her ears. Mouths and bodies. Static touches ghosting over her skin. "I've seen glimpses of your joy. I know your peace is there."

"Fool! You're...letting...those...men...infect...you. The...power...you...cling...to...is...borrowed. Without... the...courage...to...break...free...of...the...mold...the... future...will...be....more...of...the...same. You...know... I'm...right."

In a way, Adhara was right. Forgiveness and grace couldn't be offered to those on Durant's list. They lacked the fortitude to pursue redemption, and it took fungi warping their minds to get them to do the right thing. Because of Adhara, the world spun in the direction of Justice. Her destruction liberated them until it left no room for hope. When things broke, there had to be hope to rebuild something new.

What was Marisol to do with Adhara, practically a god in how she'd flooded Shadowhaven to wash away its sins? Marisol would give her a new start, the hope she was missing. She took over the computer keyboard and executed a file. "I'll carry on to prove you wrong."

The screen loaded with the programming Adhara used to take over the minds of Vincent and Grant Durant's guests. Instead of coding mind control for self-destruction, annihilation, and familicide, Diedre had reversed the orders. Marisol dug into the pocket of her jeans, drawing out a baggie of the mushrooms, which had grown in her apartment's bathroom. "You never poisoned me because you respected having a choice, so I will do the same for you. We changed the code to love, happiness, and life. Vincent can fix your exoskeleton, and Wheels is already set up somewhere swanky. She didn't leave you. We had to bail her out of county jail. You could join her and have a nice day in the sunset. Not everything will be real, but the stuff you don't have, you can pretend. Blink if you agree to this."

Adhara blinked again.

Marisol mixed the mushroom powder with the saline solution, filled a syringe, and injected it into the IV bag. She stabbed the needle into one of Adhara's brittle veins. Her husk of a body absorbed the fluid quickly. Next, Marisol helped her body into the exoskeleton—repaired, but not good as new. Its bio-fluid returned a human-like suppleness to Adhara.

Though her braids had dropped away from her brittle form, her natural, honey-blond curls shone like new. New, deep wrinkles between her cheeks and lips appeared like a scar.

Staci drove them to the airport. **Vincent**, Marisol, Adhara, and A.J. the mouse rode in the back in silence. After they stepped out of the town car, Marisol hugged Adhara before Vincent escorted the super-powered woman across the tarmac to the charter plane. A.J. perched on the woman's shoulder, heading home to peace. They reached the stairs leading up to the airplane. He drew out the gold cigarillo case to share one last smoke with his former lover, lighting one and touching the butt ends together to light the other.

"I accused you once of being trapped in your own steel box. I'm jealous you found your out, no matter what I did. Perhaps I'm finally convinced that breaking the curse doesn't mean getting rid of us." A chortle pushed a cloud of smoke out her lungs.

"I was jealous of you once. You were so free in how you carried yourself." Vincent took a long drag from the cigarillo. He had always been running from the blood and smoke, only to find more. "I'm sorry we took it away from you."

She winced as if she was fighting the urge to form tears. Short, successive puffs alleviated the pain in her expression. "For what it's worth, I didn't think the collider was going to work, much like all those other times you tried to find your way out of this curse.

Surely, you would've used it already and succumbed to the dying sickness. Because how could you have a way out and choose more life?"

His heart warmed as he looked back to Marisol patiently waiting for him. "It helps not having to do it alone."

She tossed the cigarillo to the ground and snuffed it out with her boot. "I suppose you were once a reason for me to stay, the man who unlocked the possibilities of infinity and who danced with me at the edge of a revolution."

"A better reason waits for you."

She faced the horizon, squinting at the sun. "Do you really think this is our last lifetime?"

Their lives were joy and pain, unfortunately overwhelmed by the latter. His future, cherishing his knight and queen, would bring a balance between the two. The balance that would break the curse. "I have faith that I will see you with gray hair."

Adhara hugged him. Their embrace brought comforting moments of the past. Her lips bristled against his ear as she whispered, "But I'm not your greatest sin. Do they know about the Padre?"

He grimaced as if he were standing in a belfry next to a giant ringing bell. The clanging roared through his head. Would the painful tintinnabulation of the Padre end?

She ascended the stairs, and the door sealed behind her.

Vincent returned to Marisol and draped his arm around her shoulders. Both of them stood on the tarmac until the plane disappeared into the sunset, headed to where Wheels waited for Adhara.

They entered the town car, and Marisol drew a wad of paper from her pocket. She unwrapped it carefully. The note, in Adhara's writing, read, *Ask him about Charlie.*

Vincent faced his reflection in the window. The last time he encountered Padre Juan Carlos threatened to haunt him. But with a gentle touch of his golden waves, Marisol brought him back to the present.

She said, "We'll be ready for whatever he throws in our way."

48

The Holy Trinity

When the hospital had discharged **Tobias**, he entered the care of Vincent and Marisol. They made a new home for him in the penthouse with his own bedroom and gym to physically train in as he figured out his new body.

Vincent's Research and Development Department created state-of-the-art prosthetics for him, a hydraulic leg, which allowed his knee to bend, and a robotic arm, which reacted to the signals in his upper arm muscles to manipulate the fingers. Getting used to his prostheses, however, was a feat unto itself, especially as having one eye impacted his depth perception. He stopped trying to learn how to grip with his new arm as he dropped glass after glass, attempting to drink. Training with Vincent, the one person strong enough to prop him up, led to many frustrating and sweaty stumbles.

Most sessions ended in his tantrums. Why did they ever think he was going to get better? And their talk of him returning to fight crime was fucking ridiculous. He didn't mind early retirement, per se, but his detective mind was going to be best behind a desk, staring at irregularities in spreadsheet data or any other mind-numbing, pencil-pushing task. Like the good ole days. But now, the only thing the electric shock setting in his new arm would accomplish was slaughtering the occasional fly.

"You're relearning your body. Everything will click, sooner than later," Vincent assured Tobias as he mopped the sweat off his forehead after he spent the morning trying to walk.

He snorted out his disgust. "Easy for you to say. You came out of this whole ordeal with additional powers."

"There's plenty I'm figuring out with this new atomic manipulation." He twirled his long fingers in the air, creating pink shapes like neon signs, which dissipated like rings of smoke.

Of course his changes led to more beauty and wonder. Tobias replied sarcastically. "A wise person said you're relearning your body. I'm even told sooner than later, everything will click."

"I can remove your tongue with a wave of my hand."

"And then I'll make you build me a bionic one."

"We could have lots of fun learning what you could do with that." Vincent's catlike grin returned.

As much as the shape of Vincent's mouth promised excitement, Tobias's new body couldn't muster much of a physical response. Useless Tobias only inhabited the guest room in their home.

At least Marisol humored him by wearing a tight vinyl, white nurse dress which pushed her boobs together. The useless feeling, however, deflated whatever desire he had left. Though she played the hot nurse for him, he treated her like museum exhibit—something to look at but not touch.

"You'll find your motivation," Marisol said, snuggling up against him after she helped him take off his prostheses.

"Your tits are quite motivating."

"Psh!" She bent down and kissed him on the temple near his empty eye socket.

He closed his eye to sleep. "Tell me a story. A happy one."

"I'm not creative, but here goes. The city is healing. While the collider is under maintenance, the people of Shadowhaven receive a stipend anyway thanks to a massive donation from one of Vincent Varian's benefactors. The relief is palpable.

"Next, your partner earned a medal for protecting the Homicide Department, but we know who should really receive credit.

"Shepherd's Watch has left the city for now. Their involvement during the night at Durant's is shrouded in secrecy, but we'll get to the bottom of it. The evildoers they were hired to protect confessed their crimes and relinquished the wealth they hoarded. Some might suggest a hero programmed mind-controlling fungus to get them to do it.

"After leaders and enforcers from the Shadows bit the dust, the dancers at the Pink Curtain are safe. The place has become a cabaret of sorts, hosted by a woman who hates platinum blond, shake-and-go wigs. I've offered condolences to a teenage boy for his most recent breakup, but only after he showed me his high school diploma.

"As I helped clean up Justice Square, I saw a teenage girl who should hate me paint a mural there. The image? A warrior woman in a domino mask shielding the city. The Saint of Shadowhaven."

"I think I know her, the saint."

Curling against him on his bed, she yawned, still telling the story. The exhaustion from physical therapy caught up with Tobias, and he fell asleep.

Tobias awoke. Marisol had left his bed in the night. Muffled screams traveled through the hallway. Vincent was in trouble.

Tobias jackknifed up in bed and scooted himself to the edge. As methodical as he would be loading his gun, he reached to the side table in the dark. No need to grope around—he found his eyepatch and looped it over his head, adjusting it over his eye socket. The smothered shouts in the other room increased. He breathed through his mounting worry, effortlessly holding his bionic arm between his thighs and slipping it over his stump. Turning on, his arm wiggled its mechanical fingers before he shoved his amputated leg into its sock, his boxer briefs allowing easier access to his amputated limb. He secured his prosthetic leg to his left thigh and gave the prothesis a pull to double-check its movement. Ready to save the day, he stood.

At first, his doubt presented itself in his uneven gait. He bounded closer toward the noise, his stride finding its balance. The blood rushing in his ears drowned the sound of struggle on the other side of the door. Not again, he vowed. No one would hurt the ones he loved again.

With his left leg, Tobias kicked the door open. Someone had tied Vincent to a chair, his wrists lashed behind him. His captor had gagged him with a white cloth, knotted at the back of his head. Vincent wriggled in his chair; his panicked screams crescendoed.

Tobias knelt before him. "Don't worry. I'm here." Reaching behind Vincent's head, he dug his fingers into the knot. The metal tips pulled at the cloth until it loosened. Vincent's cheek brushed against his, an accidental movement making Tobias suddenly aware of Vincent's bare chest mere inches from his. A heat rose within him, out of place in this moment of danger. "Who did this?"

Vincent dragged his tongue along his bottom lip and swallowed. His Adam's apple bobbed in his throat. "She did."

Tobias shot straight up. "Adhara's back? Where is she?"

Vincent's blue eyes sparked like lightning and then flashed into a faint pink. A smirk rose on his lips. "Behind you."

Tobias spun around, adjusting the buttons on his arm to the stun setting. He held out his hand as if he were signaling to stop. A purple pulse of electricity hummed throughout his arm.

And there she was. Not Adhara, but Marisol. Not really Marisol either, but masked and armored as the Silver Spirit. She stood in the middle of the bed, mattress dipping slightly under her feet. Her skin, anointed with oil, shone reflecting the candlelight surrounding them. However, she wasn't the version of the Silver Spirit he had come to know. Instead, she had stepped into a fetishized version of her alter ego, adorned in a silver chainmail bikini and a chainmail veil obscuring her lower face. The gaps in the armor's links offered glimpses of her nipples and the shadow of pubic hair. Only her mouth remained a mystery as her unflinching gaze cut into him.

He dropped his arm. The electric charge powered down. Fuck, he'd burst in on them during one of their sex games, and despite the thrall warming around his body, he was the unwelcome guest.

Marisol held out her hand, gesturing for him to stay. Tobias's mouth parted, letting in a shuddering breath. He was wanted, an inextricable force shared among them. It seemed too good to be true. He flicked his gaze down to Vincent, tied to the chair. His body glistened too, oiled with rose and frankincense, the floral and woodsy scent of prayer. It was as if they'd broken into his mind and set a trap for him. The mercy being, he never wanted to escape it.

Tobias nodded, accepting his role inside their trinity.

He turned back to the goddess, his Marisol. Her offered hand gracefully formed into a point directly at Vincent. "He's a bad boy, and he must be punished. He has to watch what a good boy can do."

She hypnotized him into a dizzying high. "A good boy like me?" He approached the bed-turned-altar and hugged around her legs. She raked her fingers through his hair, holding him against her. And he inhaled. Breathed in the holy scent of her. Breathed in the sweet smell of her thighs and pussy. What if this was a dream?

She pulled his hair. The twist of pain grounded him. Yes, all of it was real.

She sank to her knees as she took the metal veil off. It left indents across her nose and cheeks. Eye-level to him, she guided a necklace over his head. The chain glided through her fingers, gripping the pendant, the shield of Saint Michael. He held her face between his hands, one of a man's and the other machine. Each indent left by her mask, he met with his lips. He'd take away her pain with his kisses. Pulling him by his necklace, she gently sucked his lower lip before touching her tongue against his. He returned the kiss. At first gentle and then greedy, drawing her close below her waist. Lifting the chainmail above her luscious ass, he gave the ample curve a squeeze. His robotic hand joined in, powerfully grabbing a handful of her flesh.

She moaned into his mouth, deepening their kiss. He needed her mouth and tongue as if it were his source of life. With every hungry sweep into her mouth, he spelled every name to call him. *Tobias. Mine. Good boy.*

Holding her languid in his arms, he crawled over her, positioning her across the bed. Needing air, he broke the kiss, taking in her soft, fragrant skin along her neck. Her needy moans changed the goddess into a woman. "I love you," she whispered.

He unhooked the flimsy chainmail, uncovering her delicious tits. He kneaded them into peaks, studied how her body arched, and how her full mouth released sweet sounds.

"Use your other hand," she ordered breathlessly.

Every part of him was worthy. She even desired his new and scary parts. "I love you, too," he uttered, barely audible over their panting. His bionic hand cupped her breast, pinching her nipple between his fingers. She gasped. The heat of his mouth provided the balm to her tits made raw and sensitive from his fierce metallic touch.

As he laved and sucked, his gaze met Vincent's, feet away tied to his chair. The super-powered man's pretty pout agape as he watched, hard cock tenting his satin pajama pants. Tobias stared into his electric blue eyes. As he feasted on her, his unmoved focus communicated that their bodies were one. Every graze of his teeth, flicker of his tongue, he stored away for Vincent—to turn their kiss to more.

Good eye still on Vincent, his mouth sensed the path down Marisol's body, down across her belly and hip. She helped unfasten her chainmail and raised her knees to part her legs further. He held her left leg down. "He has to watch. I don't want him to miss one moment of what I'm going to do to that beautiful pussy."

She bit her lip and laughed, answering by stretching her right leg and holding it straight by the calf.

He kissed and nibbled down her sculpted leg, marking her soft inner thigh with his mouth. The curls around her sweet cunt shone with her arousal. Those wet lips begged for his nose to trace along her seam, to nuzzle into her sensitive clit until her essence lingered in his beard. Until she was all he'd ever taste.

She clawed at her tits as he sipped and savored. He dragged his tongue up and down over her clit. The pleasure of it echoed around the room as Vincent pulled against his bindings. Pride swelled in Tobias, and he flashed a smile. The pleasure he gave her compounded Vincent's ecstasy. He probed her with his warm fingers, adding vigorous strokes to his mouth's work. Her moans turned into desperate wails.

A magenta light held her hands back away from squeezing her breasts. A faint pink shimmer hovered over her nipples.

"No fair. You're not allowed to touch me," Marisol breathed out.

Bound to the chair, Vincent answered, "Technically, I'm not touching you."

Erotic, wet sounds accompanied her ecstatic cries. She clenched around Tobias's working fingers.

"Fuck, I need your dick," she whimpered. "Give it to me."

Tobias shifted his weight and hooked his thumbs in the band of his boxers. Magenta sparkles surrounded him, and his boxers ripped away as if by magic. Only one person had returned from the void with deep pink energy manipulating atoms.

"Hey." Tobias directed a scolding remark Vincent's way.

"The watcher grows impatient," he gritted between clenched teeth.

How could he deny two people wanting him right away? He crawled over Marisol, and she hugged his hips with her legs. He breathed in and rocked his hips forward, sliding inside with ease, and he notched himself further into her slick heat. Her breath hitched. In so many moments and stolen glances, he had wanted this, but his imagination hadn't even approached the sensation—love, rendering him weightless. Stilling, he said, "It took us so long to get here."

She stroked his face from his temple to his chin. "We don't have to think about that anymore."

He thrust. Her snug channel felt vivid in its pulsing heat. Too vivid. He was having her bare, an intense pressure tightening his balls. "Fuck, we're not wearing protection."

Her orgasms rendered her hoarse. Her speaking barely rose over audible. "I want to show him how you marked me. Our perfect mistake, remember?"

He drove into her. "Never a mistake with you, though. Never a mistake with us."

He picked up the pace and chased the sensation building at the base of his spine. Her legs hugged him tighter. "Come so deep in me, my love."

She wanted it deep, huh? He pushed himself off her and gave her the fleshy part of her hip a smack. "Turn over. I'll show you how a good boy fucks."

They both faced Vincent in his chair—Tobias on his knees, she on all fours. He gave her juicy ass a biting kiss, and he entered her. The depths of her clenched around him. His flesh-and-bone hand gripped her hips, guiding the speed and angle. He smoothed his bionic hand up her back and gathered the strands of her black-brown hair into his metal fist. "Show him how pretty your face is when I fuck you." A tug of her hair sent a pulse to her pussy.

"You can't just watch, can you?" she asked Vincent.

Vincent shook his head, and his super strength broke his bindings. His muscles twitched from the sudden force.

She rasped, "Touch yourself. Make him know he put on a good show."

He lowered his waistband enough to free his cock. In the dim glow of the candlelight, Tobias saw Vincent's formidable erection. Ridged with veins, dusky red in color, and angled toward the ceiling—it was perfect.

The kind he had imagined rubbing against his the one night they kissed.

Now, Vincent stroked his perfect length slowly. Tobias matched his pace. In this way, he could take his time—memorize how every quarter inch of Marisol felt different and elicited a different moan from her.

A few more deliberate and luxuriating pumps flooded Tobias with pleasure. Unable to resist the precipice, he rammed his hips into her. She gasped again, higher in pitch than before. Vincent matched his speed, as if Tobias had within him the control over Vincent's hand working his shaft. Slamming into Marisol and watching Vincent's eager fist, he came, grunting like an animal. He collapsed into her as she continued to milk him, pushing his orgasm as deep it could go. Her arms gave out, and he lay on top of her, utterly blissed out.

Beard bristling against her shoulder, he closed his eye and basked in the release. Not just coming, but letting go of all those times he held back and hid his true self. Before, he had been embarrassed by hope and love and drowned his disappointment in booze and sex, attempting to make them meaningless. Now, he wasn't afraid of imagining their child growing inside her and the alluring swell of her pregnant belly. Their child, he thought, all three of theirs. A symbol of their love as each of them made a night like tonight possible.

A force lifted him off Marisol and gently rested him against the pillows. The weight in the bed shifted next to him. He sensed Vincent in the bed.

"Come here," Vincent growled.

"I thought I was the one who gave the orders," Marisol teased, but she gasped again.

Tobias opened his eye to see magenta sparkles lift her and float her over Vincent. She straddled his lap and slowly swiveled her hips. By her sudden sigh, Vincent had entered her.

"He's made you so warm for me," he said into her neck.

She swallowed and nodded, undulating her body lazily. Riding him, she looked so powerful, the goddess Tobias always loved. Worshipping her would never be finished. And she was irresistible as she tilted her head back and sighed, exposing more of her throat. Tobias sat up, drawn to their energy like gravity. He kissed her neck. His mouth moments from Vincent's as they worked together, leaving no part of her uncherished.

"We should've always been like this," she said between her heavy breaths. She leaned back, bracing herself against Vincent's legs. Her movements increased in vigor, indulgent in their rhythm.

Tobias sealed his lips over her gasping mouth and stroked down her shoulder, ghosting his touch over her nipple. The whimper against his lips enticed him to explore her body further. He caressed her down her ribs and stomach, finding her clit again. Massaging her in rapid circles, he grazed Vincent's cock sliding into her.

A rush of guilt steadied his hand. Watching was one thing—touching, quite another.

"Keep going," Vincent uttered. He placed his hand over Tobias's and directed the motion. The greedier sweeps of Marisol's clit invited him to touch Vincent's shaft.

Marisol cried out. Her hips slammed into Vincent's as her body trembled against Tobias. Vincent soon followed after her.

Tobias scooped her into his arms, meeting the breathless wonder of her parted lips with kisses. He laid her on her back. The men surrounded her like parentheses.

"Are you a good man now?" Marisol asked.

Vincent shook his head, and he danced his fingers along the crease of her thigh, teasing along its apex. His elegant fingers dipped low, and he lifted them back up, coated in their semen. Tobias gripped Vincent's forearm with both his hands and closed his eye as he wrapped his lips around Vincent's dripping fingers. The salty, metallic taste melted over his tongue. Sucking Vincent's fingers clean sent a hungry twitch to his cock.

"Is that all?" Tobias asked dreamily.

Vincent guided Tobias's hand along Marisol's pussy. "You tell me."

Tobias's fingers parted the seam and explored inside. Her channel pulsed, drowning his fingers in more wetness. He withdrew his soaked fingers, raising them in the air the same way Vincent had. "Good boys share."

Without breaking eye contact, Vincent took Tobias's fingers in his mouth, hollowing his cheeks and swirling his tongue around them. Another twitch of his cock, and an uncontrolled whimper escaped out of

Tobias. Vincent's eyes flickered their telltale lightning blue, hinting at the future which promised both of them more.

"That was hot," Marisol said with a laugh.

Tobias stretched out alongside Marisol, "Understatement of the year." Between his god and goddess, Tobias had been utterly weakened, reminding him of his mortal state. "I don't know about you, but I'm beat."

Vincent did the same, lying on the other side of Marisol. "I have super strength and even I'm exhausted."

"I love you. Both. Always," Marisol said with a yawn.

"Yes, both. Always and forever."

"Amen."

Epilogue

Five Hundred Years After the Curse

I tuck the corner of the towel around my waist. Fresh from a shower, I study myself in the mirror. Outside the void, it strikes me how much I have changed through the years, but I still remain a man who appears in his early thirties, a sweet spot between young and old. I make faces at myself in the mirror, finding echoes of my past selves: Vicente, V., or Victor. Suddenly, the light catches something white along my hairline. I grab a pair of tweezers and lean closer toward the mirror. The tweezer's arms pinch around the white hair, and I pluck it from my head.

"What are you doing? Why aren't you in bed?" Marisol asks. She wears Tobias's dress shirt, which skims over her curves. Her dark hair has been fucked into a beautifully wild state, voluminous and wavy.

I squeeze the tweezers into my fist. "Styling my hair," I lie.

She hugs me around the waist and kisses me on the temple. "When you're sleeping, you don't have to have perfect hair."

"Vincent Varian always has perfect hair."

She runs her hands through it, mussing my wet curls. A groan sounds from the bedroom. We freeze and watch Tobias toss in bed, asleep. Marisol laughs. "He's not used to us yet."

"He'll get there."

"Bed? Soon?" After one more kiss, she disappears into the dark bedroom.

Alone, I look at the white hair I've plucked. I never had white hair before, which means one thing.

I am aging.

I look at the man in the mirror and smile.

The End

Acknowledgments

This book almost killed me. No joke.

During the greater part of 2024 and 2025, my health tanked, which coincided with me writing this book. I blame my grief over my dear dog passing. She was my last connection to my Midwest home.

However, I adopted another puppy in early 2025, and as much as her boisterous personality and needy nosing of my keyboard prevented forward progress in my writing, she helped me come back to myself. Thank you, my Baby Bubba, but how dare you chew up my Magneto action figure.

My next thank you is to Mr. Elise. He patiently kept the house together as I furiously wrote, edited, and formatted.

My comrade in superhero romance, TF Author, provided encouragement and a beta read, giving me the ego boost I needed. Meredith, my other beta reader, helped me strengthen Adhara as a character.

Because I write weird and complex superhero romances that just so happen to hold a mirror to society and explore history, philosophy, and religion, I'm not exactly the most widely accepted author in Romancelandia. But Ana Hansen of Sparks Editorial provided the understanding and encouragement I so desperately needed. With her as my cheerleader, I felt celebrated as the masher of genres and ideas that I am.

Finally, I would like to thank my readers. The occasional tag and DM with support gave me my reason why when I often wondered if I should quit this book thing. If you want to stay updated on my latest projects and musings about fandom, books, and Romance, subscribe to my <u>newsletter</u>.

I had nuggets of ideas about *Deus Ex Umbra* when I was writing super early drafts of *Saint of the Shadows* back in January 2020—back when the story wasn't femdom and Tobias was a complete goober who obviously was the odd one out in the love triangle. I knew at the root of Vincent's history was a woman. She would return after many years apart (and would be hiding how her long history had permanently damaged her). At first she would've been a traditional romantic rival, rocking Marisol's trust in Vincent. But as I realized this woman's history would've driven her to a radical thirst for Justice, a woman who became Marisol's idol and mentor formed in my mind. I made vision boards of her alongside my early vision boards of Marisol, Vincent, and Tobias. As I approached this story, her name and image kept changing until she formed into Adhara. Her final name change (of over nine) occurred early spring 2025.

Also early in those 2020 ideas for the sequel was a *Terminator*-style assault on a police station and a city coming together to protest against injustice. Then the

Summer of 2020 happened. I emailed a friend that I wished the United States wouldn't steal my book ideas.

Similarly, I wrote what became my first Grant Durant chapter in the spring of 2022 as an exercise to get me back into writing after experiencing a season of profound discouragement.

My point in sharing these is that I never intended for this book to be a reflection of our NOW, yet as drafts of this story progressed, I thought of that early email to my friend. *Reality, quit getting to my ideas first!*

However, if there is one thing I wish reality would plagiarize is the hope of a community healing and a future progressing to be better for the generations after me.

This book is also a love letter to all the shows and stories I grew up with. *Batman: The Animated Series*, *X-Men*, *Gargoyles*, *Buffy the Vampire Slayer*, *Interview with the Vampire*, and *Back to the Future 2* have fingerprints all over these pages.

Book three is stirring in my brain as I write this acknowledgement. Much like this book, particles of ideas have been floating about since book one's inception. Does it have a title? Maybe. Will the Padre return? Yes. It will also have Vincent aging, and Tobias claiming his own superhero alter ego name so that he is no longer the Patron Saint 2. If you have any ideas about the latter, feel free to email me, because I am currently at a loss—as in, I know what I want out of that man's superhero name, but I can't find what I'm looking for.

Yet, I am manifesting for myself improving health and embracing hope as book three comes to existence.

Also by Jonesy Elise

About the Author

Jonesy Elise is a bisexual elder millennial who writes romance inspired by the Saturday morning shows she watched growing up. Her stories are real genre mashers—sci-fi fantasy with gothic vibes, spicy romance, dystopian monster. Safe to say, she loves composing paranormal/sci-fi/romance mashups.

No matter what she writes, the FMC will come to voice, the characters will be memorable, and they'll get their HEA (or HFN). She likes her romance spicy. So, read with a glass of milk.

Jonesy is an Iowa transplant living in the Bay Area with her family and energetic dog. She loves karaoking to Alanis Morrisette, completing yoga with all the props, and attending rock concerts with cool people. She is an unabashed caffeine addict and orders her sugar-free vanilla latte with an extra shot of espresso and a sprinkle of cinnamon.

If she isn't sharing the same HILARIOUS raccoon and possum memes repeatedly, you'll find her making goofy videos to promote her books or share about her author life.

Follow her on social media, subscribe to her newsletter, tell your friends!